Shock Wave

"Intense, unique, and frighteningly real. A standout!"
—**Marc Cameron,** *New York Times* bestselling author
of Tom Clancy "Jack Ryan" novels

"In *Shock Wave*, war correspondent Al Pessin brings
back Faraz Abdallah—a hero in the war on terror for
our generation—in the explosive third book in the Task
Force Epsilon Series. His novel *Blowback* is a tough act
to follow, but Pessin does so, bringing us on an intense,
non-stop ride with characters, action, and geopolitical
intrigue written with authenticity and emotion possible
only from someone who has been there and seen it
firsthand. Pessin proves himself to be a master
storyteller in this authentic, heart stopping thriller
that is sure to be one of the best reads of the year.
Don't miss this one!"
—**Andrews and Wilson,** international
bestselling author team

"Al Pessin is the perfect blend of Daniel Silva
and Lee Child."
—**Dave Zeltserman,** Shamus and Derringer
Award-winning author

"Action, intrigue, and adventure—all wrapped up
in extraordinary characters and a gripping story.
Pessin has it all!"
—**JD Allen,** award-winning author of
the Sin City Investigation Series

Sandblast
TOP-FIVE SELECTION, UNPUBLISHED BOOK OF THE YEAR,
2018 ROYAL PALM LITERARY AWARDS;
SHORT-LIST SELECTION, 2017 BOSQUE FICTION PRIZE

"Al Pessin escorts you through thrills and chaos,
writing with the sure hand of authority.
This guy knows his stuff."
—**Richard Castle,** *New York Times* bestselling author
of the Nikki Heat thrillers

"In *Sandblast*, Al Pessin has crafted a taut action-
thriller that really pulls you in. You'll feel like you're
right beside the main character, on an increasingly
perilous journey filled with impossible choices
that threaten to change him at his very core.
The plot is highly original, and I felt like I was there.
It's a great book."
—**Henry V. O'Neil,** author
of the Sim War Series

"*Sandblast* is the definition of a terrific military
thriller—straightforward, precise and devastating. This
timely, realistic story—with its authentic and knowing
voice and courageous main characters—propels readers
to the peak of white-knuckled brinksmanship
and will be awarded top marks by fans
of Alex Berenson and Vince Flynn."
—**Hank Phillippi Ryan,** Mary Higgins Clark, Anthony,
and five-time Agatha Award winner

"Al Pessin brings a lifetime of frontline experience to a novel that could have been taken from today's headlines. Utterly compelling and a cautionary tale for our times."
—Retired Admiral James Stavridis,
author, former dean of the
Fletcher School at Tufts University, former
commander of NATO forces and media commentator

"*Sandblast* vividly depicts a close-to-real scene, which makes the story more entertaining, real and educating."
—Ali Ahmad Jalali, author, former interior minister of Afghanistan and Afghan presidential candidate, distinguished professor at the Near East South Asia Center for Strategic Studies (NESA) at the National Defense University in Washington, D.C.

"The author writes with incredible authenticity . . . exceptionally well plotted . . . complex and consistent . . . each chapter adds a new hook . . . the story will appeal to a broad range of readers. We met the people, felt their anxiety, sweated with them in their decision process. This is a deeper story than it appears . . . the inner turmoil of the protagonists propels the story. The reader is pulled along, seeing lives lived, lost, and changed. Faraz is a heroic character of sequel deserving merit."
—Statement of the judges, the 2018 Royal Palm Literary Awards

Books by
AL PESSIN

Sandblast

Blowback

Shock Wave

SHOCK WAVE

A
TASK FORCE EPSILON
THRILLER

AL PESSIN

PINNACLE BOOKS
Kensington Publishing Corp.
www.kensingtonbooks.com

PINNACLE BOOKS are published by

Kensington Publishing Corp.
119 West 40th Street
New York, NY 10018

ISBN: 978-0-7860-4675-1

First Pinnacle paperback printing: February 2022

10 9 8 7 6 5 4 3 2 1

Printed in the United States of America

Electronic edition:

ISBN: 978-0-7860-4676-8 (e-book)

For Ezra

PART ONE

Chapter One

The lone passenger felt every whitecap as the small boat crept toward the desert shore. He thought he might be sick, but he was determined not to show any weakness.

He looked out the porthole. The moonless night revealed nothing.

The man was sweating in the stagnant, hot air of the small forward cabin. The old, rusting bench with thin, plastic-covered cushions provided none of the creature comforts to which his unique capabilities had entitled him these many years.

The cabin brought to mind the tiny Beirut apartment where he'd grown up, where he'd learned of his father's murder, where his mother had died for lack of medical care. He had worked hard to forget that apartment through the decades of plush furnishings and air conditioning. He shook off the memory.

A swell hit the boat and nearly knocked him from his seat. He put a hand on the bench to steady himself and let another wave of nausea pass.

How had he come to this—on this scow, hat in hand,

virtually on his knees begging for the seeds to regrow his operation? Begging for his life.

Not long ago, this all would have been done with a phone call and an electronic transfer. Now, calls were more dangerous than ever. Moving money was, too. Damn them.

His anger and shame fueled a new determination to succeed, to impress his masters, to get back to the air conditioning.

If they let him live.

A member of the crew opened the cabin door. "Two minutes, *sayyid*." He spoke in Arabic and retreated without waiting for an answer.

Still clinging to the bench, Saddiq Mohammed Assali thanked God that he had survived the voyage. "*Allah hu akbar*," he whispered. God is great. But his tone was more sarcastic than reverent. Surviving this far was a victory, but perhaps a fleeting one.

Assali stood, something a taller man would not have been able to do in the low-ceilinged cabin. His ample belly made it hard to balance in the rolling sea and strained the fabric of his sweat-stained traditional Arab *qamis*, an untucked long-sleeved white shirt that reached not quite to his knees and was buttoned all the way to his neck.

He wiped his three-day stubble. He ran a hand through his combover. It came out greasy. Disgraceful. But such was life on the run. He had only his small travel case, half a bottle of water and an empty plastic bag that once held German pretzels. He wished he hadn't eaten them.

Assali put on the suit jacket he'd bought not long ago at the priciest men's tailor shop in Amman. He picked up the carry-on, put the water bottle in a side pocket and stepped to the cabin door, crushing discarded candy wrappers and cigarette butts as he went. For the first time he could remember, he had smoked his last. Perhaps, if this is the end, they'll at least give him one before the execution.

He mounted two of the three steps to the deck. His face caught the breeze, which blew away some of the staleness and refreshed him.

They called this the Red Sea, but all he could see was black. The small cabin cruiser was painted black. The three-man crew wore black. And they had turned off the lights. Looking toward the rear of the boat, he could hardly see anything.

They had engaged the electric motor and so were running almost silently. They were invisible and inaudible. At least that was the theory. Who knew what technology the enemy might have?

Assali mounted the final step onto the deck and turned to look around. His fist closed on a rail and he peered into the darkness. In the distance to his left, there was a glow in the sky—the lights of Eilat and Aqaba, he reasoned. Otherwise, there was darkness in all directions. Staring ahead and not blinking, he forced his pupils to dilate. The shoreline appeared, dark gray against the blackness, maybe a kilometer away.

"How can you be sure this is the place?" he asked.

"From the satellite, *sayyid*," the captain assured him. The man's face was barely visible in the dimmed lights of the instrument panel.

Assali looked toward the shore again and shrugged.

He could only hope these men knew what they were doing.

The next wave tossed the boat and splashed over the rail.

Assali turned away but tasted the salt as water hit the deck. He had two hands on the rail now and was more concerned about going overboard than about vomiting. This had to be the longest kilometer in the world.

Finally cresting the last wave, the boat surfed down to the shore and ran aground.

This time, Assali's "*Allah hu akbar*" was sarcasm-free.

"Here, *sayyid*," the captain said. He lowered a small ladder over the stern.

"Into the water?" Assali asked. This would be the final indignity. Final for now, anyway.

"It is only half a meter," the captain said, not bothering to conceal a derisive smile.

Assali frowned and moved toward the back of the boat.

The sky brightened, as if from a distant bolt of lightning. All eyes turned north, toward the glow of the cities, in time to see a second flash. Then the sound reached them—a low rumble, barely audible. They felt it as much as heard it. The boat bobbed in the surf.

Assali snorted at the irony that he was close enough to feel the impact of what he'd done. That would be a first. And also a last, he hoped. He preferred to run his operations from a safer distance.

"It is done, then," the captain said.

"Yes. So it would seem."

"*Allah hu akbar.*"

Assali nodded but did not repeat the blessing. His look said, "Give Allah credit if you want. This was my doing."

He took a deep breath and shook off the last of the claustrophobia and nausea. He might yet survive this night.

Assali took hold of the ladder's handles and hefted himself over the rail. He let out a curse, then eased himself down into the warm water. His designer leather loafers hit the sand. His gaberdine dress pants were wet past the knees. The hem of his *qamis* touched the water, but, praise Allah, his suit coat was spared. He held his bag high on his shoulder.

As he made awkward steps toward dry land, the headlights of three vehicles blinked from behind the mangroves at the edge of the beach.

Assali did not turn to wave or thank the crew. He climbed the beach incline and walked toward the cars with as much dignity as he could muster, his pants dripping, his shoes and socks caked with sand, his heart pounding.

He was sweating again, but not from the heat. A week ago, he would have been welcomed as an honored guest. Now, even after what he had just done, he wasn't sure whether he would make it off the beach alive.

CHAPTER TWO

"What the hell do you mean three days ago?"
President Andrew Martelli stood over his guests, rather than sitting in his usual chair between the Oval Office's sofas. The renewed threat of terrorist attacks and the looming election campaign had combined to crack his practiced academic-turned-politician demeanor.

"He disappeared? Is that what you're telling me? That he's a goddamned magician, or a ghost maybe?"

Martelli's target worked hard to maintain his composure under the withering assault of a presidential dressing-down. The man picked a spot on the carpet across the room, stared at it and didn't say anything. In his peripheral vision, he could see that the young aide sitting next to him was doing the same.

Lieutenant General Jim Hadley had not experienced such an outburst in decades. If anyone had tried, they'd have gotten an earful. But this was the President of the United States. So even the three-star head of the Defense Intelligence Agency had to take it. And the tirade was not entirely unreasonable. It was Hadley's news that had set the president off. He had told Martelli that one of his agents reported seeing the president's most-wanted terrorist at a fishing village in Yemen, but that was three days ago.

The president's chief of staff, Greg Capman, spoke up from the other sofa.

"And you're sure it was Assali?"

"Liz?" Hadley said, handing the question to Liz Michaels, thinking it might be harder for the president to yell at her curly hair and flared skirt pulled down to cover her knees. Liz was the acting head of Task Force Epsilon because Hadley had sent her boss to Iraq, where she'd hitched a ride on an operation in Syria and gotten herself shot.

"Ninety percent, sir," she said, her voice tentative.

"And now?" Capman pressed. "Any idea at all where he might be?"

"No, sir."

Hadley could see Liz's fingertips turning white under short, keyboard-ready nails as she gripped her notebook hard.

"Mr. President, if I may?" Defense Secretary Marty Jacobs was the senior person in the room after the president. He sat in a beige, upholstered Queen Ann armchair, facing Martelli the long way across the coffee table. "We believe this man, Assali, was responsible for the attacks in Eilat and Aqaba last night."

Martelli turned toward his old friend. The left sleeve of Jacobs's jacket was pinned to the shoulder. He had lost most of his left arm to a Taliban mortar during a visit to Afghanistan a year earlier. The president looked like he was working hard to modulate his response.

"Marty, I don't need the world's biggest military and intel apparatus to know that."

Jacobs absorbed the low-key but pointed blow without responding.

"He's the only one left after our sweep, isn't he?" the president asked.

"The only one we know of," Liz said, then seemed to realize she shouldn't have spoken unless spoken to. She looked back at the floor.

Hadley covered for her. "The only one with that sort of capability, sir. Although it's worth noting that the bombs were relatively small—moderate damage to one tourist hotel in each city, total of five killed, a couple of dozen injured. Could have been much worse and likely would have been if we hadn't done what we did to cripple his operation."

"He's giving us the finger, isn't he?"

"Sir?"

"He's telling us he can still hurt us even after we arrested or killed most of his pals last week. I also don't need your experts to tell me these attacks are not random and they're not Assali's last hurrah. They're a warning, a taunt." The president moved left and made a circuit of the sofas. "After all we think we accomplished, that asshole has the ability to do something like this just a few days later."

"That's true, Mr. President," Hadley said. "But we may not be his only audience."

"What do you mean?"

"After what we did, Assali can't be popular with his backers. He may need to show them he's down but not out."

"You mean the Gulfies?"

"Yes, sir. The money trail points that way but gets lost somewhere between Switzerland and cyberspace."

"Not good enough, General. How many years have you been working this?"

"Too many, sir."

"Damn right. Find the end of that money trail and you'll find Assali. Or trace it the other way and tell me exactly who is funding him. Whichever way it works, shut them down. Without that, it's whack-a-mole as usual. And if he's restored his credibility, he'll be looking for cash for something bigger. I will not have it on my watch, damn it! Not again. Find this guy, General. Use every resource. Push every asset. Break some knuckles if you have to."

"Yes, Mr. President."

"Now, I need to talk to these guys in private, and you and Ms. Michaels have work to do."

As the two DIA officials left, Defense Secretary Jacobs couldn't help shaking his head. Even mentioning "breaking knuckles" was very not-Martelli. It was less than a week since they'd celebrated what they thought was a decisive blow against the terrorists. After two small bombings, the president's reaction felt excessive.

"You were pretty tough on them," Jacobs said.

"Maybe I haven't been tough enough. We can't give these terrorists enough space to strike back, especially not now."

"Poll numbers are good, Mr. President," Chief of Staff Capman said.

Martelli sighed and shook his head. "Why is it these things always happen in an election year?"

"Nothing like a good Middle Eastern war to boost your ratings," Jacobs said.

"What the hell, Marty?"

"I was joking, Mr. President."

"Not funny."

"Sorry, sir. But I guess my point is that there's a fine line between launching a covert offensive against terror groups and their financiers versus sending the marines."

"It's not a fine line, it's a broad bold line. If we have to send the marines, we'll send them, but we have lots of intermediate options, including Epsilon."

"And it's early," Capman said. "You don't have to worry about the primaries, and the general is nearly a year away. The crackdown was a big boost, and I don't think Eilat and Aqaba will have much impact."

"I'm not worried about Eilat and Aqaba," Martelli said. "I'm worried about what comes next."

CHAPTER THREE

The *tap-tap* of his dress shoes was amplified as it echoed off the polished floors and painted walls of the wide corridor. He lengthened his stride to keep up with the petite, energetic sergeant who was escorting him. She was rattling on with some sort of patter about the history of the building and what was where and how you could get a coffee less than a seven-minute walk from anywhere if you knew the shortcuts.

Lieutenant Faraz Abdallah was ignoring her. He was perspiring, though people passed him wearing sweaters against the supercharged air conditioning. His eyes darted from side to side, as if looking for threats. The brand-new dress uniform they'd given him chafed against his skin, and the weight of the jacket caused shooting pains along his injured shoulder.

He held his hat under his other arm, revealing the bandage in the small, shaved area on the side of his head, not very well covered by his fresh army haircut. He was clean-shaven for the first time in more than a year.

Faraz experienced a rush of panic. He should turn around and run, get the hell out of there. He imagined that everyone who nodded collegial greetings as they passed was IDing him as a terrorist, passing the word to arrest him, torture him, put him in a dark, fetid shed.

He blinked it away, wiped his face with his hand, and followed the sergeant into an elevator. She pushed the button for 2B, the second basement.

The elevator doors opened on a bland vestibule with gray walls and no decorations. The sign above the double steel doors in front of them read DEFENSE INTELLIGENCE AGENCY, COMMITTED TO EXCELLENCE. Two Pentagon Police officers sat at a small table.

The sergeant held out her ID and Faraz did the same. One of the officers nodded and entered a code on a keypad by the doors. They opened on a smaller vestibule, with two more steel doors on the other side. Faraz and the sergeant went in, and the doors clanged shut behind them. His escort looked up at a camera mounted at the top of the wall.

"Sergeant Collins with Lieutenant Abdallah."

Faraz heard the whir of an electronic lock. A light turned from red to green, and Sergeant Collins pushed one of the doors open.

The sterile waiting room, with padded metal chairs, white walls and service logos on the walls, was small enough to be a holding cell. He'd spent too much time in those lately. This one at least had a smiling receptionist.

"Have a good day, sir." Sergeant Collins went to the far end of the room, swiped her ID and disappeared through a door with a sign that read AUTHORIZED ACCESS ONLY.

"Good morning, Lieutenant," the receptionist said in a mild Southern accent. She was retirement age, and makeup couldn't camouflage the pallor that Faraz figured came from the best part of forty years working down in this hole. "Please have a seat. General Hadley will be with you shortly."

"Thank you, ma'am." Faraz chose a chair under the army logo and picked up an old magazine so he could look at something that might distract him from where he was.

He had been working for the DIA, in essence, for two years. But he'd never been here, never even close to here. Faraz ran a finger across his neck under the shirt collar and tie. He flipped a page of the magazine but had no interest in it.

All he wanted to do was get this meeting over with. He had met Hadley once before. Nice enough for a general, said he owed Faraz some medals. And that was before this last mission. Faraz would take the medals, the handshake, the pat on the back. Then, he'd ask Hadley to let him return to his old unit—the 101st Airborne—the one his cousin Johnny had been part of.

That's the reason Faraz joined the army. To honor his cousin. In fact, Johnny was much more than a cousin. He was a friend. A mentor. When Faraz graduated from UCLA, years after Johnny was killed in action, he still felt the draw.

The 101st had been Faraz's army home until he'd let himself get talked into this mess. And that's where he wanted to return.

Not likely. After the two jobs he'd done for the DIA, they were not going to give him up without a fight. He would have to defy a three-star general. Faraz had faced down terrorists, survived an air strike, killed a man in hand-to-hand—done other things he preferred not to think about. So why were his knees bouncing now? He put his feet flat on the floor to regain control.

The receptionist took a call and turned toward Faraz. "Lieutenant?"

"Yes, ma'am."

"The general has been delayed at the White House. He'll be back as soon as he can."

The White House. The general was meeting him right after meeting . . . who? The president? No. No. This was too much. He was not ready for this.

"I don't know, ma'am."

"Sorry?"

"I need to go. I'll see the general another time." Faraz put down the magazine, stood and walked toward the doors.

"Lieutenant, please."

"Tell General Hadley I'll see him another time." Faraz grabbed the door handle, but it was locked. He pounded on it, then turned back to the receptionist. She pushed a button and the lock slid. Faraz pulled the door open and went into the holding area. He realized the outer door wouldn't open until the inner one closed, so he pulled at it against the pneumatics. The sound of the inner door's lock finally engaging was followed by the click of the outer door opening.

Faraz pushed it and walked past the policemen toward the elevator.

"Sir," one of them called after him. "You can't leave this area without an escort."

"Then escort me." Faraz stepped into the elevator and pushed the button for the main floor.

The officer rushed to join him just before the doors closed.

Chapter Four

The only civilian on the medevac flight from Germany to Washington eased herself off the gurney and pushed away the hand of the nurse who was helping her.

"I'm okay," she lied.

Bridget Davenport was an army veteran and head of a covert task force. She was not letting one lousy jihadi bullet make her an invalid, not even a big high-powered bullet.

She grabbed a handhold along the curved steel wall and took a step forward. Okay, that worked. She took another step and got a sharp pain in her right side. Left side good, right side not so much. She stopped and stretched.

The steady vibration of the aircraft and the incessant roar of the engines weren't making this any easier. And it was cold. The cavernous interior of the C-17 felt like the inside of a refrigerator—a big refrigerator that could hold more than four hundred normal refrigerators.

"Let me help you," the nurse offered from behind.

"No," Bridget insisted, holding out her left hand to block any attempt. She turned her head to look at the nurse in her flight suit and combat boots. Bridget's expression softened. "I need to do this myself."

"It's too soon, ma'am."

"Maybe. But I don't have time to wait. If I can't at least go pee on my own, how am I going to get back to work when we get to DC?"

"Honestly, ma'am, I think you need to temper your expectations on that. The surgery you had, an AK round through the side, that's serious business."

"Yeah, well, fuck all AKs. And fuck all jihadis, too."

The nurse laughed. "Yes, ma'am. Fuck 'em all."

"And fuck tempering expectations, too."

"Well, good luck with that."

Bridget smiled. She turned back toward the toilet cubicle and made her way, step by agonizing step, with the nurse shadowing her. Halfway there, Bridget stopped for rest and turned to survey the scene—long rows of gurneys bolted to the floor, each with a patient under white sheets and heavy blankets, with IV bags and medical monitors hanging. Doctors, nurses and technicians moved from bed to bed, checking, chatting, administering a med, holding a hand.

She resumed her slow, painful walk to the cubicle.

With the door finally closed and locked, Bridget leaned against the sink and winced. The pain was significant, even by her standards. The nurse was right. It was too soon, but she was not surrendering.

The bathroom mirror was unkind. They'd washed her hair at some point, but it was a tangled mess from more than a week of lying in bed. She had on no makeup, not that she ever wore much, but the scary thing was that she looked terrible. She was pale, kind of yellow in the weak bathroom light. Her eyes looked tired. She had lines on her face she'd never noticed before. A few months shy of her fortieth birthday, Bridget thought she looked eighty-five. She turned away and did what she had to do.

On the way back to her bed, she passed the nurse again. "I need my backpack and I need to get online," she said.

"Ma'am, I can get your bag, but the Wi-Fi is for aircrew and medical staff only."

Bridget sat on the edge of her gurney and put on the least nasty tone she could muster. The pain made it difficult. "When you bring me my bag, I will give you my ID, which you can show to the captain or whoever needs to see it to get me on the motherfu—" Bridget took a breath. "On the internet. Okay?"

"Sure, ma'am." The nurse sounded skeptical but, as often happens, appeared willing to let someone higher up do the arguing.

Ten minutes later, Bridget had a username and password scribbled on a yellow sticky note. She smiled. It was affirmation that she still had some clout, even bandaged and in pain at thirty thousand feet. She needed that.

Bridget logged in and opened an email from her boss, General Hadley. *"I hear you're flying back today. Safe travels. Heal up. Rest up. Hooah!"*

What the hell does that mean? Where's the "We need you back in here" line? And *hooah*, the army word for everything gung ho? In this case meaning . . . what? "You go, girl," maybe. She didn't remember Hadley patronizing her before.

Bridget opened a secure chat and pinged her deputy, Liz Michaels.

"*Hi! Great to hear from you,*" Liz responded. "*How are you?*"

"*I'm fine. How's it going?*"

"*Wait, you're supposed to be in flight now.*"

"*I am.*"

"*Cool.*"

"*So, how's it going?*"

"*We're good.*" Not exactly the level of detail Bridget wanted.

"*How was the White House meeting?*"

"*Not fun.*"

Bridget snorted. She'd had her own tense moments there. "*Anything new on Assali?*"

"*No, nada.*"

"*You think I could get something more than two-word answers?*"

"*I guess.*"

Then Liz added, "*That was a joke.*"

"*So, tell me what the F is going on.*"

"*Hadley said not to bother you with stuff.*"

It took Bridget a few seconds to decide how to respond. "*On a Pentagon line, I cannot type what I want to type right now about a three-star general.*"

"*LOL. Don't be too hard on him. He's worried about you. We all are.*"

"*That's sweet . . . I guess. But not necessary. TELL ME ABOUT ASSALI.*"

"*We don't have much new on him. We had a few bursts*

of chatter that were maybe about him or maybe about an attack or maybe about nothing. Now, it's gone quiet."

"Shit."

"Yeah, exactly." Then she added, *"Sorry for the two-word answer. Haha."*

Without phone call intercepts, the intelligence community had no way of even guessing what Assali and his remaining cohort were up to. Bridget was pretty sure he'd be up to something. She had to get back into the building, see the data for herself, push the staff in the right directions.

"Hadley says you're out two months, maybe three," Liz wrote.

"Screw that. It's what the docs say, but I'll be in the office by the end of the week if I have to shoot my way out of the hospital."

"That would be good news for me, but don't overdo it. You need to rest."

"Everybody's a doctor, now. I'll see you Friday, if not before."

"All right. Good luck. Don't shoot anyone."

As Bridget closed her laptop, the nurse appeared with her pain meds. "You should get some rest, ma'am."

Bridget glared at her. "The next person who tells me to get some rest is gonna get thrown off this airplane."

The nurse folded her arms across her chest.

"Okay, sorry," Bridget said. She took the meds.

"Listen, ma'am, you're under a lot of stress, coming off being shot, hospital time, now back to your regular job stress, whatever that is. You can snap at me. It's okay. But recognize it for what it is."

"You saying I have PTSD?"

"No, ma'am, not Disorder. That would be above my pay grade, anyway. But every patient on this plane has Post-Traumatic Stress to handle, medical staff and aircrew, too. We all get through it in our own way at our own pace, with help if needed. But half the battle is recognizing it."

"Yeah, okay. Thanks." Bridget touched the nurse's arm. "I actually am tired."

The nurse fluffed Bridget's pillow. "We have about six hours to go. I'll give you a heads-up when we're getting close."

Bridget nodded and slid along the gurney to lie down on her wound-free left side. The vibration of the plane soothed her, like one of those quarter-eating massage beds at motels in the mountains. That made her think about her boyfriend, Will, left behind in Baghdad, riding his desk job at forward Special Ops HQ. They'd had a helluva day—gone off-book, shot some jihadis, nearly gotten her killed. They'd also maybe repaired their relationship, just in time for yet another separation.

She stared at the exposed metal ceiling. Bridget knew from her army days that that's the way these things go. She knew it would be true when she decided, against all experience, to date a Navy SEAL. At least they were in a good place for their next holding pattern. She should have chatted with him when she was online. Well, who even knew what the hell time it was in Baghdad? She'd send him an email when she got to DC.

Bridget shifted to a less painful position. The next thing she knew, the nurse was waking her for landing.

Chapter Five

Assali looked particularly small in the super-king-sized bed in one of the prince's many guest rooms. The morning sun snuck through at the edges of the blackout curtains, delivering soft light to wake him.

He felt much more like himself than he had at any time in the past week, since he'd left that lovely blonde in the hotel room in Amman, minutes ahead of the Jordanian security forces and, no doubt, their American masters. Damn them for interrupting. He'd had more plans for her.

Since then, he had lived in a series of dingy safe houses and desert tents, and then the shit-soaked village and that awful boat. Last night, after a silent ride with the prince's security men, he'd taken his first shower and eaten his first decent meal in all that time. He regretted only that the prince served neither whiskey nor whores, but his regret was short-lived. He'd fallen asleep the minute his head hit the silk pillowcase.

Lying on his back, he admired the gold leaf geometric pattern on the twenty-foot ceiling. It was incongruous for a desert palace, but the walls were covered with dark green velvet and hung with fine wool carpets in flora and fauna designs.

Next to the large window to his right, twelve framed tiles depicted one of the most popular scenes in Middle Eastern folklore—three gazelles and a lion under a large tree, lush with leaves in shades of green and yellow. It was called the Tree of Life, and it originated as a mosaic on the floor of the bath in Hisham's Palace, built by a wealthy caliph in the eighth century near Jericho.

Tree of Life, indeed. One of the gazelles was being attacked by the lion and blood ran down its side. Assali had seen sanitized versions in the region's tourist bazaars, with the gazelles and the lion grazing side by side. This one, true to the original, carried the message that life is for the strong—appropriate for a caliph, he reasoned, and for the prince he would meet this morning.

Assali swung his legs over the side and dropped down to the terra-cotta floor, a full meter below the top of the mattress. He put on the plush slippers that had been provided and padded to the bathroom to prepare.

Back in his room, Assali found a sumptuous breakfast of eggs, fresh-baked flatbread and rich, dark Turkish coffee. His clothes had been cleaned and laid out for him. The attendant had found him a red and white *kufiyah*, as requested. Assali knew that was the prince's preference.

As he finished adjusting it on his head and draping the corners over his shoulders, the attendant appeared and led him to an anteroom lined with twenty identical oversized leather chairs, separated by small tables sporting woven white doilies, bottles of water and small blue vases with one fresh rose in each. The prince was flaunting his ability not only to have roses in the desert, but to waste them. Assali sat in the chair closest to the office door. His throat went dry. He opened the nearest bottle and took a sip.

Assali had been in the prince's palace before, always with some trepidation but never with the fear that gripped him now. The marble pillars, Koranic-verse tapestries and wall-sized mother-of-pearl reliefs were more intimidating than usual.

He went over the pitch he would make.

The infidel Americans had destroyed much of his capability and frozen the bank accounts he had built through years of hard work. He would have to convince the prince that his old-school, back-to-basics plan was worthy of support. It was the sole pathway to Assali's twin goals—cause maximum pain to America and its Israeli lackeys and provide himself with enough money to buy an island somewhere and live out his days in luxury. The prince shared the first goal and had indulged the second. Until now, at least.

Assali wished he'd made the move to the island before this disaster. He'd had more money than most men dream of. But neither the money nor the revenge was ever enough. Now, the Americans had made him a refugee again, and a beggar, too.

If the prince found his plan lacking, he'd be chucked out with nothing, at best, shot in a desert ditch, at worst. Or was it the other way around?

* * *

Assali expected to be kept waiting, the requisite show of power, but as his wait passed ninety minutes, his worry grew. This was humiliation. If he was lucky, it would be the worst punishment the prince would give him.

Finally, an aide appeared and without apology ushered him into the office. It was bigger than the waiting room, with the same ornate decorations. There were sofas all around, a conference table and another for meals, and four chairs in front of the desk for visitors.

In a tall-backed, green leather chair, behind the large, ornate wooden desk, flanked by free-standing poles—one with the national flag and the other with the royal standard—sat Ghassan Mohammed al-Tayyib, the prince's secretary and enforcer.

Assali exhaled, his shoulders sagged. But he righted himself—he hoped before al-Tayyib noticed. The secretary was writing something, or pretending to. He made Assali stand by the door in case there was any doubt about who had the power in this meeting.

Assali had met al-Tayyib several times. The prince's favorite henchman was short, like Assali, but maybe half his weight. Today, he looked even thinner than Assali remembered. His *qamis* was fine cotton, pristine white and, Assali knew, reached his ankles. Though it was surely tailored, it seemed to hang off of him. Al-Tayyib's sunken olive-tone cheeks gave way to a beard that would not behave as a good Saudi beard should. Behind reading glasses, his dark eyes, as always, revealed nothing. Assali had never seen the man smile.

Al-Tayyib glanced at Assali, as if noticing him for the first time, and made a gesture toward a chair in front of the desk. He did not get up. No hug, no kisses on both cheeks, no words of welcome. Not even a handshake. Al-Tayyib went back to his document, signed it, summoned an aide and handed it off.

"Tea, *sayyid*?" the aide asked.

The enforcer gave a half nod and the aide scurried away. Al-Tayyib folded his hands in front of him, took off his glasses and finally looked at Assali. He stared for several seconds, seeming to disapprove of what he was seeing. Assali sat up straight in his chair and waited for his host to speak first.

"The prince is disappointed in you," al-Tayyib said.

"It was a setback. We were betrayed, but—"

Al-Tayyib raised a hand to silence him.

"It was a defeat. You should not blame others."

"Yes. No, of course not. Please convey my deepest apologies—"

Al-Tayyib made a sound like "*Pfffft*," which, roughly translated, meant "Screw you and screw your apology."

"If not for your past record of service . . ." Al-Tayyib waved his hand beside his head, as if releasing a puff of smoke.

Assali got the message.

The aide reappeared with a shiny tray holding a tall silver pot and two glasses in silver holders. Each glass was on a saucer with sugar cubes and a small cookie. He put the tray on the desk and retreated. Al-Tayyib made no move to serve. That was unacceptably rude—another slight Assali had to take.

"*Sayyid*," Assali tried for a subservient yet confident tone, "I have a plan. We will yet achieve his highness's goals. If I could speak to him—"

"Speak to me," al-Tayyib said. He leaned back to listen

and almost disappeared into the oversized chair. He folded his hands under his chin. His index fingertips reached up to touch his lips.

Assali cleared his throat. "Last night—Eilat and Aqaba—it was a small gift to the prince."

"Small, yes."

Assali ignored the insult. "It was also a demonstration of what I can accomplish in spite of the recent difficulty, what I want to accomplish for our cause. Confronting the Americans directly in Syria was high-risk. Now, we return to a more . . . how shall I say . . . insulated approach.

"We use my old network. We kill Zionists and their collaborators. We force the Americans to help their child Israel, to stretch their resources and damage their immoral efforts throughout the region. We make the criminal Martelli look weak for the coming election.

"In a short time, when the network is fully reconstituted, we make our decisive blow—one they will never forget. And we create a situation where his highness, should he want to, could be the peacemaker—burnishing his relations with the Americans and with our brothers in the region. Or, if he prefers, he could increase the pressure, inflicting maximum pain on the Americans and taking credit with our friends in Moscow and Beijing."

"And how will you accomplish all these great things?"

"As I have for decades, *sayyid*, by making use of my brother Palestinians. They will do what we ask for their own reasons, and for little money. And we shall push them to new heights."

"And for you?"

"For me? For me, only his highness's affection and perhaps some restoration of my reputation. Of course, my commission will be reduced in light of the recent troubles."

Al-Tayyib grunted. "Yes. And no doubt you will need money up front."

"Sadly, yes. My accounts are frozen. It will cost money to set the wheels in motion, and more later for the critical battle."

"Which will be . . ."

"I have some ideas. I will be able to provide you full details when I see how the effort plays out."

Al-Tayyib looked toward a far corner of the room and stroked his beard.

Assali let the man think for several seconds. "*Sayyid*, many of my people are in hiding. It is a difficult time. But Eilat and Aqaba prove all is not lost."

"I will take your proposal to the prince. It is not much, but you are right about one thing. This is a challenging period for the jihad. We need new avenues. You will have your answer tomorrow."

The prince's gatekeeper put his glasses back on and turned to the next paper on his desk.

"Thank you, *sayyid*," Assali said. He stood, gave a half bow, and left the room, walking backward, as if al-Tayyib were the prince himself.

The next evening, Assali was in a luxury hotel room in Riyadh. Still no whiskey or women, but he had an initial payment in a new Swiss bank account and half a dozen satellite phones in his suitcase.

He opened a bag of Belgian chocolates from the minibar and dialed a number he had memorized years ago.

"*Aloo.*"

The voice brought back memories of the old days—difficult times whitewashed with nostalgia. He smiled. "I know your voice, my old friend. Do you know mine?"

"*Sayyid* A—" The man stopped himself.

"Well done, my brother. No names, please."

"Yes, *sayyid*. I am surprised to hear from you again so soon. And pleased, of course. Very pleased."

"You and your men did well."

"It was our honor to again serve the jihad. And we thank you for the opportunity."

"Now, you shall have another opportunity."

"*Allah hu akbar.*"

"Yes, yes." Assali laid out his plan—a small-scale but bold strike that would achieve two goals. It would keep up the pressure on the Zionists and Martelli. And with luck, it would provide him with the men he needed for what was to come next.

"We can do it," the man on the phone said.

"Good. I thought perhaps you were ready to retire, as an old man should."

The man laughed. "I am not as old as you, *sayyid*."

Assali snorted. "I will send you some funds. You must move as quickly as you can."

"Yes, of course, *sayyid*. And *sayyid*, I am glad we are back. When I read the news last week, I was afraid . . . You know."

"Do not fear, my friend. I am like a cat, although by now, maybe only four or five lives remaining."

"*Alf sanna, sayyid.*" May you live a thousand years.

"*Wa inta.*" And you.

Chapter Six

Bridget didn't make it to the office by the end of the week, but it was only a few days past her self-imposed deadline that she managed to get out of the hospital without having to shoot anyone.

Most people would have gone straight home. Not Bridget. She told the taxi driver to take her to the Pentagon and ordered Liz to find a wheelchair and meet her at the entrance. Then, at the DIA doors, she stashed the wheelchair behind the policemen's desk so she could walk into the office—slowly, leaning heavily on a cane—to a polite round of applause from her staff.

Bridget smiled to hide the wince from the pain that shot from the wound on her side down to the tips of her toes, then raised her left hand to stop them. "All right. All right. Thanks. We'll talk later. Now, back to work."

A few approached to shake her hand or offer a gentle hug. It was awkward to be the target of their affection or pity or whatever it was, and to be at work in the oversized army logo sweatshirt and sweatpants that she'd asked a nurse to buy for her in the hospital shop.

This was about as far from her usual look as Bridget

could imagine. She had a touch of makeup borrowed from the nurse, and her hair was, well, brushed, anyway. It's not that she was vain, but she had an image to project—powerful, beautiful, in charge. She felt none of that. But at least she was there.

Bridget walked the few steps to her small office and eased herself into the desk chair. She raised the sweatshirt to check the bandage. No blood. Good. Still, she was a little dizzy. Maybe this wasn't such a good idea.

Liz appeared holding a classified file and a newspaper. "So, Superwoman, all good?"

"Definitely not 'all good.' But it will have to do." She tilted her head toward Liz's file. "What do I need to know?"

Liz looked as perky as ever, khaki slacks, white blouse, ring curls of brown hair touching her shoulders, and even thinner than Bridget remembered. The stress of temporary command, perhaps. Liz was smart and learned fast but had less than three years under her size twenty-six belt.

"It's a shit show. There's finally some movement on the comms intercepts and we caught a couple of suspicious bank transfers, but the money bounced and we lost track of it. Something's up but we don't know what, and that's worse than not knowing anything at all. The president wants Epsilon, and he wants it yesterday."

"To do what?"

"To find out what the hell is going on. We put a mission together for consideration."

Bridget took a breath and the shooting pain came again. "I have a lot of reading to do. Brief me later, okay?"

"No time. Decision meeting is in an hour in Hadley's office."

"An hour? You should have told me."

"As I mentioned, I was ordered not to add to your stress

level. No one thought you'd be here today or were in any kind of shape to be involved at long distance. And, honestly, looking at you, I'm not sure you are."

That got an irritated look from Bridget, but she swallowed her comeback, saying only, "Thanks."

"Sorry, Bridget, I—"

"No, it's okay. You're probably right. But it doesn't matter. I'm here." She shifted in her chair to find a less uncomfortable position. "Lay it out for me."

Liz sat next to the desk, facing Bridget, and opened the file on her lap. "We think Eilat and Aqaba were a clue. We've shut the terror networks down in much of the region. But the Palestinian jihadis are separate from the newer groups in Iraq and Syria."

"I know the history."

Liz flipped a page. "So, there's a jihadi group called *Al-Hakam Al-Islamiyah*, the Ultimate Islamic Judge, or A-HAI."

"We used to call them A-HOLE. This is my specialty, remember."

"Right. Sorry. So, you know they did some nasty attacks several years ago, then refused to merge with Hamas when most of the groups did. Then they fell off the grid."

"Let's get to the part I don't know."

"Well, the guy who escaped the roundup, Assali, is connected to A-HAI. He was involved in their early years. Started out as a wannabe, couldn't cut it as a fighter, became a sort of liaison-financier."

"Hmm. Okay, that I didn't know. So, you think he went back to his old buddies when we took down his operation?"

"Exactly. If Assali and his masters want to keep pressure on us, that would be a relatively easy way to do it—

use his oldest and deepest network. The Eilat-Aqaba strike would fit."

"Yes. But you seem to be long on assumptions and short on facts."

"We are. But it's all we've got. If we're wrong, at least we'll find out."

Bridget looked out her window into the bullpen of cubicles where the staff was hard at work. "So, what's the plan?"

"We put an operative in an Israeli prison, have him connect with some A-HAI guys held there. Then they all get released in a prisoner exchange so our man can find out what they're up to."

"Sounds simpler than it is. The Israelis don't like to release prisoners. And it sounds like a lot of risk on a 'maybe.'"

"It's not as bad as a 'maybe.' There's more in the file." Liz handed it over.

"Okay, but it will take months to train up an Arab-American to take this on."

"Not if we use Abdallah."

"Abdallah? Afghan-American? Just back from a brutal mission?"

"Well, I can't speak to the 'just back' part, but the profile has him arrested by the Israelis while sneaking into the country to join the jihad. He wouldn't be the first one. Should work."

"'Should work.' Jesus, Liz." Bridget leaned back in her chair.

"Give us some credit, Bridget. This is a fully formed mission profile. We didn't come up with it in the coffee room this morning."

Bridget stared at the file. "Okay. I'll have a look."

"Two more quick things." She handed Bridget that day's Style section from the *Washington Post*. It had a quarter-page portrait of Bridget in her army uniform under the headline "CAPTAIN BADASS: SHE TOOK A BULLET TO CATCH WORLD'S MOST WANTED."

"Oh, good Lord."

"Yeah. Friendly article, though. Nice picture, too."

It was the one the army had taken before Bridget's second deployment to Afghanistan—the one they would have published with her obituary. The good news was that she was ten years younger in the photo. Bad news was it felt like thirty. And the worst news was that she was famous—the last thing the head of the president's favorite covert counter-terror organization wanted.

Liz stood to leave. "And I like the new nickname, Captain Bad—."

"First person who tries it . . ."

Liz laughed. "I'll put out a warning."

Bridget tossed the paper aside. "What's the other thing?"

"Did they tell you Abdallah is missing?"

CHAPTER SEVEN

Faraz opened one eye.

The room was sideways—lit by rays from a distant streetlamp. He saw cheap paneling, a kitchenette littered with fast food wrappers and snack bags, a coffee table with more of the same plus several empty beer bottles and a nearly empty bottle of cheap vodka.

Oh, Allah.

Faraz closed the eye. He wanted to go back to sleep. But there was something he had to do first. He pushed himself off the sofa, steadied himself against a wall and made it to the bathroom.

What the hell was he thinking? He hadn't had a drink in more than a year, hadn't planned to drink ever again—perhaps one positive thing to come out of his time living as a jihadi.

That didn't last long.

One walk through the Pentagon was all it took to send him on a two-hundred-fifty-dollar taxi ride to Delaware and the best room in the cheapest motel half a block from the beach and half a block the other way from

Henry's Liquors and Convenience Store. That was . . .
well, several days ago, anyway.

Faraz's head hurt. He found a piece of cold pizza on
the counter and ate it. There was one beer left in the fridge,
and two good shots of vodka sparkled in the bottle.

But no.

He went back to the bathroom, leaned over the sink
and splashed cold water on his face. The cracked mirror
showed neither a jihadi nor a soldier. His stubble was too
short for one, too long for the other. Who was looking
back at him? Hamed? Karim? Lieutenant Abdallah?

Faraz turned toward the tub. He'd tried to kill himself
in a tub just like it a few months ago. He was not doing
that again, though the vodka had come close. He turned
on the water, took off his clothes and hoped that a shower
would make him feel human again, help him figure out
what to do next.

Half an hour later, wearing his last clean T-shirt and
the previous day's underwear and jeans, Faraz raised the
blinds to see the first bit of light in the eastern sky. The
shower had helped, but he needed to get out of this room.
He threw his things into his backpack and went downstairs, where he tossed his key into a basket on the front
desk, took a free paper cup of coffee from a machine in
the lobby and headed for the beach.

The expanse of sand at the end of the street brought
back bad memories of the Syrian desert, so Faraz raised
his gaze to take in the ocean. He turned right to walk
south and watched the sun rise. Breathing the sea air and

getting his blood flowing, he was indeed feeling more human, but he was no closer to having a plan.

Faraz heard the sound before he saw anything. There was no cover on the beach, but instinctively, he dove to the ground.

The chopper came out of the sun. He shielded his eyes as the backwash hit him with a cloud of sand. He saw it was an army Black Hawk. Strange. Why would a chopper land on the beach, and why an army chopper?

He squeezed his eyes shut. Maybe this was yet another bad dream. But when he opened them, he was still on the beach and the chopper was still there, too.

A soldier emerged, walked toward him and yelled over the noise, "Lieutenant Abdallah?"

What? How does he know my name?

The soldier reached him, held out a hand and shouted again. "Lieutenant Abdallah, sir?"

Faraz took the hand and stood, still not sure what was going on. Then another figure emerged from the helicopter.

The soldier spoke close to his ear. "Sir, Ms. Davenport needs to speak to you."

"Davenport? Holy shit."

"Sir, please." The soldier gestured at the chopper and pulled Faraz toward it.

As he got closer, Faraz could see that indeed it was Bridget, in flight suit and helmet, holding onto the helicopter door for support.

"Hello, Faraz," she shouted over the rotor noise. "You're a hard man to find."

"How did you—?"

"Credit cards. Wanna go for a ride?"

"A ride to where?"

"Fort Meade."

"The major?"

Bridget nodded.

"I don't know, ma'am."

"Faraz, we need you. This can't wait. If you can't do it, we're screwed. Your call, but, please, take the briefing." Bridget shifted her weight. It was a mistake. She winced.

"I heard you were wounded pretty bad."

"I'll survive. But the general would kill me if he knew I'd come on this little joyride." Bridget lifted her shirt to show him part of the bandage.

Faraz didn't want to go back into her world. But what choice did he have? If he refused to board, she could AWOL him and have the crew arrest him. She'd gone to a lot of trouble to find him, and he was done with that motel room. Fort Meade was at least not the Pentagon.

"No promises," he said.

"Just a briefing." She gestured toward the chopper doorway.

"All right, ma'am." He stepped onto the helicopter and offered Bridget a hand.

The Black Hawk lifted off as soon as their seatbelts were fastened. Faraz watched the beach shrink below them. They banked over Henry's and tilted forward for extra speed on a beeline for the base where he had "died."

A training accident. That was the official story. The one they gave the newspapers. The one they told his parents. When he let that happen, he told himself he could go back someday, relieve their pain. But he'd never made it. And somewhere deep inside, he had to admit that he knew even then that there was no going back.

It had taken a multi-day bender to remind him.

The proof was being on the chopper, talking about a new mission. He thought getting sucked back in should have made him feel worse, but it made him feel better. He had a purpose, a job if he wanted it.

"Just a briefing." "No promises." Those were the beginning of a new stream of lies—lies he would tell others and lies he would let himself believe.

Faraz ran his hand across his chin. That stubble would have to go. Or maybe it was a new beginning.

CHAPTER EIGHT

Five days later, ten operatives of the recently dormant A-HAI jihadist group approached an Israeli checkpoint.

Their leader, Iyad al-Hamdani, was excited to be back in the field. He was not much of an ideologue and certainly no Islamic scholar. His fuel was hatred. He'd been taught about the Zionists' theft of his homeland, including his family's ancestral home in Jaffa, since before he could understand the stories. They fled to a village in the West Bank, not far from Jerusalem, in 1948, then fell under Israeli occupation in '67.

For the last few years, lack of funds had forced him to suppress his hatred. Now, under the renewed generosity and direction of his old benefactor, Mr. Assali, he was back in business.

Iyad had enjoyed his trip to Eilat and the crossing to Aqaba for "shopping." His old comrades were happy for the work, happy to be back in the jihad, even happier to receive some of Assali's money. And Iyad had renewed his relationship with the watchmaker—"the old man in the Old City," he called him—whose skills extended to making and smuggling devices that had plagued the region for decades. Their reappearance in the two southern cities cemented the relaunch of A-HAI. Now, step two.

There were three men with Iyad in a white van waiting in line to cross from the West Bank into Israel proper. His long frame was hunched over in the front passenger seat with an AK-47 on his lap. He ran his right hand through his close-cropped salt-and-pepper hair. He pulled at the *kufiyah* he wore like a scarf, ready to raise it over his face, and peered through the layer of sand on the windshield.

The driver tapped rapid-fire on the steering wheel. The two men in the back squatted on the bare metal floor. Each had one hand on his weapon, the other on the door handles on either side.

"*Bi hudu, ya shabaab,*" Iyad admonished. Easy, boys. This was their first operation, but not his. At forty-two years old, Iyad looked like a man who had earned his premature wrinkles through years of stress and imprisonment. His dark eyes scanned for the rest of his team.

Four of them were in a gray car ahead of him in the line. The other two came from behind on foot, walking fast between the rows of cars. One of them was dressed as a woman with a pillow tucked under his floor-length traditional *abaya* dress to make him appear pregnant.

The frantic "husband" shouted in Arabic, "Please! Something is wrong. We must get to the hospital." The "wife" leaned on him and held her swollen belly.

One of the Israeli soldiers shouted back. "Stop! Stay where you are."

The couple kept moving toward him. "Please, she needs a doctor," the husband begged.

"Stop. We will help you, but you must stop."

The couple increased their speed, approaching to within two car-lengths of the soldier.

"Please, sir."

The "woman" tripped and went down on one knee. Her right hand went under her *abaya* and came out firing a machine pistol. Two soldiers fell immediately. At short range, high-powered bullets hurt like hell even when your vest saves you.

The "husband" ripped open the Velcro-ed back of his "wife's" *abaya* and unhooked an AK-47 from a shoulder strap. He used a car for cover and started shooting. His comrade dove into a gully by the side of the road, narrowly avoiding the Israelis' return fire.

The side doors of Iyad's van flew open. One of his men stepped out with a grenade launcher and turned the Israeli guardhouse into a storm of concrete shrapnel. Vests and helmets would not save those inside.

People in the other cars screamed. Iyad saw some lie down to avoid the gunfire. Others exited their vehicles in a panic, adding to the chaos and blocking the sight lines of the surviving Israelis.

The A-HAI men in the gray car got out, took cover behind the vehicle's doors and laid down covering fire. The two men from the back of the van ran forward until they reached the nearest wounded Israeli and pinned him to the ground. Iyad arrived and knelt down to be sure the man was alive. The soldier rolled over and raised his hands to defend himself.

Iyad put the AK to his head. "*B'sheket*," Iyad said in Hebrew. Quiet.

"*Yalla*," Iyad said to his men. Let's go. They dragged the soldier toward the van. He fought them. Iyad used the gun butt to hit him on the side of his head. The soldier stopped fighting and the men moved faster, bending low to avoid the gunfire from the surviving Israelis.

When they were nearly there, Iyad shouted, "*Ya, Allah!*" Damn it. He fell and grabbed his left arm. One of his men helped him up while the other pushed the soldier into the van.

While the men gagged and tied the soldier, Iyad leaned against the vehicle pressing his right hand onto the wound. He peeked around the edge to find the source of the incoming fire. He saw some Israeli civilians on the side of the road. They were armed with handguns, as many Israelis were, and they knew how to use them.

"Over there," Iyad said, showing his men where to fire. Their barrage forced the Israelis to take cover. Two men from the second team moved to get a better angle but were cut down by gunshots.

The "husband" and "wife" ran toward Iyad between vehicles. Iyad heard the report of a rifle and saw the wife's head explode. He looked toward a hill two hundred meters away. Another bullet pierced the van's side, sending Iyad's men diving to the floor. The Israelis apparently had a sniper he hadn't accounted for in his plan.

The "husband" got to the van, panting. "We must go," he said.

Iyad went to the driver's door. "Move over. I will drive."

"But your arm," the driver objected.

"Move!"

The driver obeyed, climbing over the gearshift into the passenger seat. The Israeli soldier moaned in the back.

The two survivors of the other team had already started their U-turn. Iyad followed them but continued around the back of the line of cars to make a full three-sixty. More sniper bullets hit the van and the road.

One of his men came to the front. "Commander, no! What are you doing?"

"Guns out," Iyad ordered.

Two men held AK-47s out the passenger's window. Iyad's shoulder bled into his shirt. He cursed the pain but kept his hands on the steering wheel. He floored the accelerator and threw up gravel as the van swerved onto the shoulder and sped toward the Israeli civilians taking cover in the roadside ditch. One of them got up and took a shot at them, then turned to run for better cover.

Iyad stopped the van. "*Atlaq!*" he ordered. Fire!

His men complied and he saw the Israeli fall. "Get him!"

"Commander—"

"Now!"

Two of his men scrambled out of the van's side door and moved toward the wounded Israeli.

A bullet shattered the right side of the van's windshield and hit the former driver in the face. He fell sideways onto the gearshift, without making a sound. The other men hit the ground.

"Go, go!" Iyad screamed at them. He pushed the dead man up against the passenger-side door.

The attackers got to the Israeli and started to drag him toward the van. The sniper stopped firing now, clearly unwilling to risk hitting one of his own. As they reached the side door, Iyad could see they had a woman.

She had an exit wound on the left side of her chest, high up near the shoulder. Blood soaked her white shirt. Her jeans were ripped and dirty.

The woman was unconscious but revived when they picked her up to put her into the van. "No!" she moaned. She dug her heels into the soft edge of the road, but there were three men on her. They threw her into the back of the van, on top of the semiconscious soldier, and jumped in behind her. She cried out in pain.

As the door closed, Iyad put the van into reverse and hit the gas. The vehicle lurched backward on the sand and stones of the shoulder. He turned the wheel to spin it, then shifted gears and pressed the accelerator again. The van fishtailed as it came up onto the road and moved away from the checkpoint at high speed.

CHAPTER NINE

Faraz hit the padded wall hard and fell to the floor. His jaw hurt from the blow.

"Sorry, sir," said the large man. "Was that too hard?"

Faraz was about to say "Yes," but Major Gerald Harrington spoke first. "Looked about right to me."

Harrington was watching from a corner of the small room usually used for martial arts training. He was the army's top covert operative trainer—short, wiry, shaved head, hard handshake, all business. Faraz had dealt with him several times. It was never fun.

Less than a week into his training, the beachfront bender and the promise of "just a briefing" were all but forgotten. The outlines of the mission hadn't mattered. He was "in" by the time the chopper landed among the bland buildings and boxy barracks of the fort. Before that, really.

Faraz rubbed his chin and spat. "Are we done here?"

"Not quite," the major said. "You need to look the part. One more, please, Sergeant."

The large man helped Faraz stand, shrugged, and punched him on the other side of his face.

Faraz spun around and hit the wall again. He glared at the major.

"All right," Harrington said. "That will have to do for now."

"For now?"

"We'll see how you look in a couple of days. Time to hit the books. Things are happening out in the world that could move up your timeline."

After a shower, Faraz met the major in a small windowless office with one desk and one chair.

Harrington slid an envelope across the desk. "This is the full mission brief. It doesn't leave this room. You'll have some time to study it every day. We'll grill you on it starting next week."

The major left. Faraz sat in the chair and broke the seal on the envelope. Inside was a thick file. The cover was stamped CLASSIFIED, with a lot of other terminology below it, ensuring that only a handful of people would ever see what was inside.

Across the top of the folder was the mission code name: SHOCK WAVE.

Faraz would be "Khayal Durrani," a solid Pashto name. He had immigrated to the United States from a refugee camp in Pakistan as an orphaned ten-year-old, thanks to a clean record and sponsorship from the Muslim Benevolent Association of Newark, which provided him with a foster family.

Khayal had been a troubled youth. After high school, a job in a supermarket and minimum-wage-plus-tips were not what he wanted out of life. He started saving every penny to buy a ticket to Europe so he could join the jihad. Six months later, he was captured late one night off the Israeli coast with three other men on a small boat.

As "Khayal," Faraz would be put in an Israeli prison. His mission was to infiltrate the Palestinian terror network known as A-HAI and find out what they were planning. If possible, he was to come up with a location for the current Number One on the United States' list of Most Wanted Terrorists. He was a financier, liaison and puppet master, likely luxuriating in a five-star hotel somewhere while coordinating the next big attack on America.

A grainy photo showed an overweight man with a beard, *kufiyah* and sunglasses. The caption read, "Possibly Saddiq Mohammed Assali, date unknown. Place of Birth, Lebanon. Nationality, Palestinian. Age, estimated 55 years."

Assali. Faraz had seen him once in Syria from a few dozen meters away. The jihadists treated him like royalty and called him "al-Malik," the King. He was their connection to the mysterious Gulfie money men. After Faraz reported Assali's name and link to the terrorists, the man had evaded an American-Jordanian assault team by mere minutes.

Faraz studied the image, then moved on. There was a pile of background information to memorize for the cover story, with names, places and a myriad of details. Faraz flipped to the next page and started studying.

Chapter Ten

There were bruises on the soldier's face and blood matted the hair on the left side of his head. He still wore his uniform, the shirt showing damage from the bullet that hit his armored vest.

Corporal Yuval Alon was nineteen and usually looked younger. But after fewer than twenty-four hours in captivity, he already appeared worn beyond his years. In the terrorists' video, Alon sat on a dirt floor. The woman lay next to him on a thin mat, unconscious.

On the large high-definition TV in the prime minister's office, they could see every detail of the stark scene, lit by a flickering fluorescent bulb.

By now, they knew that the woman was Maya Gerson, a twenty-five-year-old army veteran and mother of a two-year-old boy. She had no tubes or monitors attached. Half of her shirt was covered with a bloodstain. Someone, probably the corporal, had pulled her hair aside and twisted it so it would stay in place. The gray cinder block wall behind her indicated they were in a basement, or maybe a warehouse.

"We are alive and well cared for," Alon lied, his eyes

making clear that he was reading from a script. "We call on the Israeli government to accept the demands of *Al-Hakam Al-Islamiyah* and release the political prisoners in exchange for our freedom."

He looked toward Maya. "This woman was wounded and needs medical attention. We appeal to the government to make the trade as soon as possible." The screen went dark.

The prime minister sat back in his chair at the head of the cabinet table and cursed in Arabic. His first language was much better for cursing than Hebrew.

Shlomo Yardeni was a retired general and Israeli's first Sephardic leader. His family immigrated to pre-state Israel from Syria in the 1930s. He was born—the youngest of ten—in '48, the year of independence.

Yardeni's formerly black hair was gray now, but still close-cropped. His bushy eyebrows were gray, too. Life as a politician had grown his belly too large for his old uniforms. But no matter. He wore the dark suit, white shirt and blue tie of a politician—an imposing six-foot-four politician. He tried to project his former air of authority, but the government was much more difficult to command than any military unit.

"Never," came the snap decision from his foreign minister, Moshe Greenshpun, leader of the right-wing party whose support kept Yardeni in power.

"Your answer came quickly, Moshe," the prime minister said. "But not so fast that I didn't know what it would be before you said it."

The two men sparred all the time. Greenshpun's ideology gave him every answer to every problem. Yardeni preferred to consider his options, leading Greenshpun to label him "Shlomo in slo-mo" during the previous campaign.

"You would let them die," Yardeni continued, "without so much as a discussion?"

"Discuss, if you want. That is your specialty. The answer will be the same, and always has been. Israel does not negotiate with terrorists. Period."

"Except when we do."

"Except when someone makes a mistake out of weakness and strengthens the terrorists in the process."

Yardeni was used to Greenshpun's insults. He turned away from his nemesis and asked for opinions around the table.

To one extent or another, they all agreed with Greenshpun. If he was honest, the prime minister would have to admit that, philosophically, he agreed, too. But philosophy was easy. It was harder to sign the death warrants of two young Israelis. That, he was not prepared to do. Not yet, anyway.

"I want options," he said. "Diplomatic and military options. We will reconvene in two hours."

Greenshpun rose to object. But Yardeni turned his back and left the room.

That night, well after midnight, an Israeli Special Ops team moved silently through a West Bank village.

The leader, Major Yaron Drucker, raised a hand to stop them. He surveyed an alley with his night-vision goggles, then entered it and signaled for his men to follow.

They gathered at the rear door of a house. Drucker

looked at his sergeant, who double-checked the location on his GPS device, then nodded.

Drucker flipped his goggles up off his eyes and the others did the same. He gave the order with a hand signal.

His men hit the door with a battering ram and ran inside, shouting in Arabic, "Down! Down on the floor!" The team turned on their helmet lights to blind anyone who had been sleeping.

A woman screamed and ran across the hallway in front of them. Drucker followed her, pointing his Uzi. He saw her cowering in a corner, having pulled her children from their beds and wrapped her nightgown around them.

"*Ayn hom?*" Drucker demanded in Arabic. Where are they?

"*Ayn min?*" the woman replied. Where is who?

"The hostages," Drucker shouted in Arabic. He poked his rifle into her side.

The children screamed but the woman was defiant. "Are you crazy? There are no hostages here. It is only my children and me."

Drucker heard his men searching the house. "Where is your husband?"

"He is in Amman on business. Please, we are simple people. I do not know what you are talking about."

"Ach." Drucker left one of his soldiers to guard the woman and went to see what the others had found.

"The house is clear," his sergeant announced.

"Search the yard. Look inside and outside for a trap door or hidden room."

"Yes, commander."

* * *

Yardeni shook his head as he read the report and let loose another Arabic curse. The 1960s décor of the prime minister's office absorbed it. The wood paneling imported from America matched the desk, credenza and bookshelves. The Israeli government shield and the logos of the country's military units and police forces provided most of the decoration. A national flag stood in a corner.

Photos of Yardeni's four grandchildren smiled at him from a side table, implying expectations he was currently unsure he could meet.

The raid had come up empty. Indeed, the woman's husband was in Amman on business. The intel that pointed them to her house was false, likely planted by the terrorists to waste their time and damage his reputation. He had put a gag order on the information, so at least his humiliation would be limited to the cabinet room.

Meanwhile, Yardeni was no closer to rescuing the hostages and had no more intel on targets for further military operations. He looked at his watch, 6:30—early even for him. He had called a security cabinet meeting for 7:00. Greenshpun would be all over him. But even Greenshpun wouldn't leak classified operational details. Probably.

Greenshpun's grand entrance was at 7:10, and he made it look like he had to use all his strength to throw the morning newspapers onto the cabinet room's polished wood conference table, where they slid toward the prime minister.

"Sickening," Greenshpun declared.

Yardeni looked up from his conversation with the

social affairs minister. He glanced at the array of clocks on the wall. "Good of you to join us, Moshe. Perhaps now we can begin."

The officials settled in their seats, representing the group's permanent members—the foreign, defense, police and finance ministries. The head of military intelligence, General Oded HaLevy, was also there, as were a few others who had been working on the kidnapping.

"It is an abomination," Greenshpun declared. "More than half of the papers are calling for a prisoner swap. I will not be swayed. And I warn you, Shlomo, I will not be part of a government that capitulates to terrorists. It is a matter of principle and national security."

"You would be wise not to lecture me on either," Yardeni shot back, slapping his hands on the table and standing up to confront Greenshpun. "I was on the front lines when you were on the back benches of the Knesset plotting political maneuvers." He said the last words with evident disdain.

"I take second place to no one on these issues!" Greenshpun's face turned red, setting off his white hair. He was a foot shorter than the prime minister and half his weight. He wore a gray suit and the skullcap of a religious Jew. He glared up at Yardeni for a few seconds, then sat down and ceded the floor.

Stills from the hostage video were plastered on the front pages that lay scattered across the table, along with pictures of the distraught Alon and Gerson families and a blurred-out portrait of Maya's son.

Yardeni turned to Social Affairs Minister Sara Fridman, who would not usually attend a security cabinet meeting. "Sara, tell us about your visits last night."

Fridman was the youngest member of the government and not accustomed to addressing the senior leaders. She wore a gray sweater, a black skirt that reached past her knees and sensible shoes. Behind dark-rimmed glasses, her eyes looked like she hadn't gotten much sleep.

She stood, smoothed her outfit and looked down at the table. "It was difficult." Her voice was soft, almost inaudible. She cleared her throat and continued with as much confidence and volume as she could project. "Of course, the families are upset, frantic, actually. They want their loved ones back. They want you, us, to do whatever is necessary. When I left the second home, Maya Gerson's house, the police had to help me through the crowd. The people were angry, shouting curses and insults, and calling on the government to bring the hostages home."

"I am not surprised." It was Greenshpun again, with exaggerated disgust. "She lives in a liberal area, your supporters, Shlomo. How things have changed. Not so long ago, when attacks and kidnappings were more frequent, the country was united. Now, half of them, your half, have gone soft."

"We do not have soft generals." It was General HaLevy, the intelligence chief, speaking up for his old friend and former commander Yardeni. He stared Greenshpun down, daring him to insult the prime minister again.

Greenshpun snorted. "Ha. We shall see. It may be that the prime minister is more interested in having his ego stroked by calls from the White House than in making the hard decisions we need to fight terrorism. Giving in to the terrorists will lead to more terrorism."

"Enough." Yardeni raised a hand and looked around the table. "We all want to defeat the terrorists, and we will. That is a different question from how to protect the lives of these two young people."

"No, it is not," Greenshpun said. "And if they are killed, the terrorists will face a retaliation like none they have seen before."

"No amount of retaliation would bring back Maya and Yuval. And I'm not as sure as you are whether compromise or defiance would lead to more violence in the long term."

"Compromise? You can't—"

Yardeni pounded the table with his fist. "You will not give me orders! I have heard your opinion—and your threats and your insults—and I will make my decision. Meeting adjourned."

CHAPTER ELEVEN

In the major's sparse office, Faraz went through the by now familiar process of shedding his identity. His new IDs, credit cards, the last of his cash—all fit into a manila envelope. He thought of the duffel he had packed with his belongings the first time around. He had no idea where it was now. No use for it, either.

This ritual meant he had only a few more days of training—to be assaulted by the sergeant, to study his backstory, to get used to the idea of becoming a terrorist again.

He gave the major the dress uniform he'd worn that one day at the Pentagon. "Maybe it'll fit the next guy," he said. He thought he sounded dejected, though he didn't mean to.

"Put this on," the major said, handing Faraz a pair of black plastic sandals, white boxers and a blue Israeli prison jumpsuit. "We had it flown over specially for you."

"Now?"

"Schedule change, Lieutenant. You leave in an hour."

That got Faraz's attention. So much for having a few more days. He held up the jumpsuit. "All right, sir."

Harrington provided no privacy, so Faraz turned his back and changed. He tossed his clothes onto a chair.

The speakerphone on the major's desk buzzed and his secretary's voice came on. "Call for Lieutenant Abdallah, sir."

"Put it through," Harrington said.

"Faraz?" It was Bridget.

"Yes, ma'am. You're on speaker with Major Harrington."

"Sorry about the schedule change, but the Israelis could be moving toward a prisoner exchange. There's high-level pressure in play and we have to get you into position. Are you ready?"

"I have to be. It would be good if I could study the file on the plane, though."

"Major, let's make that happen."

"Already thought of it," Harrington said.

"Good. Faraz, I'd have come up, even with the short notice, but the general ordered me not to miss any more medical appointments."

"No problem, ma'am. Take care of yourself."

"Hey, that's my line. Be careful, Faraz. Stay safe."

"I'll check, but I don't think that's in the mission profile."

Bridget laughed. "Goodbye, Faraz. See you soon."

"*Insha'Allah.*"

At the flight line, Faraz said farewell to the large man who had provided his camouflage of bruises.

"I hope you're all right, sir."

"I hope they don't hit as hard as you did."

The sergeant laughed. "All due respect, sir, that was warm-up level."

"Good thing I got my 'Get into Jail Free' card, then." Faraz shook the sergeant's beefy hand.

Major Harrington handed Faraz the mission file and gave him one of his too-strong handshakes. "There's an open safe on board. You put these papers inside and lock it before you leave the plane. They'll bring them straight back to me."

"Yes, sir."

"Happy landings, Lieutenant. Good hunting."

"Thank you, sir." Faraz mounted the stairs toward the smiling air force flight attendant standing at the doorway of the small jet. Not many "prisoners" got assigned one of those.

"Good afternoon, sir. Welcome aboard."

Faraz settled into a wide beige leather seat. He stared out the window. As the plane began to taxi, he turned away from his last look at America and opened the file.

Fifteen hours and one refueling stop later, Faraz stowed the file and shielded his eyes as he stepped off the plane at an Israeli desert airstrip. He could see a road in the distance, a small building with a flight control room on its roof, a dark blue van bearing the logo of the Israeli Prison Service and little else.

Faraz got a casual salute from an officer at the bottom of the stairway. He noted that it would be his last.

"Welcome to Israel. I'm Captain Ilana Zemer."

"Thanks. Good to meet you." Faraz shook her hand.

Zemer looked him over. Taller than Faraz, with black

hair pulled back into a bun, wearing trousers and shirt the same color as the Negev sand, she spoke to him like he was a new recruit. Or a prisoner.

"You know you will not receive special treatment." She cocked her head toward the van. "Once you are inside the facility, you are a terrorist prisoner, like any other."

"Yes, ma'am. I understand."

"Are you sure you want to do this?"

"We all have our orders."

"I must ask."

"Yes, ma'am, I'm sure."

He wasn't, really. Who could be, in a situation like this? Was there any other situation like this?

"I will be like any other prisoner. But you're aware of the code word."

"Yes, but it is only to be used for urgent communications or if your life is in danger. We have translated it for you, which may be useful depending on your situation." She handed Faraz a piece of paper with the words in English and transliterations of the Hebrew and Arabic. "They will take this from you when you arrive at the prison. You have ten minutes to memorize it."

"And I will be placed into the necessary grouping?"

"Yes. We are aware of the contacts you need to make. That is why you are here at this prison."

Captain Zemer walked Faraz to the van and spoke to the three-man crew. "This is Khayal Durrani, prisoner number 2082-2708. He is an American who joined the jihad. Put him in solitary."

Faraz shot her a look.

"Some time in solitary will raise your credibility and

make you look more like a prisoner and less like, well, what you are."

Faraz pointed to a bruise on his face. "But we already—"

Zemer shook her head. "Solitary. Then we will release you into the general population to make your contacts."

That was not in the mission brief, but the Israelis were in charge now.

The guards cuffed his hands in front of him and put shackles on his ankles, connected by a short chain. He flashed back to his time in Syria, where he had worn a similar set just a few months ago.

One of the guards grabbed his arm. "Get in."

Faraz complied. He sat on a bench on one side of the van, under a small, barred window, clutching the piece of paper.

The van doors slammed and the vehicle moved off across the tarmac.

Faraz studied the words in the light from the window. "*Hazat 'Ardia*" in Arabic. "*Gal Helem*" in Hebrew.

In English, "Shock Wave."

Chapter Twelve

Bridget limped into General Hadley's office, leaning on her cane. While his staff worked in the second basement, the director of the DIA got a suite upstairs near the secretary's and a view that included the Washington Monument and a corner of Arlington National Cemetery.

"We're going to Tel Aviv," he said before she could sit.

"Hmm, okay. I thought you wanted me to move into Walter Reed." Bridget sat on a guest chair in front of Hadley's desk.

"You look better and the docs say you can travel."

"Do they now? You're getting medical reports on me?"

Hadley's right index finger tapped the three stars on his left shoulder.

"And, what's our mission, exactly?" Bridget asked.

"We'll meet with my old running buddy General Oded HaLevy, head of Israeli military intelligence. The White House wants to get Abdallah launched, but the president feels he can't count on the prime minister to agree to a prisoner exchange. It's on us to push the general to push the PM, or to make something else happen."

"Make what happen?"

"Whatever it takes."

"You're surprisingly eager on Abdallah, considering that he bailed on his meeting with you."

"I'll survive the slight. I guess he needed a minute or two. He's back on task now, according to Harrington. You got any better options?"

Bridget knew that Hadley knew she didn't have any better options. "When do we leave?"

"Tonight."

The van was cleared through the double fencing around Israeli Prison Service Facility Number Seven.

The back door opened and Faraz shielded his eyes from the desert sun. The driver stepped in and took the piece of paper from his hand. "From here, no one knows who you are. They only know what to do if any prisoner says the code word."

"Got it."

"Ready?"

Faraz took his last breath of freedom. "Yes."

The driver and the other guard each grabbed an arm and pulled Faraz from the van. He stumbled when he hit the ground, and the driver kicked him. "Up, terrorist!" the man shouted.

Faraz stood. They took his arms again and marched him into the prison.

Bridget and General Hadley got to Israel twenty-four hours after Faraz. At Ben Gurion Airport's VIP terminal, a protocol officer met their military executive jet—the same type Faraz had used—and sped them to the defense ministry headquarters in a three-vehicle motorcade.

They went through the entrance reserved for official visitors, with no security check, and took an express elevator to the top floor, where a conference room door stood open, revealing green cushioned chairs and pale-blue walls decorated with portraits of Israel's past defense ministers.

"James, it is good to see you." General HaLevy met Hadley at the doorway and put him into a bear hug. "And I'm pleased to congratulate you in person on your promotion." The general was a hair under six feet tall and not much overweight for a man in his sixties, with puffy jowls and hands the size of rib eyes.

"Thank you, Oded," Hadley said, disengaging from the embrace. "It's good to see you, too. This is Bridget Davenport, director of Task Force Epsilon."

Bridget was relieved that she got a simple handshake.

"Ah, the famous task force and the famous Captain Ba—"

"An honor to meet you, sir." Bridget cut him off before he could use her new moniker.

"And, James, perhaps you remember my covert operations chief, Colonel Ariyeh Ben-Yosef."

"Of course. I first met him when he was a cadet," Hadley said. He leaned across the table to shake Ben-Yosef's hand.

"Do not admit that," HaLevy said. "They will make you retire immediately."

"Don't tempt me." Hadley turned to Ben-Yosef. "I knew your father, Colonel. He was a good man."

"Thank you, sir." Ben-Yosef's smile disappeared for just a moment.

"And I remember, Oded, that you took young Ari under your wing after Lebanon."

"Yes, but I promise, I did not personally promote him."

Ben-Yosef gave Bridget the once-over without bothering to hide it. He was early forties, with olive skin, slicked back dark hair, crow's feet and a casual confidence that could easily slide over into arrogance. He wore tan desert camo, which contrasted with the older men's dress uniforms. Bridget shook his hand. He gave her a smile that she thought belonged in a hotel bar.

Bridget pursed her lips and looked away, catching a glimpse of the view toward the Mediterranean, a mile and a half away, before the general's aide closed the heavy curtains. When the aide retreated, the four of them settled into their seats, two by two—like in the Bible, Bridget thought—on either side of the conference table.

Hadley had asked for the meeting, so he opened the conversation, "I know you're in the middle of a crisis, Oded, so I appreciate your meeting with us. As you know, we have a plan in motion, and we need your help."

"We are always in the middle of a crisis, and of course, you will always have my help. But in this, I am not the one to decide."

"But you meet with the prime minister daily. No?"

"More or less. But, James, this is a longstanding problem for us and a longstanding policy. We cannot release these terrorists and we cannot encourage more kidnappings. I told you this on the phone."

"My understanding is that there could be some flexibility

in the case of these hostages and with our operation as an added incentive."

"The prime minister only seems flexible compared to his coalition partners. I do not believe he will do it, in the end."

Hadley asked Bridget to present the intel about A-HAI and Assali and to lay out the spike in comms intercepts and bank transfers.

"I know all this," HaLevy said, waving a hand to cut her briefing short. "And you know, James, we do not negotiate with terrorists."

"I also know that you have done so when it suited you and that you have hundreds of low-level prisoners you could release with little impact."

"Not hundreds. And they would not accept those men, not without the high-level terrorists who we will not release."

"Many in Israel believe getting your people back is the priority in this situation."

HaLevy scoffed. "Will you teach me Israeli politics now James? Many people believe many things, but they do not have the responsibility to keep the state safe. And as for keeping America safe? Well, you may have to find another way this time."

Bridget spoke up. "General, this is not just about stopping the next attack on America. We believe Assali will use his Palestinian network to attack Israel as a way to put pressure on us. Eilat and Aqaba, the kidnapping, these are the beginning of something bigger."

"Perhaps," HaLevy said. "But we have dealt with such waves before. The cabinet believes releasing the prisoners would only make it worse, and honestly, I agree. I recommended putting your man in place in the prison as a favor to you. The prime minister agreed in case things change. But I do not expect it."

Bridget felt Colonel Ben-Yosef staring at her and did her best to ignore it, focusing her gaze on the general.

"Perhaps there is a way," Ben-Yosef said.

Now, Bridget had to look at him, as did the two generals. "What way?" HaLevy asked.

"There could be many reasons we release one prisoner or a small group—illness, humanitarian grounds, even end-of-sentence. We could get the American into position without any connection to the kidnappings. I'd be happy to liaison with Miss Davenport to see if we can work something out." He smiled a "gotcha" smile.

Hadley seemed not to notice and turned back to his counterpart. "Oded, this is a high priority mission. The president wants it to happen. Whatever you can do to get our man launched will be much appreciated."

"How long are you staying in Israel, General?" Ben-Yosef asked.

"I have a couple of meetings at the embassy and then I'm off. But Bridget can stay to coordinate, if that would be helpful. Can't you?"

Bridget shot Hadley a look. They hadn't discussed that. She'd brought exactly one change of clothes, which she'd already put on before landing. She still wasn't used to dealing with the three-star version of Jim Hadley. "Yes, sir," she said, trying to make clear she wasn't happy and knowing it wouldn't matter.

"Good." General HaLevy appeared relieved that the meeting would end at something other than loggerheads. "Colonel Ben-Yosef and Ms. Davenport will work the issue for us. James, we will stay in touch. And next time, stay a little longer. It's been too long since that time I took you to my favorite hummus restaurant in Hebron."

"With two armored vehicles and a Special Ops team."

"The price one pays."

There was a knock on the door. HaLevy's aide stepped halfway into the room. "General, your, um, other visitors are here."

"Ah," HaLevy said. "Perfect timing. Send them in."

The aide opened the door all the way, and a woman came in with a girl about six years old. The child took tentative steps at first, but when she saw General HaLevy, she ran to him.

"*Sabah*," she shrieked.

HaLevy caught her and lifted her into his arms. "James, this is my granddaughter, Tali, and my daughter Rivka, who you met many years ago, I think."

"Of course." Hadley half stood from across the table.

Rivka walked past her father to Colonel Ben-Yosef and leaned over to give him a kiss. She was petite, with tight jeans, a white scoop-neck T-shirt and shoulder-length light brown hair streaked with blond.

Hadley smiled. "So the colonel is your . . ."

". . . son-in-law. Yes. They have been together since that difficult time when he became an unofficial member of our family. Some years later, they made it official."

Ben-Yosef spoke to Tali. "You have kisses for *Sabah* but none for me?"

"No!" The girl rolled her eyes and put her arms around the general's neck.

"I'm sorry for the interruption, James, but it is Take

the Kids to Work Day, or whatever they call it. Another American import, I think."

"Well, it's very nice to see Rivka again and to meet Tali, but we need to get to the embassy." Hadley got up and reached across the table to shake HaLevy's hand. "Thank you, Oded. Let's make this happen."

HaLevy stood with Tali in his left arm. "If it is in any way possible, I'm sure we will."

Bridget handed a business card to Colonel Ben-Yosef. "You can reach me on my cell or through the embassy."

"I'll do that." With his wife in the room, the colonel was suddenly projecting a professional demeanor.

Bridget smiled at Rivka, who had a proprietary hand with blue-painted fingernails on the colonel's shoulder.

After the meetings at the U.S. embassy on the Tel Aviv waterfront, Bridget walked Hadley to his car.

"Sorry for the short-notice assignment," he said.

"No notice, you mean."

Hadley looked out toward the beach crowded with sunbathers catching the afternoon rays and young people in bathing suits playing volleyball. The sun shined from a clear blue sky over the Med. "Yeah, well, there are worse duty stations. You were in one of those not long ago."

"True that, sir. This definitely looks like an upgrade."

"Well, don't get too comfortable. I need you back in DC ASAP. Meanwhile, the embassy doctor will track your progress. And stay away from the volleyball. You don't want to open your wound."

"Yes, sir." She shook his hand and Hadley got into the

car. Bridget waved as his vehicle and security team rolled out of the driveway.

Back inside, Bridget settled into a small office on the military liaison's floor. She had a desk, a chair, a secure computer and not much else. Her narrow window looked south along the beachfront promenade. If she pressed her head to the glass, she could see the Med. Bridget looked at the backpack sitting on the floor, her luggage for what was supposed to be a six-hour visit. It held her toiletries and the clothes she'd worn on the flight.

On her personal email, Bridget found a note from Will in Baghdad. *"Hi. Strange to have you so close and yet so far. Why not swing by on your way home? It's pretty boring here without you."*

Bridget had hoped for a reunion when he rotated out in a few weeks. Now, if he got to DC on schedule, they might yet again be on different continents.

She switched to a chat app. *"Hi. Got your email. Looks like I'll be here for a while."*

"Cool. How about date night? We'll break some rules, get mad, make up . . ."

Bridget was glad Will was sounding more like himself. The leg injury he sustained in Afghanistan had landed him in a desk job, possibly for good. The months of separation and the stress of his slow rehab had just about ended their relationship.

In all, they'd known each other for less than two years and been apart for most of it. Then, he showed up in Baghdad. They had a big fight, went on a barely legal operation together and she nearly died. And right after they made up in her clinic room—with only a kiss to seal it—she'd flown off on the medevac to Germany.

"*Sounds like fun. You're good at commandeering choppers. Come on over for dinner.*"

"*BE RIGHT THERE!!! Ha ha. I WISH! Watch out for those Israeli guys.*"

"*Roger that,*" she replied. It was like he had ESP. "*How's the leg?*"

"*Cane has been under my bed for the last week. Plan to keep it there.*"

"*Excellent!*"

"*So, why Tel Aviv?*"

"*Um . . .*

"*Need-to-know basis, as usual?*"

"*All you need to know is that I miss you. Now, let's see how soon we can both get back to DC.*"

"*Yes, ma'am.*" He sent her a salute emoji.

Bridget sent him back a thrown kiss and closed the app.

She opened her classified email to write to Colonel Ben-Yosef. If she was staying in Tel Aviv to coordinate with the Israelis and press them to help launch Faraz's mission, she was going to have to deal with him. She'd fended off plenty of men like him during her military and Pentagon careers. She was very good at saying no, and her martial arts training was there to back her up. Also, he was married. With that adorable little girl.

She found he had already written to her. "*I'm happy we will be working together. Let's meet for dinner to discuss.*" He named a waterfront restaurant and suggested eight p.m.

And there it was.

Right, let's discuss a classified mission and Israel's strategy on the hostages at a crowded restaurant, likely one with romantic lighting and a good wine list. Or maybe enjoy our dinner without any work talk and discuss the classified material later in my hotel room. Bridget rolled her eyes.

She wanted to write "You've got to be kidding me" or "Great, please bring your wife." But she couldn't afford to alienate him, so she typed, *"Thanks, but my day started twenty-four hours ago on the other side of the pond. Tomorrow at eight a.m. Your office or mine?"*

Ben-Yosef didn't give her a hard time. *"My office,"* he wrote back a few minutes later. *"Ten a.m. I will put your name on the security list."*

Bridget sat back and stretched. It had, in fact, been a long day, with no more than a catnap on the plane. Cat. Damn. She fired off an email to the cat sitter. Between her travel and hospital time, poor Sarge probably thought he belonged to the sitter.

The embassy had booked her at an American chain hotel within walking distance. It was early, but there wasn't anything more she could do until the meeting with Ben-Yosef. A shower and a bed sounded awfully good right now. She'd stop to buy some clothes along the way.

CHAPTER THIRTEEN

The solitary confinement cell was considerably nicer than the putrid shack where Faraz had been held in Syria. His new accommodation had a toilet and a hard bench for sitting and sleeping. There was enough room to exercise and he was not in chains. The food was edible.

Faraz was reciting his mission plan to himself when the bolt slid open and two large Israeli guards came in, shouting at him in Hebrew. They grabbed him, threw a burlap bag over his head and dragged him down the corridor. Faraz's shoulder hit the side of a doorway and they pushed him into a chair. His ankles were shackled to the chair legs and his wrists were cuffed behind him.

They left him alone, with the bag still on his head. Faraz worked to keep his breathing steady and sucked the material as close to his mouth as he could. The more air he could breathe in from outside the bag, the better. Otherwise, he'd breathe an increasing amount of carbon dioxide and become lightheaded—good for the interrogator, not so good for him.

It was easily an hour before Faraz heard several people come into the room. Someone pulled the bag off his head and he squinted at the light. The two large guards were on either side of him, and across a small table sat a thin, balding Israeli soldier in a uniform with no rank insignia or name tag. Faraz almost smiled. The blank uniform reminded him of Major Harrington.

"Good morning," the man said in accented English. He opened a notebook and took out a pen. "You are Khayal Durrani of Newark, New Jersey. Is that correct?"

"Um, yes."

"You sound unsure. Are you Khayal or not?"

"Yes, of course, I am."

"Good. You were arrested after arriving by boat on a beach south of Ashkelon two days ago. Why did you come to Israel?"

"Tourism."

One of the guards approached and slapped Faraz hard across the face. He spat blood.

"This will become tiresome and rather painful for you. We have treated you well, so far. That can change. I urge you to answer truthfully. Why did you come to Israel?"

"I came here to join the jihad."

"That is better. And who is your contact?"

"I have no contact."

The guard hit him again, so hard that he would have fallen off the chair if his ankles hadn't been attached to it.

The interrogator stared at him, waiting for a better answer.

"I had no contact in Israel. My contact in Cyprus I knew only as Mohammed. He arranged the boat for me and two others."

"And then what happened?"

"We were told we would be met on the beach, but we

were not. We split up. I was captured. I don't know what happened to the others."

"And who were the others?"

"We were told not to give each other our names."

"Three men rode a small boat from Cyprus, with a captain and maybe others, and never called each other by name?"

Faraz hesitated. This time, the other guard hit him in the back of the head.

"Hesitation means you are trying to think of the next lie. Now, tell me, what were their names?"

"I don't know. We followed the order not to tell."

The officer snorted and wrote something in his notebook. Without looking up, he said, "Take him."

The guards put the bag back on Faraz's head, took off his leg irons and pulled him out of the room. They led him along a corridor and down some stairs. He heard a cell door open. The guards took off his handcuffs, removed the bag and pushed him into his new accommodation. It was some sort of punishment cell, with a dirt floor, a thin mat for sleeping and a squat toilet in one corner. It was all of six feet by twelve, with a low ceiling and water dripping from a crack near the middle.

Faraz figured the Israelis wanted to soften him up for his next interrogation. Or maybe they were doing what the captain from the airfield said, making him look more like a prisoner. Either way, the theory was confirmed when his lunch came—a stale pita, a dollop of terrible hummus and a small glass of water. Well, this would give him something to talk about if they ever put him in the general population.

* * *

Bridget arrived at the defense ministry a few minutes early to allow time for security and to get up to wherever she was meeting with Colonel Ben-Yosef. But that was unnecessary.

The colonel came out of the gate as her embassy car pulled up. He greeted her with a too-long handshake and a smarmy smile, handed her a temporary ID and escorted her past the checkpoint with a hand on her upper arm.

In the elevator, he asked whether she'd slept well and how she was liking Israel, and he renewed his invitation to sample some local food.

Bridget was glad she'd opted for professional and modest clothes during her quick shopping trip the day before. She wore beige pants and a long-sleeved pale-yellow blouse buttoned nearly all the way to the top under her blue travel blazer.

The colonel's office was large enough to have a sofa and an easy chair, and it sported the same sea view as the conference room. Ben-Yosef told her to sit on the couch and made a show of extracting two cups of coffee from a machine on a side table. The aroma was impressive for a coffee lover like Bridget.

He delivered the drinks to the small table in front of her and sat in the easy chair. "Please . . ." he urged.

Bridget sipped.

"Do you like it?"

"Mmm. Deep and sweet. Very good, Colonel."

"I'm glad. And if we are going to be working together, I am Ari. And you are Bridget. Yes?"

"Yes, of course." She took another sip.

"May I say, it's hard to believe that photo is from over ten years ago."

"Photo?"

Ben-Yosef took a copy of the *Washington Post* Style section from an end table. He held it up and looked from Bridget to her picture. "Beautiful, in either version."

In Washington, Bridget would have had him busted down to corporal for a line like that. But the rules seemed to be different here and she needed his help. He was looking straight at her, his smile something between amorous and lecherous. Bridget figured he succeeded more often than he failed. He was good-looking and had the air of casual confidence she found attractive.

But Bridget was not in the mood or the market. She had nearly gone down that road in Baghdad, and it almost ended her relationship with Will. Was that really less than three months ago? She was not doing that again.

And she had a firm policy regarding married men. Pretty firm.

She wanted a different kind of action from Ben-Yosef than he wanted from her. So she smiled and forced the conversation back to the mission.

"Colonel—"

He looked at her sideways.

"Sorry. Ari, please tell me if you've made any progress toward finding a way to get our agent launched."

"We are taking good care of him, preparing him, in case we find a way. I am working on a proposal to have him released with some low-level prisoners even if the big exchange doesn't happen. But approval will take time."

"We don't have much time. We believe Assali will move quickly to restore his reputation."

"There have been many miracles in this land. Perhaps this will be the next one. But with all my abilities, I cannot move as quickly as . . ." he gestured toward the sky.

Bridget was not amused, but she smiled.

"Why don't we have lunch tomorrow for an update?"

Bridget declined and said she'd come back to his office instead.

She was not enjoying the game as she normally would. In the flirting war, she had the power. But on the mission, he did. She couldn't risk shutting him down or bruising his ego, not until the job was done, anyway.

Chapter Fourteen

The sand-covered Toyota pickup, with ripped seats and shock absorbers long since blown by desert roads, hammered its passengers without mercy as it bounced toward the camp.

In the front passenger seat, holding the window frame for dear life, Assali seethed. This was not his usual ride.

His new home came into view in the distance—a small compound with wooden outer walls. The gate opened. Without slowing, the vehicle passed through and skidded to a stop in front of the camp's only building.

It took Assali several seconds to get out, his bones aching with every movement. He straightened himself and his clothes as best he could, raised his chin and inspected the courtyard in front of the building. He nodded at various fighters who stopped what they were doing to offer small bows.

Disgusting. And hot. Very hot.

He should be at the hotel in Riyadh—or better yet, London—telling men in places like this what to do. Alas, in his present circumstances, he was forced to be in the middle of the Saudi desert, twenty kilometers off any paved road, and to literally get his hands dirty. And his suit. And the new pair of designer shoes that had replaced the old ones, ruined during his humiliating trudge through the surf.

His security chief got out of the truck's backseat and followed, carrying Assali's suitcase. Salim was short and muscular—the strongest man Assali had ever known. But more important, he had demonstrated unfailing loyalty for more than a dozen years, since well before the Syrian debacle.

Salim had an encyclopedic knowledge of the interlocking terror groups and seemed to know every fighter by name and reputation, a skill that earned him adoration and a vast network of informants. Salim was, in fact, the one who had called to warn Assali that night at the hotel in Amman.

Assali mounted three steps to a small front porch. This would be his sorry home and headquarters until he worked his way out of it—or rather, until other men sweated and died so he could get out of it. He looked out at the open-air kitchen, half-dozen tents, and vacant field ready for more. In the far corner was a wood and canvas partition in front of what he assumed was the latrine. Assali shuddered.

Salim put his bag on the porch.

"Inspect the camp and give me a report. We must be ready on time and we need several dozen trained fighters. From the look of it, we have a lot of work to do."

"Yes, *sayyid*." Salim rushed off to comply.

In the building's vestibule, Assali was greeted by a small, elderly man with a gray beard and skin darkened by decades in the desert sun. He wore a tattered gray *qamis*.

"Welcome, *sayyid*. I am Mustapha, at your service."

Assali snorted, barely looking at the servant. He wanted to say, "Whiskey, neat." But he knew that was impossible and this man might report him to the palace. So, instead, he said, "Tea, sweet."

"Of course, *sayyid*." Mustapha retrieved the bag and led Assali along the hallway. "Your office is here, *sayyid*, in the front. Your bedroom is at the end of the hall." They walked the few steps to the back of the building. "I hope everything is to your liking." Mustapha put the case on the bed and left.

Assali walked to the room. Nothing was to his liking. The bed was narrow and made up like a combat cot. The nightstand and dresser were worn and pitted. The light was a bare bulb that hung from the ceiling on a wire. A small air conditioner mounted in the window was on full blast and the room was still too hot. A generator growled somewhere outside. The idiots had put it close enough to disturb his sleep.

He moved to the office. Adequate. At least there was a desk chair large enough for his girth, though its padding was escaping through a slit on one side. On a small table, an old black metal fan whirred and swung side to side, doing little to cool the room. There were two visitor chairs and an old leather sofa, where he would like to have taken a nap.

But time was short.

Assali had promised the prince, through that trouble-some snake al-Tayyib, that the attack would be ready for the festival. In the meantime, he needed to recruit and train the team and conduct preliminary attacks to continue building the pressure and to, yet again, prove himself to the prince.

Mustapha delivered the tea just ahead of Salim's return. The servant was clever enough to provide two cups and to leave after he put the tray on the desk.

Assali saw that Salim did not look happy. "Tell me."

"*Sayyid*, we have fewer than fifteen men, various levels of training, with only a few who have any competence. It is hard to see how we can be ready in a few weeks."

"But we will be." Assali did not leave any room for discussion. "You worry about the training. I will find you men."

"Yes, *sayyid*." Salim downed his tea and headed out to get to work.

Assali pushed himself up from the chair and went to the bedroom. He opened his suitcase and took out one of the satellite phones. Al-Tayyib could send him to this shithole, but he could not expect him to manufacture men from sand and sunshine. Now that the prince had approved the plan, perhaps Assali had some leverage.

He dialed the palace and sat on the bed. Al-Tayyib's assistant put him on hold. Assali hit the speaker button and leaned against the pillow. He waited fifteen minutes, at ten dollars a minute satellite charges, he assumed. But money was nothing to these people. Unless it was Assali asking for it.

Assali was nodding off when the assistant came back on. "Mr. al-Tayyib will speak to you now."

"*Shukran*." Thank you. There was a further wait and some clicking on the phone line.

"*Aywah*." Yes.

"It is Saddiq Assali."

"I know who it is. What do you want?"

"I want to fulfill the prince's wishes."

"I am a busy man. Do not play word games with me."

Assali feigned contrition. "I am sorry, *sayyid*. I am not playing games. I cannot fulfill the prince's wishes with a small bank account and fifteen untrained men."

"More money will be provided, as promised. What of your plan to force the Zionists to provide you with men?"

"It is in progress, as you have seen. They will comply. But these things take time. Meanwhile, perhaps—"

"Then I suggest you speed the process. The prince's patience is not infinite. You have failed him before. Do not do so again. And do not miss the target date."

"Yes, *sayyid*. Of course."

Al-Tayyib ended the call.

Assali was stuck. If the prince would not send him men, he would have to do something more to make the Israelis comply with his demands. Many of his best men were still in their prisons.

He picked up a different satellite phone and dialed Iyad.

Chapter Fifteen

Faraz was filthy and starving after twenty-four hours in the punishment cell. He hadn't been outside. Human contact was the *slide-clang* of the food slot in the door of his cell.

He sat on the mat and leaned against the wall, his knees up, his head between them. He felt duly softened up.

Faraz breathed as slowly as he could. It was stifling hot in the cell. The only air circulation was provided by a small metal grate near the top of the back wall.

The two guards burst in, shouting in a mix of Hebrew and English. "Liar!" the larger one screamed in his face. He pushed Faraz against the wall and the other one punched him in the stomach. He doubled over and one of them hit him with a forearm in the back of the neck. He went down hard.

The men kicked him, injuring the ribs that had not yet recovered from similar treatment at the hands of his captors in Syria.

One of the guards stepped on the small of Faraz's back with considerable weight. The other pulled his hair, stretching his neck. "You will tell us the truth, terrorist. Make it soon." The man pushed Faraz's face back to the floor, and they left as abruptly as they had arrived.

Faraz lay there breathing hard. Was this part of the plan? Or had something gone terribly wrong? He needed to experience this, and to look like it, so he could blend in with the other prisoners. But for him, the charade had already gone too far.

Bridget sat in Colonel Ben-Yosef's office for the second time.

Since their last meeting, twenty-four hours earlier, she had declined invitations to join him for dinner, drinks, coffee and a tour of Old Tel Aviv.

The message must have gotten through. On this visit, she'd gone through normal security and been escorted by a low-level soldier on the regular elevator. And she had been waiting alone on the office sofa for twenty minutes.

When Ben-Yosef finally came in, he treated her like an unwelcome salesperson, which she was. Maybe it was part of his battle plan.

"I have nothing new for you," he said, foregoing the courtesies and the flirting. He sat behind his desk.

"Colonel," Bridget began her pitch, opting for formality over first names, "it is imperative that we insert our man into the terrorist network—imperative for your security and ours." She moved to a visitor chair to be closer to him. "A major attack is coming, and unless you have a better way to find out what it is, we need to get our man in there. The president believes the best way—the most credible to the terrorists—would be through a prisoner exchange."

"The president believes?"

"Yes."

Ben-Yosef's eye roll indicated to Bridget that she had gone from intriguing to tiresome in his eyes. Perhaps her rejections had gone too far. Or maybe he was just a macho man with a fragile ego, like so many she had encountered over the years.

"Well," his tone was patronizing, "the prime minister believes it is not in Israel's interests to negotiate with terrorists. He has told that to the president personally. At this time there is no other credible way to release your agent. Meanwhile, he is in solitary, and I'm told, starting to look like a prisoner. When this crisis is over, we will try to find a way."

"Solitary?"

"Yes."

"He needs to be in the general population so he can make contacts before the exchange."

"There will be no exchange!" Ben-Yosef's anger flared. "If a longer timeline is not acceptable, perhaps it's better to take your agent out rather than expose him to danger in the general population. If they figure out what he is, the code word won't help him. He'll be dead before we can intervene."

"Colonel . . . Ari, the question of the exchange is above our pay grade. But preparation for the mission is not. You need to get him out of solitary in case the prime minister changes his mind."

"He won't change his mind." Ben-Yosef was exasperated now, but he settled himself. "All right. If you want to take the risk, we'll have him moved. If anything happens to him, it's on you."

"Understood."

"Anything else?" Ben-Yosef seemed to be as eager to get rid of her as he had been to get close to her.

"No. But please confirm to me when our man has been moved."

"I will have someone take care of it. Now, I have a meeting. Good day, Ms. Davenport." Ben-Yosef said her name like it was an insult. He picked up a file and left the office. The soldier appeared to escort Bridget out of the building.

Faraz's hands were cuffed behind his back as he walked along the row of cells between two guards to the sound of assorted Arabic catcalls. It was a one-level cell-block, part of a cluster of prefabricated buildings forming an octagon around a central courtyard. The complex was surrounded by twelve-foot fences topped with razor wire. The last time Faraz had seen a fence like that, Guantanamo Bay had been on the other side. This time, there was nothing but desert.

The trio stopped in front of a cell and one of the guards shouted something in Hebrew. The bolt slid and the lone prisoner inside moved to a back corner.

A guard pushed Faraz and he stumbled into the cell. The guard unlocked the cuffs, then retreated, closed the gate and shouted again. The bolt slid and the guards departed.

The cell was ten feet wide and slightly longer. Bunk beds on the left took up a significant amount of the space, with a toilet and sink behind. There was a fresh bedroll on the top bunk and a towel. The cinder block walls were beige and pockmarked.

Faraz looked at his new cellmate. Every man Faraz had seen during his short walk through the prison looked the same—midtwenties-ish, thin, muscular, olive skinned, bearded, greasy haired, angry.

Not this guy.

His first contact among the Palestinians was a dough boy—Faraz's height but chubby, fair, and younger than the others, maybe twenty-two. He was struggling to grow a few wisps of beard and was also, quite clearly, afraid.

"*Ana Khayal*," Faraz said. I'm Khayal. "*Min America.*"

The guy relaxed a little. "Ayman," he said. "What the hell are you doing here?" Ayman took a tentative step forward from his corner.

"You speak English. Great." Faraz held out his hand and Ayman shook it.

"So? Tell me." Ayman had an accent somewhere between Midwestern and Middle Eastern.

"Arrested entering the country." That was as much of the cover story as this guy needed to know, at least for now. "They say I'm a terrorist, but I say it was 'Tourism While Being a Muslim.'"

Ayman laughed. "Serious crime. I see they worked you over for it."

"Yeah. I'm fine."

"And you're from . . . ?"

"New Jersey. Previously Afghanistan."

"Oh, wow."

"Where did you learn your English?"

"We had a teacher from Chicago for a couple of years.

He was a cool guy, taught us to speak like real Americans. That's what he said, anyway."

"Well, he did a pretty good job."

"Thanks."

"So, what are you doing in here?"

"Well, it's complicated, you know. I guess you could say it's 'Political Activism While Being Palestinian' and also 'Being a Member of the Wrong Family.'"

Faraz forced a chuckle. "What family is that?"

"Al-Hamdani." Ayman straightened up when he said it.

"Sorry, I guess I should know the name, but I don't."

Ayman showed irritation for the first time. "Well, you're not very well informed, then. We have been freedom fighters for four generations. Two of my uncles and several cousins are in jail. My father was murdered seven years ago by the Israelis. He and his brother were at a meeting in Gaza when they dropped a bomb. Many of my relatives have given their lives for the jihad."

"*Allah yarhamom*," Faraz said. "May Allah bless them. "Again, sorry, I guess I should have known."

"Yes. And you should have heard of my cousin Iyad. He is the leader of the movement my father created, *Al-Hakam Al-Islamiyah*. In English, they call it A-HAI."

Now, alarm bells went off in Faraz's head. He had read about A-HAI for the first time a week ago in his briefing papers. Someone did a good job putting him in a cell with an A-HAI operative.

"Wow, yeah. Obviously, I've heard of A-HAI. You're part of it?"

Ayman lowered his voice. "I am Iyad's right hand. I

handle the political side—run our internet presence, write statements, plan strategy."

"Impressive." The guy could be exaggerating or lying outright to impress Faraz, but the fact that they'd put him in this cell provided some credibility. "You know about the kidnapping? They say it was A-HAI."

"Of course, I know. We have no news in the prison, but we hear things. I'm sure my cousin planned it, probably did it himself. The Zionists will never admit it, but I bet he has demanded a prisoner release, including me."

"Your cousin sounds like an important man. I hope to meet him someday."

"He is one of the most important men in Palestine. Our fathers were murdered sitting side by side. Now, we stand side by side to lead the movement."

"I also had a cousin who was a mentor for me. But he died when I was a boy."

"In jihad?"

"No." Faraz stifled a laugh. "We don't do much jihad in America."

"How, then?"

Faraz had talked himself into a corner. How might Johnny have died if he hadn't joined the army right out of high school and been killed in Afghanistan not long after 9/11?

"Motorcycle accident. He used to ride like a wild man."

"Sorry to hear it."

"It was a long time ago." Faraz went quiet.

His mind traveled back more than a dozen years. He was playing catch with Johnny, going to the movies with him, riding on the back of a borrowed Harley. Johnny was wearing his dress uniform, saying goodbye to young

Faraz and his parents before he left for Afghanistan, letting Faraz try on his beret, thrilling the boy by saying, "Keep it up, little man." Faraz was crying on the sofa with his mother when the men came a few weeks later to say Johnny was dead.

His mother. Faraz took a breath. He could not allow himself to go down that rabbit hole. She died thinking he was dead—the lie he let the army tell his parents so he could go under cover. It still haunted him.

"Stand back," came the order on the loudspeakers in Arabic, Hebrew and English.

"We need to stand against the wall," Ayman explained. "They will bring our dinner."

Faraz was grateful for the interruption. He stole a look at his cellmate. The Israelis had chosen well—Ayman was connected and not intimidating. Good start.

Chapter Sixteen

Iyad had never hesitated in carrying out an order before. But this time, he thought the job might, in a way, do itself.

Now, as midnight approached, it still hadn't. He would have to do as instructed.

He sat on an upholstered chair salvaged from a trash heap in an abandoned and crumbling storage building in the middle of an olive grove outside Halhul, a militant town near Hebron on the West Bank. The roof was corrugated metal. The walls, what was left of them, were wood.

The location had two advantages. It was remote and it had a cellar.

They had been safe there with the hostages for almost a week, much longer than planned. The Zionists led them on with covert messages and promises of secret negotiations, but nothing came of them. And the failed raid proved they were only playing for time until they found the real hideout.

A few hours earlier, Assali had told him they must

act to force the Israelis' hand. For Iyad, it would not be the first time. But it would be the first time with a woman.

He stood. Two of his men were lounging on random pieces of furniture. Another was sleeping on the floor. "*Yalla*," he said.

"What?" the previously sleeping man asked.

"You stay here and keep watch. You two, with me."

Iyad opened the trap door and picked up a flashlight from the floor as he went down the ladder. The cellar was lined with gray cinder blocks and divided into two rooms, with a small vestibule in between. Iyad used a key to open the lock on the wooden door to his right and shined the light into Corporal Alon's eyes.

"Take him out," he ordered. The men grabbed Alon by the arms. He was weak and dehydrated. He had washed no more than his hands and face since they'd taken him. His wrists and legs were shackled.

"Where are you taking me?" Alon demanded.

"Put him in there," Iyad said, indicating the other room.

"No! I must stay with her." The corporal refused to walk, so the men dragged him across the vestibule and threw him into the room. One of them slammed the door and slid a bolt lock. Alon kept shouting, but they ignored him.

Iyad went into the room on the right and knelt down next to Maya. The blood on her shirt was dry. The mat she lay on stank of sweat, urine and feces. She was unconscious. Her breathing was shallow, her skin pale.

"I cannot wait for you any longer," he said. Iyad closed her nose with his left hand and put his right over her mouth. He extended his long arms and leaned into the task.

Her body jerked, but had little strength to fight him. Her eyes remained closed.

Iyad's wounded arm hurt, but he pushed harder. He rallied himself to the task. You Zionist bitch. You fired at me. You deserve to die. He put a knee on her hips to keep her still.

It didn't take long.

A few minutes after six a.m., Baruch Kaplan walked his Labrador through the main gate of the remote West Bank settlement carved out of a rocky Judean hillside, where he lived with his wife and two daughters. He waved a greeting to the security guard on duty and turned right on the main road.

The town was surrounded by Palestinian villages, and Baruch's wife had warned him many times about walking beyond the fence. But he was a former wrestler and had the muscles to prove it. He had also been a commando in his day and always kept his gun under his belt in the small of his back. In Baruch's view, this was his land and no one was going to keep him off of it. Not the terrorists. Not even his wife.

Baruch pulled his jacket close against the morning chill and turned right onto the two-track path that led toward a neighboring village. He played out the dog's leash to let it explore the rocks and wildflowers. The village's farm fields were ahead of him, and the construction site for another new settlement was to his left.

The dog pulled hard on the leash. Baruch stumbled.

"*Ha'aht, ha'aht*," he urged. Slowly, slowly. But the dog kept pulling.

Twenty meters farther along, the dog stopped and crouched down, as if unsure whether to proceed, staring at some tall weeds by the side of the path.

"What is it, boy?" Baruch approached, shortening the leash as he went. When he caught up with the dog, he saw what was in the weeds.

Baruch had been through two wars, but he gasped at what he saw. The woman was lying faceup, wearing a bloodstained white shirt and jeans. Her arms were over her head. Light brown hair covered half of her face. But he could see one eye, open, staring at the sky.

He recognized her from the news reports.

The men held at Prison Number Seven were on their morning exercise break in the courtyard. Ayman introduced Faraz to some of his friends, all of them more in the mold of fighters. Still, they showed deference to Ayman that Faraz would not have expected. Perhaps his boasts were legitimate.

"We will be out before long, I promise you, my brothers," Ayman said, to nods of approval. "*Insha'Allah*, of course." If it is God's will. "My cousin is arranging it as we speak," he bragged. "Perhaps we will even take you, Khayal, so you can get back to 'tourism.'" He said the last word like it was a big joke, and the others laughed on cue.

"I hope you're right, Ayman," Faraz said. "And as for tourism . . ." He lowered his voice. "I'm sure there is much you and your cousin could show me."

Now Ayman laughed. He slapped Faraz on the back.

"Yes. Aqsa Mosque . . . Western Wall . . . Israeli prisons."
Ayman led the others in a renewed burst of laughter and
Faraz joined them.

Ayman's friends switched to Arabic. Faraz made his
way to the edge of the crowd and leaned against a wall to
catch a narrow strip of shade. Although it was early
spring, the desert sun was harsh, even at ten a.m.

He watched a soccer game on a too-small field with
not enough players and lines in the sand for goal markers.
He assessed the various cliques. Most looked the same
as Ayman's friends, but some were older and more intimidating—hard men with jihadi beards and the scars to
prove their commitment to the cause.

As Faraz was looking to his left, three men came from
his right. One of them, tall and thin, bumped him hard.
When Faraz righted himself, the man was bending forward, nose-to-nose with him. "*Min inta?*" Who are you?

Faraz stepped back against the wall. "*Khayal Durrani,
min America.* English please."

"Ach," the man spat. "American." He reminded Faraz
of the jihadis he'd met in Syria—untempered aggression
and bravado beyond their capabilities, relying on superior
numbers to back up their intimidation.

Faraz stared him down. "I came to join the jihad."

The man burst into exaggerated laughter, then translated for his colleagues, and they did the same. He held
out his hands as if trying to reconcile two opposites.
"America. Jihad. America. Jihad." The men laughed as if
it were the funniest thing they'd ever heard.

When they calmed themselves, their leader said, "I am
Suleiman. This is my place. What I say, you do."

"Your place?"

Suleiman moved half a step closer, nearly touching Faraz now. His men stood behind him, blocking Faraz's view of the rest of the yard and anyone else's view of him. All Faraz could see was Suleiman's face, his scraggly beard, the large scar on his left cheek.

"Do you doubt me?"

Faraz kept his eyes on Suleiman's. "No, I do not."

"Good. You stay with al-Hamdani?"

"Yes."

"He is a dog and his father was a dog and all his family are dogs."

Now, this was interesting. Faraz wished he'd had more time to study the intricacies of the Palestinian terror network. He was sure his surprise showed, but maybe that was appropriate for his cover.

"He thinks he is the president of Palestine and his cousin is the general and all his family are the ministers. But they work only for themselves. They reject the leadership of the movement and they worship the king of Saudi Arabia. For them, jihad is politics and money. You should choose your friends wisely, American." Suleiman jabbed a finger into Faraz's chest to emphasize his point.

Faraz found himself sweating. He blamed the heat. He had faced down tougher men than Suleiman. But here, he felt alone, vulnerable.

Suleiman spat again, then stared at Faraz. "I know jihad. Al-Hamdani has nothing like this." He pointed to his scar. "He is a soft boy. You should not be fooled by his sweet words."

"If you say so, I believe it," Faraz said.

"Ha." Suleiman grunted. His breath hit Faraz's face. "I

will show you." Suleiman cocked his head and his friends followed him to Ayman's group.

They barged through the crowd until Suleiman came face-to-face with Ayman. "Are you spreading more lies, Mr. President?"

Ayman stepped back. He managed a nervous laugh. "That is a title you will never have, Garbageman."

Suleiman pushed Ayman hard and he staggered into another man. Two of Ayman's friends moved to confront Suleiman.

"Easy brothers," Ayman said. "Soon we will all be free men, thanks to the true leadership of the movement. We have no need to fight the *tafah*." The riffraff.

Suleiman lunged, but Ayman's two men held him back.

"Careful," Ayman teased. "If you get hurt, you won't be able to help your mother haul shit when you get out."

"How many men do you need to protect you from me?"

"None!" Ayman shouted. He put his hands on his friends' shoulders and pushed them apart.

Suleiman glared at him. He half-turned to walk away. Then, with Ayman's guard down, Suleiman turned back and lunged at him.

Ayman went down with Suleiman's hands on his throat. Two men grabbed Suleiman's arms to pull him off but were stopped by his friends. Ayman twisted his big body, but Suleiman held on.

The scuffle triggered a melee involving a dozen men, with fists, dirt and a few primitive weapons. Faraz had to make a quick decision. He would rather have stayed out of the fight, but he saw it for the opportunity it was.

He ran into the center of the crowd. Suleiman was on top of Ayman, holding his throat with one hand and punching his face with the other. Faraz put a forearm around Suleiman's neck and squeezed hard. When Suleiman's hands came up, Faraz pulled him off of Ayman, threw him to the ground and fell on him with a knee in his groin.

Ayman struggled to his feet and landed a kick to the side of Suleiman's head before the water hit him.

Sharp streams of high-powered spray came from six spigots around the compound, knocking men over and forcing everyone to focus on his own safety rather than fighting. Faraz went into fetal position next to Ayman. Suleiman rolled onto his stomach and covered his head.

The water stopped. A voice on the loudspeakers said, "Stand up. We have no more water to waste on you. Anyone who touches another man will be shot."

Faraz looked up. Israelis with automatic rifles faced them from the cellblock rooftops. He was breathing hard. Ayman's face and neck were bruised. "Can you get up?"

"Yes, I think so. Do not help me." Ayman stood and wiped the water off his face. He winced when he touched the bruises.

The voice said, "If you are injured, move toward the door or raise your hand for assistance. Others stay where you are."

Ayman turned to head for the door. "You saved me, Khayal. I will not forget it."

CHAPTER SEVENTEEN

The outcry from the death of Maya Gerson was intense. By noon, when the security cabinet met, her family had already been all over the TV broadcasts crying, and calling for revenge on the terrorists and consequences for the prime minister.

The preliminary report indicated she had not been injured beyond the gunshot, but she had not received medical care, either. Still, the chief pathologist believed the wound was not fatal and suspected another cause of death. He needed more time to be sure.

Foreign Minister Moshe Greenshpun needed no more time. "She died because you failed her," he shouted at the prime minister.

"Calm down, Moshe." Prime Minister Yardeni was working hard to hold his temper. "You will not bring her back to life by raising your voice."

"You failed to provide sufficient security. You failed to make the terrorists' costs so high that they stopped attacking us. And when she lay bleeding in a terrorist cell, you failed to rescue her."

Yardeni slammed his hand on the cabinet room table.

"Sit down! A few days ago, you opposed a plan that would have had her safely at Hadassah Hospital by now. But I do not say you failed her. Have you forgotten we are all defenders of the state? All of us. Even young mothers doing their shopping. Maya was a hero. When the terrorists started shooting, she could have run away. But she raised her gun to defend her fellow citizens."

Greenshpun did not sit and was poised for another tirade.

The prime minister raised a hand to stop him. "Ladies and gentlemen, we will have a moment of silence for Maya Gerson, daughter of Israel, defender of the state. May her memory be a blessing. And then we will carry on the fight for which she gave her life. Will we not, Mr. Foreign Minister?"

Without responding, Greenshpun lowered his head as the other security cabinet members stood to pay their respects.

An aide rushed in, but stopped short when she saw what was going on. As soon as Yardeni said, "Thank you" and sat, she moved to his side and showed him a document.

The prime minister slumped in his chair, then leaned forward, elbows on the table, holding the piece of paper in both hands. "Ladies and gentlemen, I have been informed of another disturbing development. The medical examiner reports a gruesome discovery. Prepare yourselves." He paused and took a breath. "Inside the throat of Maya Gerson, they found a finger."

There were gasps around the table.

"Fingerprints are being analyzed, but they believe it belongs . . . belonged . . . to Corporal Yuval Alon."

Hands went to faces. Jaws dropped.

"There was also a scrap of paper, on which is written in Arabic, '*qiteat qitea*.' It means 'piece by piece.'"

Cabinet ministers let loose a mix of curses, and there was a general murmuring of horrified responses.

Yardeni tapped the table with his right hand. "My friends. Corporal Alon is nineteen years old. His life is in our hands. Let us put away bravado and consider our options. I have spoken to President Martelli. He has an operation in motion. A compromise now might save Alon and give us a chance for a greater strike against our enemies in the future."

That night, Bridget lay shaking with fear, bleeding and dying on cold ground in the middle of a jihadi gunfight, when the harsh ring of her hotel room phone shocked her back to reality. She sat up straight, sweating, and peered into the darkness.

She found the phone on the second ring.

"Sorry to wake you," Colonel Ben-Yosef said. "You will be picked up in half an hour. There have been some developments."

"What developments?"

"It took all day to negotiate it through a long line of intermediaries, but to my surprise, you may be getting your wish."

The line went dead. Bridget got out of bed, her head still half in Syria. She opened the curtains, hoping for a flood of sunshine, but it was still dark. The lights of the city twinkled along the coastline. She checked her watch. 0450.

* * *

Two hours later, Faraz was halfway through his meager punishment cell breakfast—thanks to his participation in the fight—when he heard a commotion in the hallway. Prisoners were calling to each other and there were shouts of "*Allah hu akbar*" and other phrases Faraz did not recognize. Men were banging metal water cups against their cell doors.

A couple of minutes later, the bolt slid and his door opened to show two grim-faced Israeli guards. "Come," one of them said. "Move, move, move."

Faraz went to the doorway. They grabbed him by both arms and marched him to the exit, then pushed him into the morning chill of the yard, where he found a celebration in progress.

"What's going on?" Faraz asked the nearest man.

"Freedom," the man said. "We are going home."

Bridget watched the celebration sitting next to Colonel Ben-Yosef in an Israeli military command bunker just inside the Green Line—Israel's pre-1967 border that marked the division between its original territory and the former Jordanian land west of the Jordan River that Israel had seized in the Six Day War.

The West Bank, which Jews called Judea and Samaria, was home to large Palestinian cities like Hebron, Nablus and Bethlehem, and countless villages. Now, decades after Israel occupied the area, there were dozens of Jewish settlements, too.

Much of the command center was underground, with

the entry floor on the surface made of steel-reinforced concrete that, Bridget reasoned, was built to survive a direct hit from any type of missile the Palestinians, Arab states or Iran was likely to have.

A plaque on the door indicated the first facility on this site was built in 1946 by the Jewish paramilitary group called the Haganah, during its fight for independence from Britain. The updated command post reminded her of the many American ops centers she had been in. It had the same basic design and much of the same equipment and software.

The room was wide and held four rows of desks packed with computers and comms gear. Bridget and the colonel sat in the back row, raised a foot above the others to provide a clear view. They faced a wall of giant screens that displayed the key locations for what was about to happen.

On the left, a live feed from a drone showed Prison Number Seven, where the gray exhaust of two buses wafted over dozens of men jumping up and down and embracing each other. Half a dozen prison guards were stationed on two rooftops, weapons at the ready. Outside the fence, two armored vehicles waited.

The middle screen showed a remote intersection in the southern West Bank. By agreement, there was nothing on the roads for five kilometers around.

The third screen showed the courtyard of another prison, where men were lined up to board buses.

The controlled frenzy of the bunker was familiar, even though Bridget couldn't understand the words. What sounded like orders and confirmations flew across the room. Technicians keyed in computer commands. Soldiers delivered documents, maps and coffee.

Bridget noticed a commotion on the screen on the left.

Faraz lifted himself on tiptoes to see what the cheering was about. He saw Ayman coming out of the clinic with his forehead bandaged and a broad smile. Ayman pumped his fist into the air, setting off chants of "*Allah hu akbar*" and "*Hak-Is*," the Arabic shorthand for A-HAI.

Ayman waded into the crowd, accepting hugs and kisses. Halfway across the compound, he spotted Faraz and moved directly toward him. Ayman hugged Faraz and kissed him on both cheeks. Then he turned and presented Faraz to the crowd.

"Allah sent this man, Khayal Durrani, all the way from America to save me from the arrogant garbageman yesterday." Ayman's voice was hoarse. He put his right hand on his neck. "I cannot talk much now."

"Good," someone shouted from the back of the crowd. The men laughed and cheered.

Ayman smiled. "Yes, okay." He raised a hand to quiet the men. "I just want to say, he is one of us now!"

The men cheered and moved in to congratulate Faraz.

They had no sound on the video feed in the bunker, but it was clear the men were celebrating. Bridget put on a headset that connected her to Sergeant Esti Peretz, Ari's aide, who sat against the wall behind her.

"Can you hear me?" Peretz said.

Bridget gave a thumbs-up.

Ben-Yosef was not flirting. He was focused on the task at hand. For the first time since she'd met him, he was wearing glasses, which gave him a more intellectual look. He leaned forward to read his computer screen. When the blue phone on his desk rang, he picked it up instantly and spoke in Hebrew.

The translation came into Bridget's headset. "Yes, sir. Got it." Ari hung up and raised his voice to issue an order. Peretz repeated the words in English, "The operation is authorized. Load the buses."

CHAPTER EIGHTEEN

An alarm went off in the prison courtyard, and a voice came through the loudspeaker with instructions in three languages. "Prisoners, line up at the buses."

That quieted the celebration. This was really happening.

"We prefer to defy Zionist orders," Ayman said. "But I think we should follow this one."

That set off another round of cheering as the men made way for Ayman to get to the front of the crowd. He brought Faraz with him.

The voice came on the loudspeakers again. "You will board the buses. Anyone making trouble will be left behind."

The men settled down and formed two lines. Someone started one more chant in a whisper, "*Hak-Is, Hak-Is.*"

Ayman took the first window seat on the bus labeled *shamal*, north, and pulled Faraz in next to him. Faraz had to squeeze in. Ayman's girth took up more than half the bench. The other men shook their hands and slapped Faraz on the back as they boarded. The noise built again as the bus filled up.

In the rear, there was a section separated by a double

chain-link fence. An Israeli guard came on board through the back door, brandishing a rifle. "Quiet! No trouble on the ride or we turn back." Another guard joined him.

When the men settled, the driver boarded through his own door and took his seat inside a steel cage.

Faraz saw Suleiman and his friends move toward the other bus labelled *janub*, south. He pointed them out to Ayman, who grunted his disdain.

"What is this hatred between you two?" Faraz asked.

"Suleiman's father fought beside my father, was with him in Gaza. He was a good man. But when they were martyred, Suleiman thought he should be the leader of *Hak-Is*. The other families chose to follow my father's wishes, with a council of elders and Iyad as our captain. Suleiman was angry. He took his family out of the movement. It created a sort of north-south divide, but we are the bigger group."

"That was seven years ago?"

"Yes. But that is nothing in these feuds. We will hate each other for generations, unless we kill them all first. It would have been better to leave Suleiman and his friends behind, but these things are always a matter of negotiations."

Outside, Suleiman was last in line to board the other bus. He paused and took one final look around before stepping in. His eyes locked on Faraz and Ayman. A guard gave him a shove through the door.

"And what was that about his mother hauling shit?" Faraz asked.

Ayman chuckled. "Their family business is garbage collection. When his father died, Suleiman had no interest, so his mother took it over—not a proper thing for a woman to do. She should have sold it or let one of Suleiman's uncles run it. But she took it on herself. We call her 'the garbagewoman' and 'the mother of all shit.'" Ayman laughed again. "All shit, including Suleiman."

Faraz forced a chuckle.

An officer two rows ahead of Bridget stood and turned to say something to Ari. "Prison Seven ready," was the translation that came into her headset.

Ari responded. "Send the first buses."

The officer nodded, sat down and typed something into his computer. On the video screen, Bridget saw one of the guards at Faraz's prison take a phone out of his pocket. He checked the message against a piece of paper and showed it to a colleague for confirmation. Bridget could sense some reluctance as the man stepped forward and paused before gesturing to the drivers.

The prison's gate opened and the buses moved out. The first turned north, led by one of the armored vehicles. The other bus and escort went south.

Twenty minutes later, Faraz's bus and its police vehicle pulled to the side of the road, one kilometer outside a Palestinian village. The driver said something into his radio handset. The speaker crackled and the reply came.

The driver keyed the radio again and said a few more words. Then he put the handset back on its hook and pushed a button to open the main door. "*Min huna, tamshun*," he said. From here, you walk.

At first, no one moved. Then, from the back came a voice, "*Yalla shabaab. Huriya.*" Let's go, boys. Freedom.

Nervous laughter rolled through the bus, then shouts of "*huriya*" and "*Allah hu akbar*." Faraz stood and stepped aside to let Ayman lead the way. Ayman turned to the men, pumped his fist in the air in rhythm with the chanting, and went down the steps.

Outside, the men formed a crowd around Ayman and jumped for joy. They cheered and chanted and shouted insults at the Israeli guards. Some knelt down and kissed the ground. There was much hugging and kissing on both cheeks.

"Come," Ayman shouted. His voice cracked as his bruised throat refused to cooperate. He switched to a whisper. "I am sure there is a party waiting for us."

Ayman put his right arm around Faraz and waved with his left for the others to follow them to the village.

The Israelis watched them for a few seconds, then turned the vehicles around and drove away.

The command post's left screen was split on the diagonal now. The upper part showed Faraz's bus. The lower one had the other bus, outside a village in the southern West Bank.

Bridget, Ari and everyone at the command center saw the two groups of prisoners released simultaneously, as planned. The blue phone rang. Ari hit the speaker button, and they heard the senior security officer's terse report.

Sergeant Peretz delivered the translation, "Prisoners delivered. Mission complete."

"*Kibalti*," Ben-Yosef responded. Got it. He raised his voice. "Send the second signal."

All eyes moved to the middle screen—the remote intersection—where nothing happened for several agonizing minutes.

Then two vehicles approached from the west. One was a black Toyota Crown sedan, the type favored by third world diplomats whose budgets would not pay for a Mercedes. It had Egyptian flags flying from small poles above its headlights. The other was an Israeli ambulance. They stopped short of the junction.

"What's going on?" Bridget asked.

"We must wait until the prisoners walk to the villages and the terrorists get confirmation," Peretz said.

"They do not have drone video," Ari added with clear irritation. He sounded like he had lost patience with Bridget, along with all interest. "They will have ten minutes to deliver our soldier to the Egyptian ambassador. Only when our soldier is released, alive and well, will the buses move from the other prison." He gestured toward the third screen.

"And if he is not released?"

Ben-Yosef lowered his chin, rolled his eyes to the top of their sockets and looked at her above the rim of his glasses. "We are ready for that, too."

They both turned back to look at the screens. It took a long time for the prisoners to cover the short distances to their families and friends waiting in the villages. Or maybe it just seemed that way.

The silence in the room, and especially between Bridget and Ari, got heavier as the wait dragged on. She wanted to cut through the awkwardness. "I'm sure a prisoner release is not your favorite type of operation."

Ben-Yosef shot her a look and didn't respond.

On the left screen, the prisoners were about halfway to the villages. On the other screens, the Egyptian ambassador and the additional busloads of prisoners waited.

But, unless there was a problem, for Bridget the waiting was over. She leaned forward to look for Faraz in the crowd, but she couldn't find him.

"Our agent is there?"

"Yes, as promised."

Chapter Nineteen

When the former prisoners turned the corner toward the village square, with Ayman and Faraz in the lead, the crowd of more than a thousand burst into cheers. Dozens of people ran forward to greet their loved ones. Women cried and ululated a *"loo, loo, loo"* singsong. Some of the men cried, too.

The crush of bodies pushed Faraz to the side. He saw a row of television crews on a set of risers—Palestinian TV next to Israeli TV and international networks. He moved into position to be sure they got a shot of him. As he did so, he passed Ayman, who grabbed him. "Come, Khayal, you must meet my family."

Ayman dragged Faraz through the crowd and introduced his mother and sister. Mrs. al-Hamdani touched the bandage on her son's head. "You should go home and lie down."

"It is nothing, Mother," Ayman said. "Today is not a day to lie down." He started a chant of *"Fi-la-steen, Fi-la-steen!"* The men jumped in rhythm, fists in the air, faces toward the cameras.

When the celebration died down, family groups started

leaving the square, some walking home, others getting into cars.

"Come, Khayal, my mother has prepared a feast."

"Are you sure?"

"Of course, the man who saved my life will get the biggest portion—after mine, of course." Ayman laughed and put his arm around Faraz, escorting him toward a large house in a prosperous-looking neighborhood.

Bridget decided it would be bad form not to wait for the end of the operation.

Just ahead of the ten-minute deadline, a white van approached the remote intersection. It made a U-turn thirty meters from the Egyptian ambassador's car. A side door opened and a man in an Israeli uniform was pushed out.

He fell to his knees, blindfolded, hands tied in front of him. He turned and spat toward his kidnappers but the van was already moving.

Four soldiers and two medics stepped from the ambulance and ran toward the man. One of the soldiers removed the blindfold and spoke into a radio.

"*Ze hu. Ze Alon.*" It's him. It's Alon.

Lunch at Ayman's house was lamb, rice and roasted vegetables, with the finest sweets from Nablus for dessert. Several cousins and some neighbors joined the festivities. The house was two stories, with a large living/dining room taking up the right half of the main level. The floor was tile, covered here and there by traditional rugs. A tacky overstuffed brown L-shaped sofa took up one corner, with a semicircle of matching chairs facing it. There was a large TV next to a picture window with a view of the backyard. The wooden coffee table and side tables had white doilies on them and vases with plastic flowers.

The dining table was long and had another table added to it for this special occasion. Ayman introduced Faraz to everyone as "the man who saved my life," so he became the star of the event. The story of the thirty-second fight with Suleiman and his friends was told and retold as if it were the greatest battle of the jihad.

Ayman's sister, Maysoon, helped her mother in the kitchen, and other family women joined them. Faraz noticed that their headscarves were not pulled tight. And while they were dressed modestly, here that meant long skirts and loose blouses of various colors, not the dark *abayas* and *chadors* of rural Syria and Afghanistan. Only Ayman's mother, a widow, wore black.

Maysoon had on jeans and an untucked man's shirt that covered her bottom. She had a scarf wrapped around her long black hair, but much of it was visible, anyway. With no veil, Faraz could see her plump cheeks and her smile as she delivered food to the men. Her dark eyes met his—another thing that would not have happened in his previous postings. She seemed younger than Ayman, around twenty, and her English was better.

"You are from New York?" she asked as she brought a plate of vegetables.

"Newark, but close by."

Maysoon gazed through the front window into the distance "I want to go to New York, the city that never sleeps." Maysoon looked back at Faraz. "Here, we are in the village that never wakes." Her laugh soared two octaves and insisted that everyone join in.

"You want to go to New York. I went to a lot of trouble to get out of there and come here," Faraz said.

That brought Maysoon up short, but she recovered. "Well, Khayal, that makes one of us a fool." She laughed again and moved back to the kitchen, her shirttail swinging behind her.

By early afternoon, Faraz was stuffed and tired. He turned to Ayman. "Can I use the toilet."

"Of course. Down the hall, last door on the right."

Faraz headed for the back of the house. He passed a stairway leading to the second floor and went along the hallway. The walls were painted brown on the bottom, beige from waist level to the ceiling. There was a closed door on the left and an open one a little farther that revealed a bedroom. Beyond was the bathroom, with the back door at the end of the hall.

When Faraz returned to the front of the house, he saw that the men had moved to the yard. He needed to press his lifesaver status to ensure that the "President of Palestine" became his entrée into the jihad. Faraz found Ayman regaling yet another group of men with their prison exploits.

"Thank you, my friend. It has been great to be part of your family for a few hours."

"From now, you will always be part of my family."

The hook was in.

"I hope so." Faraz took Ayman's arm and led him to the edge of the crowd. He lowered his voice. "I came here to join the jihad. Five minutes in an Israeli prison did not change my mind."

Ayman smiled. "I am glad to hear it. You will sleep here tonight. Tomorrow, we will go to meet my cousin, Iyad. He could not show himself here today. But we must thank him, and he will be pleased to meet you."

"The man who saved your life."

Ayman doubled over with laughter. "Yes, yes. The hero." He put his arm around Faraz and led him inside. "You will sleep in the guest room on this floor. The family sleeps upstairs."

After an early breakfast of strong coffee and fresh pita with salty white cheese, Ayman's mother gave them a basket of food for Iyad. "Do not eat it along the way," she admonished them.

Ayman left the kitchen and came back carrying two light jackets—one for Faraz, one for himself. "Finish your food and put this on, Khayal. Our brothers will be here in a minute."

Mrs. al-Hamdani fiddled with the fresh bandage on Ayman's head. "Be careful, my son. I have only one of you."

"Yes, Mother. But we have important work to do."

She kissed him on both cheeks and held his hands, releasing them only when he moved toward the front door.

Faraz stood. "Many thanks for your hospitality, *sayyidat*."

"You are welcome here anytime, Khayal."

"Thank you. And please thank Maysoon for me."

"I will." There were tears in Mrs. al-Hamdani's eyes. She explained without being asked. "Ayman just got

home. He is injured. Now, he is leaving again and I don't
know when I will see him."

Faraz put his hand on his heart and made a small bow.
"I will keep an eye on him."

Ayman's mother smiled. "Thank you."

"Khayal, let's go," Ayman shouted from outside. His
voice was stronger, getting close to normal.

Faraz nodded farewell to Mrs. al-Hamdani. As he
came through the front door, he saw two of their fellow
former-prisoners arrive in a beat-up pickup truck.

The men set off over dusty roads heading northeast.
After twenty minutes, they pulled into a repair garage in
a village.

"Problem?" Faraz asked.

"No problem," Ayman said. "But we cannot go straight
from my house to Iyad's hideout. The Zionists may be
watching. We walk now. But first, jacket off."

Faraz and Ayman exchanged jackets with the other
two men, who left by the shop's front door. Ayman took
the food package and led Faraz out a side door, across a
narrow alley and into another building. They continued
through businesses and homes, spending as little time
outside as possible, until they reached the edge of the
village. A box truck with a caterer's logo was waiting with
its cargo door open.

The two men jumped in and moved past boxes of
canned goods and packaged items. A man came in after
them and hugged Ayman, kissing him on both cheeks. He
was fiftyish, Faraz thought, thin, with an unkempt beard,
a trucker's well-worn clothes and a poorly tied *kufiyah*.

"It is good to see you, abu-Hakim," Ayman said.

"I am happy to see you as a free man."

"Thank you, my friend. Iyad will be grateful for your help."

"It is my duty and my pleasure."

Ayman introduced Faraz and abu-Hakim gave him a hug. Then he passed Ayman a handgun. "For any emergency," he said. He clasped Ayman's shoulders one more time, jumped out and pulled down the door.

Faraz and Ayman took seats on the boxes. The only light came from two small air vents, high up on each side.

"Impressive security," Faraz said.

"We must. Iyad is the most important man in our movement. The Zionists want him badly, but they won't get him. He is too smart."

"Where are we going?"

"I do not know. Our next driver will know where to take us."

"Next driver?"

In the half-light, Faraz saw Ayman smile.

Their third ride was two motorcycles. Faraz held on as his driver followed Ayman's along a dirt road between groves of lush olive trees. The fruit was small and pale green, hidden among the oval leaves, still months away from harvest. But the trees made a canopy over the road, protecting them from prying eyes in the sky.

Faraz couldn't help thinking about his first motorcycle ride, with his cousin Johnny. They'd both gotten in a lot of trouble for that one, even though Johnny had bought a kid-sized helmet for him. He could imagine what his mother would say even now about him speeding along a dirt road without a helmet. The thought gave him a chill. He had to keep such things out of his mind.

The bikes veered off the road and zigzagged along a path between the trees. Faraz ducked to avoid low-hanging branches. After a few minutes, they arrived at a one-story wood-frame building—some kind of oversized shack, where a farmer might have stored his equipment. Some sections of its walls were missing. It had a corrugated metal roof.

Ayman dismounted. The gun that abu-Hakim had given him stuck out of the back of his waistband, pushing his trousers down enough to show the top of his buttocks. He thanked the driver and took his mother's care package from the bike's saddlebag.

"This is our safe place," Ayman said with a broad smile. "Now you will meet my cousin." He was almost giddy with anticipation. He led Faraz toward the shack's door, guarded by two armed men. Faraz counted eight more among the olive trees.

A man appeared in the doorway. He was tall and thin. He wore jeans, a black cotton sweater and a well-used baseball cap that shaded his trimmed beard and broad smile of bad teeth.

"Iyad!" Ayman shouted, and ran the last few steps to embrace him.

"*Ibn eami*," Iyad said. My cousin.

They did the left-right-left three-kiss greeting, then Iyad held Ayman away to have a look at him. "You are more of a man after a few months in prison," he teased, touching Ayman's stomach. "The Zionists fed you too well."

Ayman pulled in his ample belly. "It is true. But as you

can see . . ." He touched the bandage. "I am ready to fight."

"You tell the world what we do, and I will do the fighting."

"No, cousin, this time I will fight alongside you."

Iyad smiled. "We shall see. Who is your friend?"

Ayman introduced "Khayal, the man who saved my life" and told the story of the fight.

Iyad turned to Faraz and switched to English. "You are welcome here, Khayal."

"Thank you. I did not imagine that my route to the jihad would go through a prison and an olive grove, but perhaps it has."

"Of course, it has," Ayman assured him.

The men went into the building and sat on a sofa and old chairs clustered around a small table. Iyad poured tea from a camp stove and opened the food package. "Your mother is a saint. May Allah protect her." He took out a small cake and shared it among them. "I will save the rest for later."

Faraz saw Iyad's bedroll along the back wall, under the building's only window. A backpack leaned against the wall. There was a washup basin, a soiled towel, a battery-powered lantern and a few more unmatched pieces of furniture. It seemed incongruous, but a rustic woven carpet lay on the floor in one corner.

Faraz raised his teacup toward Iyad and sipped. The tea was bitter. He followed the broad strokes of the cousins' conversation.

"You are living rough," Ayman said.

"It is temporary, although . . ." Iyad laughed. "I have been here longer than expected. Now that we have awakened the movement, I am hunted. But I leave tonight."

"Tonight?"

"Yes. There is much work to do. Our mentor has called us to action, and we will not fail him."

"Where will you go?"

"That, I cannot tell even you, my cousin. But I will be back before long. And you will know it. Everyone will know it." His lips curled into a satisfied smile.

"I will go with you," Ayman said. "We will go with you."

"I don't know." Iyad glanced at Faraz. "You are not a fighter, Ayman, and with all due respect to Khayal, I have just met him."

"I have been imprisoned as a fighter, and I have fought to defend our family honor. I am a fighter. I will do the internet work, as always, but this time I will train to go out with the team. Please, cousin, you cannot say no to me."

Iyad looked at his tea, then cocked his head toward Faraz. "And this one?"

"I vouch for him one hundred percent. He put his life on the line for me against Suleiman, a garbageman but a formidable fighter. I wish you had left him in the prison."

"I considered it. But perhaps he will yet be useful, especially since we now have money for operations."

Ayman grunted.

"I came here to join the fight," Faraz said. "Please."

Iyad looked from Ayman to Faraz and back. "We need men. The kidnapping and prisoner exchange were designed to provide them. I will think about it."

* * *

Faraz and Ayman spent the rest of the day lolling among the olive trees. Iyad huddled with two men who arrived in the afternoon. When they left, Faraz saw him pacing outside the building while talking on a satellite phone.

At dusk, a van arrived with their dinner. They settled on the floor of the shack for a meal of rice and chicken. "I have spoken to our benefactor," Iyad said. "The mission is on track. The training has begun. But he needs more men and he needs them now. You two will come with me."

Chapter Twenty

After dinner, Faraz and Ayman were sitting on the old sofa when another man arrived. He was Iyad's age, around forty, but taller and thinner. He had a full beard that crowded his prominent nose. He wore skinny jeans and a black T-shirt.

The man shook Iyad's hand and kissed him on both cheeks. When he came toward the sofa, Ayman stood and gave him a lazy handshake. No kisses. "Welcome, Ra'ed," Ayman said without enthusiasm. "What are you doing here?"

"I will go with you." Ra'ed pinched Ayman's cheek.

Ayman slapped his hand away. "I am not a child anymore."

"Really?" He pointed at the bandage. "Did you fall down and hurt your head?"

"I was in a Zionist prison, as you know."

"Ah, right. Now you are a grown man."

"I am a fighter."

"Ha," Ra'ed said. "We shall see." He rolled his eyes and went back to talk to Iyad.

"Who is this guy?" Faraz asked.

"He is an old comrade of Iyad but I do not like him. He is from the South. He stuck with us when the movement broke apart. But I always feel like he is waiting for the right opportunity to betray us to the garbageman."

Faraz watched Iyad and Ra'ed in earnest conversation. "Iyad seems to trust him."

Ayman slouched on the sofa and looked at an empty corner of the room, as if he didn't care what Iyad and Ra'ed were doing.

A few minutes later, one of the guards came in and spoke to Iyad.

"*Yalla,*" Iyad said.

Outside, it was nearly dark. The four men got into the same food truck that Faraz and Ayman had used that morning, with the same grizzled driver, abu-Hakim. The guard pulled down the cargo door, banged on the side of the truck and abu-Hakim hit the gas.

"It's early for such a movement, isn't it?" Faraz asked.

"Less conspicuous," Iyad explained. "Anything after ten p.m. draws attention. Now, it is totally normal for a food truck to be on the road."

Up front, abu-Hakim held the wheel tight and made sure he kept to the speed limit as he drove north on Route 90, paralleling the Jordan River. He was pleased that two Israeli police cars on station at the entrance to a settlement paid him no mind as he drove by.

At a well-lit intersection, an army jeep came up next to the truck, and the soldier in the passenger seat gave him the once-over. Abu-Hakim smiled and nodded. When the light changed, the soldiers turned left as abu-Hakim continued north.

The landscape turned from stunted trees and prickly bushes to a desert of sand, stones and the occasional tenacious bush. Abu-Hakim checked his mirrors. Two Israeli cars were behind him. He pulled to the side to let them pass, earning waves of thanks.

But he wasn't being courteous. He needed to be alone on the next stretch of road.

Less than a kilometer farther along, he checked the mirrors again, then veered right onto a dirt road that led to a cluster of buildings. He blew past them, continuing off the end of the road at a good clip and bouncing through a field of weeds and rocks. Fifty meters farther, the field angled down sharply toward the river.

The embankment hid them from the road but not from any aircraft. "*Yalla, b'sre*," Abu-Hakim shouted. Get going. He banged on the wall of the cargo area behind him.

Iyad raised the door and they all jumped out.

It was dark outside now and the truck's lights were off. The four of them stood behind the vehicle and peered into the darkness to the east. A small light flashed. Then again.

"This way," Iyad said.

Faraz lowered the door and banged twice on the side of the truck. Abu-Hakim turned hard left and found the right angle to climb the bank without tipping over.

Iyad led the men down to the water. The light blinked again. This time Faraz could see that it illuminated a young man standing next to a small wooden boat. Iyad jogged to the man and greeted him. He was barely more than a boy, short and barefoot.

"*Achooee.*" My brother. Iyad greeted him. "We are ready."

"Come," the boy said.

They boarded the boat—little more than a raft, really—and Ra'ed helped push it off the bank. Ayman and Faraz rowed, while the boy handled the rudder. Iyad sat in front.

The ride was short, with only the flashlight to show the way. The Jordan is little more than a stream for most of its length, about sixty meters wide at this point. In the summer, they could have almost walked across. But this was the end of the rainy season and the river was deep and fast. It was also well defended by both the Israelis and the Jordanians.

"This boy knows the river like no one else," Ayman whispered.

"Quiet," Iyad said.

Their young captain moved to the bow, handed the flashlight to Iyad and reached out with a pole cut at the end into a V. In the half-light, Faraz saw him catch a piece of the chain-link border fence that ran the length of the river and lift it over them. A post that should have held the fence down came up with it.

They all ducked as the boy guided the fence over them. A minute later, they were scrambling ashore in Jordan.

The young man saluted and pushed off, disappearing into the night. The four of them crouched down and waited.

At length, the signal came—two short flashes of light to their right, maybe fifty yards away. Iyad touched his index finger to his lips and tilted his head for the others to follow.

When they reached the light, Faraz could make out an ancient tractor attached to a trailer piled with palm fronds. Iyad dove in and the others followed, making sure they were completely covered.

The tractor belched and strained as it pulled them along a pitted road, or perhaps no road at all. The exhaust fumes permeated the pile of fronds. Ayman coughed.

But they didn't spend long on the trailer. Whoever their benefactor was, he had some cash, because their next ride was an aircraft.

The single-engine propeller plane fitted with large white tanks for crop-dusting sat at one end of a dirt runway in the middle of a farmer's field.

There was another round of ritual hugs and kisses before the pilot ushered them on board. Iyad sat in the copilot's seat. Faraz, Ayman and Ra'ed sat on the floor. The pilot started the engine and shouted over the noise. "Welcome to my airline," he said. "Fasten your seatbelts." Then he laughed.

They had neither seats nor belts.

The three men grabbed onto the wall and crop-dusting pipes as the pilot popped the brakes and the plane bounced forward at high speed, hitting every rut in the field. The last one launched them into the air.

The first part of the flight was rough. They stayed low and there was much banking, left and right. The plane was buffeted by air currents. The pilot gripped the controls and leaned forward. Faraz figured he was making evasive maneuvers to avoid radar and air defenses. Ayman's knuckles were white from holding on with all his strength, and his face was pale. Perhaps he was wishing he hadn't eaten that dinner.

Then the plane started climbing. When it leveled off, the pilot relaxed and twisted in his seat to face them. "You can be calm now, my friends. From here, it is . . . how you say? . . . the friendly skies."

The pilot laughed at his own joke, tossed them a plastic bag with bottles of water and energy bars and turned back to his flying.

Bridget sat in her king-size hotel room bed, cozy in the high-quality sheets and plush comforter, wide awake at two a.m. and holding her phone to her ear.

She was pissed. She should be snoozing on a plane flying back to Washington. But Hadley had emailed her orders to stay put until they had a chance to talk. This was the chance.

"I need you to stay a few days," Hadley said. "See how it plays out."

"But, sir, we saw Abdallah in the TV footage from the village. I stayed to make sure he got released and connected with the jihadis. That's done. And you said you wanted me back ASAP. We have lots of other things going on."

"This is the only thing anyone cares about."

"'Anyone' meaning . . . ?"

"Yeah, meaning you-know-who, in the house across the river."

"Oh, sir, I know he's engaged with this mission, but exaggerated expectations would not be good. Pressure leads to mistakes and—"

"I know."

Bridget shut up. She knew Hadley didn't like being told things he already knew.

"Look," he continued, "it's my job to run interference with the higher-ups, make sure you're free to do your job. But the National Command Authority does set priorities. And congratulations, you've got one."

"So, I'm here so you can tell the president that I'm here?"

Bridget heard the general breathing, perhaps a technique to avoid an outburst.

When he answered, it sounded like a forced calm. "If that were the reason, it would be enough. But there are other reasons. Our friends at Langley are convinced an attack is imminent. Comms traffic, money moving, the kidnapping to force a prisoner exchange. It all points in one direction. And your team in the basement has no argument with that analysis. Abdallah could be walking into a shitstorm, and if he is, we need him to tell us about it before it happens. Having you there is an extra level of insurance, an extra point of contact. Not unreasonable. And even if you think it is unreasonable, enjoy the rest of your stay."

Hadley hung up without saying goodbye. That had never happened before. He must be under some serious pressure. Bridget looked around. If things were that bad, a few more nights in this hotel and days in the beachside office were not the worst things in the world.

She checked her bedside clock and wondered whether Will was awake. They were in the same time zone for a change, but she didn't know what kind of hours he was working in Baghdad. She reached for her phone and tapped, "*You awake?*"

No response.

Bridget brushed her hand across the pillow next to her. She imagined her head lying on Will's muscular arm, the curly hair on his light brown chest, the smell of his shaving cream.

Oh, stop. It's just torture. They hadn't been together like that in—Bridget started to count the months but stopped. What's the use?

She looked back at the phone. Still, no response. "*Wimp,*" she typed. Then she deleted it and started again. "*I guess SEALs need their beauty rest. Talk soon.*" She added a *Z-z-z* emoji and hit send.

Bridget put the phone into its charger and slid down to get some sleep.

Chapter Twenty-one

Faraz didn't know for sure that they landed in Saudi Arabia, but he had a pretty good idea. The timing was right at their speed, and the men who met them wore white robes and red-and-white *kufiyahs*. They treated Iyad as a returning hero and took them the rest of the way in a limo, with a fridge full of bottled water and a tray of sweets.

Their predawn arrival at the desert camp caused a small celebration, lit by floodlights powered by a noisy generator. At first, Faraz hung back from the hugging and kissing, but Ayman brought him into the crowd and made introductions.

Faraz noticed a man watching the scene from the doorway of the camp's building. He was short, heavyset, bald and bearded, and wore a suit jacket against the morning chill over traditional Arab trousers.

A shiver went through Faraz and he turned away.

He recognized the man more from seeing him at a distance in Syria than from the DIA's terrible photo. At least the agency had provided his full name, Saddiq

Mohammed Assali, jihadi financier and, this would seem to confirm, the new terrorism mastermind.

Finding Assali meant Faraz had accomplished part of his mission but put the rest in jeopardy. If Assali recognized him, he'd never find out what the plan was, never have a chance to report the location, probably not survive until tomorrow.

Assali and Faraz never actually met in Syria. "The King" had been busy with more important things than paying attention to a lowly fighter. Maybe he wouldn't remember.

Faraz looked back toward the headquarters. Assali gave no hint of recognition. In fact, he seemed bored watching the celebration.

Another man emerged from the building, shorter than Assali with the demeanor of a veteran fighter. Faraz knew him from Syria, too. He had been with Assali that day. Shit.

Faraz moved to the far edge of the crowd, away from the two men. He would have to come up with a story in case they remembered him.

But what story could he possibly tell?

Faraz made it through the day without encountering Assali or the other man. They did not join the fighters for meals or training.

During a session outside the walls, Iyad commanded Faraz and Ayman's group while Ra'ed was on the other side of the camp with the more advanced fighters.

Ayman lagged behind, straining to finish the laps

around the camp and unable to perform even the most
basic hand-to-hand movements.

Iyad was tough on him. "Faster, cousin," he shouted.
At one point, he pushed Ayman aside to show him how
to perform an exercise movement. Ayman stumbled. Iyad
steadied him, then stood over him until he got it right.

When tent assignments came, Iyad put Faraz and
Ayman together. Faraz saw Ayman was not happy. As they
lay on their mats, exhausted from their long night and
day, he asked, "What's wrong, Ayman? You don't want to
be my tentmate?"

"I should be with Iyad. Instead, he shares with Ra'ed."

"They're old comrades. I guess that means a lot."

"Yes, yes. But I am Iyad's family. I have been to prison.
I play a vital role . . . or I would if there was any internet
in this damn place."

"I thought you wanted to be a fighter."

"I am a fighter! And I will go on the operation. Iyad
promised me that."

"What operation?"

Ayman didn't answer immediately. "I do not know. I
should be with Iyad, helping to make the plan. And the
men should see that I am by his side."

"Yes. Of course. I hadn't thought about it that way.
But don't worry, Ayman, the men respect you. The rest
will come."

Ayman grunted. "You're a good friend, Khayal. We
will rise up in the organization together." He rolled over.
"After we get some sleep."

* * *

The next morning, Faraz came out of his tent and almost ran into one of the men he didn't want to see. He rushed past him.

"Wait," the man said. "I am Salim, chief of security. But you know me, or at least I know you."

Faraz turned back and searched his brain for the proper Arabic response. "*La aetaqid, sayyid.*" I don't think so, sir.

Salim stood in front of him to get a good look. He was a couple of inches shorter than Faraz. He had a thin face with a rough gray stubble and deep-set dark eyes. His brow had prominent lines, made more so by his current frown. Salim looked to be in his fifties, testimony enough to his toughness in his chosen line of work.

"But I do think so," Salim said, switching to English. "What is your name?"

"I am Khayal."

"American?"

"Yes, sir."

Salim scratched his beard. "I do not know many Americans, but I know you. Have you been a fighter before?"

"No, sir. I had just arrived from America when the Zionists arrested me."

"I know I have seen you." He leaned left and right to look at Faraz's face from different angles. "Perhaps it was at a disco in Las Vegas."

Faraz stared at him, confused.

Salim burst into laughter. "Yes, that is it. I met you at the disco." He laughed some more and moved on toward the headquarters. "See you later, Disco Boy."

Faraz watched him walk away. Salim had not risen to be security chief for a terrorism boss by letting things go.

Faraz was sure he would turn it over and over in his mind until he remembered.

During the following days, more men arrived from the prisoner release, but Assali and Salim seemed unhappy with the numbers and the quality. Faraz avoided the two leaders as much as he could. He made sure to sit with his back to their table at mealtimes. He turned away if he caught Salim looking at him during training. Or, if he couldn't, he made a mistake or fell down to disrupt Salim's concentration and demonstrate he was not an experienced fighter.

The evasive maneuvers made it impossible for Faraz to eavesdrop on the leaders' conversations. But Ayman often imposed himself on Iyad and Salim at mealtimes. He would approach their table near the headquarters, and usually they invited him to sit. This further enhanced his status among the men. And if Faraz played it right, it also made Ayman his field agent.

One day during a water break, Faraz said, "So, Ayman, what's happening? With all the time you spend with Iyad and Salim, you must know the plan by now."

Another fighter joined the interrogation. "Yes, please, Ayman, tell us."

"You shall see when the time is right, my brothers," Ayman replied, putting down his water cup and walking away. "It is our job to be ready when my cousin calls upon us."

Ayman was relishing his position as a confidante of the leaders and channeling it through his tried-and-true PR phrases. He was sounding like the internet propaganda he used to write. But Faraz thought it was likely that Ayman simply didn't know the plan.

That afternoon, the men built a mock village out of plywood and practiced attacking it. Iyad divided them into teams of eight and designated a leader for each. Faraz could not see any logic to the selections. The leaders were not necessarily the best fighters, nor did they have any long-term connection to the movement, except Ra'ed and Ayman.

Faraz was on Ayman's team. In their first run at the target, they approached the front door, looking right and left for any threats. Ayman kicked in the door and the others ran inside. For the exercises, they carried real weapons but didn't waste ammunition, instead shouting, "*Bahm, bahm, bahm.*"

Ayman went in last and pretended someone came at him. "*Bahm, bahm, bahm,*" he shouted, and announced, "Got him. All clear." Faraz was sure Ayman had seen the move on some American television show.

As the training went on, Ayman proved he was not much of a fighter, as expected. His extra weight slowed him down, and he was all thumbs with his AK. His turns on the target range were a disaster.

Ra'ed's team was the best, and everyone was required to watch whenever it was their turn to attack the house. It was clear to Faraz that Ra'ed had formal training, as well as experience.

More men joined them every day from the prisoner release. Some performed well upon arrival. Others seemed to be trying to become the men the Israelis had accused them of being.

And many of them did. Even Ayman was performing

better, now. The small-unit movements were coordinated and effective. The men cheered each other on after each assault on a succession of faux villages, like boys at summer camp preparing to face their rivals in the big game.

But here, the big game was life or death. Faraz didn't know where they were going or when, but people were going to die, and he didn't see how he could stop it.

Chapter Twenty-two

On Faraz's fifth day in the camp, Iyad added something odd to the training. The men were taught basic commands in Hebrew—*tsmol, yemin, kadima, tirah*. Left, right, forward, shoot and a few others. Faraz asked Ayman why, but he turned and walked away.

When it was time to assault the mock houses, Salim took charge. "No more *bahm, bahm*," he announced. "Today, you shoot." He paused and looked over the gathering. "Try not to kill each other."

The men collected their ammunition and began a series of live fire assaults on the plywood village. Salim watched from a safe distance, shouting criticism or encouragement as needed.

Ra'ed's team went first, setting the example. Ayman's team was next, and Faraz made sure to stay behind Ayman so as not to get shot. But they did well. Ayman made the right moves and gave the right commands in Hebrew. They got a polite round of applause from the men.

Assali and Iyad joined Salim to watch the final round of assaults on the now decimated faux village. When the shooting stopped, the men gathered in front of the leaders.

"In three days, we will strike our first blow," Iyad said. "This is not the big attack you have heard about, but it is important. We will create the conditions for what we need to do. Train hard, my brothers. Your lives and our success depend on it."

The men cheered and hugged each other and fired their remaining bullets into the air. In the evening, they built a bonfire of broken plywood houses.

That night, Faraz lay in the tent while Ayman paced outside. Faraz poked his head through the flap. "What are you doing?"

"I must speak to Iyad. Something is happening. I should know what it is."

Faraz went back inside. If Ayman was gathering intel, that was fine with him.

After a few minutes, Ayman called out, "Iyad, I must speak with you." Faraz heard footsteps as Ayman hurried to intercept his cousin.

When Ayman crawled back into the tent he went straight to his mat and turned away from Faraz without saying anything.

"So?" Faraz asked.

"I cannot tell you."

"What is the operation?"

"I cannot tell you."

"You cannot tell me, or Iyad did not tell you?"

Ayman swung around and glared at Faraz. "Of course,

he told me. He asked my advice. I gave him . . . what do you call it? Input. I had input."

"Wow. Good for you." Faraz guessed Ayman would not require much prodding to further demonstrate his superior position. "So, we attack?"

Ayman didn't answer.

"We return to Israel to attack?"

"Think about it, Khayal. Where are the Zionists? Should we strike at them here? In Saudi Arabia? Maybe in Iran? Of course, we will return to Israel . . . eventually."

"But not this time?"

"Be patient. I am grateful to you, but I cannot tell you all of the plans for our jihad."

"Allah's jihad."

Ayman's anger flashed now. He pushed himself up on his right elbow and emphasized his points with his left hand. "Of course, it is Allah's jihad. Do not pretend you know more than me, Khayal. Our movement, Iyad's and mine, is Allah's jihad in Palestine. Do not believe that you are my equal in the organization."

Faraz made a show of contrition. "Of course, my friend. I'm sorry."

"Your questions will be answered soon. Very soon." Ayman rolled away from Faraz again. "You came here to join the jihad, Khayal. I hope you are ready."

As the training progressed, Faraz saw a change in the men. They took every exercise more seriously. There was more helping and less taunting of the weaker recruits. There was more time for target practice. Men cleaned their weapons without being told.

At dawn on the third day after Iyad's pep talk, team leaders distributed new clothes—olive green trousers and shirts with no markings, and combat boots with socks. This was also strange. In Faraz's experience, jihadi fighters used their own clothes and no one cared what they wore.

"Put these on," Ayman ordered his team. "Bring your weapons to the front of the camp. We leave in ten minutes."

His XXL uniform buttons straining over his stomach, Ayman led Faraz and his six other men as they walked through the front gate, where they found a pickup truck and two large, air-conditioned tour buses. This was the five-star Saudi jihadi experience, a significant contrast to the primitive camp they had been given. The buses had no markings on the sides, and Faraz noticed that their license plates were covered.

Salim came through the gate right behind them. "Line up," he ordered.

The men fell into sloppy formation next to the buses and Salim walked the line. He told one man to button his shirt properly, another to tie his boots. When he came to Faraz, Salim said, "You look like a fighter, Disco Boy. Your uniform is right. You stand in proper position. Your weapon points to the ground. You did not learn this in Las Vegas."

Faraz shifted his position. "It is only by accident, *sayyid*." Beads of sweat formed at his temples despite the cool morning air.

"Ha!" Salim looked at Faraz for a few more seconds, then moved on.

When Salim finished the inspection, he issued the order to board the buses and the men loaded up. Faraz sat next to Ayman as usual in the first row of the first bus. He saw Iyad and Salim board the pickup truck to lead the small convoy.

Faraz twisted in his seat and saw Assali and the servant Mustapha standing by the gate to watch them go. As the convoy started to move, Mustapha gave an enthusiastic wave. Assali offered a skeptical glare.

They rode all morning, arriving around noon at a desert camp of sand-colored tents and camels, where a sheikh in white robes and matching *kufiyah* greeted Salim and Iyad as they got out of the pickup. The sheikh put his arms around the visitors and took them to the largest tent. Ayman jumped off the bus and jogged toward them, clearly hoping for an invitation. But the sheikh's tent flap snapped shut behind them.

Ayman recovered by taking charge of the rest of the men, hurrying them off the buses and following a teenage boy, who guided them to the latrine. From there, they walked to a row of basins where they could wash.

Midday prayers were in a tent with traditional carpets on the sand and all its side flaps open. Lunch was in the same tent, served by more teenage boys—fresh pita, rustic hummus and hard-boiled eggs, with desert well water to drink. Other than the sheikh, Faraz saw only one man, who supervised the boys. He saw no women.

After lunch, the man said, "Which one is Ra'ed?"

Ra'ed stepped forward.

"You are wanted in the sheikh's tent. You men rest now."

Ayman seethed as he watched Ra'ed walk to the main tent. Faraz would also have preferred for his "agent" to be in there. They appeared to be on the verge of launching a terrorist attack. And Faraz didn't know where he was or where he was going.

He found a spot to lie down on a carpet where he could see the sheikh's tent. Ayman paced behind him.

"Are you nervous, my friend?" Faraz asked.

Ayman stopped and put his hands on his hips. "No. I am not. Do you think this is my first fight? I am more ready than you are, Disco Boy."

"So that's my nickname, now?"

"If Salim says it is. It fits, anyway."

"Ha. Okay. Anyway, I admit I'm nervous. But you are the one who can't stop pacing."

As if to prove that he could stop, Ayman sat and leaned against a tent pole. His right hand played with some sand that came up between the carpets. "There, are you happy, now?"

"I am happy," Faraz said. "Do you know where we're going?"

Ayman threw a fistful of sand out of the tent and got up to start pacing again.

Chapter Twenty-three

After nearly two weeks of waiting to hear from Faraz and trying to do her actual job from six thousand miles and seven time zones away, Bridget gave herself a day off. One advantage of her temporary deployment was that she could get in a full day of tourism and be back at her desk before noon Washington time if necessary.

She took a bus to Jerusalem and followed her tour book's admonition to visit the Western Wall first, lest, God forbid, she should be in Jerusalem and for some reason miss it. She marveled at how much smaller it looked than its place in history would seem to require. From the stairway leading down to the wall's open plaza, she was more impressed with the two mosques that towered above it on the Temple Mount, their gold and silver domes instantly recognizable as the symbols of the city.

Bridget moved toward the wall's women's section on the right and reached into her bag for the scarf she'd brought—another piece of advice from the tour book. Her slacks with long-sleeved untucked button-down shirt covering her rear end passed inspection by the self-appointed gatekeeping orthodox Jewish women, and she approached the ancient stones.

Bridget wasn't much for praying, but somehow it felt like the thing to do. The place had a spirituality to it—the ancient stones, the history, the people all around her saying their blessings, making their pleas. Bridget prayed for her parents' health, for Will's safety, and for Faraz's, too. And she prayed that his mission would end soon so she could go home—selfish perhaps, but she figured she might as well get it out there if she was on a direct pipeline to God.

Turning to leave, Bridget put twenty Israeli shekels in a charity jar but didn't take the small pencil and scrap of paper offered in return. She knew the tradition was to put a prayer into the wall's crevasses, but she'd said her piece.

She consulted her map and zigged right, then left toward the Church of the Holy Sepulchre. She was awed by the architecture and found a pillar to lean on as tourists flowed past her. She stared at the ceiling and contemplated the church's significance to so many people over the centuries, right down to her parents' deep faith.

Her tour book told her that Christian teaching said this was the site of both the crucifixion and the tomb from which Jesus rose, and also told her not to necessarily accept that. The faithful believe the site is authentic, historians are not so sure. Ordinarily, Bridget would side with the scientists, even social scientists. But like at the wall, there was an undeniable feeling of something.

Bridget shook it off. Maybe it was the musty air. She rejoined the line snaking through the church between velvet ropes and took the first exit she saw.

She was planning to walk the stations of the cross but

Al Pessin

had had enough religious experiences for one morning. What she needed now was a coffee.

A few turns on the cobblestoned alleyways brought her to the unmistakable smell of cardamom. She traced it to a tiny coffee shop on the edge of the *souk*, the Old City market. She sat on a low stool at a small octagonal wooden table outside the shop, with barely enough room for people to pass by.

A boy, maybe ten years old, wearing jeans and a red T-shirt with a Power Ranger on the front, came to her table. "*Aywah.*" Yes.

"Coffee, please," she said.

"Sweet?"

Bridget was unsure.

"Medium?"

"Yes, medium, *shukran.*" Thank you—one of her three words of Arabic, the others being *hammam* and *salaam*. "Toilet" and "peace," the latter also being good for "hello" and "goodbye."

While she waited for the coffee, she watched the crowd go by—men in Western clothes, women in *abayas* with casual head coverings, younger people in jeans and flip-flops. A few tourists with backpacks and noses in guide-books.

One man in a sport coat and eyeglasses stood out. He looked like he must be a teacher or some sort of profes-sional. He dodged right and flattened himself against a wall as a two-wheeled cart came the other way, piled im-possibly high with household goods. The attendant pushing it was unable to see ahead. He shouted in Arabic—must have been something like "coming through," Bridget figured. The "teacher" dusted off his jacket and moved on, not in the least bit perturbed.

The boy returned with Bridget's coffee in a double-sized shot glass on a saucer, with a tiny spoon and a small pastry. The first sip was both sweeter and hotter than she had expected, and her reaction must have shown it because three old men sitting outside a café down the alley got a good chuckle. Bridget raised her glass as a toast. They looked embarrassed to have been caught staring at her, but one of them raised a glass in return. Then he said something to his friends and went inside.

Bridget blew on her coffee and took another sip. The cardamom gave it a unique flavor and aroma that said, "Middle East." It occurred to her that her only previous trips to the region had been in uniform and body armor, and she'd had little contact with locals. True, she had been living in Tel Aviv for the last two weeks. But that felt more like New York. This alleyway was firmly in the Middle East.

The man at the café came back to his friends with an Arabic-language newspaper. He pointed at it and the men nodded their agreement. One of them looked toward her wide-eyed, but the man with the newspaper said something and the gawker turned away.

That was strange. Something in the news about . . . what? America? Europe? Western women?

Bridget shrugged and took another sip of her coffee — that one-sip-too-many that got her to the grounds at the bottom of the cup. She winced and looked up to see if her faux pas had been noticed. It hadn't been. The men were ignoring her now, and the newspaper was gone.

She summoned the boy and made the international sign for "check please" with her right index finger.

The second half of Faraz's trip was a high-speed dash westward through the Saudi desert. They veered left off the road and slowed to pass through a double chain-link fence, where a bus-sized hole had been cut.

"Where are we?" Faraz asked.

Ayman stared straight ahead, clinging to the metal bar in front of them. "Jordan."

"But how . . . ?"

"*Sayyid* Assali has many resources."

Ayman leaned forward, straining to see ahead. It was almost dark now, and the vehicles used only their running lights.

Bridget was also on a bus, approaching the Tel Aviv station. It had been an exhausting but exhilarating day. Her stop in the *souk* had turned into three hours of meandering and making conversation with merchants, all of whom wanted to serve her tea and give her terrific bargains. She netted T-shirts for Will and her father, a colorful knit hat for her nephew, and fine wool shawls for herself and her mother. She'd also had the best shawarma sandwich of her life.

It was late. Bridget had stayed out longer than planned. She was tired and in need of a shower. But this was the other side of the time zone coin. It was still only midday in Washington, and she was sure that even though the team knew she had the day off, urgent messages were piling up in the secure comms system.

Bridget joined the taxi queue and consulted the Hebrew cheat sheet in her tour book. When it was her turn, she struggled with the words, "*Shagriroot Amerikayit.*"

The driver turned and shot her a "give me a break" shrug. "U.S. embassy, then?" he said in an Australian accent.

Well inside Jordan, the buses pulled to the side of a dark road. Iyad got onto Faraz's bus, Salim went to the other.

"Brothers," Iyad announced, standing in the front with his AK over his shoulder. "We will soon launch our operation. For many of you, it will be your first time. Do not worry. Allah is with us. We have chosen a soft target, but there may be some resistance. Brothers, it will be difficult. There will be civilians—women and children, Arabs. Pay no attention. Do your jobs. It is essential that we increase pressure on the Zionists and distract from our coming operation. Return to the buses when ordered. Team leaders stand."

Half a dozen men stood up, including Ayman and Ra'ed.

"Follow the orders of these men," Iyad said. "And this is important— do not speak. Only the team leaders will speak. And they will speak only Hebrew. You know the commands."

The synapses in Faraz's brain were firing. Attacking Arabs in Jordan? Speaking Hebrew? This is crazy. At least the unit leader selections made sense now. Those men were the best Hebrew speakers. He had no time for further analysis. The bus was moving again.

"Weapons ready," Iyad said.

The desert on the right side of the road gave way to a chain-link fence surrounding a slum of ramshackle houses—wood and metal shacks clustered along narrow streets. A web of electrical wires hung overhead on poles that looked as if they might fall at any moment. Goats were tied to stakes in small backyards. Some yards had chicken coops.

The compound was huge, well over a kilometer along the road and deep enough that Faraz could not see the other side. A refugee camp? A Palestinian refugee camp? This made no sense.

"Remember your orders." Iyad said. "No talking except the team leaders."

Still standing, Ayman nearly tipped over when they turned onto the road that led to the neighborhood's entrance. Faraz saw the sweat beading on Ayman's forehead. The sides of his shirt were already soaked through.

The driver gunned the engine and the bus blew through a gate arm, startling two unarmed guards who had no chance to stop them. At an open area, some sort of village square, Faraz's bus veered right and he saw the other one go left. They screeched to a halt in a cloud of sand and the doors flew open.

"*Kadima, kadima,*" Iyad shouted in Hebrew. Forward, forward. He jumped down the three steps to the ground and started shooting. Ayman led the men off the bus and crouched down.

Iyad pushed him toward an alley. "*Laych, laych.*"
Go, go.

Faraz came off the bus behind Ayman and grabbed his
arm, urging his team leader forward. Ayman got his body
moving and started firing at random houses as they went.
Faraz glanced over his shoulder and saw Iyad directing
other teams to various parts of the camp, while Salim
took three fighters toward the gatehouse.

Ayman's men were running through the alley now, as
fast as Ayman could lead them. They fired through the
windows of houses as they went. The homes were small
and irregular, made of whatever materials their owners
could find. Some walls leaned against neighboring houses
for support. Faraz fired, too, making sure his bullets
went high.

The scene was lit by streetlamps at irregular intervals
and light from houses as residents turned them on to see
what was happening. Smarter people left the lights off.
But some panicked and ran from their homes, screaming
and waving their arms, some directly into the gunfire.

One man ran toward them, cursing the Zionists. The
team member next to Faraz cut him down with a short
burst.

"*Yemin, yemin,*" Ayman shouted. Right, right. They
turned into an alley that led to a cluster of homes. Faraz
stopped at an intersection, pretending to reload, and
waved his colleagues past him. Then he turned left, made
two more quick turns and kicked down the door of the
next house he came to.

A woman cowered on a mattress in the far corner of
the one-room hovel, protecting three children behind her.
Once Faraz closed the door, the only light came from the

room's one window, which caught some rays from a streetlamp. The sound of gunfire was loud and close.

"Please," she screamed in Arabic. "Please do not shoot us."

Faraz pointed his rifle at them and put a finger to his lips. He struggled to find the right Arabic words. "Quiet, Mother. I will not shoot. Where is your telephone?"

"Please, please. My children."

"Telephone!" Faraz repeated, and he shook his weapon at them.

"There," the woman said, pointing. "On the table." She pushed her children farther back into the corner.

"Do not move and you may survive this night." Faraz grabbed the phone and dialed the Ops Center.

Bridget had picked a good day to take off. Although there were dozens of emails, some needing answers, she hadn't missed anything truly urgent. She kicked off her shoes and settled in to fend off the latest nag note from General Hadley.

Although it was late, the office was not empty. Apparently, hers was not the only department that demanded immediate answers, until at least five p.m. Washington time.

The secure phone rang. The caller ID said "Unknown." Maybe Will was on duty and calling on the secure system, even though he shouldn't. She smiled and picked up the handset.

"Hello, sailor."

"Ma'am, this is the Ops Center. You have a call. Codeword: Shock Wave."

* * *

Faraz squatted next to the mattress and kept his weapon trained on the woman. He met her eyes to make clear she should not get any ideas about moving or crying out.

The phone line issued a click every two seconds, providing reassurance he hadn't been disconnected. Procedure dictated that if they could not reach his primary contact in thirty seconds, the operator would take his report. Right now, that felt like a crazy amount of time to wait.

Bridget sat up straight and pulled herself closer to the desk. "Put it through."

She knew the system would record the call. Still, she opened a secure document on her computer to take notes.

Bridget held the receiver between her ear and shoulder. The line beeped, and she said, "This is Shock Wave contact. Go ahead."

Hearing Bridget's voice, Faraz relaxed a little. He hadn't realized he was breathing in rapid, shallow breaths and holding his rifle so tightly that his knuckles were turning white. He moved his finger off the trigger and pointed the gun at the floor.

Faraz covered his mouth and whispered into the phone. "Training camp, Saudi desert. Assali on site. Working on an MTO, details unknown. Preliminary attack now underway. Possibly a refugee camp somewhere in Jordan. Attackers are jihadi but speaking Hebrew. Over."

"Hebrew?"

"Yes, and Israeli-style uniforms, some sort of subterfuge."

"Copy. Assali location?"

"Eight hours driving east of attack site, through a fence, possibly Saudi-Jordan border."

"Got it. Thank you."

Faraz moved the phone from his ear and listened to the gunfire outside. It was moving away from his position. He would have to get back to the bus soon.

"You were right to connect me with the al-Hamdani family. Ayman's cousin Iyad is a key player, along with a friend of his named Ra'ed, last name unknown. Also, Assali's security man, Salim."

"Excellent. Anything at all on the MTO?"

"Only that it's happening soon."

"Do you need egress?"

"Negative. I'll return with them to report further."

"Great. Thank you." Bridget paused. "It's good to hear your voice."

"Yours, too.

An explosion shook the flimsy walls and the children cried out.

"What was that?" Bridget asked.

"Attack in progress. Sorry, I gotta go." Faraz ended the call and deleted it from the phone's history. He walked to the woman and put the barrel of his AK against her chest. "I was never here," he said in Arabic.

She nodded and covered her face with her hands.

Chapter Twenty-four

Gunfire raged in the distance and a nearby house was on fire. Faraz would have to find Ayman or link up with another group. He opened the door enough to look out. In the light of the streetlamp, he saw nothing to the right, toward the buses. He had no view to the left but had to take a chance.

Leading with his weapon, Faraz stepped out and moved toward the buses.

"You, stop!" The familiar voice came from behind. Faraz turned to find Salim pointing his AK at him. "Disco Boy. What were you doing in that house? Hiding from the fight?"

Faraz lowered his weapon but kept his finger on the trigger. "No, *sayyid*. I was clearing it. There is no one inside."

"And where is your team?"

"We were separated. I hope to find them at the buses."

Salim came closer and looked up at Faraz. He tilted his head to change the angle. "Step into the light," he said, pointing with his gun toward the streetlamp.

Faraz complied.

"I do know you." Salim brought his left hand up to steady his weapon. "I never forget a face. You were in Syria with al-Souri."

"No, *sayyid*. I have never been to Syria."

"Do not lie to me." Salim took another step toward Faraz, turning his gun to the side so he could get closer. He seemed to be putting the pieces together as he moved. "Yes. It was an American who betrayed us. You were there when they attacked. You were the sp—"

Salim did not finish the word. Faraz's bullet hit him in the stomach at point-blank range. Salim staggered back, his eyes wide. Faraz shot again, higher this time, hitting him in the chest. Salim twisted and fell on top of his rifle.

Faraz looked around. They were alone in the alley. He stepped into a narrow walkway between two houses. He was breathing hard and his heart was pounding. But he had no time to calm himself. He didn't want to be caught near Salim's body. Faraz looked at it one more time. Salim was facedown, not moving.

His exit wounds were large and had spewed blood in the street and against the wall behind. Faraz squatted, reached out and put two fingers on Salim's neck. No pulse. He looked around again, then ran through the passageway between the houses and came out on a parallel alley.

Faraz turned toward the buses. When he got to a larger street, he fell in behind one of the teams and fired the rest of his bullets as they went, without causing any damage. He boarded the first bus and found Ayman agitated in the front row.

"Where were you?" Ayman demanded, his adrenaline apparently surging. He half stood up under the luggage rack. "I thought you were dead. Or were you hiding somewhere?"

Faraz was also keyed up and had no trouble feigning anger. "I lost you in the alleys. I ran with another team for a while, firing all the way, then followed them back here." He unclipped the magazine from his AK and tossed it at Ayman. "You see? Empty. You're not my father. Don't scold me. I did my job."

For all his bravado, Ayman backed off. He put his gun, butt down, between his feet and looked out the window. "They need to get back. We must get out of here."

"The men are coming. Don't worry. And don't point that thing at your head."

"It is empty anyway," Ayman said.

Faraz sat down. His heart was pumping. Through the windshield, he saw Iyad directing the men. Most boarded the buses. One team established a security cordon in case any of the residents launched a counterattack.

"Any casualties on the team?" Faraz asked.

"None dead. Some wounded. There is an AK in every house. But they were no match for us."

Two fighters ran up to Iyad, shouting and waving their arms. Iyad had a physical reaction, bending forward, putting his left hand on one of the men's shoulders.

When he recovered, he shouted some orders in Hebrew and headed off at a run with the two fighters and two other men. Ra'ed took command of the courtyard.

Ayman got off the bus and ran over to Ra'ed. "What's going on. We need to leave."

"I do not know. Iyad told me to get the men on the buses and wait for him. So, get on your bus, Ayman."

"If Iyad is not here, I am in charge."

"You were sleeping and he gave the job to me. Now load up." Ra'ed raised his AK a little to show he was serious.

Ayman turned to some other men, the last to arrive back at the buses. "Go, go," he said. "Load up." He herded them onto the bus, got on last, pushed past Faraz and sat down hard by the window.

"What's going on?" Faraz asked.

"It is not your concern. We will leave when Iyad returns."

With all the fighters except the security cordon and Iyad's team on board, what had been violent chaos a few minutes earlier turned to quiet tension. The drivers gunned their engines. All eyes watched the perimeter of the small square for any threat.

Two minutes went by. Three. The refugees would not cower forever.

One of the men on the cordon turned to an alley and pointed his weapon. "Someone is coming," he shouted.

Ra'ed and the rest of the team turned their guns in the same direction, and several rifle barrels poked through windows of the buses.

Iyad appeared at the alley's exit, holding up a hand. "It's me. Load up."

Faraz saw the other four fighters behind Iyad, carrying Salim's body between them.

Palestinian news reports said Israeli commandos attacked a refugee camp in southern Jordan without provocation, killing dozens, including women and children, and wounding hundreds.

Television footage showed bullet-riddled shanties, bodies in the streets, women wailing and men screaming for revenge. The bloodstain Salim left got considerable airtime. Witnesses reported that the attackers wore Israeli-looking uniforms without insignia and spoke Hebrew.

The camp was known as a hotbed of militancy, so to Palestinians, and many others, the narrative made sense. Never mind that if Israel ever did conduct such an attack, it would use different uniforms and likely order its soldiers not to speak Hebrew.

In an effort to tamp down the expected violent response, Prime Minister Yardeni went on Arabic satellite channels to deny involvement and to offer condolences and aid. In his Moroccan-accented Arabic, peppered with excessively intellectual words, he tried to appeal to ordinary Palestinians. He said Israel had no reason to attack the camp and would never target civilians. He blamed Palestinian extremists working with foreign support to stir anger.

Of course, he knew that was true, thanks to Faraz's call, but he couldn't offer the proof.

Up against gruesome cell phone videos, eyewitness reports and the long history of bad blood, the prime minister's TV appearances had no impact, except to fan the flames.

Within hours, two Israeli settlements were attacked and a bomb destroyed a coffee shop in Jerusalem, killing an Israeli Arab man who worked in the kitchen. Governments around the world condemned Israel. President Martelli called for an investigation and threatened to veto a U.N. Security Council resolution that Arab states were already circulating.

* * *

The buses arrived back at camp in late morning. The men got off and gathered around the pickup truck while Iyad, Ra'ed and two others lifted Salim's body, his bloodstained clothes now crusted with a layer of sand. They laid him on a white bedsheet on the ground.

Assali came out of the headquarters. The men moved aside so he could get to the front of the crowd. He re-coiled half a step when he saw Salim.

"He is our only martyr, *sayyid*," Iyad said. "Shot by someone at the camp. I know he was your friend. *Inna lillahi wa inna ilayhi raji'un.*" Indeed we belong to Allah, and indeed to Him we will return.

Assali stared with a blank expression, appearing unable to move or speak. It was the first time Faraz had ever seen the boss show any demeanor other than supe-riority.

But it wasn't long before he recovered. Assali turned away from Salim to face Iyad. "The mission was a success, from what I hear on the radio." His voice was unsteady.

"Yes, the men did well and also maintained the decep-tion. This will lay the groundwork we need."

Assali nodded. When he spoke again, his voice and demeanor were back to normal. "Good. Prepare Salim. We will give him the martyr's funeral he deserves."

Bridget was still at the embassy, her "day off" having morphed into a work all-nighter that extended into the fol-lowing morning. She had Liz and the DIA team scouring comms intercepts in search of any clue about the big attack Faraz said was coming. So far, they had nothing.

Her one success was to order a playback of satellite tracking that showed the buses speeding away from the refugee camp. She saw them cross into Saudi. And she got a location on Assali's camp.

Bridget sent the info and called Hadley, who was still working at midnight in DC.

"I see your report," he said. "Good work."

"Thank you, sir. I called to suggest that we not share the camp location with the Israelis. Faraz is there, and we need to let his mission play out. They might prefer a retaliatory strike."

"I see your reasoning. But they'll find out eventually, and my old friend Oded will be apoplectic—their whole government will be, understandably."

"Yes, sir. But an air strike won't shut down the network, might not even stop the attack. If we're going to achieve our broader goals, we need to buy Abdallah as much time as we can. We certainly can't let the Israelis drop a bomb on him."

"Agreed. I'll run it up the chain. But it will be hard to keep this genie in the bottle."

Chapter Twenty-Five

It didn't take the genie long to get out.

"You lied to us." Those were the first words Colonel Ben-Yosef spoke when he called Bridget just after noon.

"Excuse me?"

"You told us about your man's call, but not about the satellite tracking."

"I'm not required to tell you everything. I didn't want—"

"You didn't want us to do exactly what we are doing right now. Fortunately, you are not our only source of information."

"But, Colonel . . ." Bridget did a midcourse correction. "Ari, our man—"

"Now, I am 'Ari,' because you want something from me. I know—your man is there and he has a mission. He should not be there. He should have escaped last night. And his mission should be to stop the next attack, which is what we are doing in . . ." He paused, ". . . in about forty-five minutes."

"In daylight?"

"This cannot wait. It is an advantage of having options other than risking pilots' lives."

"The camp is in the middle of Saudi Arabia."

"I am aware of that. They will deny it. We will deny it. The game will be played. And the threat will be eliminated."

"The current threat will be eliminated. Maybe. But our man's intel could do more than stop the next attack. You can't—"

"Do not tell me what we can't do." Ari was angry now. "We will do what is needed to protect our people. Your man was not able to stop last night's attack, and I doubt he can stop the next one. We can. And we will. The prime minister has informed President Martelli. And I am telling you so you have a chance to get a message to your agent."

"And how am I supposed to do that? Skywriting? Carrier pigeon? I need more time."

"There is no more time. If you can't reach him, that's unfortunate. Perhaps his training will save him. But stopping the next terrorist attack is the absolute priority. Goodbye, Ms. Davenport. And although I do not, at least for now, have the authority to tell you to leave Israel, I honestly believe it would be best if you did."

The line went dead.

Bridget was not the type to panic, but this was pushing the limits of her self-control. It was hardly worth going through her options for reaching Faraz because she had none. She couldn't call her contact in Saudi military intelligence and tell him she was running a covert op on his soil and the Israelis were about to attack. Even if she did, there wasn't time for him to rescue Faraz, assuming he'd be willing to try.

Also, Ari said Martelli knew about the Israeli plan. He apparently hadn't put his foot down to stop it.

Apparently.

She picked up the handset of her secure phone and dialed Hadley's cell.

"They're what?" Hadley said after Bridget's as-brief-as-possible summary of the situation. His voice was clear now, after the expected sleepy "Hello." It was a few minutes past five a.m. in Washington.

"We've got maybe forty minutes. Probably less for a safe abort."

"I got nothing from HaLevy, my so-called 'old friend.' That tells you how pissed he is."

"Sir, can you possibly check with the White House to make sure the president is on board with this? That's what Ben-Yosef told me, but it's hard to believe he'd let them attack with our man on-site."

Hadley grunted. "All right. On it." He hung up before she could say thank you.

Faraz was on the gravedigging team. He and another man dug while two others rested. Then they switched. It was hard, sweaty work in the early afternoon sun. He was already exhausted and drained of adrenaline from the operation and his encounter with Salim.

He wanted to spit in the grave, but there were too

many men around. His sweat would have to be disrespect enough.

Faraz felt a shadow over him and looked up. It was Iyad. "Good. That is enough. Go and clean up for the funeral."

Iyad offered Faraz a hand as he climbed out of the grave. When Faraz got to the top, Iyad said, "Someday, we will all be martyrs."

Faraz took a beat, then replied, "*Insha' Allah.*" The phrase usually meant, "If it is God's will." But it could also mean, "May it be God's will."

"Do not be too eager, Disco Boy. But yes, *insha' Allah.*"

Twenty minutes later, Faraz stood next to Ayman in front of the grave and the pile of dirt that would fill it. They were in the first row with Iyad and Ra'ed. The other men were arrayed behind. Salim's body lay on the ground in front of them, wrapped in the bedsheet.

Ayman was more upset than Faraz expected about the death of a man he barely knew.

"Are you all right, my friend?" he asked.

Ayman shot him a look, clearly not happy that his emotions were showing. "It could have been any of us," he whispered.

Iyad called the men to attention, and they waited for the arrival of Assali.

Bridget watched the seconds tick by on the government-issued analog clock on the workspace wall. "Come on," she said out loud. She dared not call Hadley back. She knew he didn't like to be pestered, and he could be talking to the president. But the forty-five minutes were running out.

She jumped when the phone rang.

"Davenport."

"Sorry, Bridget. The prime minister was not taking 'no' for an answer."

"He refused the president's request to protect an American soldier?"

"I don't know the word-for-word, but I woke up your old friend Jay Pruitt, who was on call for the NSC—his second call of the night. He said he'd awakened the president to speak to Yardeni less than an hour earlier. Pruitt monitored the call and took notes. He told me there was some discussion and the prime minister said he was aware of the situation and was calling as a courtesy, not for consultation. Jay said he sounded pretty pissed about not getting the intel sooner. He told Martelli to order his soldier to keep his head down, or some bullshit like that."

Bridget sat back in her chair. To her unpracticed diplomatic ears, that sounded pretty strong coming from junior ally to senior ally. "Wow," was all she said.

"Yeah. Pruitt apologized, but there was apparently nothing the president could do. I asked for a call to be sure Martelli understood this strike could kill Abdallah. Pruitt got a little testy at that point, said they understood perfectly well, and that in the absence of new information, he was not waking the president a second time to raise the same issue he'd already dealt with."

"Shit."

"Yeah. All we can do is hope the first bomb doesn't hit Abdallah. He knows how to protect himself after that."

"In a desert camp with no cover."

"It's a tough situation, damn it. I wish we could fix it, but we can't."

"And then what?"

"I assume the Saudis will send in troops and pick up any survivors."

"They will be royally pissed."

"That's the only way Saudis get pissed. If he survives, and if the Saudis find him, we'll get him back eventually. Right now, that's the best we can hope for."

"And his mission?"

"Yeah, well, if the strike kills Assali, that'll hurt them. But we'll have to find another way to get at the rest. You will, that is."

Assali emerged from the headquarters wearing traditional pants with his suit coat and *kufiyah*, and he appeared to Faraz to be putting on a show of grief. His attendant, Mustapha, was close behind.

Assali walked the fifty meters to the gravesite, paused over the body and bowed his head. After a few seconds, he turned to the men and spoke.

"Salim Abu Thawra was a good man, a strong fighter. He was loyal to Palestine and to me. All of you should work to be like Salim."

The men stood in ragged formation, many with their heads down.

Assali continued. "Now, by Allah's will, Salim is a martyr." He said the *Shahada*, the affirmation of Muslim faith. "*La ilaha illu-lah, Mohammed rasulu-lah.*" There is no God but God. Mohammed is the messenger of God.

Iyad and Ra'ed stepped forward, lifted Salim's body and lowered it into the grave, then stepped back for a moment of prayer.

The drone-launched supersonic American-made Hellfire missile outran the sound of its engine.

Chapter Twenty-six

The explosion obliterated the headquarters building and sent pieces of it flying in all directions. Several of the men at the back of the funeral gathering were hit. Faraz and the more savvy fighters, like Faraz, Iyad and Ra'ed, dove to the ground. Others, including Ayman, stood frozen.

Assali took a middle approach, squatting down but apparently reluctant to get his suit dirty.

Faraz raised himself enough to dive at the boss and tackle him into the grave. Salim's body cushioned their landing, but Faraz's head glanced off a rock protruding from the side. Another explosion rocked the camp, and shrapnel flew across the top of the hole, through the space where Assali had been crouching a moment earlier.

"What are you doing? Get off me." Assali's arm came up to push Faraz off of him.

"Stay down, *sayyid*. It is the safest place."

A third explosion shook the grave and convinced Assali to bury his face in the dirt next to Salim's feet. Faraz heard a thud and saw Ayman's big body hit the ground. His head and shoulders hung over them. He was unconscious.

A hail of sand rained on them as debris from the explosions came down. Faraz lay on top of Assali and put one hand over his own head. Assali's *kufiyah* was off and his mostly bald head was covered with earth.

There were several more missile hits, but none close to them. Then, all went quiet. Assali raised his head and looked at Faraz.

"Not yet, *sayyid*."

Assali didn't argue.

Several seconds went by. Ayman dangled above them, his eyes closed, blood trickling down the stubble of the beard he was trying to grow.

Faraz pushed himself off of Assali, stood up and looked over the top of the grave.

What he saw was a testament to the power of American weapons and the accuracy of Israeli targeting. The entire camp was flattened. The walls were down. The tents lay in twisted heaps. The kitchen equipment had been blown to random locations. All of the vehicles were seriously damaged and two were on fire, as were the ruins of a storage shed that held their weapons and supplies of food and water.

The destruction of the buildings and vehicles caught his eye first, but as he looked at the detail, he saw the bodies. Most were camouflaged in a layer of sand. Few were moving. As the echoes of the explosions receded, he heard the moaning and the desperate calls of "*saeadni*." Help me.

Faraz moved to the other side of the grave and checked

Ayman. He was breathing, and he moaned when Faraz touched him. "Stay there, my friend. I will help you."

He turned to Assali. "I think it is over, *sayyid*. I will help you up." Faraz intertwined his fingers to form a step.

Assali stood and brushed himself off. He looked at Salim's body, its sheets now dirty and in disarray. "Salim saved me several times. And now he has done so again." Assali glanced at Faraz and let out a short breath through his nose. Then, he put his hands on the edge of the grave, stepped into the boost Faraz provided and, with considerable help, hefted himself onto the surface, belly first.

Assali stood and looked around. Faraz saw his jaw slacken. His right hand came to his chest.

"*Sayyid*?" Faraz said.

Assali looked down at him. Faraz held up a hand, seeking help to get out of the grave. After a second, Assali said, "Yes, yes, okay." He set his feet and reached down to give Faraz a pull.

As Faraz came up, Iyad approached from behind what was left of the mound of dirt next to the grave, with Ra'ed close behind.

"*Sayyid* Assali, are you all right?"

Assali took stock of himself and wiped off his jacket. "Yes, I am fine. This man . . ."

"Khayal," Faraz said.

"Khayal. He helped me. We were . . . in there."

Surprise, irritation and, in the end, respect crossed Iyad's face. But he didn't give Faraz the satisfaction of a compliment. Instead, he spoke to Assali. "*Sayyid*, please find a place to rest. I will assess the damage and attend to the wounded. Khayal, Ra'ed, come with me."

Iyad took one step past Assali and saw his cousin on the ground. "Ayman!" Iyad went to his knees beside Ayman's prone body, pulled him away from the grave and turned him over. He took Ayman's wrist, feeling for a pulse.

Faraz knelt and put his ear to Ayman's nose and mouth. "I think he is breathing."

"Yes, he has a pulse."

"Praise Allah."

Ayman moaned again.

"He will be all right," Iyad said. "Come, we must check the others."

Faraz followed Iyad and Ra'ed as they assessed each man. Most of them were dead.

Two hours later, with no idea whether or when they might be rescued, Faraz and half a dozen other survivors strung a canvas remnant on stray tent poles to create some shade and lay down to conserve their energy. Assali was pacing in front of what used to be his headquarters.

Ayman was on a salvaged sleeping mat. He had a head wound with a blood-soaked *kufiyah* wrapped around it. He was conscious but not moving much. Iyad sat next to him.

"Water, cousin," Ayman said. His voice was soft and raspy.

"We have none," Iyad replied. "Rest now."

Other men had various shrapnel wounds that Faraz and Iyad had wrapped as well as they could. Two bled out despite their efforts. Faraz's head injury, a bump and some scratches, merited no attention compared with the others.

Ra'ed and another survivor stood watch, brandishing the two serviceable AKs they had found. They had also found Assali's satellite phones, but all three were damaged and unusable.

Assali stopped pacing and sat under the shade, his back against the twisted remains of one of the vehicles. He brought his knees to his chest—as close as he could with his belly in the way. His fancy black shoes were caked with sand. One had a bloodstain.

There was no one to clean it. Mustapha was among the dead, his body laid out with the others near Salim's grave. The survivors had no energy to bury them.

Assali took a handful of sand and rubbed the stain, to no avail.

"What will we do now, *sayyid*?" Faraz asked.

"They will come for us," Assali said, without shifting his gaze.

"Who will come?"

"Our friends." Assali looked at him now. "Our friends who failed to protect us. We still have a job to do."

"But how—"

Assali waved a hand to cut him off. "Our benefactor will not take this lying down. The Zionists and the Americans will pay a heavy price."

When he finished talking, the camp was silent again, except for the labored breathing of the wounded.

Bridget rested her chin in her left hand and her elbow on the desk. Her right hand gripped the computer mouse.

She hit refresh on her classified email as frequently as the system would allow—about every two seconds.

She was waiting for the satellite video of Faraz's location. If she had been at the Pentagon, she could have watched the Israeli air strike in real time. But in Tel Aviv, she had to wait for the secure uploads, ten-minute segments that took longer than that to arrive.

She had already seen the attack itself. Not surprisingly, the Israelis were highly skilled. They put six missiles, from three drones, she guessed, in a standard pattern, devastating the small camp. Bridget saw that there was some sort of gathering at one end of the camp just before the missiles hit and the smoke and debris obscured her view. She assumed Faraz was there, out in the open, with the others.

Like fish in a barrel.

Now, Bridget was refreshing for the upload of the next ten minutes, which she hoped would show the extent of the devastation.

A ping heralded the file's arrival and she double-clicked it. At first, she couldn't see anything. But toward the end, the image cleared and she saw what she expected—the buildings and tents destroyed, bodies on the ground, no movement. Then, the video ended.

Bridget was out of patience. She called the imagery assessment unit.

"Simons," said the senior analyst on duty.

"Patty, hi. Bridget Davenport here. I need you to look at something for me."

"Shoot."

"Starting ten minutes after the Israeli air strike, which I've seen, do you have any movement in the camp? Anything on infrared?"

"Hang on."

Bridget tapped her pen on the desk and worked to control her breathing. She was waiting for Simons to tell her whether there was any chance at all that Faraz was alive.

The wait dragged on. She heard computer keys clicking.

"Um, yeah, I got some movement on that next file at zero plus three twenty-two. Coupla survivors, anyway. I can get you more details in half an hour or so."

Bridget let out a sigh of relief. At least, she had some hope to cling to. "Thanks, Patty. Put a rush on it. And that file is on its way to me, right?"

"Yes, ma'am. Unfortunately, I can't put a rush on the electrons."

Now, what? Now, nothing. Bridget was pretty sure the attack wouldn't be on the news. The Israelis wanted to keep their capabilities secret. The Saudis would not want the world to know their air defenses had been breached. And A-HAI had no interest in publicizing its setback— probably no way to even know about it yet. The camp was remote enough that there likely would be no villagers with cell phones posting video.

She'd have to wait for the next file and, later, the Saudi mop-up operation They'd be reluctant to share info, but maybe Hadley would trade some of the satellite video.

Faraz heard the sound first. He raised himself on one elbow.

Assali noticed. "What is it, Khayal?"

"Vehicles." Faraz stood and moved to protect Assali.

At the edge of the camp, Ra'ed and the other fighter raised their weapons. Iyad ran to join them.

Faraz saw a cloud of dust approaching. The vehicles

moved fast along the dirt track that led from the highway to the camp. As they came into view, he saw the convoy was led by two Saudi Army Humvees, followed by an ambulance, a sedan, two box trucks and more Humvees.

Faraz appreciated the irony. American-made missiles attacked them, and now American-made vehicles were rescuing them. If that's what this was.

Assali grabbed Faraz's arm, pulled himself to his feet and moved toward the gate. "I told you," he said. Then louder, "It is all right. They are friends. Put down your weapons."

The limo and its escort came to a halt in front of the remnants of the camp. Assali approached the lead Humvee as a Saudi officer got out. The officer left his sidearm in its holster, but a dozen soldiers emerged from other vehicles with an array of weapons at the ready.

"Praise Allah you are here," Assali said, stopping a non-threatening distance from the officer. The man grunted and took in the scene with evident disdain.

A soldier approached the limo and opened one of the rear doors. A small man got out, wearing an immaculate white ankle-length *qamis*, red-and-white *kufiyah* and aviator sunglasses that were too big for his face.

"*Sayyid* al-Tayyib," Assali said, rushing over to the prince's secretary. "I did not expect you to come personally."

Al-Tayyib spat into the sand. "Neither did I." He looked around at the mess that had been Assali's operation, the spearhead of the prince's plan. His gaze paused on the survivors, their clothes ripped and bloody, their faces dirty. He looked past them toward the row of bodies.

Then the secretary looked Assali up and down. "I see

you have survived when you should have died yet again. You possess a unique mix of incompetence and good luck."

Assali's body language shifted from contrite to confrontational. "*Sayyid*, our capabilities did not include air defenses." The comment hung in the air.

Al-Tayyib looked toward the lead officer. Faraz thought he might order Assali shot on the spot, and the rest of them right after. But instead, the visitor gestured and the officer issued an order. Two of his men carried cases of water to the survivors, and the ambulance crew moved to check on the wounded. Al-Tayyib looked back at Assali and said, "Walk with me."

The two men moved away from the convoy. Faraz accepted a bottle of water, opened it and took a long swig. He wiped his hand along the condensation and used the moisture to wipe his face. He kept his eyes on Assali and the visitor. Faraz couldn't hear what they were saying, but he saw Assali nod several times, then put his hand on his heart in a gesture of thanks.

Assali turned back toward the men. "Iyad, Ra'ed, come here." They jogged over, water bottles in hand. Iyad carried an extra one for Assali, but the boss didn't open it. Maybe he didn't want to show any weakness, even thirst. Perhaps he believed his survival depended more on his image than on water.

There was more talking Faraz couldn't hear. A medic came to check him, but he shook the man off. Another one was tending to Ayman, who was sitting up now and finally had the drink of water he wanted.

Assali was explaining something and pointing at Ra'ed. Iyad and Ra'ed nodded, then shook hands and kissed on both cheeks. Al-Tayyib and Ra'ed walked toward the convoy. Ra'ed got into one of the Humvees and Al-Tayyib got into his limousine. The two vehicles made a U-turn and took off down the dirt road.

Iyad and Assali walked back toward the men. "These soldiers will take us to our new camp," the boss announced.

"Where did Ra'ed go?" Faraz asked.

"He went to . . ." Iyad hesitated. ". . . to seize an opportunity. Our friend brought important information. The details are not your concern."

"More men will join us," Assali said. He had regained his command demeanor. "As I always told you, our mission is important and time is short. This setback does not change that. Our benefactor will not allow the Zionists to defeat him. He will provide what we need to succeed, and even more. This will be beyond even my imagining. Now, board the trucks. The soldiers will bury our dead. We have work to do."

The men looked at each other. To Faraz, it seemed that this was already more than any of them had bargained for. But no option was presented.

Assali turned for the vehicles. Healthy fighters helped the wounded. Two members of the ambulance crew carried Ayman on a stretcher.

CHAPTER TWENTY-SEVEN

An hour later, a fresh batch of satellite video showed the Saudi convoy arrive and then leave in two pieces. The first part, a limo and an escort, turned back toward Riyadh. A few minutes later, the rest of the vehicles headed south, toward Mecca, deeper into the desert. The satellite lost them at dark amid rolling hills.

Bridget pressed everyone she could think of for information about whether Faraz was among the survivors and where the missing convoy had gone. No one had anything.

By eight p.m., her body was demanding sleep. She had to admit she was too old for consecutive all-nighters. And she was still expending energy healing her wound, which ached when she got tired.

She called Colonel Ben-Yosef one more time. He made her wait on hold, then answered with, "Yes, what is it?"

"Sorry to bother you again, Colonel. Just checking whether you've been able to get anything on my agent from your Saudi sources."

"I told you I would call you if I had anything."

"But you are best placed—"

"Yes, of course, we have some sources. But we are not burning any of them to find your man. Face the facts. He's probably dead. And if he's not, he will be when we find the new terrorist camp and hit that one, too."

"The Saudis might strike back if you do too many of those."

"Not likely. They will not risk war for the jihadis. The royal family sees them as useful tools. Nothing more."

His tone reflected his anger, but Bridget knew he was right. "Listen, Ari, I'll make a deal with you. I'll leave the country if you find my agent."

"You should leave, anyway. Now, I have work to do." He hung up.

Bridget stared at the handset. Amazing how rejecting his advances and then withholding intel could turn off a man's interest.

She looked around. She'd spent too much time in this bare little office with its narrow window. She picked up her purse and backpack and headed out.

Beyond the embassy's bulletproof glass doors, the evening air refreshed her. Bridget felt guilty inhaling the aroma of the sea and looking forward to her cozy hotel bed, but there was nothing more she could do for Faraz until someone provided her with some intel. Maybe not even then.

She turned right on the beachfront promenade and trudged toward her hotel.

* * *

Bridget was back at her desk before dawn, which meant she could catch Hadley via secure line before he went to bed in DC. She hesitated in the middle of dialing. It was Sunday morning for her, Saturday night for him. But she was pretty sure he would not be out late or sleeping.

"Nothing new," he said instead of "Hello." "I've told the night staff to call you immediately if we get anything, so you don't have to wake me every hour on the hour."

"Yes, sir. Sorry. Have a good night."

Bridget decided to call the one person who couldn't tell her to buzz off. The encrypted line clicked as it connected her with the Pentagon's second basement.

"Liz Michaels." The voice always sounded too cheery for the job, even close to midnight.

"It's me."

"I know. I could set my watch by it. And before you ask, no, I'm sorry, we don't have any news on Abdallah or anything related."

"No chatter, finance, travel?"

"Yeah, of course, there's all three. I can even say there's a slight uptick. But nothing we can put a finger on."

Bridget was silent. She hadn't expected anything different. The call was hope triumphing over experience, and experience had made its usual comeback.

"Listen," Liz said. "We could really use you back here. If Abdallah is gone—"

"Liz—"

"Sorry, but it has to be said. If Abdallah is gone, we need a strategic re-eval and a new plan, or several. And we need you here for that."

Bridget took a beat. "We're not there yet."

"Well, again, sorry, but we're getting close. It's obviously your call, Bridge. He's your guy. And he might turn up even if you're not sitting in Tel Aviv, you know. Just think about it."

Bridget refused to acknowledge the premise of Liz's suggestion. "I have the watch, Liz. You should get some sleep."

After they hung up, Bridget stared at her screen as if some info about Faraz might pop up. Her priority had been to get back to the Pentagon, but she felt that if she left now, she'd be abandoning the young soldier she'd put in harm's way.

Twelve hours later, Bridget was no closer to finding Faraz. Colonel Ben-Yosef was dodging her calls. Hadley was in meetings all day. Liz and the team had nothing.

Bridget needed to clear her head, and she hadn't eaten anything other than what the embassy vending machines had to offer in two days. She pushed back from her desk and looked out the window. The sun was a good hour from setting into the Mediterranean. She grabbed her purse, jacket and cell phone and headed for the exit.

The beach was about a thirty-second walk. The waterfront was breathtaking. Several serious volleyball games were underway and cafés with tables and chairs in the sand were starting to fill up. It was striking that such an idyllic scene played out right next to the antiseptic atmosphere of the embassy and the world of horrors she lived in through her computer.

The sunshine and sea air washed over her. Bridget was

tempted to grab the nearest table and order a large glass of wine. She thought she'd fit right in with her new Israeli outfit—the same beige pants and pale-yellow blouse she'd worn to her first one-on-one with Ari more than two weeks earlier. But she wanted to get away from the embassy. She had her comfortable travel shoes on, so she put her jacket over her arm, turned left and started walking south along the beachfront promenade.

With the sea on her right, a mix of tired pre-independence buildings and modern skyscrapers played out on her left. The evening rush of customers browsed in trendy shops or lounged in upscale bars and restaurants. But every Hebrew sign, every snippet of conversation, made her think of Colonel Ben-Yosef—his creepy advances and his disregard for Faraz's safety. She moved on.

Bridget was glad to be walking without too much pain. The broken ribs and head gash from the terrorist attack in DC five months earlier were healed. But the newer injury—the AK wound that had hobbled her—still hurt. Her body was not bouncing back like it should have. Like it used to.

The doctors had warned her, reminded her she wasn't twenty-two and fresh out of West Point anymore. That seemed like a lifetime ago—graduation, her commission as an intel officer, two deployments to Afghanistan. Now, this assignment might keep her away from home on her fortieth birthday. Forty. Jeez.

What happened to her three-stage plan: career, husband, kids? She had only fulfilled the first part. To make matters worse, she wouldn't even be able to celebrate her birthday with Will, which meant no chance to make progress on the second part. And Part Three was, well . . . tick-tock.

Will. Damn. She should have called him before she left the office. She'd have to remember to try later.

After half an hour of walking, Bridget's side ached. But she pushed on. The sun kissed the Med as she came to the end of the beach, and she continued on narrow lanes. Zigging and zagging to stay near the water, she entered a different world—one more like the Jerusalem *souk* than Tel Aviv, with stone buildings, old houses and lots of Arabic on the signs.

She came out of the maze back at the water. There was no beach here, but rather a marina for small fishing boats. This was Old Jaffa, and somehow she felt more comfortable here, at least tonight.

Bridget stopped in front of a seafood restaurant with a view of the water. It was on the land side of the beachfront road, with a small park across the street and the marina beyond. White metal tables with red plastic chairs beckoned. It was getting dark, and she needed some chow.

A thin, well-wrinkled man in an apron sat at a table nursing a glass of tea. He stood when she approached.

She pointed at a table with a good view of the water. He nodded. "*Ahlan wa sahlan.*" Welcome.

"*Shukran,*" Bridget said. She sat and put her jacket and purse on the chair next to her. "English?"

"Yes, yes," the man said, and he retreated into the restaurant.

He emerged a minute later with a bottle of water, a glass, a basket of warm pita bread and an English menu.

"Wine?" Bridget asked.

"No." The waiter shook his head. He pointed at the symbol on the menu that indicated it was a Halal establishment that adhered to Islamic law.

Ah, well. The perils of being adventurous. Bridget let him pour her a glass of water and perused the menu. With the boats in view, the logical choice was to order fish. She pointed at her selection so the waiter could see. He smiled. She added a Greek salad. He nodded and scurried away.

Bridget devoured the salad crisp greens, sharp onion, and salty olives and cheese, with a little too much vinegar and olive oil.

She smiled at other patrons as they arrived. There was a couple with two rambunctious children, who took a table on the other side of the patio. Then three Arab men in dress shirts, polyester pants and black shoes sat down with the waiter to discuss something over cigarettes and Turkish coffee.

Bridget put the main course well into her top ten. The fish was perfectly salted and grilled. The rice was flavored with a spice she didn't recognize. And the French fries were so crisp that she couldn't resist having a few.

The waiter approached. "Is good?"

"Yes, very good. *Shukran.*"

The waiter smiled, placed his right hand on his heart and went back to the kitchen.

Bridget's mind wandered as she finished her dinner. She thought about Will grabbing some chow at the base in Baghdad. She thought about her parents in Florida, likely out for a walk on a spring afternoon. She thought about her poor cat, Sarge, staying at the sitter's studio apartment for weeks on end. She thought about anything except Faraz. But the harder she worked to push him out of her mind, the more he loomed over whatever else she thought about.

It was dark now. The fish was only a skeleton, and Bridget had eaten as much of the rice and fries as she intended to. The scene was lit by small bulbs strung over the dining area and a row of streetlamps down by the water. All that was missing was a bottle of wine. And Will. Time to get back to the hotel and call him.

She looked up to summon the waiter. She wanted a coffee and a taxi.

But he wasn't around. Maybe he was inside, fetching someone's food. Then she noticed that she was alone. The three men had disappeared, as had the family, although they couldn't have eaten by now. Maybe they ordered takeaway?

Bridget raised her voice. "Hello? Sir?"

No response. That was strange. He'd been so attentive. "Hello—"

She was interrupted by a black van approaching fast on the waterfront road. The vehicle jumped the curb and screeched to a stop not five feet from her, knocking over one of the tables. She jumped back. Her brain was catching up to what was happening, but her first instinct was to avoid getting run over. She stood and her chair tumbled behind her.

The van's side door slid open and two men came at her. She raised her hands to fend them off. The first one punched her in the jaw, shocking her and sending her head spinning to the right, spewing spittle and blood. The other man put a cloth bag on her head. It was putrid, distracting her from what she had to do.

Bridget screamed and used a martial arts move, but missed. The men grabbed her arms and pushed her to the ground. Pain shot through her side. She kicked at them, but missed again. They dragged her toward the van.

"Let me go!" she screamed, and tried to pull her arms free. But her words and her effort had no impact.

More hands were on her as they lifted her into the van. Her back slammed onto the vehicle's floor.

"Stop it! Goddamn you!" Bridget flailed and twisted, but at least two men put their body weight on her.

The door slammed. The van dropped off the curb and sped away.

A hand pushed the bag against her nose and mouth.

"Quiet," a voice said in English.

A kick to the head silenced her.

PART TWO

Chapter Twenty-eight

Bridget woke up on a dirt floor with her hands and feet cuffed. The bag had been removed from her head and the room was lit by a single fluorescent bulb. She blinked a few times and saw that the space was large and had no windows. She was near a cinder block wall. The place smelled of damp and body odor and something else. Olives, maybe.

She sat up, straightened her back and legs, and brought her hands to the left side of her head where the man had kicked her. It was painfully close to her previous injury. She moved her hands to her jaw and winced when she touched the spot where she had been punched.

Bridget didn't have any other new injuries. Her side hurt, but there was no blood.

Her last round of army POW/hostage training was more than a decade in the past. Since then, she'd been a graduate student and a desk jockey. She folded her hands in front of her and focused on her breathing.

She remembered. Rule Number One: don't panic.

Bridget heard footsteps on a stairway, coming down from above. A bolt slid and three men came into the room. Two stayed by the door. A tall man with a bushy beard and prominent nose walked across the room and stood above her. Bridget raised her hands to defend herself.

"I am in charge here. You will do as I say and if your government also does as we say, you will live."

"I think you made a mistake. I—"

The man squatted and slapped her in the same place where she'd been punched. Bridget cried out and fell on her right side. She barely prevented her head from hitting the floor.

"You will not lie to me. We know who you are. We know what you are worth. We will have our price, or it will be my pleasure to kill you."

Bridget nodded. She believed him.

He walked away and said something to the other men. They started setting up lights and a video camera.

General Hadley was not following Rule Number One.

When Bridget didn't show up for work on Monday, no one at the embassy noticed. She made her own schedule, didn't answer to anybody in the building. But ten hours later, well into Washington's workday, when she didn't answer emails and calls, Hadley's instincts and paternalism conspired to raise his alert level. He pulled rank on the embassy's army attaché to get him to personally go to Bridget's hotel, where he found nothing and reported no one had seen her.

Hadley called General HaLevy at Israeli military intelligence. At first, HaLevy was nonchalant. "Maybe she made a friend last night. Or maybe she went to the beach. Or maybe she's on a plane heading home. Her mission is over, I think." Then he added, "Very sadly over."

"First of all, we don't know that her mission is over because you have not provided any assessment on your air strike. And second, Oded, I know this woman. She does not take a day off or board a flight without reporting in."

"Well, since we're doing 'first' and 'second'—first of all, it was not my turn to watch Ms. Davenport. And second, it's not my job to find missing persons, if that's what she is."

"Goddamnit, Oded, you dropped half a dozen bombs on one of my men two days ago, and now one of my people is missing in your city. Are we allies, or not?"

"Don't ask me about allies after you withheld critical information from me."

"Maybe I'll get the president to ask the prime minister about Davenport. I hear they have a call coming up."

"You're threatening me now, James? You need to calm down."

"Don't tell me to calm down! And I will do whatever I have to do to figure out what the hell is going on."

HaLevy waited before continuing. "All right, James. I can't promise anything, but I will ask Ari to make some inquiries."

"Oh, damn it."

"Pardon me?"

"Check your classified email. We have a problem. I'll call you later."

* * *

Hadley watched the video for a second time. He could feel his face turning red. When it ended, he pounded his fist on his desk and hit PLAY again.

Bridget was projecting calm, but she looked terrible. Her hair was in disarray and she had a bruise on the left side of her face. She appeared to be sitting on a dirt floor, with a gray cinder block wall behind. Her eyes were focused to the left of the camera, where Hadley assumed someone was holding a script.

She held a copy of an Arabic newspaper that had published the *Washington Post* story about her, complete with the picture. Her hands were cuffed.

"I am Bridget Davenport, American spy, head of Task Force Epsilon," she said. "I am being held by the brave fighters of *Al-Hakam Al-Islamiyah*, who are fighting for justice and freedom for the Palestinian people. The fighters will release me when they receive fifty million dollars, and two hundred Palestinian prisoners are released. The list of names and the bank account details will be attached to this video."

Bridget stopped.

Hadley heard a man's voice off camera. "Read it," he ordered.

"You have until twelve noon Friday to meet these demands. Otherwise, I will be killed."

She swallowed and took a breath.

"The cause of *Al-Hakam Al-Islamiyah* is just. I urge my government and the Zionist occupiers to comply with their de—."

The video ended abruptly, which Hadley took as a reflection of the terrorists' poor editing skills. He didn't want to think they had done anything they didn't want the world to see.

His desktop intercom squawked. "Sir, the Task Force Epsilon team is here."

"Send them in."

Hadley stood as Liz Michaels led four colleagues into his office. They were some of the DIA's top experts in terrorism, Arabic, and satellite imagery analysis. They were grim-faced and Hadley figured he looked the same.

They had a tall army colonel with them. "Lionel Watkins, sir," he said. "Army Hostage and POW unit."

Hadley came around the desk and shook his hand, then nodded at Liz and the others. "You all look like I feel," he said.

There was not even a chuckle in response.

"Let's sit." Hadley took a seat at the end of his coffee table. Liz sat on the sofa with Watkins. He had his feet on the floor, hands on knees, leaning forward to indicate he was ready. The other team members brought over chairs from the conference set.

Hadley spoke first. "Liz, what do we have?"

"Sir—" Her voice cracked. She cleared her throat. "Sir, the video is authentic. It was routed through too many servers to track its origin, which is usual for these things. The room where—" She paused again. "The room where Bridget is being held appears to be the same room where the Israeli soldier and civilian were held, where their video was shot."

"Anything on the male voice?"

"We're running analysis on it, but nothing so far."

"These guys are serious, general," Colonel Watkins said. He was African American, early fifties, gray hair.

He wore a service dress uniform with several rows of ribbons. One of them was black in the middle with vertical red, white, and blue stripes on the sides. At some point in his career, he had been held by enemy forces.

"This group, A-HAI, took some hostages years ago, when they were more active. They don't mess around, as we saw with the kidnapped Israelis. They will kill Davenport if they don't get what they want."

Liz shifted her position. The others looked away.

Watkins continued. "Sir, the good news is that they have actually released hostages when their demands were met, building credibility for a moment like this."

"Fifty million and two hundred prisoners," Hadley said.

"Yes, sir."

"Not likely. How did Davenport look to you?"

"As expected, sir. Bruised but overall in good shape so far. I checked her file. She's had the training, but it was some time ago. In these situations, mental toughness is the key. She was up to speed when she was on active duty, but we don't have a good measure of her current status, especially after her last mission and injury."

"So, you're saying . . . ?"

"Sorry, sir. I guess it's obvious, but I'm saying the sooner we get her out of there, the better."

Hadley resisted the temptation to say he didn't need a full bird colonel to tell him that. He turned to Liz "What do you make of the deadline. Four days is a long lead time."

"It is. But they may realize they're asking for a lot. Also, it will be a Jewish holiday called"—she checked her notes—"Purim. They have parades, festivals, costume parties. As far as we can tell, the terrorists chose a day that's stressful from a security point of view, that they can potentially make more stressful."

"Spreading the Israeli forces."

"Yes."

"Distracting from something?"

"Possibly. We're looking at it."

Hadley's intercom crackled again. "Sir, there's another Epsilon team member here. She says it's urgent."

"Send her in."

A thin young woman holding a laptop joined them. Her face was flushed, clashing with her short, henna-dyed hair. And she was breathing hard, as if she'd run up the two flights from the second basement, along the E-Ring corridor and up another flight to Hadley's office. She was dressed like someone who expected to spend her day in the basement—ripped jeans, a plain gray sweatshirt and old-school pink sneakers.

Liz stood. "Sir, this is Patricia Simons from our video section. Patty, what's up?"

"The video." Simons struggled to catch her breath. "Whoever their video editor is sent us the wrong file."

"What do you mean?" Hadley said.

Simons knelt down and put the laptop on the coffee table. She opened it and hit a few keys, then swung it around so Hadley, Liz and Watkins could see. The others gathered around.

The screen showed the video's opening frame, with Bridget holding up the newspaper. "He . . . she . . . whatever. Probably he . . ." Simons was confident in her keystrokes, less so in her presentation. "He edited the video, right? We all saw the bad cut at the end. He should have exported the part he wanted and created a new MPEG-4. But he didn't. He made the cut, then he saved the file as an H.264."

"English, please," Hadley said.

Simons scratched her head and took a breath, apparently struggling for the non-tech version. "He should have sent the edited file, but he sent the whole thing."

"But we all saw the video stop," Liz said.

"Right, but when I loaded it into editing software, I was able to drag the trimmer to the right." She got blank stares. "I mean, I was able to undo the edit. We can see the part he wanted to cut out."

Colonel Watkins slid forward to get a better look. Liz leaned in. Hadley moved his chair. "Play it."

The video ran as before. Bridget identified herself, said she was being held by A-HAI, gave their demands, the deadline and the threat to kill her. Then she got to the final sentence.

"The cause of *Al-Hakam Al-Islamiyah* is just. I urge my government and the Zionist occupiers to comply with their demands. Do not worry, I am being treated well. This is the only communication you—"

During those final sentences, Bridget slipped the middle finger of her left hand in front of the newspaper. A man stepped into the frame, his back to the camera, and smacked her before she finished. She fell to the side and hit the ground hard. The man moved left, turned slightly, kicked her in the stomach and shouted something in Arabic. Then the video ended.

Liz gasped and covered her mouth.

"Play the last part again," Hadley said. When it finished, he asked, "What did he say?"

"Curse words," Liz replied. "He called her 'daughter

of a whore,' etcetera. Any particular army POW meaning to the finger?"

Watkins responded. "No. Just what you'd think. 'I'm not really being treated well and screw these guys.'"

Hadley looked around the room. "You have more now for voice analysis, and we saw an overgrown beard and a bit of his cheek and nose. Get on it."

"Yes, sir." Simons closed her computer and was the first through the door, with the rest of the team close behind. Hadley gestured for Liz and the colonel to stay behind.

"I'll get on with the Israelis. Send me whatever you get ASAP."

"Yes, sir," Liz said. "What about Shock Wave?"

"The Saudis didn't find Abdallah's body, as far as we know. I choose to believe he left with the others. So, his mission continues, but we have no way to reach him or monitor him. He'll be in touch when he can. For now, Bridget is the priority."

Hadley's secretary poked her head into the office. "You have a call waiting, sir. Secure line from Baghdad, a Commander Jackson."

Liz gasped. "You know who that is, sir?"

Hadley exhaled. "Yes. You two get to work." As they left, he went to his desk and picked up the phone.

"This is General Hadley."

"Sir, this is Will Jackson. I'm—"

"I know who you are, son. So, you've heard what happened?"

"Yes, sir. It's all over the news, as well as classified channels."

"We're doing everything we can."

"I'd like to help, sir."

"We have all the—"

"I *need* to help, sir. I'm only a short hop from Israel. I can be your man on the ground. I can rustle up a whole SEAL team if you need one."

Hadley forgave the interruption. He might have cut off a superior officer, too, if his girlfriend had just been kidnapped by terrorists.

He thought it over. Without Bridget, he had no reliable eyes and ears in Tel Aviv. The four-star head of Special Ops would be pissed if DIA poached one of his men from Baghdad. But Hadley figured that having a team member taken hostage should give him any extra scratch he might need.

"I don't think we'll send a SEAL team, Commander. The Israelis have assets of their own, if it comes to that. But a man on the ground could be useful."

"All I need are orders, sir. I'm ready to move."

CHAPTER TWENTY-NINE

The first day in Assali's new camp, conditions were primitive. But the fighters had hot food made on a camp stove and all the water they could drink, with plenty left over for washing. They set up their tents and a camouflage net on four poles that provided some shade for eating and praying. There was one oversized tent for the boss.

In addition to Iyad and Assali, there were eight fighters, all with at least minor injuries. Faraz's scratches were scabbed over and the bump was half its original size. Ayman was the worst off. But the food revived him enough that, with Faraz's help, he got off his mat and made a slow walk around the camp in spite of the afternoon heat.

"I'm glad you're feeling better," Faraz said.

"Thanks. That was rough." He had an arm over Faraz's shoulder and leaned on him for support.

"Scary, for sure," Faraz said. "But your injury looked worse that it was. Head wounds always bleed a lot."

Ayman pushed him away. "I was unconscious. I nearly died."

"Yes, yes, well, here, we should be safe."

"Why would you say that? We thought we were safe at the other camp."

"Well—"

"We are exposed here. The Zionists could attack again. And even if they don't, it is as if we do not exist. The world does not know what we are doing. We have no web presence, no media contact."

"Our mission is a secret, even from us."

"You do not understand how these things work. We do not need to know. It would be dangerous for us to know. But I should be laying the groundwork online, building our support."

"You won't get online out here."

"That is my point. If I am a leader of the movement, I must be a fighter. But if the movement is to succeed, people must know we are back, fighting for them. Injured, I cannot fight. Here, I cannot get online."

They turned back toward the front of the camp. Faraz looked at Ayman's bandaged head. "So, what will you do?"

"I need to be in a place with internet. I might have to go home, only for a short while, to make some posts."

Damn. The time for extracting intel from Ayman might be coming to an end. Faraz decided to ask the key question that had been on his mind since Iyad had refused to answer it the day before. "Where did Ra'ed go?"

Ayman didn't answer.

"Ayman?"

"I do not know," Ayman snapped. "Iyad tells me nothing."

* * *

As Faraz and Ayman headed back to their tent, a convoy arrived. There were two busloads of men and several trucks.

Iyad went out to greet them. First off the buses was a long-haired man with dark eyes and a trimmed beard. The man shook hands with Iyad and seemed to be introducing himself. There was some pointing and nodding, then the new arrival started issuing orders to the men in his bus while Iyad took charge of the other bus.

They started unloading the trucks, and Iyad called out to his men to help.

Ayman excused himself from the work, due to his injury. Faraz and the rest of them stacked boxes of food, kitchen items, clothing, weapons and ammo.

The new men found their tents in one of the trucks and got to work setting them up. Iyad took a group to expand the latrine and create a kitchen area. Some of them looked like they'd never left home before. But the ones working with the long-haired man appeared to be hardened fighters, some with accents from Iraq, Syria and other places Faraz couldn't identify. He counted forty, maybe fifty new arrivals in all.

The same Saudi officer who had led the original rescue also escorted this convoy. He sat in Assali's tent sipping tea. The tent flaps were up for air. "More tea, someone," Assali called out.

"I've got it," Faraz shouted. He jogged to the camp stove to collect a pot and two glasses, then headed for Assali's tent.

"Come in," Assali said. "Colonel, this man tackled me during the attack, pushed me into a grave, injured my hands and neck. Should I have him punished?"

Faraz put the tea tray on the ground.

The officer smiled. "But I see you still have your hands, and your neck still has your head on it. Perhaps you should have him rewarded."

Assali had to laugh at the joke at his expense. "And what do I have to reward him with? A cup of tea?"

"It was my honor to help you, *sayyid*," Faraz said.

"Yes, of course. Now go."

Faraz's plan to overhear some of their conversation failed. They said nothing more until he was a safe distance away.

He noticed that the work had stopped. The long-haired man was leading some of the fighters in prayers.

Faraz approached Iyad. "Who is the new commander?"

"His name is Bashar. He is from a Lebanese group. I have heard of him. He is an experienced man."

After the prayers, the convoy left and Assali summoned Iyad, Faraz and Bashar.

Ayman was pacing under the shade. Even at some distance, Faraz could see that he was angry not to be included.

"Our friend Ra'ed has done well," Assali said. "The pressure on our enemies grows. He is preparing the ground for our attack, which must be done on schedule in four days' time."

"We will be ready," Bashar said.

Iyad appeared skeptical. "Your men are up to the task?"

"Do not worry about my men. Worry about your own."

"Enough," Assali said. "Bashar is here because he is known to our benefactors and they believe he can help us. There is no room for argument. Khayal, you will work with Iyad to get the rest of the men trained. Now, go, all of you. There is no time to waste."

Faraz caught up with Iyad outside. "I'm happy to be working with you."

"You know nothing about our work. You somehow make people think you are something special—first Ayman, now Assali. I am not convinced." He stepped in front of Faraz and blocked his way. "I have been working toward this all my life. My father died for this. Do not get in my way."

Back in the tent, Ayman stood to confront Faraz, despite the pain it clearly caused him. "What was that about? I should have been included."

"You're leaving, aren't you?"

Ayman scoffed. "It is not yet approved. What did they tell you?"

"We must train hard for an operation on Friday. Also, Ra'ed did well on whatever he went to do. Raising the pressure, Assali said. That's all."

Ayman waved his arms in frustration. "I can have no impact in this shithole. I must get out of here." He turned and limped out of the tent.

CHAPTER THIRTY

Bridget's right cheek was on the ground and her head was throbbing. Her knees were drawn up to her chest. The room was dark and she was shivering.

She touched her left cheek where the man had hit her—twice now—and winced in pain. She planted her cuffed hands on the floor and pushed herself into a sitting position. A wave of dizziness hit. She fell back and knocked her head on the wall. That hurt, but it revived her.

Why had she been so stupid? Sure, be Captain Badass. Flip the jihadis the bird. Stupid. If Rule Number One was "Don't panic," Rule Number Two was "Stay alive and healthy." She should not have invited her captors to punish her. She was in this for the long haul. Four days, they said. Seemed like an eternity. And then . . . what? They chop her head off and send the video to her parents? No. She could not let her mind go there. Hadley wouldn't let her die in this dungeon. He wouldn't.

Bridget wiped her hands across her shirt and then

rubbed her face. She heard the men coming down the stairs.

Colonel Ben-Yosef sat at the central desk in a room full of workstations at the Israeli military intelligence tech center, in the basement of a nondescript building in a working-class suburb of Tel Aviv. He was watching over the shoulder of the technician in front of him, whose screen was scrolling lines of numbers faster than any human could read.

This was the last place Ari wanted to be. He was a soldier and a field operative. He'd done everything possible in his career to avoid windowless holes like this. He was tapping on the desk with a pen, an old tick he had mostly suppressed.

"Anything?" he asked.

"When we have something, it will stop," was the obvious answer from the man at the computer, who was leaning back, flipping through something on his phone. He wore the uniform of a corporal, but Ari knew he was much more than that. He was Ephraim Golani, one of Israel's tech rock stars, head of a data-crunching startup that the newspapers said would soon be worth a hundred million dollars.

Golani's black curly hair covered his ears and hung down over his shirt collar. In his rush to get there when Ari summoned him for emergency reserve duty, he had forgotten his army boots, so he wore the bright white running shoes he'd had on in his office at a renovated warehouse in a remote corner of the Negev three hours earlier.

The scrolling stopped, and ten digits were highlighted in the middle of the screen. Ari recognized it as Bridget's cell phone number. He leaned forward. "That's it."

"Yes." Golani sat up and ran a finger along the line of digits. He paused on a time code and wrote it on a pad of sticky notes. "That is the time of the last signal." He continued scanning the numbers and stopped again on a grouping on the right. "This is the tower code."

He turned to another computer, entered the number in a search window, hit RETURN and read the result, "*Old Jaffa Port.*"

The three men came into Bridget's dungeon and turned on the TV lights to blind her. She pushed herself against the wall, raised her knees and arms to protect herself and covered her face with her hands. Through a space between fingers, she saw the tall man approaching.

He slapped her hands away. She looked up at him and blinked several times. The man moved right and left, looking at her injuries. When their eyes met, he smiled. Then he spat at her.

His spittle hit her cheek.

"You were foolish," he said in English. "You know I cannot kill you, at least for a few days, so you defied me. But your time here can be more"—he searched for the right word— "unpleasant. It can be unpleasant or it can be more unpleasant. Yes. I like this word. Unpleasant. Do you understand?"

He moved to the side so Bridget could see the other

two men. The large one held a crowbar, the smaller one leered at her and grabbed his crotch.

"Yes, I understand," Bridget said.

The man squatted down to her level. She could see the pores on his cheeks above his beard and the tobacco-stained teeth below his overgrown moustache. She could smell his breath—garlic and cigarettes.

He grabbed her cuffed wrists. "I have killed many like you—American dogs, Zionists, occupiers of the Holy Lands." With each phrase, he squeezed harder and moved his head closer to hers. Then his left hand came up and grabbed her throat. Bridget took hold of his arm, but he leaned in, pushed her against the wall and squeezed.

"I would be happy to kill you, too, or to let those men do what they want. And yet, I am your only friend."

Bridget gagged. Her eyes begged him to let go.

He released her and stood. He brushed off his shirt, wiped his hands on his pants and turned to leave the room.

Bridget held her throat and gulped for air. "May I know your name?" Her voice was hoarse.

He stopped and turned back to her. "I am Ra'ed. Do not test me again." He walked past the men by the door.

The smaller one, who had not stopped staring at Bridget, took a water bottle from his back pocket and threw it at her. She flinched when it hit the wall next to her head, then scrambled to retrieve it.

Corporal Golani led Ari along a narrow corridor, dodging people coming the other way. They took two quick turns and stopped in front of a door labeled *HASHGACHA*.

Surveillance. Golani swiped his key card but got a red light. He stepped aside for Ari to try. The colonel's card did the trick.

Inside, a sergeant turned to see who was coming in. "Corporal, you are not authorized—"

"But I am," Ari said, stepping past Golani.

"Yes, sir. I'm sorry. I didn't see you. How can we help you?"

"You can do whatever this man says."

Within a few minutes, they had a team of technicians reviewing footage from dozens of security cameras around the cell tower in Old Jaffa Port for an hour before and after the time code Golani had written down—the last signal from Bridget's phone.

"Got her," came a voice from a corner of the room. Ari and Golani rushed over. The technician, a middle-aged woman with a senior sergeant's insignia, pointed to a female figure in beige pants and a yellow blouse, holding a blue jacket over her arm. She was in an alley, walking away from the camera, past a bakery and a pharmacy.

The sergeant clicked her keyboard. Bridget appeared on the next camera, walking toward them, rounding a corner onto the sidewalk in front of the marina and stopping to look around. The technician paused the feed and zoomed in.

"Is that her?" Golani asked.

"Yes," Ari said. He noticed her smile. She looked more relaxed than he had ever seen her. "Roll it."

The sea breeze caught Bridget's hair and she brushed it off her face. She resumed her walk, passing under the camera. With a few more keystrokes, the technician found her in front of the restaurant. Bridget turned her back on them and walked into the restaurant's patio area. When she sat down, she was facing the camera. It showed her from a high angle, likely a light pole across the street.

Ari ordered fast-forward. "We don't need to watch her eat," he said.

The restaurant's comings and goings sped by. The family arrived, then the men. The waiter scurried back and forth. Then it all went black.

"What happened?" Ari demanded. "Camera failure?"

"That's strange," the sergeant said. "Let's roll back and go normal speed."

They saw the waiter check on Bridget, then on the other tables. The men got up and left. The waiter lingered with the family, seemingly explaining something. Then the screen went black.

"Slow motion," Ari said.

They watched again. There was burst of static just before the feed ended.

"Looks like someone cut the wire," Golani said.

"Find me another view."

The woman brought up an index and checked the angles of several cameras. The fourth one she looked at had a long view of the waterfront street. The restaurant's sign was in the distance, but they couldn't see the seating area.

A black van turned onto the street and approached the restaurant at high speed. It jumped the curb and stopped. Even with maximum zoom, they could only see its rear doors. Its license plate was covered.

Fewer than thirty seconds after it stopped, the van moved off and turned a corner to go out of frame.

"Follow it," Ari said.

All of the technicians reconfigured their searches. Golani moved among the workstations to organize the work.

"I found it," someone shouted from across the room. "I'll send it to you."

The black van appeared on the sergeant's screen. She followed it on several cameras through the narrow lanes, then lost it when it turned onto a back road as it left the city.

Ari turned to Golani. "Security cameras, satellites, everything. Find me that van."

CHAPTER THIRTY-ONE

Ari was outside the tech center for a smoke when Corporal Golani came to find him. "We have something interesting. Please come inside."

Back in the surveillance room, Golani showed him video of a black van entering a parking garage. "Now watch," Golani said. "I move ahead two minutes, and . . . there."

Half a dozen vehicles emerged from the garage and went different directions. There were cars, SUVs, a green pickup truck—none of them particularly noteworthy.

"We checked. In the hours before and after, hardly any vehicles enter or leave."

"Where is this garage?"

"Road 465, two kilometers inside the Green Line."

"Follow them all," Ari ordered. "Call me with locations." He was out the door by the time he finished talking.

Half an hour later, Ari stood in the parking garage outside the black van while a police crime-scene team scoured it for evidence. Major Drucker, the assault team commander, stood next to him.

"Your people have been to the restaurant?" Ari asked.

"Yes. No sign of Miss Davenport or her attackers. The place was hosed down. Routine cleaning, they said. And of course, no one who was there last night can be found, and those working today have confirmed alibis. We closed them down. That will put pressure on the owners, but not as much as the terrorists will put on them."

"A hair," one of the investigators announced from the back of the van. "Light brown, thirty-two centimeters. Also, blood."

Ari cursed. He took out his phone and walked to the edge of the structure to catch some signal. He called Corporal Golani and got the destination of the first vehicle that had left the garage.

In the room above Bridget's prison, Ra'ed and the two other men lounged on the old furniture.

"Let us go down, Ra'ed," the small one said. "What does it matter?"

"Do not ask me again, Naji." Ra'ed gave him a look that made clear his answer would not be changing.

They heard a vehicle approach. The men stood and grabbed their weapons. It was not necessarily trouble, but they always had to be ready.

Outside, Ra'ed found the catering truck, with abu-Hakim at the wheel. Two men were unloading their meals.

Abu-Hakim looked agitated. "What news, my friend?" Ra'ed asked.

"The Zionists found the van. They are mounting an

operation. It is not huge, as we have seen before. It seems they want to keep it secret for now. But our people report they are coming. Before long, there will be roadblocks. I may not be able to return. You are not safe here."

The caterer's helpers got back into the truck. "Allah be with you, Ra'ed." Abu-Hakim turned the wheel hard left and drove away.

Colonel Ben-Yosef insisted on driving, shunting Sergeant Peretz to the passenger seat. He was clocking better than a hundred kilometers an hour on side roads beyond the Green Line, heading for the destination of the first vehicle out of the parking garage.

Peretz held onto the dashboard and armrest. "Sir, these roads ahead have many turns. And the team won't be there for another eight minutes. You might want to slow down."

Ari gave her a look but eased off a little. The village was at the southern tip of the West Bank, on a dead-end road—a good location to hold a hostage.

"Tell them to hurry," Ari said. "And get me General HaLevy on his secure line."

Peretz keyed her phone and put the call on speaker.

The general answered on the first ring.

"We will make the raid in a few minutes," Ari said.

"Be careful."

"Yes, sir."

"You have some reason to believe that this is where she is being held?"

"No, sir. Only the video footage. We had no time to

prioritize. We are hitting them all. I'm nearly at location one."

"All right. A moment, please."

They heard the general's voice as he turned away from the phone. "All right, sweetie. I don't know what's wrong with Queen Esther, but if you want to be the Little Mermaid, I'm sure you can work it out with your mother.

"I'm sorry, Ari. I have Tali on the other phone. She and Rivka are fighting about her Purim costume, and since you are on a mission and can't be reached, in addition to my duties securing the state, I am the referee."

Ari laughed. "Once again, your mission is more difficult than mine. You worry about the Little Mermaid. We will take care of our American Cinderella."

"Good luck."

Peretz ended the call. "Sir, we are two kilometers out. We should wait here."

Ari stopped the car under an olive tree by the side of the road to wait for the team.

"Eat quickly," the guard said as he dropped a paper bag in front of Bridget. She had given Ra'ed's accomplices names. This one, who constantly undressed her with his eyes, was Slimy, the other was Ballou, big and quiet.

Ra'ed and Ballou left. Slimy stayed by the doorway and watched her. He was short, maybe five-two, but looked like he spent a lot of time in the gym working out his frustrations. Bridget thought that, given the chance, she could take him. But maybe not. She knew success in the martial arts studio didn't necessarily mean success here. And she'd never practiced with her hands and feet in shackles.

She looked up and met his eyes. He left and locked the door.

The bag had a pita bread, a hard-boiled egg and a bottle of water. Bridget heard the men moving around upstairs. Something was up. She followed the advice and ate.

Within a few minutes, all three men came in. She pushed herself against the wall and prepared to fight. Ballou swatted her hands away from her face and put the canvas bag on her head. Two men grabbed her arms and pulled her to her feet.

"Do not make noise," Ra'ed said. "Do not fight us. Your life depends on it."

Ari and the assault team sped up to the first house at the edge of the village. There was a green pickup truck in the driveway.

Their vehicles blocked any escape from the front, and one of them crashed through a fence into the back garden, scattering several chickens.

The men dismounted and took cover. There was no reaction to their arrival. Major Drucker raised a bullhorn. "Come out with your hands up," he said in Arabic. "You will not be harmed."

No response.

Ari nodded at Drucker, who whispered a command. Two men in full armor approached the front door. They put a device shaped like a box fan on the porch and retreated, playing out a cable as they went.

When they were back behind the vehicle, they looked at Drucker. "Fire," he said.

Al Pessin

The device jumped as it shot a dozen pellets into the door all at once. The door swung open, hit a wall and swung back.

Drucker took the lead, five-foot-ten and all muscle, popping a wad of gum. He moved to the house, bent at the waist, his Uzi pointing at the door. Six men followed.

Ari waited behind his car with Sergeant Peretz. It was frustrating, but that was the protocol. It felt like a long time, but it was only a minute or so before Drucker came to the door and called out, "All clear."

Ari ran to the house. "Are you sure?"

"Yes, we are sure."

"Check the yard."

"We did."

"Check it again."

Ari went inside. He took a crowbar from one of the soldiers to pull up floorboards and break drywall wherever he thought it might be useful. Or to work out his anger. By the time he came out, the assault team was packing up and a forensics unit was checking the pickup for evidence.

"Nothing so far, sir," the unit's chief reported.

"Drucker," Ari shouted. "Load up. Follow me."

Ari threw the crowbar into the backseat of his car and got behind the wheel, alongside Sergeant Peretz. "What's our next destination?"

"Reports from the other targets are coming in. All are empty. There is only one remaining."

Ari put the car in gear and made a tight U-turn, the rear wheels skidding as he went. "Direct me."

* * *

The men pushed Bridget up the steps, across a small room and through a doorway. She tripped on the door-jamb, but they held her up.

Ra'ed pulled up the bag and put his face so close to hers that his beard brushed her chin. "Remember, quiet and alive, or loud and dead."

Bridget nodded. It was getting dark outside, and she was standing behind a car with its trunk open. Ra'ed shoved a gag into her mouth, then pulled the bag back down, pushed her into the trunk and slammed the lid.

Bridget braced her shackled hands and feet against the sides, but the ride was brutal. Wherever they were going, they seemed to be taking dirt roads.

There was a big bump now, as if they'd hopped a curb. The road got smooth and the car accelerated. Ra'ed said something in Arabic and the driver slowed down.

He switched to English, his voice coming through into the trunk. "I have a gun pointed at you. If you make noise or we have any problem on the road, you will be the first to die."

Chapter Thirty-two

Commander Will Jackson could not imagine what kind of clearances were needed for a short-notice, direct Baghdad–Tel Aviv flight, and he didn't care. All he cared about was how fast the C-37A military executive jet could fly.

His ride was on loan from the senior American general in Iraq. The pilot told him they'd make the trip in an hour and a half. It would have taken Will a full day to catch a military transport to Germany and connect to a commercial flight to Israel.

It paid to have the three-star head of DIA as your travel agent.

Most passengers on such a flight would have leaned back into the plush leather seat, popped up the footrest and enjoyed their soda and peanuts, maybe caught a nap. But Will sat forward and stared out the window. He checked his watch every few minutes. His right leg bounced up and down in his desert cammo trousers. His twice-injured left hip ached, but he was determined to ignore it.

* * *

Somewhere below him, Bridget's left hip ached, too. She had been lying on it, as far as she could tell, for something like an hour on the hard floor of the trunk. Her head also hurt from rebreathing the same air, along with car exhaust and dust from the road.

The car slowed down, turned onto a gravel surface—maybe a driveway—and stopped.

"Stay quiet," Ra'ed said from up front.

The car doors opened and closed. The men greeted someone. She heard a woman's voice.

It was dark as Ari, Peretz, and the assault team sped along a two-track road through a West Bank olive grove, following the satellite track of the last vehicle on Corporal Golani's list.

They stopped in a cloud of dust at an old storage building, and the team members ran from their vehicles with weapons up. Drucker took cover with Ari and Peretz and gave his warning through the bullhorn.

As before, there was no response.

He repeated it. "Come out with your hands up."

A voice came on Drucker's radio. "Target vehicle in the back, sir."

Drucker looked at Ari, who nodded. Drucker spoke into the radio, "Go."

Two men moved forward and broke through the door with a small battering ram. Drucker and the rest of his team ran inside. Ari broke protocol and went in behind them.

It was one large room, so the All Clear didn't take long. Ari walked to the hodgepodge of furniture. He saw the leftover food and the bedrolls on the wooden floor. He smelled the cigarette smoke.

"This building is for storing olives at harvest time," he said. "Why would they have furniture and bedding?"

"For rest maybe," Drucker said.

"But it is not harvest season." Ari picked up a piece of pita. "And this bread is fresh. Someone left in a hurry and not long ago."

Ari moved to the far corner. There was a rough carpet thrown at an odd angle. He kicked it. The carpet slid to the wall, revealing the outline of a trap door.

The soldiers were immediately on alert. They surrounded the door, weapons pointing at it. One man put his hand in a small opening and lifted. Hinges creaked. The soldier pulled hard and flung the door onto the floor at Ari's feet. Someone shined a light down the stairway.

Drucker pointed to two men and they led the way. He held Ari's arm to prevent him from following. Doors were opened and closed downstairs. Then, a soldier called to them, "All clear, but you should come and look, sir."

Ari ran down the steps into Bridget's prison. From the doorway of the room on the right, he saw her sleeping mat and the remains of her dinner, the disturbed dirt floor with a small stain of dried blood, and the cinder block wall that had been in the background of her video and the one of the captured Israelis. He let out a string of Arabic curses, banged his fist on the open door and took a step into the room.

Major Drucker grabbed his arm again. "Let the forensics team in there first, sir. There's nothing more for you to find."

Ra'ed opened the trunk and pulled the bag off Bridget's head. He was brandishing a handgun. Ballou and Slimy stood behind him. They were in a carport next to a house, lit by a light above a door.

"You have done well, so far," Ra'ed whispered. "Do not change that."

Through the gag, Bridget grunted her assent. He put the bag back on her head and pulled her out of the trunk. Her foot caught the edge and she fell onto the gravel. Stones cut into her knees and forearms.

Ra'ed pulled her to her feet and led her around the car, pressing the gun into her ribs.

"Up," he said. Bridget reached with her right foot and found a step, then another with her left. Ra'ed shoved her ahead. She heard a door open. "Now, down."

Ra'ed pushed and Bridget stumbled down a flight of stairs into the cool air of another basement. He came down behind her. "Head down."

Bridget complied. Ra'ed led her forward a few steps, then removed the bag. Bridget blinked.

The space was small, a quarter the size of her previous room—more like a prison cell, with a low ceiling and lower doorway. It was lit by a single bulb in a broken fixture. The floor and walls were unpainted concrete. The air was stale but dry. There was no furniture, no bedroll, no window.

Ra'ed stood uncomfortably close and looked directly

into her eyes. "You know what I will say. Stay quiet, stay alive. Do not be stupid."

Bridget nodded.

He removed the gag and stepped back.

"I need water and a toilet," she whispered.

Ra'ed did not respond. He used a key to take off her handcuffs but left the leg shackles in place. Outside the room, he hung the key on a wall hook, then closed the metal door and slid the bolt.

Will's plane rolled to a stop in a remote corner of Ben Gurion Airport. He was surrounded by a maze of multi-colored runway markers, and he could see the lights of Tel Aviv in the distance. A hulking 747 flew low overhead, coming in for a landing.

The flight attendant opened the door and unfolded the stairway.

"Thanks for the ride," Will said.

"Anytime, sir. Good luck."

Will put his duffel on his shoulder and went down the stairs toward an Israeli army sergeant alongside a pale green army SUV. Her blue eyes and bun of blond hair were not what Will expected. He was probably not what she expected either—six-foot-two, milk-chocolate skin and close-cropped tightly-coiled black hair.

The sergeant saluted and waited for the noise of a departing aircraft to subside.

"I am Sergeant Esti Peretz, sir. Welcome to Israel. I will take you to Colonel Ben-Yosef."

Chapter Thirty-three

Faraz lay alone in the tent and stared at the V-shaped ceiling. He was now some sort of training officer for A-HAI, preparing men for an attack, what the Americans called an MTO, a major terrorist operation.

And he had no idea what it was. And no way to report it if he had.

Faraz thought about his next move. Assali probably had a new stash of satellite phones, but there was no point taking the risk to steal one with nothing much of value to say. His one consolation was that, from what he could tell, he had a few days to figure it out.

Ayman burst into the tent. He grabbed a small canvas bag and stuffed his new, Saudi-supplied spare set of clothes into it.

Faraz sat up. "What's this?"

"I am going home. Iyad agreed. We discussed the plan. I cannot participate injured. I will do the political work that I always do."

"I thought you wanted to be a fighter."

Ayman turned on Faraz, reached down and pushed him onto his back. "I am a fighter! I told you this already.

I was in a battle. I was injured. I may fight again, but now I cannot. The political work is important, especially as the day gets closer. Assali agrees. I am needed elsewhere."

"Okay, okay. So, you know the plan?"

Ayman stood straight and winced in pain. "Of course, I do."

"Tell me, please."

"I cannot. Do not think you are my equal, Khayal. You arrived a few days ago and are helping to train a few men. I am a leader of the movement."

"Yes, of course."

"You will know when you need to know."

Ayman turned to leave.

"You will go tonight?"

"More supply trucks are due any minute. I will return to their base with them, then go home from there."

Sergeant Peretz took Will to a low-rise apartment complex two blocks off one of Tel Aviv's trendy avenues of bars and restaurants. The building looked like all the others on the street—stucco fronts with small balconies protected by wrought iron security bars that rose to the floor of the next level.

The buildings were raised on stilts, and the sergeant pulled into a guest parking spot underneath.

"This is the colonel's home?" Will asked.

"No, sir. This is one of our army flats. He lives outside the city, stays here when he has to."

Peretz led Will up three flights of steps to the top floor, where there were two apartment doors. She knocked on the one on the left. When no one answered, she took a key from her pocket and they went inside.

The apartment was sparsely furnished with one comfortable chair, a wood-frame futon sofa and a combination TV stand and liquor cabinet. The kitchen was small but tidy, with a coffeemaker and kettle. Will could see a bathroom door along a hallway and another door beyond, presumably the bedroom.

"The colonel will be here soon," Peretz said. She opened a cabinet to reveal a basic set of plates, cups and glasses. "There are cold drinks in the fridge. Please help yourself to whatever you like." She handed Will a sticky note. "This is my phone number. I will be waiting in the car to take you to your hotel."

Twenty minutes later, Will sat on the sofa with a glass of whiskey Ari had poured him.

"*L'chaim*," Ari said.

Will gave him a quizzical look.

"It means 'to life.' We Jews always drink to life."

"*L'chaim*." Will took a sip.

Ari sat in the leather chair, his uniform pants muddy from the field, his boots carrying dirt from Bridget's cell. He gave Will an update on the search. "I saw the place. It was not pretty. We will send you the full report."

Will had his elbows on his knees, the whiskey glass in both hands, his head down. "And no idea where she is now?"

"We are checking the satellites, but no. They were

smart to hide in an area with many trees. Difficult to trace movements."

Will looked up. "So, what do we do now?"

"We?"

"Yes. I'm here to help."

Ari stifled a yawn. "Commander—"

"Will."

"Okay, Will, I am tired. I agreed to meet you because the general told me to, because he is friends with your general, who was also friends with my father. So, welcome to Israel. But I don't see what one American can do to help. We will find her."

"You'd be surprised what one American can do, especially with a three-star general taking his calls."

"I can't think why he would take your calls or why he would send you here. Maybe you can tell me."

Will didn't want to answer that, not yet, anyway. "Like I said, I'm here to help. I will be ready first thing in the morning, earlier if needed. I think you'll find that you have orders not to shut me out." Will stood and took the final swig of his whiskey. "I might even be useful. Thanks for the drink."

Within a few hours of her arrival, Bridget had a thin mattress, a blanket and even a pillow with a clean pillowcase. There was also a chair, like one from a 1950s kitchen set, shiny steel with light blue plastic-covered padding on the seat and back support. And they'd brought her a bottle of water and a metal bowl that looked like a spittoon to serve as her toilet.

The breakfast was orders of magnitude better than what she'd been given at the previous place—scrambled eggs and vegetables with fresh pita and a mug of tea. And the meal was hot. That meant they were cooking upstairs and there was at least one new person in the mix, probably the woman she'd heard when she arrived.

Her suspicion was confirmed by a snippet of muffled conversation she caught. The woman raised her voice, and Ra'ed responded, shutting her up. At one point, Bridget thought there was a second woman's voice, but she couldn't be sure.

Bridget did some squats and push-ups. Her side wound stopped her on her first sit-up attempt. She stood and lifted the chair ten times with her right arm, then her left. And repeat. It wasn't hard to get a light sweat going with no fresh air coming into the room. She poured some of her water onto her right hand and rubbed her face. Her bruises still hurt, but only when she touched them.

She would look for an opening to escape, of course, but that was unlikely. Bridget had to rely on Hadley and the Israelis to find her or to reach some compromise on the terrorists' demands. She thought about Will. Did he even know she'd been kidnapped? A SEAL assault team would be useful right about now.

Bridget sat on her mattress and leaned against the wall. Was it good to think about such things or bad? She needed a mental project but couldn't think of one. The only thing she could come up with was to relive her runs along the Potomac from her apartment south past the airport. She envisioned the parking lot, the path down to the road, the tunnel under the parkway. She tried to see every building, every tree. She imagined people passing her coming the other way.

Her adrenaline waned. Bridget finally felt the effects of the last thirty-six hours. She put her head on the pillow and fell asleep.

Chapter Thirty-four

Ayman's ride pulled up to his mother's house in late morning. He'd been lucky. He caught a wee-hours military flight from the Saudi base to a Jordanian one and crossed the river to the West Bank with the boy-captain before dawn. Abu-Hakim, the caterer, was there to meet him.

What a difference twelve hours make. From desert camp to his mother's embrace and the aromas of her kitchen.

"Ayman! Oh, praise Allah," Mrs. al-Hamdani said when he came through the door. She ran to him with arms wide. But when she kissed his cheek, she pulled back, looking at his injury. "Are you all right? You must sit down."

"It is nothing, Mother. We were in a fight. I was wounded. But it is nothing."

"It is not nothing. Sit. I will clean it and make a fresh bandage."

She led him to the table and pushed him into a light-blue chair. He noticed there were only three, instead of the usual four.

His sister, Maysoon, came into the kitchen and kissed him on both cheeks. She whispered in his ear, "It is good you are here."

Ayman was about to ask why when Ra'ed appeared in the kitchen doorway.

"*Ya, Allah*!" Ayman said. "What are you doing here?"

Bridget couldn't understand the Arabic shouting match. A young woman's voice joined in, which made the men shout louder. Someone pounded on a wall and that ended things.

Then there were footsteps on the stairs.

The bolt slid and the door started to open. Then it was pushed shut and the bolt slid back. There was more shouting and a scuffle. Then she heard the distinct sound of a slap.

A series of words she was pretty sure were curses followed, and one person went up the stairs, followed by the other. The upstairs door slammed.

"It is my house!" Ayman slammed his fist on the kitchen table.

"It is all right," his mother said. "It is for the movement."

Maysoon was with them, but Ra'ed had gone to the guest room he shared with the two other men, the same one Faraz had used.

"It puts you in danger," Ayman said. "It risks Maysoon's place at the university, everything." He was close to tears.

"Iyad called me from a satellite phone," Mrs. al-Hamdani said. "He told me it was an emergency. They had nowhere else to go. The Zionists will not look here. This house has not been important to them for years, since they murdered your father. Ra'ed is a hard man but he has been respectful. And he promised to move as soon as he finds somewhere to go."

"He is a liar."

"Perhaps, but there is nothing we can do. Please, do not fight with him. I fear what he might do."

"I can handle Ra'ed."

"Yes, I am sure you are right. But let us not provoke him. Calm yourself, I will make you some food."

After the meal, Ayman stomped up the stairs to his room and got to work on his old laptop, drafting a press release and some online posts. He wished he could reach Iyad, get him to order Ra'ed out of the house. But that was not possible.

He could not get rid of Ra'ed, but he could do his job. He set up his usual series of internet bounces, sending the communiques through multiple servers worldwide, making them untraceable. With an energy drink in his hand, he settled in to monitor reactions.

An hour later, a vehicle pulled into the driveway. Ayman looked out the window to see Ra'ed greeting a tall man with a scar on his left cheek. "*Ya ibn sharmouta*," he muttered. Son of a bitch. It was Suleiman, the garbageman.

He ran down to the side door to intercept them. "He will not come into my house," Ayman declared, blocking the doorway.

Standing in the carport, Suleiman cocked his head and

looked at Ayman like he was a child. "You want us to speak outside where Zionist spies can see us?"

"I don't think so," Ra'ed said. He pushed Ayman out of the way. Suleiman's two companions glared from their rusted SUV, its driver's door dented and the outside mirror missing.

Ayman grabbed Ra'ed's arm. "You cannot bring this man into my house. He opposes our movement. He attacked me in the prison. He has no respect."

Ra'ed shook him off. "He may not respect you, but he and I go back a long way, to your father's time. We need him for a mission that I cannot do and you certainly cannot do. You will get out of our way and let us work."

"What mission?"

Ra'ed turned away and led Suleiman to the guest room.

Ayman paced in the hallway, from the kitchen to the back of the house, past the doors to the guest room, bathroom and basement.

He caught snippets of the conversation. "It is done . . . the word is out . . . do not worry . . . enough men." When he heard them coming out, Ayman returned to the kitchen. Suleiman smiled as he passed him on the way to the side door.

"Do not come here again, Garbageman."

Suleiman stopped and took a step toward Ayman, as if to attack him. Ayman flinched. Suleiman and Ra'ed burst out laughing.

"Yes, Mr. President," Suleiman said. He waved his hand in front of him and made a ceremonial bow, triggering another round of laughter from Ra'ed.

The two fighters embraced, and Suleiman headed out, letting the screen door slam shut behind him.

On Faraz's first day as a trainer, Iyad gave him a dozen men and a section of the field outside the camp.

"Whatever I do with my men, you do the same," Iyad said. "Do not allow weakness. Time is short. The job will be difficult."

Faraz did as instructed. The training involved general skills—weapons handling, attack formations and the like. He used all his Arabic fighting vocabulary and learned a few new words.

In one exercise, he taught them how to attack in waves, with three men moving forward, firing into a building or open area, then the others coming in behind. They carried AKs without ammo.

"*Hujum, hujum, hujum*," Faraz shouted. Attack, attack, attack.

The men were eager but green. They had trouble getting the sequence right, pointed their weapons at each other, failed to watch for counterattacks. But as the day wore on, they improved.

Bashar was with his men about a hundred meters away. He had not exaggerated. They were well trained and had clearly worked together before. They were also the only ones who stopped at prayer times.

It was Tuesday evening in the Middle East, midmorning in Washington. More importantly for President Martelli, it was day two of the small window in which they might save Bridget Davenport from being executed by terrorists.

As expected, the Israeli cabinet had rejected any payment or prisoner exchange. The hostage was American and had been advised to leave the country. That made it easier for them to hold the line.

Even though he had his answer through official channels, the president insisted on a call with Prime Minister Yardeni.

"You must consider some sort of offer," Martelli said, "if only to buy time. Davenport is a senior and very important part of our covert operations structure, and I know her personally. You cannot leave her to die."

"Andrew, I'm sorry, the cabinet will not do it. And honestly, my friend, we must all face the fact that they will never release her for exactly the reason you stated, because she is such a senior intelligence official. I'm sorry to say it, but she may be dead already."

"Nonsense." Martelli's stress level was starting to show. "You know it wouldn't make sense for them to kill her before the deadline. How is it you gave in to their demands for your soldier but won't even discuss it for my operative?"

"Again, you give the answer within the question. We made the trade, and as my opponents predicted, the terrorists did the same thing again with even greater demands. I cannot argue for another concession, even if I wanted to. We have already put our men at risk in attempts to rescue her, and we will continue to do everything possible. But I cannot do what you ask."

"Shlomo—"

"In a few days, this will be over, one way or the other,

and we will continue to hunt them down. For now, there is nothing more I can do."

As he did whenever his duties allowed, General HaLevy was visiting the Ben-Yosef house north of Tel Aviv for dinner. He sat on the sofa while his grand-daughter, Tali, played with a Little Mermaid doll and an assortment of plastic sea creatures while singing, it seemed, the entire score from the movie. The smell of lentil soup made with his late wife's recipe wafted through the air.

"Wine, Papa?" Rivka called from the kitchen.

"A small one, thank you, sweetheart."

HaLevy's gaze fell on a family portrait from three years earlier, taken at a nearby beach. That was the last one with his wife, who died of cancer a year later. He smiled. She loved these dinners at Rivka and Ari's house. HaLevy used to tease her, saying she liked Ari better than him.

"Here you are, Papa," Rivka said, delivering the wine. "It's a new one from the Golan Heights." She had put on a blue, knee-length dress for dinner with her father, and Tali wore a matching green one.

"Thank you, my dear. You look lovely, tonight." The general clasped her hand.

"I see the look in your eyes," Rivka said. "You were staring at the picture of Mama."

"Guilty. But all I really need to do is look at you."

Rivka leaned down and kissed him on the cheek.

"And how did you convince Tali to change out of her costume?" he asked.

"I told her this is what the Little Mermaid wears for dinner with her *sabah*."

Father and daughter shared a laugh, and Rivka headed back to the kitchen.

"Will Ari be home for supper?" the general called after her.

"I should ask you. But I doubt it. They had a planning meeting about security for the Purim parades in Jerusalem. But you know that, right?"

"Yes, yes, of course."

"Tali will march with her class."

"I wish I could see it, but I will be stuck in Tel Aviv."

HaLevy's phone rang. The tone of Ari's voice made him put down his wine and sit up straight. "Yes. . . Okay. . . And it's confirmed? Of course, yes, you have authorization. Be careful, Ari. Report back to me as soon as it's over. Take the American, but don't let him get into the middle of it. Good luck." The general ended the call.

"That doesn't sound like a meeting." Rivka said.

"Don't worry. It's nothing."

She stared at him.

"Nothing I can tell you about. But believe me, no need to worry."

Fifty miles and a world away, Ayman used the same line on his mother. "No need to worry. I will be back in a few hours, or perhaps tomorrow morning at the latest. I have some internet work to do, and Munir can help me. You remember my friend Munir."

"Yes, of course."

"It's not far. Have a rest. I will be back before you know it."

Ayman stood in the kitchen with a small backpack containing his computer and assorted attachments. The house was still filled with the smells of the dinner Mrs. al-Hamdani had fed them.

"You leave us here, with these men?" Maysoon said.

"You were alone with them before I got home. They will not hurt you. Ra'ed knows I would not tolerate it. Iyad would not tolerate it."

Mrs. al-Hamdani's shoulders sagged. "Still, I would prefer—."

"Mother, there is much work to do for the movement. Father would be proud." He leaned down and kissed her cheek, then nodded at Maysoon and left.

Chapter Thirty-five

Will sat on a bench in the Israeli Special Ops team's ready room inspecting the handgun Ari had issued him. He was with a dozen men in various stages of undress as they prepped for the rescue. Will wore his SEAL desert camo uniform and a borrowed set of body armor. His left leg hurt more than usual, maybe from stress, maybe from his inability to sit still since he'd heard about Bridget's kidnapping.

Ari and an Israeli major walked over. "This is Yaron Drucker, unit commander," Ari said.

Drucker held out a hand to shake, then reached farther and ripped the American flag patch off the plastic fasteners that held it to Will's uniform. "Leave this here. Your insignia and nameplate, too."

"Right."

"When we get there, you stay back with Colonel Ben-Yosef."

"But—"

"Commander, I respect you and the navy SEALs. But being in a unit like this, you should understand, we have procedures. You would be in the way. You will wait until the site is secured or you will stay here."

"You know he's right," Ari said. "I will also wait with you."

Will looked from one to the other and saw no room to negotiate. "Yes. All right."

Bridget was feeling the effects of two days in captivity. As she sat leaning against the cell wall, her body ached. She hadn't washed beyond putting water on her face. Fear of what came next was starting to overwhelm her mental exercises.

She pulled at her shirt, which stuck to her body. She stank, even she could smell it. She put her head in her hands. She needed a plan.

Bridget jumped when Ra'ed came in to deliver her dinner. She saw Ballou by the door. Ra'ed handed her a lovely plate of rice and chunks of meat. It was steaming hot, and the aroma cut through Bridget's malaise.

The idea hit her so fast she had to blink her eyes to think it through. She wasn't sure what it would accomplish, but she only had a few seconds to implement it. Somehow, the dinner had presented her with some leverage she might be able to use on this man.

"I need to speak to the woman," she said.

"What woman?"

Bridget nodded toward the plate.

"Why?"

"Woman's problem," she said, and she looked down as if embarrassed.

"Oh." Ra'ed took a step back.

"Please."

He looked away, then turned and left in a hurry.

Bridget smiled.

It was dark by the time Will stood outside the Special Ops building with the Israeli team while they got their mission brief alongside three armored personnel carriers, a command vehicle and Ari's SUV. Sergeant Peretz stood behind Will to translate.

"We have received a tip from one of our informants in the West Bank that identifies a house not far from Jerusalem," Drucker said. "The interior layout is standard for such homes of that age." He rolled out a schematic on the tailgate of one of the vehicles and shined a light on it. "The design is familiar to all of you."

Will saw the soldiers nod.

Drucker continued. "Surveillance confirms suspicious activity. We will approach in standard formation. Other units will secure the neighboring houses. Our information is that she is lightly guarded to avoid suspicion. We must assume she is in the basement or perhaps in a bedroom upstairs. Be quick but careful. Anyone inside is an enemy except the hostage. Any questions?"

There were none.

"Load up."

Will got into the SUV with Ari, and they fell in behind the armored vehicles, heading east.

"No matter how good your men are, the jihadis will have time to kill her," Will said.

"We will scan with infrared and insert microcameras

to assess the situation before we strike. Usually, they hold captives in a locked room. The hope is that they are too busy staying alive to take the time to get to her."

"Hope."

"That is our experience. Frankly, sometimes we are right, sometimes we are wrong. It is better than leaving her there."

Will watched the darkened landscape speed by, desert hills dotted by ragged Palestinian villages that looked like they hadn't changed in a hundred years—except for the electrical wires and satellite dishes—and Israeli settlements freshly sandblasted and painted, dotted with solar panels and ringed with barbed wire and security lights.

"I will do it," Maysoon said, taking her mother's hand at the kitchen table.

"No, my child. It is too dangerous."

"How is it dangerous? She cannot hurt me."

"We should wait for Ayman."

"What can he do? She wants to speak to a woman. Can you imagine why? And you know when he goes to Munir's house to do internet work it always takes longer than planned. It is hard for Ayman to be here with Ra'ed. Let him stay there. If she has a 'woman's problem,' I will help."

Her mother had no more strength to argue.

Ra'ed came into the kitchen.

"I will get some things," Maysoon said, pushing past him and going up the stairs toward her bedroom.

* * *

Bridget had finished her dinner by the time the bolt slid to the open position. Ra'ed came in and stepped aside.

"Stay where you are," he said.

Bridget looked past him. She had been expecting an older woman, someone who had spent a lifetime honing her cooking skills, probably wearing an *abaya* and a headscarf. What she saw was a young woman, a girl almost, in jeans and a baggy shirt, with a scarf tied casually around her black hair. She was short, barely five feet tall, with dark eyes and plump cheeks. Her black-rimmed glasses gave her a studious look. She clutched a gray plastic bag to her chest.

The girl took two tentative steps into the room. She winced at the smell.

"Thank you for coming," Bridget said, sitting on her mattress. "Do you speak English?"

"Yes." Hearing Bridget's voice seemed to have an effect on the girl, perhaps made her realize the hostage was a real person. She lowered her arms.

"I need . . ." Bridget looked at Ra'ed, then looked away.

The girl got the message. She spoke to him in Arabic. He objected. She insisted.

Ra'ed looked back and forth between the women. "Remember," he said in English. "Do not do anything stupid." He backed out and shut the door, but did not lock it.

"I see that you brought what I need," Bridget said. "Thank you."

The girl handed over the supplies.

Bridget put the bag aside and made eye contact. "What is your name?"

"I am Maysoon."

"I'm Bridget. I'm pleased to meet you."

Maysoon didn't answer.

"You are a very good cook."

Maysoon let out half a chuckle. "That is my mother."

"Ah. Well, please thank her for me."

"I will bring you more supplies tomorrow."

Bridget lowered her voice. "You must help me. They will kill me. Please."

Maysoon recoiled. "You are the enemy," she said.

"Look at me. I am a woman, like you. I am loyal to my country, like you. Believe me, I want peace and justice for the Palestinian—"

Maysoon spat on the floor. "Do not play mind games with me."

"It's not a game, Maysoon. It's my life." Bridget lunged, grabbed Maysoon's wrists and pulled her to her knees. She spoke in an urgent whisper. "What I'm telling you is true. I only want to go home, to be free, to raise a family, just like you."

Saying all that out loud hit Bridget hard. Her voice broke. "Do you want my death on your conscience? You will never forgive yourself if you let them kill me."

Maysoon pulled away. She stood over Bridget, seeming unsure what to do or say. She turned and left, startling Ra'ed as she pushed the door open.

On the outskirts of a village, Will and Ari stepped aboard Drucker's command van. Two technicians and the major faced a wall of screens and computers.

They had a live feed from the helmet camera of one of three recon soldiers who had gone ahead. The target house was set back from the road. It had two stories and a gravel driveway with a rusty and beat-up SUV under a carport. Five steps led up to a porch.

"Are you sure she's there?" Will asked.

"As sure as we can be," Ari said. "The information is from a solid source. We will know more shortly."

The recon guys were crawling now through bushes between the house and its neighbor. The main display switched to a distorted fisheye view.

"That is the remote camera," Ari said. "It is on a monopod they will raise up just enough to give us a look inside through a window."

The camera showed a close-up of the side of the house, then it came over a windowsill and stopped. The soldier fixed the focus and turned the camera left and right.

They saw a kitchen. Two men sat at the table, one with an AK on his lap. The other one's weapon was on the table. He leaned the chair back on two legs and sipped tea. The camera's microphone picked up a muffled voice from elsewhere in the house.

The man who was leaning back called over his shoulder. "*Kul b'khayr.*"

Ari translated. "He says, 'All is well.'"

Drucker stood and looked at Ari. He appeared as relaxed as a man can be at a moment like that, but his dark eyebrows were furrowed. "It's a Go, then?"

"Yes. Good luck."

Drucker left the van. On one of the monitors, Will saw him board the lead armored vehicle. A few seconds later, it moved off toward the village along with the second one. The third stayed behind for backup.

"I hate sitting here while they go in," Will said, his leg bouncing.

Ari didn't reply. He stared at the monitors and gripped his Uzi.

Bridget inventoried the supplies—four pads, some clean towels and a bottle of water. She closed the bag and tossed it against the wall. She had made her point with the girl, but she wasn't optimistic. There was no reason to think she would have any interest in helping "the enemy" or would take the risks necessary to do so, or could possibly succeed against the men. The girl might even tell Ra'ed about their conversation, and he would make Bridget suffer for it.

Another stupid plan. But it was the only one she had.

Bridget picked up the bag. She didn't think anyone would check when she returned it, but just in case, she would have to find a way to cut herself so she could stain the pads.

Chapter Thirty-six

The Israeli commandos hit fast and hard. The feed from a camera on the lead vehicle showed a rocket-propelled grenade fly through a window and obliterate the kitchen. The commandos poured out of their vehicles, firing, with Drucker in the lead.

There was no return fire from the house, so they moved forward, some mounting the steps to secure the main floor, others running along both sides of the building to block any escape from the rear.

The team on the left was hit first.

An explosion destroyed that corner of the house, and the facing wall of the neighboring house, and killed four of the Israelis. Two survivors lay exposed on the ground.

The bomb on the other side went off a second later. Will and Ari saw Drucker launched off the porch into the front yard while more of his men fell.

Through the smoke, a lanky man with a scrawny beard and a large scar on the left side of his face led half a dozen jihadis out of the house with their AKs on automatic.

* * *

Suleiman laughed as he fired and screamed in English over the gunfire, "Die Zionist dogs!"

He and his men sprayed the yard with 7.62-millimeter bullets—an inch and a quarter long and a third of an inch in diameter—each one capable of blasting a fatal hole in a body or a significant dent in its armor, especially at short range.

Suleiman went down the steps one at a time, picking his targets among the Israelis who were still alive.

"They were ready for us," Ari said inside the van.

"No kidding." Will was already up and opening the door.

Ari grabbed him. "You stay here."

"Bullshit."

"I have orders."

"Fuck your orders. Bridget could be in there." Will pulled his arm free and jumped down from the van. He took off running behind the backup team's vehicle, which was already speeding into the village. He heard Ari's footsteps behind him.

When the vehicle stopped, Will ran past it to find Drucker and his surviving soldiers taking cover behind the second vehicle.

"You all right?" Will asked.

"Yeah, mostly. Hurt my back, but I'll live."

Ari joined them as the lead vehicle exploded from an RPG hit. The force of the blast and the flying shrapnel and debris sent them all to the ground. Will saw that two of the Israelis did not get up.

The backup team was firing, but outnumbered as

more terrorists came out of the house or fired through the windows.

"RPG," Drucker ordered.

"No!" Will said.

But two soldiers raised a launcher and fired.

Suleiman and his men saw them. His team dove for cover, but his adrenaline overwhelmed his judgment. Or maybe he had made his decision beforehand.

He swung his AK toward the RPG team and fired.

The bullets pinged off the armored vehicle, interrupted by the whoosh of the rocket-propelled grenade and then the boom.

The projectile hit the terrorist team leader in the chest, slicing his body in half and exploding when it hit the stairs behind him. Two seconds later, gunfire resumed from inside the house.

"We have to get in there," Will said.

Ari held him down.

Drucker keyed his radio and said something in Hebrew.

Ari translated. "He called for air support."

"You can't do that," Will said.

A voice came through the radio. Ari translated again, "They refuse due to possible hostage on site."

"Damn right."

Drucker let out an Arabic curse. He turned to Will and Ari. "We need to withdraw. We don't have enough men to take the house. We need to get our wounded out of here."

"You're kidding me," Will shouted at him. "They could kill her any second."

"We have men down. We need to get them and go."

Will looked at Ari.

"He's right," Ari said. "If they haven't killed her, or if we haven't, we can only save her by withdrawing."

Will pushed past Ari, grabbed an American M4 rifle from a fallen soldier and ran toward the alleyway on the right.

"Jackson!" Ari shouted.

A hail of bullets sent Will diving to the ground behind some bushes. Pain shot from his injured hip down to his foot. He raised himself onto his elbows and fired, then got up and ran toward the back of the house while the Israelis kept the jihadis busy in the front.

When Will went down for cover a second time, he felt Ari land next to him. "Damn it, Jackson, get back to the vehicle."

Will ignored him and looked into the backyard. He saw the three Israelis from the recon team down and not moving. "Cover me."

"No!"

But Will was already on the move. Crouching low, he stayed near the wall and made his way to the back door. With the jihadis' attention focused on the team in front of the house, Will was able to stand up enough to look through the screen.

The hallway was clear. Will opened the door as little as possible and slipped through.

Ari's voice came from behind him. "Jackson, get out of there."

Ahead, there was a stairway leading up, so he couldn't

see the front of the house. He checked the bedroom and bathroom near the back door. Empty.

Ari stood outside and called to him in a loud whisper. "Jackson!"

Will put his fingers to his lips and pointed to a third door in the hallway. He opened it and found the basement stairs. He gestured to indicate he was going down.

Halfway there, something moved behind him. He turned to see Ari standing guard at the top of the stairs. "If you must do it, move fast."

Will bent over to get a better look into the basement. It was dark and there were no sounds to guide him.

He reached the bottom and took cover behind the stairs. He grabbed the standard-issue high-powered flashlight from his belt, pressed its lens to his leg and turned it on. He moved it enough to let a small amount of light into the room, then a little more.

The central part of the basement was piled with the usual junk a family might discard—boxes labeled in Arabic, old electronics, a girl's pink bicycle. He shined the full force of the light around the room. There was no one there, but to his right he saw a bolted door.

Ari came halfway down the stairs. Will held up a hand to stop him. He pointed to his eyes, then to the door. Will approached it and slid the bolt. The door creaked open.

"Bridget?"

There was no response.

Five seconds later, Will was back at the stairs.

"She's not there," he said.

"What?"

"You heard me. This was a setup. Your intel was bull."

"Damn it!" Ari banged his fist against the bannister.

"We have to get out of here." Will tried to push his way past Ari, but the Israeli held him back.

"I'll lead."

At the top of the stairs, Ari looked right, toward the front of the house. The gunfight was raging, likely tying down all of the terrorists. He turned left to lead Will out the back.

As Will neared the top of the steps, he was brushed back by a burst from an AK.

Ari fell in the hallway.

A jihadi appeared above him in the basement doorway, pointing his rifle toward Ari for a finish-off. Will raised his weapon and fired.

The force of the bullet at close range threw the man against the wall. His body twisted from the impact, and Will saw the look of surprise on his face, the last emotion he would feel. His body sagged and he slid down the wall to the floor.

Will waited. The hallway was quiet. He climbed the last few steps as quietly as he could and peeked toward the front. The guy had been alone.

To his left, Will saw Ari lying facedown. The rear plate of his body armor had taken three hits, and he was bleeding from wounds on his right arm and leg. Will felt for a pulse. Maybe. It was hard to tell and he had no time to wait.

He went to the back door and opened it. Drucker and four other Israelis pointed their weapons at him. He raised his arms.

"It's me. The colonel is down. Help me."

Without a word, Drucker mounted the steps. He and

Will dragged Ari out of the house. Two of the soldiers carried him to the alleyway.

"The basement is clear," Will said.

Drucker gave an order in Hebrew and three of his men went upstairs. They returned a few seconds later. The lead man shook his head.

Will's shoulders sagged as the reality hit him. Bridget was still being held. Somewhere. Or maybe she was dead.

Drucker said something in Hebrew into his radio. Then he turned to Will. "Air support is on the way. We need to go."

Bridget sat on her mattress with a collection of pebbles in her hand. She had gathered them from the corners of the room, hoping to find one sharp enough to do the job. She picked out the sharpest one and pressed it to one of the cuts she'd gotten on her right knee when she fell on the gravel.

Nothing.

She put her weight into it, rubbing back and forth, pressing the edge into her flesh. It hurt more than she had expected. Luckily, her tetanus shot was up to date.

Finally, a drop. Bridget took one of the pads and poured some of her precious water onto it, then held it under the cut. She pressed the pebble a little more and got enough blood for her purpose. The dark red faded toward pink as it diluted on the pad. She put it down and grabbed another.

When she finished, she admired her handiwork. It was good enough to fool the men, possibly not the women.

Chapter Thirty-Seven

Well after midnight, Will sat with Major Drucker in a waiting area at Jerusalem's Hadassah Hospital Ein Kerem shock trauma center. They were both still dirty from the field. Drucker's left arm was bandaged. Three of his men were dead. Half a dozen others had serious injuries. He had sent the rest home to clean up and rest.

The polished floors and antiseptic smell reminded Will of his long stays at hospitals in Germany and Bethesda getting surgery and treatment on his leg. According to the docs, he wasn't ready to go on ops yet. He'd argued with them plenty. But as he sat there with the old pain returning, he had to admit they were right. Admit to himself, anyway.

Will got up to stretch and walked the length of the room. When he turned back, he saw Drucker looking miserable. "I'm sorry about your men. I've been where you are now. I know it's tough."

Drucker looked at him, then looked away. His men had died trying to rescue Bridget. Will knew there was nothing more he could say about that.

"It's my fault the colonel got hit," Will said.

Drucker looked at him again. "You want me to say no, that it's not your fault? Of course it is, up to a point. Both of you should have stayed in the command vehicle. But the colonel is an experienced soldier. He made his own decision, as you did."

A doctor emerged from the STAFF AND FAMILY ONLY door with a woman and an Israeli general. The woman looked shell-shocked. The general held her arm.

Drucker made introductions. "General HaLevy, sir, Rivka—Mrs. Ben-Yosef—this is Commander Jackson."

The doctor started in Hebrew.

"English, please," Will said.

The man seemed annoyed but he did as requested. "The colonel is alive. His body armor protected his vital organs. But he lost a lot of blood from his leg and arm wounds, and the multiple bullets that hit the body armor caused severe bruising across his back. He is moving from surgery to intensive care. I cannot say when he will return to duty, but he will survive."

Rivka glared at Drucker. "How did you let this happen? He is not a commando anymore."

"It was a bad situation. He ran to the gunfire. We should not be surprised."

Rivka turned to Will. "And you were there?"

"Yes, ma'am."

"How is it that you two are standing here and my Ari was nearly killed?" Her voice caught.

"Rivka, please," the general said.

She took a couple of breaths and disengaged from her father's arm. "Yes, all right. It is really Ari that I'm mad at." She moved toward the hallway.

HaLevy looked at Will. "I have not told her, but I read the report. He followed you into the building."

"Yes, sir."

"You were to wait in the vehicle."

"It was an ambush, sir. The hostage—"

"I think this is the end of your mission."

"But, sir—"

"On the first flight."

General HaLevy walked past them to catch up with his daughter.

At sunrise, Faraz emerged from his tent to the sound of the men whooping and hollering outside the dining area. They had opened several boxes from the previous night's supply delivery and were holding up adult-size Halloween costumes—clowns, superheroes, fairy-tale characters.

Faraz walked over. One of the men held up a pirate outfit and danced around waving his plastic sword. Another, half-dressed as an astronaut, shot him with a ray gun that made a grinding noise and had a flashing red light.

Iyad stood at the edge of the crowd, smiling and holding two costumes wrapped in clear plastic.

"What's all this?" Faraz asked.

"Our . . . shall we say . . . uniforms." Iyad laughed.

"What?"

"We do not have Disco Boy, so I chose this one for you." Iyad slapped a costume into Faraz's stomach.

The outfit was printed with a dark suit, white shirt and blue tie. The plastic mask was a smiling white man with gray hair. It took a moment for Faraz to recognize the face.

"Bill Clinton?"

Iyad burst into laughter. He slapped Faraz on the back and headed for Assali's tent. Faraz hurried to catch up. When they got there, Bashar was already inside, deep in conversation with the boss.

"It is a good plan," Bashar said. "They will not expect it. We will have maximum impact."

"Yes, brilliant," Iyad said. "Even living my entire life under Zionist rule, I would not have thought of it."

The men laughed.

"Sorry," Faraz said. "Can someone explain?"

Assali leaned back in his chair, his paunch straining the new tunic the Saudis had provided. The man had been stressed ever since Faraz met him. This was the first time he saw him smile.

"Did you know any Jews in America?" Assali asked.

Faraz was not expecting the question. "A few, I guess."

"They have many holidays," Assali said, waving a hand to dismiss their importance. "They won a war, they eat some food. They won another war, they eat some different food."

"It is all about the food," Iyad said through another round of laughter.

"On Friday, they will eat triangle cakes, but we focus on a different tradition. They dress in costumes. They act out the story of the holiday they call Purim. A king fell in love with a Jewish girl and saved the Jews, blah, blah, blah. But these days, they do not limit themselves to those characters. They dress in all sorts of costumes. And so will we. There will be parties and parades. That is when we will strike."

Maysoon brought Bridget's breakfast along with a bag of fresh supplies. Ra'ed looked in briefly, then closed the door. Bridget held up the original bag with the soiled pads, its handles tied together. When Maysoon bent down to retrieve it, Bridget whispered, "Will you help me?"

"I cannot."

"Cannot or will not?"

"It is the same."

"It is not the same. You can distract them. You can unlock the door. You can save my life, Maysoon. Only you."

Ra'ed's voice came from outside the room. "How long does it take to discuss women's problems? Come. Get out of there, Maysoon."

She moved toward the door.

"Think about it, Maysoon. My life is in your hands."

When Maysoon came up from the basement, she found Ayman eating and working on his computer at the kitchen table. She did not greet her brother but went out the side door to put Bridget's bag in the trash. Then she walked back past Ayman to pour herself a cup of tea at the counter.

"What time did you get home?"

"It was late. I am not a child. What is the matter, Maysoon?"

"It is nothing." Maysoon put the teacup down and did

not turn around. "I have seen the woman, twice now. It is upsetting."

"Yes, Mother told me. Do not worry. This will all be over soon. Meanwhile, look at this. It might make you feel better." Ayman swung the computer around.

Maysoon sighed and turned to look at it.

"It is a statement. In English, they call it a 'manifesto'— a grand word. It says *Al-Hakam Al-Islamiyah* is the leader of the Palestinian movement and that we will soon demonstrate our power."

"By killing the woman?"

Ayman laughed. "It is easy to kill a woman. And maybe we will kill her. But our power will be in what she gains for us, and in what we will do, in any case, in two days' time."

"And what is that?"

Ayman smiled. "I cannot tell you."

"You cannot tell me or you do not know?"

"Of course, I know." Ayman answered too quickly and looked away. His lower lip quivered.

His sister knew the signs. He was lying. Normally, she would tease him until he confessed. But this morning, she didn't have the stomach for it.

"So, what will you do with your manifesto?"

"I will publish it to the world. It will land like a missile in the middle of the political landscape. It will change everything. Watch this."

He reached around the computer, closed the document, then dragged its icon into a window shaped like a maze. A graphic appeared, a mouse running through the maze, back and forth, back and forth. Then, it appeared to explode.

"You sent it?"

"Yes." He sat back in his chair with a satisfied smile.

"But can't the Zionists trace it back to here?"

"Never. I am too clever. The manifesto will go through dozens of servers all over the world before it appears on our website. No one will know where it came from. That is what Munir and I were working on. Now, I will go back to his house. We will watch the football match and monitor reaction to the manifesto."

"Be careful. There will be patrols. You heard what happened last night?"

"Yes. The garbageman is a martyr. Disgusting."

"You should say '*Inna lillahi*' for him."

Ayman went back to his breakfast. "You say it if you want."

The A-HAI document caused the stir Ayman had hoped for when it hit the internet in the wee hours of Washington's Wednesday. Its politics were a stale rehash of Palestinian claims, and its allusions to great things to come were vague. But following Faraz's report and Assali's disappearance into the Saudi desert, it further increased concern about an MTO.

General Hadley scanned his ID and barreled through the Pentagon's South Entrance. Rather than go up the stairs to his executive office, he turned left and walked— more like stormed—down the hall to the elevator that would take him to the second basement.

It was six a.m., but the Task Force Epsilon offices were full. The team was working flat out to find the manifesto's origin and to figure out whether it held any clues about what was coming. The only thing they knew for sure that A-HAI might do in the near term was murder Bridget.

Hadley barged into Liz's office without knocking. Actually, it was Bridget's office—the photo of her with her parents was still on the desk, her emergency outfit was still hanging on a wall hook in its garment bag.

"What do you make of it?" Hadley asked.

"We're working on it, sir. Seems like a lot of empty threats, except for the obvious." Liz looked away and wiped her hand down her face to regain control.

Hadley took a breath and softened his tone. "What do you know so far?"

Liz turned back to him. "The writing is in the same style we've seen from them before, maybe written by the same person."

"And do we know who that is?"

"No."

"Well, let's find the hell out."

Someone came up behind Hadley and knocked on the open door.

"Excuse me." It was the IT specialist, Patricia Simons. "I think you should both see this."

Simons laid two pieces of paper on Liz's desk. Each had lines of letters and numbers. Every other line had an arrow at the end.

"What are we looking at?" Hadley asked.

"This is our trace of the A-HAI upload. Well, so far. It was sent through lots of servers before it was posted, which we would expect. Whoever did this is good, but I don't think he's as good as he thinks he is."

"Go on."

"It's hard to explain, but when you send something

over the internet, it gets a sort of electronic postmark. It announces to each computer along its path, 'Hey, it's me, I'm from wherever and I need to go to wherever.' Then that server creates the link and lets the file pass through. It all takes nanoseconds. Most times, the pathway is easy to trace, but it's also easy to encode the postmark, which is what this guy did."

"But you can break his code?"

"In the last few hours, we broke some of it, traced the transmission back a few levels, which you see here. But we don't know how far it goes—how many bounces there were—so we don't know how close we are to the origin. And the code is getting more complex with each jump. It will take time, and we may not be able to track it all the way to the source. But it's worth a shot."

"You pull in whatever resources you need from the team," Liz said.

Hadley corrected her. "From the whole agency, the whole damn building."

CHAPTER THIRTY-EIGHT

That evening, Maysoon sat alone in the kitchen. Her mother was lying down while the dinner she'd prepared for the terrorists and their hostage simmered on the stove. Maysoon was reading a book, nursing another cup of tea and trying not to think about Bridget.

She was supposed to hate the enemy. And she did. Why had meeting one in person made it impossible for her to concentrate on her reading?

"I am a woman, like you," she said.

Ha! It was a ridiculous notion. The hostage was an oppressor. Maysoon was a victim and a freedom fighter. Of sorts.

Still, the woman's words lingered.

"My life is in your hands"

"You will never forgive yourself if you let them kill me."

Maysoon knew what the men did, what attacks they carried out. She knew A-HAI had kidnapped the soldier, killed the young mother, conducted countless deadly operations over the years for the liberation of Palestine. It was jihad. She was conditioned not to feel empathy for the people on the other side.

But she had never met one before.

Sure, she encountered Israelis every day. She'd even met some Americans. But not like this. Not at the cutting edge of the war. Not who might be the next to die. In her house.

This was so different from watching the jihad on television. She had been proud when she saw bombed-out buildings, cafés and buses. She felt no sadness when she looked at pictures of hostages and watched the families crying at their funerals. She thought about the Palestinian refugees whose homes and land had been stolen. She thought about the children growing up in camps, the men languishing in prison, the martyrs. Her father.

But she'd never been to the scene of an attack, never met someone chained in a basement waiting to die.

In her house.

The shorter of Ra'ed's accomplices came in with his AK hanging by its shoulder strap. He smiled at Maysoon and gave her a formal greeting. "Good afternoon, Miss al-Hamdani. How is your health?"

The laws of Arabic etiquette required her to respond in kind. "Praise Allah. And you, Naji?"

"Praise Allah."

Naji went to the stove and opened the lid of the dinner pot. The aromas of cumin and nutmeg filled the room.

"Leave it," Maysoon ordered. "It is not time yet."

Naji complied, then sat down on Maysoon's left and leaned his rifle against the cabinets behind him. "Your mother is an excellent cook. Has she taught you her skills?"

Maysoon looked toward the hallway door. "Where is Ra'ed?"

"He has gone out. I am in charge." Naji leaned toward Maysoon, showing off his slimy smile and cigarette-stained teeth. He was wearing a soccer shirt that needed washing. He folded his hands in front of him, so his right elbow was close to her left arm.

"And the other man?"

"In the basement. I will relieve him later so he can sleep."

"What do you want, Naji?"

"I want to talk to you. You are a fine young woman—smart, I hear. I am a respected fighter in the group founded by your father and now led by your cousin. We should get to know each other."

Maysoon rolled her eyes. "I don't think so."

Naji looked at her, his mouth curling into that smile again. "Of course, we should." He put his right hand on Maysoon's arm.

She pulled away. "If you touch me again, my cousin will have you cut into little pieces."

Naji put his hand on his heart. "My apologies."

"And if you are in charge, shouldn't you be on patrol or something?"

Naji didn't move.

"Or would you rather I tell Ra'ed you sat with me without an invitation or a chaperone, and—?"

Naji held up a hand to stop her. "All right, all right. I heard you were tough, and it seems the information was correct." He stood and picked up his AK. "But I am also tough. In time, we shall see who is tougher."

Maysoon glared at him. After he left the room, she

muttered a string of curses not appropriate for a young lady.

Assali's fighters continued to play with the costumes at dinner, wearing masks and speaking in strange voices.

Faraz had enough intel now to make a report if he could get ahold of a sat phone. The device would provide their location. He now knew when the attack would happen and that the men would be in costume. He still didn't know where they would strike, but this was more than enough.

He sat at a picnic table with Iyad and Bashar, eating dinner and thinking of how he could get the full attack plan out of them. As the men continued to joke around, Faraz shook his head.

"What is wrong with you?" Iyad asked.

"They are like children," Faraz said. "We have a job to do. We cannot do it with five-year-olds."

"They will settle down," Bashar said. "At least, I can say my men will settle down."

"They will all do what needs to be done," Iyad said. "They are tense as the day of the attack approaches. We must let them relieve the stress in this way, unless our friends in Riyadh are sending a busload of women."

Iyad and Bashar laughed at that one, so Faraz joined in.

He decided to take the direct approach. "And what exactly is the attack plan?"

Iyad stopped laughing. "You will know when you need to know, Disco Boy." He left the table and went into Assali's headquarters.

Faraz sat in silence with Bashar as they finished their meals. He considered a nighttime operation. He had a bayonet. He could slip into Assali's tent, kill him and make a call. But it was high-risk. With so many men in camp, someone was always outside, having a smoke or making a trip to the latrine.

In the absence of any better plan, he might have to try it.

Iyad came out of the building and walked straight to the table. He leaned forward toward Faraz and Bashar and spoke in a quiet voice. "After the meal, tell your men to prepare for departure."

Maysoon and her mother sat at the table finishing their dinner. Ra'ed came through the side door scowling and slammed it behind him. Then he noticed the women. "I am sorry," he said. "*Salaam aleikum.*"

"*Aleikum salaam*, Ra'ed," Maysoon's mother said. "Have some dinner,"

"Yes, thank you, *Sayyidat* al-Hamdani." Ra'ed went to serve himself.

"What is the matter?" Maysoon asked.

Ra'ed closed the pot and threw a fork onto his plate. "Suleiman's operation did not convince the Zionists to cooperate. They will not release prisoners for the life of the woman." He turned to take his meal to the bedroom, but stopped at the doorway. "And your son's so-called manifesto did not help—the bragging, the threats. The whole world is on alert, and the Zionist government made a statement saying it will never deal with such an organization. Where is Ayman, anyway?"

"He is visiting a friend," Maysoon said.

Her mother stood. "You would do well to remember my husband founded the movement. My son and my nephew Iyad are the leaders now. They respect you, but do not overstep."

Ra'ed scoffed and started down the hall.

"Ra'ed," she called after him. He stopped and turned. Mrs. al-Hamdani walked to the doorway and spoke in a stage whisper. "Not in my house."

"What?"

She pointed a finger at him for emphasis and spoke a bit louder. "You heard me. Not in my house."

"I understand. But I cannot promise. We will do what we have to do."

Mrs. al-Hamdani started to argue, but Ra'ed turned away, went into the bedroom and closed the door.

Faraz was herding his men toward the buses. Their mood had turned serious but some still wore their costumes. Many of them carried their toy weapons along with the real ones. It was dark. The area outside the camp was lit by the glare of the vehicle headlights.

Iyad stood next to the lead bus shouting for the men to hurry. Assali emerged from his tent holding his suit coat and a small valise, looking like he was about to board a commuter flight. The crowd of men near Iyad parted as the boss walked through and took the front row seat.

Even from a distance, Faraz could hear him yell at the driver to turn up the air conditioning. He hoped Assali had the sat phones in his bag.

Faraz directed his men to the third bus and went to speak to Iyad. "We attack tonight?"

"No. We have a long way to go."

Maysoon sat on her bed wearing gray sweatpants and a sweatshirt with the Birzeit University logo—an olive tree with the motto "Building a Better Palestinian Future."

Her plan was to not think about Bridget, to not see her again. Maybe Ayman could convince the men to take the woman out of the house. Then, whatever happened would be out of her hands.

But she knew that was not likely. Ra'ed had told them they wouldn't have come here if there had been anywhere else to go. Now, the Zionists were on alert. Movement was impossible.

For Ra'ed to close the bedroom door in her mother's face, he must be under a lot of pressure. Still, his rudeness would be punished. But when? Ayman couldn't stand up to him and she had no idea when Iyad might return.

Maysoon rocked forward and back, grasping her blanket in both hands.

The words would not go away.

"You can save my life, Maysoon. Only you."

"You will never forgive yourself if you let them kill me."

Maysoon was not a particularly religious girl, but

without meaning to, she recited the *Salat al-Istikhaara*, the Prayer for Seeking Counsel. *"Allah, humma innee . . .*

O Allah, I ask guidance from Your knowledge, and power from Your might . . .

She squeezed her eyes shut and tightened her fists on the blanket. She couldn't remember the rest of the prayer. She tried, but no. It wasn't there.

Maysoon threw the covers out of her hands and opened her eyes. She would have to make this decision without Allah's counsel.

It was still midafternoon in the Pentagon's second basement. Patricia Simons jogged to Liz's office, skirting desks and colleagues as she went.

"We finished."

"Wait," Liz said. She hit speed dial for Hadley's office and the secretary put her right through. "Sir, Simons has something."

"Go," Hadley said.

Liz nodded at Simons.

"Um, well sir, we played the trace out as far as we could. Long story, lots of bounces."

"Ending up where?" Hadley asked.

"We can't get an exact location. It's a neighborhood, a service node east of Jerusalem."

"How big?"

"I can't say for sure, hundreds of subscribers, I'd guess. Maybe over a thousand. The Israelis would know."

"Send me the details."

"This could be it, sir," Liz said.

"Don't get your hopes up. Sounds like a large area. And this is the internet guy, not Bridget. Unless they're in the same place, we'd have to find him, take him alive, hope he knows where she is and that he'd tell us."

"Or that the Israelis could convince him to tell us," Liz said.

"Yeah, in a short time frame. Anyway, it's something to work with." Hadley hung up.

Chapter Thirty-nine

Will holed up in his hotel room all day. He'd sent a secure email to Hadley to pass on the word that General HaLevy had ordered him out of the country. The reply was, "Sit tight."

Without saying where he was, Will texted Drucker for an update on Ari. The report was good. The colonel was awake but would have to stay in the hospital at least one more night.

Will emailed Liz Michaels, who told him there was no new intel on Bridget. He was about ready to bounce off the walls. He dialed Hadley for at least the tenth time.

The secretary answered. "As I told you last time, Commander, and several times before that, the general is working the issue. You are to wait for his call."

"All right. Sorry. Thank you."

Will paced the room. He had the Israeli news on the TV in case Bridget's picture popped up. But it hadn't.

His phone rang.

"This is Hadley. We have something." He told Will about the trace of the A-HAI manifesto. "We're working with the Israelis to narrow it down. I got you a twenty-four-hour reprieve from General HaLevy. Stay where you are. You'll be back in the mix when the time is right."

Will sat on the bed. Outside his window, the Mediterranean was dark except for a tourist boat with multicolored lights running down the coast. On the promenade, the nightlife was in full swing—happy people strolling, laughing, drinking.

But somewhere out there, probably not far away, the woman he loved was in a terrorist hellhole. And if she wasn't dead already—please God, no—the deadline for getting her out was now only thirty-six hours away.

Maysoon sat with her head in her hands.

Damn them. Damn them all—the Zionists, the Americans, and damn Ra'ed and Iyad for their stupid plan and for bringing it to her house.

Idiots. Palestine will not achieve freedom by killing that woman.

Maysoon got out of bed and looked at herself in the mirror above her dresser. She appeared tired, stressed out. She wanted to be a midwife, or maybe a doctor. How could she, if she let this happen?

In her agonizing, Maysoon had conceived a plan. She hadn't meant to, but even thinking of helping the woman led her mind to explore how she could possibly do it. She had no way to judge whether her plan was any good. And she couldn't say for sure whether trading her honor for her soul was a good bargain.

But something told her that with her limited resources,

it was the right approach. In any case, she'd made her decision and she had no other ideas.

Maysoon thought about putting on a more attractive shirt but decided it was too dangerous and almost certainly not necessary. She brushed her hair and put on a headscarf, making sure it didn't cover much. She put on her glasses, packed another bag for the hostage, and went to the door.

Yes, damn them all.

Maysoon took a breath and let it out. She would be punished. But it would be nothing compared with how she would punish herself if she let this happen.

She opened her bedroom door and went downstairs. The hallway was empty. Maysoon heard the by now familiar sound of two men's rhythmic snoring in the guest room. She opened the basement door and went down.

Naji was sitting outside the storage room but stood when he saw her.

Maysoon smiled as if she was glad to see him. "I have more things for the woman."

"I don't know—"

"The others are sleeping. That means you are in charge, right?"

"Of course."

Maysoon smiled again to help him decide.

"All right. I will allow it." He slid the bolt and started to open the door.

Maysoon saw Bridget inside, curled up on the floor, her eyes closed. The handcuffs were off, lying against the wall. But her feet were still chained together. Bridget's face and clothes were filthy. Her breathing seemed shallow. She looked terribly alone and helpless.

The girl's resolve strengthened. She looked at Naji. "I am sorry I was rude to you earlier. This has all been so stressful." She lowered her gaze. "I am afraid."

"Do not worry. We will protect you. I will protect you."

Maysoon looked at him. They were about the same height and standing only a few inches apart. "Yes. I know. Thank you." She took the bold step of touching his arm. His breath caught.

She let a second go by. "May I go in, now?"

"Of course." Naji moved out of the way and pulled the door open so Maysoon could enter the cell.

Bridget sat up straight. She was surprised to see the girl. There were still plenty of supplies from her visit a few hours earlier.

Maysoon pulled the door closed behind her and crossed the room. She put down the bag and whispered, "When you hear the bolt slide open, wait one minute, then move fast, and as silently as you can. I will distract Naji."

Bridget's eyes widened. She nodded, then pointed at the shackles and chain on her feet.

Maysoon's body sagged but she recovered. "Naji."

"Yes." He answered from outside.

"You must remove the leg chain."

"It is not allowed."

Maysoon walked to the door and opened it.

"Are you in charge or not?"

"Yes, I am in charge."

"Then take off the chain. It is necessary."

He hesitated.

"Please, Naji." Maysoon cocked her head to the side.

"All right. I will do it for you."

Naji took the key off the hook and unlocked the leg irons. Then he left and closed the door, clearly not wanting to spend any more time than necessary in proximity to "women's problems."

Bridget rubbed her ankles. "Thank you."

"At the top of the stairs, go left, out the back. Then . . . I don't know. Climb the fence and run. It is the best I can do."

Bridget took Maysoon's hand. "It's a lot. Thank you. Come with me."

"No. I will not abandon my family or the movement."

Bridget nodded. "All right. Be careful. You are very brave. To save a life is not a small thing."

When Maysoon came back out of the storage room, Naji slid the bolt to the locked position.

"Again, I am sorry about earlier," she said. "You are not a bad guy. We should talk sometime."

"How about now?"

Maysoon paused as if to consider the idea. "Okay." She lowered her chin and let her eyes roll to the top of their sockets. She blinked. She did not have a lot of experience at flirting, but it wasn't her first time, either.

Naji grinned. "What shall we talk about?"

"Over there. Away from the woman." Maysoon indicated the other side of the stairway, a dark corner of the basement.

Naji smiled more broadly and took Maysoon's hand.

She pulled away. "Talk. Only talk. Over there."

Naji chuckled. "Of course. Talk." He turned, wasting no time moving to the other side of the room.

Maysoon reached behind her back and slid the bolt. She walked toward Naji, blocking his view of Bridget's door, resigned to what she would have to do.

Bridget started counting the seconds. She moved to the door and listened. There were voices in Arabic some distance away. The guard said something. The girl giggled and replied.

Twenty-five, twenty-six, twenty-seven. Bridget hoped the girl was counting, too.

Naji put his right hand on Maysoon's left forearm and rubbed up and down.

"What are you doing?" she teased. But she made no move to stop him.

"I like you. And I think you like me."

"Yes, but—"

"But, what?" Naji took hold of her arm.

Maysoon put a hand on his chest. It was not yet time for her full humiliation. She pushed him and moved to her right so they spun around. Now, her back was to the wall. And his back was to the cell.

Forty-six, forty-seven, forty-eight.

Naji put his left hand on Maysoon's waist. "What's the harm? I think you want to as much as I do." He pulled her in. His breath fogged her glasses.

Maysoon stopped counting. Her time was up.

Chapter Forty

Fifty-eight, fifty-nine, sixty.

Bridget pushed the door open. She put her head through and peered into the darkness. Just barely, she could see the slimy one's back. "Naji" the girl had called him. Maysoon stood in front of him, looking over his shoulder.

Bridget nodded.

Maysoon leaned toward Naji and they kissed. She put her hands on his head to hold him in place.

Bridget moved to the stairway and went up three at a time. She turned left in the hall and reached the back door in a few steps

As Bridget took hold of the door handle, someone grabbed her hair from behind and pulled with such force that she fell flat on her back and banged her head on the floor. She was dazed.

Ra'ed fell on her, put a knee on her chest and took hold of both her wrists. He leaned in, his face over hers, his hair matted from sleeping, his nightshirt hanging loose. He spat in her face.

Bridget's head throbbed. Her side wound ached. She

raised her right leg to hook Ra'ed's head, but he evaded the move. All his weight was on her chest. She had trouble breathing. Her vaunted martial arts skills failed her.

Naji came to the top of the stairs out of breath, his eyes wide. Ra'ed shouted something at him in Arabic. Then Maysoon came up behind Naji. Her headscarf hung off her hair. Her face was flushed.

"Ahhh," Ra'ed said. It was clear in any language that he understood what had happened.

Ra'ed flipped Bridget over and put his knee in the small of her back. She fought, but he was too strong. He pulled her right arm up between her shoulder blades. "Do not move or I will break it. I swear by Allah." He pulled harder.

Bridget cried out in pain and stopped fighting him.

Ra'ed issued an order. Naji pushed Maysoon out of the way and ran down the steps. Ra'ed used his free hand to pull Bridget's hair and twist her neck so she was forced to look at Maysoon.

"I see that you had help. We will deal with her, also. Maybe I will let you watch."

The large man Bridget called Ballou came out of the bedroom, looking half-asleep. Ra'ed said something and Ballou reached into the room to get a rifle.

Naji returned with the handcuffs and leg irons. He and Ra'ed put them in place, cuffing Bridget's wrists behind her back this time. She let her body go limp on the floor.

Ra'ed stood and brushed himself off. "Stand up, American bitch."

Bridget struggled, using the wall for support. As soon as she was up, Ra'ed slapped her with the back of his hand. She staggered. Maysoon let out a small scream, cut off by a look from Ra'ed.

As Bridget recovered, he took hold of her throat and pressed her against the wall. His beard dripped with spittle. The veins on his forehead looked like they might burst.

"If you do this again, I will kill you and everyone in this house. Do you understand?"

Bridget didn't respond. Ra'ed squeezed her neck harder.

"Yes, yes." Her voice was raspy. She glanced at Maysoon. The girl was leaning against the opposite wall shaking. "She did nothing," Bridget said.

"Ach!" Ra'ed pulled Bridget forward by the neck, then slammed her against the wall again. "Even now you lie to me."

He issued another order and Ballou took hold of Bridget. Ra'ed went to Maysoon and slapped her. She cried out and collapsed. Her glasses flew down the hallway and hit the far wall as an older woman came around the corner from upstairs, pulling her robe tight around her nightgown. Maysoon ran to her.

Even though it was in Arabic, Bridget could more or less follow the shouting match that came next. The woman was angry at Ra'ed first, then at Maysoon, then at Naji, then back to Ra'ed.

Then the woman moved toward Bridget with her fists raised and screamed at her in English. "What did you do? You used my daughter. Now we are all in danger!"

Ra'ed held the woman off and forced her back to Maysoon. He turned to Bridget. "The woman is weak and her daughter is a whore, but she is right about that."

While Naji and Ballou pointed their guns at Maysoon

and her mother, Ra'ed forced Bridget down the first few steps to the basement. Bridget tripped on the chain and fell the rest of the way. With her hands cuffed behind her, she had nothing with which to soften the fall. Her left shoulder hit the concrete floor, but somehow her head was spared.

Ra'ed kicked her in the stomach. "Get up."

Bridget couldn't.

Ra'ed kicked her again, then grabbed her hair and one arm and dragged her into the cell. He dropped her in the far-right corner, away from her things. Then he took the mattress and half-full water bottle and threw them out of the room. He dumped the bag of supplies Maysoon had brought and stomped on them, then kicked them in Bridget's direction.

"Do not move." Ra'ed stormed out of the room and returned a few seconds later with a hammer and a large nail. He pounded the nail into the floor between Bridget's feet, put a link of the leg chain over it and used the hammer to bend the nail down until its head dug into the concrete.

Ra'ed stood and looked at her, out of breath and red-faced. He went to the hook outside the cell and came back with the key. He uncuffed Bridget's hands and recuffed them in front of her. "That is your only privilege. Do not lose it."

He went out of the room again but reappeared with a large metal bowl. He threw it at her, and she had to raise her hands to deflect it. That shot a pain through her shoulder. Ra'ed turned off the light and closed the door. Bridget heard the bolt slide.

She fumbled in the darkness for the bowl and threw up into it. She put it between her knees, pushed the hair off her face and retched again. Bending over the bowl, she breathed in short, uneven bursts. She put her hands over her nose and mouth to prevent hyperventilation. It took some time for the feeling to pass.

Bridget leaned back against the wall, sweating and shivering. Her shoulder and head throbbed. The bare floor was cold. The room was pitch black and she couldn't reach the light switch.

She moved the bowl to the side, stretched her legs and reached up to touch the tender spot on the back of her head. None of her physical conditioning or POW training had prepared her for this.

Bridget thought about what Ra'ed might do to Maysoon. She kicked at her leg chain. The girl had done a brave thing and now she would pay for it. She did it because Bridget had convinced her. Bridget was good at convincing people to do things they didn't want to do, things that would hurt them and their families.

She kicked the chain again. Bridget needed to put such thoughts out of her mind. She had done what she had to do and it almost worked. There was no way she could help Maysoon now.

Bridget had to go back to basics—don't panic, stay healthy, stay alive. But for what? It seemed more likely than ever that she'd never get out of that house.

In the hallway, Maysoon held onto her mother, but it was a one-sided hug. Mrs. al-Hamdani was busy staring down the two fighters and was showing no sympathy for her daughter.

Ra'ed came up from the basement. "Come. We go upstairs."

"That is my bedroom," Mrs. al-Hamdani said. "You will not—"

"Go!" Ra'ed leaned in, nose-to-nose with her, screaming and spitting. "Go or I will kill your daughter the traitor right now."

Mrs. al-Hamdani pushed him away, daring him to hit her. But she complied. She picked up Maysoon's glasses and led the girl to the stairs.

The men followed them up. Ra'ed went into the master bedroom and searched it. He opened every drawer of the faux-Louis XVI dresser and threw the contents onto the floor. He ripped all the clothes off their hangers and rummaged through the boxes on the closet floor.

He picked up a framed photo of Mrs. al-Hamdani's late husband, the founder of A-HAI, and took it to the doorway where the women waited. "He would be ashamed." Ra'ed smashed the frame against the doorpost, sending glass flying in all directions, then tossed what was left into the closet.

In the night table drawer, he found a small pistol and a box of ammunition. He put them in his pocket. Then he picked up the phone, yanked its wire out of the wall and threw it out of the room.

Ra'ed moved to the attached bathroom and came out with a scissors and a nail file. He walked up to Maysoon in the hallway. "Your cell phone."

She stared at him as if in a daze, unable to face what was happening, what she had caused.

Ra'ed slapped her. "Phone!" Her hand trembled as she gave it to him. He turned to the guards. "Let them in."

The two men stepped aside, and the women picked their way through the debris to sit on the green-and-white frilly comforter on Mrs. al-Hamdani's bed.

Ra'ed stood in front of them. "My obligation to respect you and your house has ended. Any problem—any problem—and I will do what I have to do."

He left the room and closed the door.

Maysoon's mother looked at her with more anger in her eyes than the girl had ever seen. "How could you?" she asked through clenched teeth. Then she slapped Maysoon in the same spot Ra'ed had hit.

Maysoon stopped breathing. Her mother had never struck her before.

"You betrayed the movement. You betrayed me. And you betrayed yourself. Now, what will become of us?" Mrs. al-Hamdani put her face in her hands and burst into tears.

"*Umi*," Maysoon said. She put her hands on her mother's shoulders but the woman pushed them off. Mrs. al-Hamdani turned to look at her daughter. Her anger gave way to disappointment, then despair. Then she couldn't look at her daughter at all anymore.

Mrs. al-Hamdani lay down and turned away. Maysoon stayed on the edge of the bed, tears streaming down her cheeks.

A few minutes later, there was hammering, first at the bedroom door, then at the door from the bathroom to the hallway. She saw Naji climbing up a ladder outside the window. He raised a hammer and nailed it shut.

"*Umi*, what will we do?" Maysoon sobbed.

Her mother didn't move or open her eyes. "Pray, stupid girl. Pray that Allah eases Ra'ed's anger before he kills us."

Maysoon composed herself. "Ayman will be home in the morning. He will get us out."

"Oh, Allah!" Mrs. al-Hamdani opened her eyes now and pushed herself up on one elbow. "I hope he does not come home. Ra'ed is more likely to kill him than to kill us." She lay back down and started sobbing again.

Maysoon's body slouched. She lay down next to her mother. How could she have been so stupid? So, so stupid. She let the enemy use her. She turned her back on her people, put her family in danger, debased herself by kissing that worm, Naji, and maybe ensured that the hostage would be killed.

No. She would not spare a thought for that woman. She was evil, and Maysoon had her own problems to worry about. Even if Ra'ed didn't kill them, she would have to live with the betrayal, the humiliation. What would she say to Ayman? To Iyad? Maysoon would be an outcast with no future, no education, no husband. It would be better to die. At least then, they would have to honor her.

How had she not thought of all this before?

She looked at her mother. She had never seen her so angry. But the anger wasn't the worst of it. The disappointment in her mother's eyes was far worse.

Maysoon put her glasses on the nightstand, turned her face to the pillow and prayed for the second time that day. "*Allahuma aghfir li . . .*" O Allah, forgive me all my sins, great and small . . .

She had been a good girl all her life. Surely, Allah would forgive her, provide her with a way to be free of the shame she had brought on herself and her family. Surely, he would.

Chapter Forty-one

Faraz's overnight stop was a tent city in a remote corner of a Saudi military base. They kept the A-11AI men well away from the soldiers, but Faraz saw the lights of the base buildings and the efficient perimeter security. And the American weapons.

He sipped tea with several of his men as Saudi soldiers handed out breakfast bags with bread and hard-boiled eggs. Pots of tea brewed on camp stoves. The buses idled nearby.

The men ate and checked their weapons without being told. They had been ordered to put their costumes away. Iyad made clear it was time to get serious.

Assali arrived in a Humvee from his night of relative comfort, courtesy of the base commander. There had been no chance for Faraz to get anywhere near a sat phone.

The boss joined a conversation between Iyad and a Saudi officer well away from the rest of the men. The officer seemed to be explaining something, pointing to the men and the buses, then toward the road that led north out of the base.

Assali nodded and said something to Iyad, who made

a half-bow to the officer, then walked toward Faraz and the other men.

"*Yalla shabaab.*" Let's go boys.

Will's wakeup call from Liz Michaels came at five a.m. He was downstairs and dressed for action when Sergeant Peretz pulled up in an SUV half an hour later.

"They wouldn't tell me anything on the phone," he said through the window.

"All I know is that with help from your people in Washington, our technicians have identified a target. I will take you to the tech center."

Will squeezed into the passenger seat. "Any update on Colonel Ben-Yosef?"

"He is awake and he is angry."

"Angry?"

"He wants out. General HaLevy has ordered him to stay in the hospital, for now."

At the tech center, Will found Major Drucker with Corporal Golani, the internet wizard. He was pointing at the shaded area of a map on his computer screen.

"This is the node your people found. And"—he zoomed in—"we have identified this area as the sub-circuit from which the file originated. There are a hundred and twenty-seven subscribers." Golani widened the view again. "You can see the location, the northeastern edge of what we call Greater Jerusalem, maybe eight kilometers from the Old City."

"Looks like a densely populated area," Will said.

"Very hostile, too," Drucker told him. "We need to narrow it down."

"This is not a tech issue," Golani said. "We have gone as far as we can go. Now it is an intel issue. We need to know who lives there that might do this."

"Ha," Drucker said. "Any of them might do it."

The buses stopped in late morning at a sunbaked crossroads. Faraz saw only sand and hills in all directions.

The last road sign they'd passed indicated twenty-five kilometers to *"Al-hudud Al-Urduniya,"* the Jordanian border.

The heat hit Faraz as he emerged from the bus to consult with Iyad and Bashar. Assali stayed in the air conditioning.

"We wait here," Iyad said. "Not long, I think."

"Wait for what?" Faraz asked.

"The rest of the men."

Half an hour later, a long line of assorted vehicles arrived—sedans, station wagons, SUVs—in various states of disrepair. Many were dented and some belched gray smoke. Most had Jordanian license plates. They were empty except for their drivers.

"What's this about?" Faraz asked Iyad.

"We cannot drive into Israel on tour buses. We split up, go into Jordan in small groups, then cross into Israel tomorrow. Some will be stopped, but whoever gets through will rendezvous at a safe house for the attack. Gather the men. I will provide the details."

* * *

It turned out that the question of who in the communications subcircuit might have sent the manifesto was at least partly a tech issue.

Will watched while Corporal Golani downloaded a file of subscribers sent over by the service provider. Then Golani ran a comparison of that list with Israel's list of suspected or known terrorists.

Drucker's cynical view was not exactly true, but it wasn't far off. Of the hundred and twenty-seven subscribers, eighty had surnames that were on the watch list for one reason or another.

"They could be terrorists or distant cousins of suspects or not related at all," Drucker said. "It will take hours to sift through and figure out if any of them is a realistic potential source of the manifesto."

"Send it to our people," Will said. "If they work on it, too, the process should go faster. They might even know some things about those folks that you don't."

Golani looked doubtful. "I will ask for permission."

Iyad led the effort to distribute the men among the vehicles, made sure their weapons and costumes were hidden in the cargo holds or under seats, and gave out a limited number of counterfeit IDs. The documents looked amateurish to Faraz, but Iyad assured him they were sufficient for the first border.

"You are with me in this one." Iyad pointed to the lead SUV.

"Shouldn't I be with the men I trained, to make sure they do their jobs?"

"No, Disco Boy, you will be with me."

Faraz decided not to argue. Best not to raise Iyad's suspicions any higher, although this would make it more difficult to get away or make a call. He got into the SUV as ordered. He sat in the backseat, alongside one of Iyad's fighters, a quiet but competent man named Jamal.

The twenty-something driver twisted in his seat, showing Faraz a broad smile, and reached back to shake his hand. "I am Waleed. You are the American?"

"Yes. Khayal. How did you know?"

"Everyone has heard of the American jihadi who saved Ayman al-Hamdani from the garbageman."

"I think the story has grown with time."

"Of course! Enjoy it." Waleed was clean-shaven, short and wiry, with unruly black hair and good English.

"And where are you from?"

"Jerusalem. My Israeli ID card should get us across, no problem."

"How do you have an Israeli ID?"

"I was born in East Jerusalem, which they call 'Israel.' So, if we are born in 'Israel,' we have the right to be there. It is different from the card a Jew gets, but mostly I can go where I please."

"That sounds useful."

"Yes, very useful." Waleed laughed. "But they also know every time I cross a checkpoint. Right now, they think I'm visiting my grandmother in Jordan." He chuckled. "Poor Granny has been ill, you know."

Iyad got into the front seat. "Yes, Waleed's granny has had many illnesses. And yet, she moves house often—

Amman, Irbid near the Syrian border, recently Aqaba."
He and Waleed laughed.

It struck Faraz that Waleed was the kind of unassuming
guy that security forces would overlook, unlike Iyad and
Ra'ed, who looked like fighters, and Bashar, whose long
hair and pious attitude tagged him as an ideologue or guru.

Iyad reached his hand out the window, waved and
thrust it forward. "*Allah hu akbar*," he shouted. The chant
undulated down the convoy and came back to them.

Waleed put the SUV in gear and hit the gas, letting the
wheels spin and throw up sand until they caught some
traction and shot the vehicle forward.

At the Jordanian border, Faraz watched as half a dozen
of their vehicles moved through without any problems.
The guards took a quick look at the documents and made
only a cursory inspection of the cargo areas.

"Where are the others?" he asked.

"Up and down the border," Iyad said. "Some official
crossings, some not."

Waleed and his ID and his passengers were waved
through. "It is good to see you, my brother," he shouted
at the guard as he drove by without stopping.

Once inside Jordan, the men relaxed. Waleed passed
around a pack of cigarettes and told them, "We are good
now, until tonight."

They sped north on Jordanian Highway Number Five
and blew through the market town of Ma'an. They skirted
the Dead Sea and held their noses at the sulphury smell.
An hour later, they arrived at a farmhouse off an unmarked
dirt road.

Bridget hadn't eaten anything or had any water since dinner the previous evening, before the escape attempt. She had spent a lot of time pulling at the nail that held her leg chain to the floor, but Ra'ed had done a good job hammering it deep into the concrete. She decided not to waste any more of her waning energy.

It was dark in the storage room. Bridget had slept, but she didn't know for how long. It must be afternoon by now. She had no way to really judge it. Her shoulder felt better, but there was a bump on the back of her head where it had hit the floor.

Ra'ed burst in and turned on the light, blinding her. She curled into a protective position. He came halfway to her and stopped.

As Bridget's eyes adjusted, she saw him recoil from the stench. She had used the metal bowl twice, and it reeked.

"Food." Ra'ed tossed her a paper bag and turned to go.

"Please, I—"

"Ach." Without turning around, he turned off the light and slammed the door.

Ra'ed returned to the bedroom he shared with the other two men.

"What will we do now?" Naji asked.

"We wait. Nothing has changed."

"We should kill the hostage and go," Naji said. "Maysoon may have betrayed us to the Zionists. Let us go down. We will take care of the woman for you."

Ra'ed crossed the room and slapped him. "You are not giving orders! You were fooled by a girl. Now, you want to have your way with the woman. Stop thinking with your *zabr*. We stick to the mission for the good of the movement. Tomorrow, if something needs to be done, I will do it."

After spending the whole day at the tech center, Will was eating a meal of vending machine snacks in the staff lounge when Corporal Golani appeared at the door. "Commander, please come. I have something to show you."

He followed Golani to the surveillance unit, where a screen showed a satellite image of the subcircuit.

Golani sat down and clicked the mouse. The image zoomed in to a two-block radius. He drew a red circle with his cursor. "We dismissed this house at first because the internet account is in a name that's not on our terrorist registry. But your people figured out that it is a fake name. The person does not exist. So, we dug deeper to see who the original owner was and cross-referenced the name with our terror database. Decades ago, the owner was a close friend of Marwan al-Hamdani, a founder of the A-HAI terrorist group, who was killed in Gaza years ago. This set off alarm bells at the top of our military intelligence and at the DIA, but they won't tell us why. Anyway, the widow still lives there. The son was among the prisoners released last week. A nephew is the group's military leader."

"You think they maybe have sent the Manifesto, maybe have Davenport?"

"More than think. We pulled the satellite video and local surveillance cameras." Golani made some keystrokes and showed a series of videos tracking a black sedan through the neighborhood to the house and into its carport.

Will was leaning over his shoulder. "A car arrived. So what?"

"We traced where it came from." Golani opened another window on the screen. It showed a map of the central West Bank and Jerusalem. "This red dot is the house. The blue line is the track of the car. We cannot trace it back farther, but it comes into our surveillance two kilometers from the storage building in the olive grove, about an hour before you and our team raided it."

Will stood up. "Where's Drucker?"

"On his way to a rendezvous point. Sergeant Peretz is waiting outside to take you. Good luck, Commander."

CHAPTER FORTY-TWO

The rendezvous was in an alley on the edge of a village that had been absorbed by Jerusalem's urban sprawl. This time, the Israelis were taking no chances. The force was three times the size of the one that got ambushed.

Will arrived at dusk to find Major Drucker consulting with Colonel Ben-Yosef, who sat on the bumper of an armored vehicle. The upper part of Ari's right arm was wrapped in a bulky cast and strapped to his body. His wrist was in a sling. The right leg of his camo pants bulged from a bandage underneath.

"Colonel, how are you?"

"I'm all right."

"I'm sorry about what happened. I—"

"Forget it. We have work to do." Ari had his fatigues on but no body armor.

"With all due respect, you probably shouldn't be here," Will said.

"Everyone tells me that, but I should say it to you. You showed that you cannot follow orders."

Will had no reply.

"Tell me, Commander, why are you really here. What

is your connection to Ms. Davenport, or, as you called her the other day, Bridget?"

Will hesitated. "Colonel, our bosses have an arrangement. I'm here on the authority of— "

"Yes, yes, a three-star general. You will sit with me in the command truck while the team goes in for your . . . what? Shall we say 'friend'? If you make a move to go off on your own, I'll have you arrested. How's that for an arrangement?"

Will was taken aback but recovered. His personal feelings, and Ari's, were irrelevant. "Look, I apologized for getting you shot, but it was your bad intel that got us there and it was your decision to follow me in. This time, our people confirm the intel, and I'll be damned if I'm going to sit in a truck half a click from the action with you and Sergeant Peretz."

Drucker spoke up. "You'll be the next to get shot."

"Major, I commanded a unit like this. I don't expect to be out front. Second wave, rear position, but I will be up there."

"I cannot authorize—" Ari started.

Will took out his phone. "Fine. This is a high-profile mission. I'll call the White House, and the president will call the prime minister, and you will get your orders."

It was a bluff. The best he could do was call Hadley, and there was no time to play phone tag.

Ari looked at Drucker.

"Second wave," Drucker said. "You stay back until called forward."

"Agreed."

"I see you have the pistol I lent you," Ari said.

"Yes. I could use something bigger."

"No. And the gun is only for self-defense."

"But—"

Ari raised a hand to cut him off. "I said no. One more thing, Commander. We are not going gently this time."

"Meaning?"

"Meaning we are going to assume that if Miss Davenport is there, she is being held in the basement. This house has the same design as the other, same as thousands in the West Bank. We will stay clear of the basement. The rest of the building will be the hot zone."

"That's a big risk."

"We already lived through the alternative. We will not do that again."

"You seem pretty confident. Corporal Golani said you know something you're not telling me."

Ari looked like he was about to answer but changed his mind. "Your people will have to tell you."

Will boarded one of the backup team vehicles and it moved into position behind Drucker's unit. Six exhaust plumes rose into the evening air.

Will's right leg bounced. *Come on. Come on.*

"Assault team is coming," his driver said.

Will turned to see an Israeli Humvee with a missile launcher mounted on its roof speeding up the street. The vehicle went past him, heading straight for another one coming from the other direction, fitted with a large machine gun.

The two screeched to a halt in front of the target house, about a hundred meters from Will, and opened fire.

The first missile shattered the window to the left of the

front door and devastated the kitchen. The second hit the other side, exploding in the dining room where Faraz had had lunch and destroying the tacky sofa and TV just beyond.

Fire from the heavy machine gun sprayed high and low across the width of the house, shattering windows and piercing walls.

Ra'ed heard the vehicles. He ran out of the bedroom in his underwear and was blown back into it by the first explosion. He landed on the floor, and when he stood, he was nearly knocked down again by the second blast.

He finally emerged into the hall to find the larger of his two colleagues dead on the floor. Ra'ed's first thought was to go to the basement and use the hostage as a shield. But how far could he possibly get? And his survival was not the objective. Pressuring and distracting the Zionists was the objective and, if possible, getting the ransom. That was gone now.

This was jihad. He would take as many of them with him as he could.

Ra'ed shouted an order to Naji in the basement. "*Aqtulaha, aqtulaha alaan!*" Kill her, kill her now.

He took cover behind what was left of the kitchen wall and said the *Shahada*. Then, Ra'ed raised his AK and came around the wall firing. "*Allah hu akbar,*" he shouted. "*Huriyat li-Filasteen!*" God is great. Freedom for Palestine.

Large caliber bullets from the vehicle-mounted machine gun threw him back. He was dead before he hit the floor.

* * *

Bridget heard the explosions and gunfire and knew what was happening. At least, she hoped she knew. She pulled her chain to the maximum and pressed herself into the corner in case the house came down around her.

She also heard Ra'ed's order. She didn't understand the words, but the tone was enough. The next burst of shots made her cringe, and something, or someone, hit the floor above her cell.

Bridget steeled herself in the darkness. She ran her hands along the floor to her left, searching for the metal bowl.

The bolt slid and the door flew open, flooding the room with light. Bridget shielded her eyes with her forearm and saw Naji raise his AK.

Her movement was awkward with her hands still cuffed. There was a sharp pain in her side when she twisted to the left. But she came back around with all the speed she could muster and flung the contents of the bowl at Naji.

He flinched and turned away, then wiped urine and vomit from his right cheek. He cursed, threw down his gun and ran at Bridget, his eyes wide. She swung the bowl and hit him on the right side of his head.

Naji went down, dazed. Bridget raised the bowl again and took a bead on his forehead. As she swung the bowl, Naji raised a hand to stop her. He got hold of her wrist and squeezed. She fought him, but her strength was depleted. He pushed her back and slammed her onto the floor. The bowl rolled away.

* * *

Will was out of patience. He left the vehicle and took off at a run, ignoring the young officer who commanded the backup team. He took cover behind the assault Humvee as it launched another salvo into the house.

Drucker shouted a command and the big weapons went quiet. Twenty Israeli commandos ran forward, with Will right behind. He caught up with Drucker at the front door.

"Jackson, get down, stay back."

"Bullshit." Will pushed past him.

Naji was on top of Bridget now, holding both of her cuffed wrists above her head with his left hand. She raised a knee, but the chain only allowed it to get a few inches off the floor.

He leaned into her, pressing himself against her. His right hand groped her breasts, and he smiled that smile Bridget and Maysoon had come to hate. He said something in Arabic and grinded into her.

Bridget squirmed to the left, looking for an angle to head-butt him. Naji put both his hands on her throat and squeezed. His eyes bored into hers. Bridget grabbed his wrists but couldn't move them. She twisted her body to throw him off balance, but he was too strong. She was gagging, struggling to breathe.

Naji straightened his arms and put more weight on her neck. Her head exploded with pain. He cursed. His spittle hit her cheek.

The pistol shot was deafening in the small space.

Naji collapsed onto Bridget. His blood splattered her face. What remained of his head fell to the right of hers. His hands loosened on her throat. She gulped for air.

Someone crossed the room and threw Naji off. A large man stood over her, silhouetted against the light coming from the doorway.

Bridget's hands rubbed her neck, as if to open her windpipe. She blinked. Her brain could not process what her eyes were telling it.

She spoke, but it came out more like a croak. "What the . . ."

Will knelt down and cradled her head, wiping Naji's blood from her cheeks with one hand, pointing his gun toward the doorway with the other. "Yeah, it's me. Just breathe."

Bridget closed her eyes, then opened them. Will was still there. She managed a couple of breaths, reached out to touch him. She started shaking.

"Easy, now. It's all over." Will helped her sit up and pulled her head to his chest.

Bridget put her hands on his cheeks. The handcuff chain caught on his chin.

"It's not . . . a dream?"

Will smiled. "No, kiddo. But it would be a good one."

"How is it possible?"

"You've got friends in high places. And you've got me. You should be asking what took us so long."

Bridget took hold of his shirt and pulled him close. She started sobbing.

Someone came to the doorway. Bridget cringed and

sought cover behind Will. He lowered his gun when he saw Drucker.

"It's okay," Will said.

"The house is secure," Drucker reported. "And I see you have the hostage."

"Yes, I do."

It took a couple of minutes for Bridget's breathing to return to normal. Will took a water bottle from outside the cell, gave her a drink and rinsed her face. He found the hammer and pried up the nail that held her to the floor.

"You think you can stand?"

Bridget took his hands and made it to her feet. She was unsteady and leaned on him as they walked out of the cell.

"The key," Bridget said, looking toward the wall hook.

Will got the cuffs and leg irons off. "Need a lift?" he said, indicating the stairs.

"Maybe an assist." Bridget took hold of his forearm and climbed the steps one at a time.

In the hallway, they sidestepped the two bodies and found Ari directing the troops.

Bridget stopped short. "Colonel."

Ari smiled. "I told you to call me Ari."

Bridget smiled back. "Ari. Thank you. You're wounded."

"It's nothing."

Bridget looked at the two terrorists dead on the floor. She pointed at Ra'ed. "That one was the leader."

Will put his arm around her and got a knowing look

from Ari. "Come outside," Will said. "The docs should have a look at you."

"Wait. What about the women?"

"Upstairs," Ari said.

Bridget walked past him to the foot of stairway.

Ari put a hand on her arm. "I wouldn't."

Bridget shook him off. "No. I need to." She went up, with Will close behind.

From the master bedroom doorway, she saw Maysoon lying faceup in her mother's bed, her eyes closed, her mouth open. The girl's body was riddled with shrapnel and gunshot wounds. There was so much blood, Bridget could barely make out the university logo on her sweatshirt.

Maysoon's mother was on her knees on the floor with her back to Bridget. An Israeli medic tended to a wound on her head, while another soldier stood over her, rifle at the ready. The woman reached up with one hand to touch her daughter. "Maysoon, Maysoon," she wailed.

The floor creaked as Bridget stepped into the room.

Mrs. al-Hamdani turned. "You!" She lunged, but the soldier blocked her path with his rifle. She screamed and cursed until her words devolved into sobs and she collapsed onto the floor.

Bridget walked to the bed. Maysoon's face looked peaceful despite the carnage to her body. Her long, dark hair was splayed on the pillow, the first time Bridget had seen her without a headscarf. Her plump cheeks made her look younger than she was. Her eyeglasses were undisturbed on the nightstand.

"She tried to help me," Bridget said. "She was . . ."

Her voice trailed off.

Will put his hands on Bridget's shoulders. She felt him breathing behind her, his chest against her back.

They stood there for several seconds. Then Bridget swallowed hard and turned away. "Please. Take me out of here."

Chapter Forty-three

There were a dozen people gathered around Liz Michaels's desk in the Task Force Epsilon director's office. They had a live audio feed of the Israeli operation on her computer, with Sergeant Peretz translating from the command van.

They heard the explosions and gunfire. They heard the report that "the American" went in against orders. They heard voices call "all clear" from various parts of the house.

Then there was nothing for several of the longest seconds Liz had ever lived through.

Finally, two words in Hebrew and Sergeant Peretz's translation. "Hostage secured."

"Yes!" Liz shouted. She pounded the desk with both fists. The folks behind her cheered and clapped. Liz blinked away tears. She stood to hug Patricia Simons and everyone else she could get ahold of. Someone produced a bottle of champagne and opened it. An array of paper cups and coffee mugs competed to catch the foam.

Liz's phone rang. The caller ID indicated it was Hadley. She dried her eyes with one hand, hit the speaker button with the other.

"Sounds like a party," he said.

"Yes, sir. Care to join us?"

"Maybe later. Well done, all of you."

"Thank you, sir. All we need now is to see her face, hear her voice. I'll ask for a video call."

"That might have to wait a while. Bridget is on her way to the hospital. She's okay but I hear she's had a tough time of it. We'll get you a call when we can, but it'll likely be a few days before we can get her home."

The crowd quieted. "Of course, sir."

"And let's not forget we have a high-priority mission in progress. Intel indicates some strange movement in Saudi and Jordan. We have a lot of work to do."

The Jordanian farmhouse was abandoned, but Waleed had brought some food—bread, potato chips and cookies. While he and Jamal dug into the stash, Iyad went outside for a smoke.

Faraz followed. "What's going on?"

"Some of the men have papers. They are crossing at regular checkpoints. The rest of us will cross where we can."

"But Waleed has papers."

"We don't want the Zionists to know he's back."

"And where are we going?"

"*Al-Quds.*" The Holy—Arabic shorthand for Jerusalem.

Will held Bridget's hand in the back of the Israeli ambulance all the way to the hospital.

The crew started an IV and treated the bruises where

the terrorist had hit her. They put a fresh dressing on her Syria wound, which somehow had stayed closed through the ordeal.

There was nothing they could do about the smell.

"Stay with me," Bridget said through the oxygen mask they made her wear.

"Count on it."

Ayman sat on a beanbag chair in his friend Munir's bedroom, amid stacks of technology magazines, video game cartridges and Islamic texts. His head was down, his hands clasped behind his neck. A soccer game played on the TV, on mute. Their computers auto-scrolled comments on the manifesto. Ayman had given up on not letting his friend see him cry.

News of the raid on his house had reached them in a panicked phone call from a neighbor. It took an hour until the details were confirmed. His sister was dead. His mother arrested. The house destroyed. The Zionists had a manhunt on for him.

"Maysoon . . . dead," was all Ayman could say. He rubbed his eyes.

Munir sat in his desk chair, as shaken as Ayman. "Maysoon was the sister I never had. She was a great person. A patriot." His voice cracked. "Maysoon is a *shahida*, now." It was the rarely used feminine form of martyr.

"I never imagined that was her destiny. Mine, perhaps. But not hers."

"Allah has chosen our path and we struggle to find it," Munir said. "That is the essence of jihad."

Ayman wasn't sure he believed that, but he needed

something to hold onto, so it would have to do. He nodded and rocked forward and back. Why had he let Ra'ed keep the hostage at his house? Why had he not contacted Iyad?

He knew why. Because Iyad had no doubt authorized the move. How could he do such a thing?

No matter, now. It was done. It was jihad. His sister was gone. He would never see his mother again. But the jihad would go on.

Munir leaned forward and put his hand on Ayman's shoulder. Physically, Munir was the opposite of Ayman— short, thin and bookish, without noticeable fat or muscle on his body. He had a moustache and goatee and needed a haircut. "Ayman, this is an unspeakable situation, but you cannot stay here."

"But you are my friend." Ayman had known Munir since grade school. They learned computer skills together during long hours in the room where they sat now. Video game skills, too.

"Yes. But it is suicide for you to stay here and dangerous for me and my family. They know we are friends and we are barely two kilometers from your house. The Zionists will come looking for you, and soon."

Ayman sat up. "You are right. Damn all Zionists." He took out his phone. His mother and sister smiled at him from the lock screen. Each held a Ramadan pastry. He had snapped the photo only a few months earlier. Ayman put two fingers of his right hand to his lips, then touched the screen. Then he turned the phone over, removed the battery and SIM card, and put the parts back into his pocket.

"I have somewhere I can stay tonight," Ayman said. "Tomorrow . . . well, tomorrow I will have more options."

"What options?"

"Never mind. Get the keys to your father's car and grab some food and water. I will leave, but you must take me."

General HaLevy opened the front door of his house south of Tel Aviv to let Ari in. "I told you to stay in the hospital."

"My apologies."

"Maybe you are spending too much time with the American, learning to ignore orders."

"I stayed back until the end. I'm fine."

They went into the living room and sat. The room had yellow wallpaper printed with small desert flowers, chosen by the general's late wife. Souvenirs of their travels and family pictures filled every surface. Ari could see himself, smiling, in every direction, along with Rivka and Tali.

"You want tea? Maybe something stronger?"

"No, thank you. I won't stay long."

"How is your arm?"

"It's fine, unless I want to punch someone."

HaLevy chuckled. "And I see you are limping. Please, sit. It was a good day, Ari."

"Yes, but I'm worried. Our guys and the Americans report lots of movement on country roads in Saudi and Jordan. The al-Hamdani boy is on the loose. Tomorrow is Purim. It doesn't feel right."

"You are going to say we should cancel the parades."

"From a security point of view, yes."

"But you know the government will not do that. It's not our way. Life goes on in spite of threats, in spite of attacks."

"I know. I believe in that, too. But—"

"You have a good security plan. Use extra units if you have to."

"Reserves?"

"No. Calling up the reserves would create a panic, spoil the holiday. And it's not necessary. Take whatever units you need from the active force and the police."

"All right." Ari paused. "I didn't expect you to ask the prime minister for reserves, but it was worth a try."

HaLevy smiled. "If you're up to it, you're in charge in Jerusalem. Keep me posted. I'll be at headquarters in Tel Aviv to monitor the whole country and liaise with the cabinet, if necessary. Now, go home to your wife and daughter and get some rest."

Ayman and Munir parked next to an Israeli pickup truck on the edge of a gas station on Highway 90 in the Jordan Valley, well outside the glare of its lights. Ayman put his phone back together, turned it on and tossed it into the back of the pickup. "Go, go," he ordered.

Munir pulled back onto the road and headed north for ten minutes.

Ayman directed him to turn east off the highway onto a dirt road, then left onto a two-track through scrub land. Munir's father's old sedan bumped over the rocks and through the ruts dug out by decades of water runoff. In the passenger seat, Ayman held a bag of snacks and bottles of water between his feet.

After a few minutes, the headlights illuminated an olive grove.

Munir slowed down as the road became rougher, then swung right. In front of them in the clearing was the now empty storage building.

"Here," Ayman said.

They got out. The latch on the door hung loose. Ayman went inside and found the light switch.

The room had been ransacked. The furniture was overturned. Plates and plastic cups were strewn on the floor. The carpet was crumpled against the wall and the trap door to the basement was open.

Munir walked in. "What is this place?"

"It is, well, many things. My cousin Iyad has used it for operations several times. It looks like the Zionists have been here."

"What if they come back?"

"Why should they? They have searched it, passed it by. I only need to be here for a few hours. Help me." The two men lifted the back of the sofa and set it on its legs.

"I should go," Munir said.

"Yes. Thank you, my friend." Ayman embraced Munir and kissed him on both cheeks. "And you never saw me. You don't know where I am. My life and yours depend on it."

"Yes, of course. Good luck."

Ari slipped into bed fresh from washing up as best he could without getting his bandages too wet. He had succeeded in not waking Rivka so far, but now he slid over and embraced her from behind.

She jumped. "Ari! I did not expect you home tonight."

"Should I go?"

Rivka turned to face him and they kissed. His leg bandage rubbed against her. She touched the one on his arm. "Does it hurt?"

"Not so bad." His hands reached around to hold her close. He'd had a helluva forty-eight hours. He needed to hold her, to feel something other than pain and stress. He pulled her in and pressed his body to hers.

"Oh, Ari." She rubbed against him. "I see you have some adrenaline left over."

"Are you complaining?"

She shook her head and reached down to touch him.

Ari started to roll on top of her but winced in pain.

She pushed him onto his back. "Let me."

Chapter Forty-four

"You remember the boy who brought us across?" Iyad was crouching next to Faraz in some bushes near the Jordan River, a little after one a.m. Friday. The other men were a few meters to their left, a bit bleary-eyed, having had only a couple of hours sleep. "You are about to meet him again."

Iyad flashed a light into the darkness.

Two flashes came back.

Iyad shined the light again. "*Yalla.*" He stood and jogged toward the river.

Faraz, Waleed and Jamal followed. Where the field sloped down to the water, the boy greeted Iyad with a handshake and kisses on both cheeks.

The small boat sat low in the water with five of them and their weapons on board. The boy pushed off for the short, dark ride to the West Bank.

Will woke up on a chair in Bridget's hospital room. It was still dark outside, and the only lights in the room came from the machines monitoring her vital signs. On the surface, she seemed okay—a few bruises and dehydration. Will knew her most serious wounds were likely not visible. He could tell from how she shook when he first held her, from what she said in the ambulance, from how they had to pry her hand off of his in the ER.

The docs made sure she'd get some rest with a pill that knocked her out before they let Will into the room. He got up and looked at her, so peaceful after so much trauma. And so beautiful. Maybe it was time for his emotional release. He took a big, halting breath to prevent it.

Will pulled the chair closer to the bed, sat down and took Bridget's hand. She moaned and squeezed it. She licked her lips and opened her eyes.

"Hi," Will said. "How you feeling?"

Bridget took a second before answering. "Okay, kinda. Thirsty."

Will reached for a cup on her rolling tray and held it so she could get the straw between her lips.

"Thanks. That was so . . . weird to see you in that place."

"Yeah. Long story, but we've been looking for you for days—me, the colonel, lots of others. Your team was working 24/7."

Bridget squeezed his hand. "Thank you."

"Don't mention it. I did it for me, actually. You think I have girlfriends lined up waiting?"

Bridget let out a half-laugh. "Definitely not."

Will leaned in for a kiss. Bridget wrapped her arms around him.

When he sat back down, she said, "Do you know . . . ? No, I guess you wouldn't know anything about the mission I was supposed to be running."

"No, sorry. But you need to focus on you right now."

Bridget shifted her position and winced. "Not my strong suit. I need to know what's going on."

Faraz, Iyad and the other men lay prone on the western bank of the river and peered over the edge. They could see little in the darkness. Iyad crawled ahead through the river grass. "There," he whispered, pointing to the left. He stood and signaled for the others to join him.

The old black SUV looked abandoned. It was dented and rusty, but the key was in the ignition.

"Waleed will drive and I will sit with him. You two, into the back."

Faraz and Jamal climbed into the cargo area and covered themselves and the weapons with a tarp. They braced for a rough ride.

Fifteen minutes later, Iyad called out, "We are clear, now. You can sit up."

There wasn't much to see through the windows except olive trees.

After a few more minutes, Waleed stopped the SUV in front of a farm building Faraz recognized. As they got out, a voice came from inside.

"It is all right. It's me, Ayman."

The building's door opened and there he was, illuminated by the SUV's headlights. He looked pale, no doubt from spending all his time at the computer. His tousled hair nearly covered a small piece of gauze on his head wound. But his face was grim. As Iyad approached him, Faraz thought he saw Ayman's lower lip quiver.

"What is it, cousin? Why are you here?" Iyad went for a handshake and cheeks kiss, but Ayman embraced him.

"What? What's wrong?"

Ayman let him go. There were tears in his eyes. "Maysoon is dead."

"What? No."

"Ra'ed and the others, too. My mother is in prison. The Zionists destroyed my house."

Iyad was stunned for a moment. Then he put his hands on Ayman's shoulders. "My beautiful cousin has been martyred. May Allah welcome her in His embrace."

Ayman pushed him away. "Why? Why did you let them use my house?"

"We had no option. I did not imagine—"

"You were wrong." Ayman was angry, but also seemed to be on the verge of tears.

"I will take that mistake to my grave. You must know how sorry I am. But, in the end, Maysoon is a *shahida*."

The men looked at each other. Faraz thought Ayman might attack Iyad. But he softened. "I know. It is jihad."

Ayman let Iyad embrace him again.

"Somehow," Ayman said, composing himself, "they freed the hostage before the boys could kill her."

Iyad cursed.

"Hostage?" Faraz asked.

"That is what Ra'ed went to do," Iyad explained. "He was a great fighter and I knew him for many years. It is a big loss. Surely, he and his men have also been welcomed as martyrs. They had an important job—to distract the Zionists, make them give us men and money for the future. But Allah had a different plan."

Faraz stepped forward and hugged Ayman. "Maysoon was a lovely girl. Smart and committed. Now we know she was brave, also."

"Yes, brave. Thank you, my friend."

Faraz let go and stepped back.

Iyad put an arm around Ayman's shoulders. "Come. Let us go inside."

Waleed and Jamal brought the weapons from the vehicle. They all sat around Ayman on the sofa and chair and wooden crates the Israelis had left behind. He told them what details he knew and shared what was left of his food.

"Who was this hostage?" Faraz asked.

"An American spy," Iyad said. "They held her here, but had to move when the Israelis swept the area."

"A spy?"

"Yes, a stupid spy who had her name and picture in the newspaper, Bridget Davenport."

Faraz's blood ran cold and it must have shown.

"Have you heard of her?" Iyad asked.

"No. How would I hear of her?"

"You look upset."

"For Maysoon. I'm upset for Maysoon . . . and for the men, and that the hostage escaped."

Iyad did not look convinced, but he turned back to Ayman to press for more details of the Israeli raid.

Faraz worked to compose himself, then stood. "I'll be back."

"Where are you going?" Iyad asked.

"To a tree," Faraz said. "Is that a problem?"

Iyad waved a hand to dismiss him.

Faraz went outside and stood behind one of the trees as if he had to pee. He ran his hand through his hair. Bridget. A hostage in Ayman's house. How did that happen? At least she's free now. But Maysoon. . .dead.

It was a lot to take in. Meanwhile, the attack would

happen soon and involve a lot of men. And he still had no comms.

But he was back on the West Bank. He should be able to get hold of a phone. He could keep walking through the trees, find a road, get to civilization. Faraz looked around to see how far the trees went.

"Khayal!" It was Iyad at the building's door. "How long does it take? Get back inside. We must be extra careful now."

Iyad waited until Faraz got back into the building. He closed the door and leaned a chair against it to keep it closed. Waleed and Jamal were lying on the floor.

"Get some rest," Iyad ordered. "You will need all your strength in a few hours."

Faraz went to lie down near Waleed and Jamal, but kept his eyes and ears open.

Iyad went back to his conversation with Ayman. "Why would you do that, cousin?"

"For Maysoon. For my father. For . . . everything. Be honest. I am not good at fighting skills, am I?"

Iyad did not answer.

"The Zionists are after me. I do not want to go to prison for the rest of my life. I never saw it before, but now . . . yes, this is my destiny."

"But your mother—"

"My mother will never get out of prison. Already, I'm sure she is respected by the other prisoners. This will make her the queen, the most respected woman in Palestine."

Iyad rubbed his forehead.

"Do not say no, cousin," Ayman begged. "When we get to the city, I will go to the watchmaker."

Chapter Forty-five

"Yalla, time to go." Iyad roused the men. "This is an important day, my brothers, the day we have been working toward."

It was dawn Friday—the Jewish holiday, and also the weekly Muslim holy day.

"Costumes?" Waleed asked.

"Not yet."

Outside, the men washed at a spigot and made use of the olive grove for their morning routines. Faraz came back to the house at the same time Ayman came from the other direction.

"How are you doing?"

"I'm okay." Ayman walked past him and stood alone on the edge of the clearing.

Faraz followed. "Come on, Ayman. We're friends. Talk to me."

Ayman sighed. "I must accept the new reality. The Zionists murdered my sister and my father before her. My mother is also taken from me. I have a new life now. A life with Iyad and the movement." Ayman turned and stared into the trees. "You know I never liked Ra'ed."

"Yes."

"He was arrogant and, it turns out, incompetent. What he did destroyed my family, my life. He killed no Zionists, not even the hostage he had in his hands. But he died a martyr. He will always be remembered for that. He will have his place in paradise. Even Suleiman, the garbage-man, died a martyr. His mother is now respected beyond her wildest dreams."

"And so?"

"And so, I will surpass them."

There wasn't room for Ayman in the cargo area of the SUV, but he squeezed in anyway, half his weight on Faraz. The ride on the dirt road was particularly painful. Not long after they got to the highway, they turned off again.

"Hold on, boys," Iyad called from the front seat. "We must go on the back roads."

Faraz kept track of the turns as best he could. Ten agonizing minutes later, the vehicle slowed and went through a series of turns until it backed up and stopped. Iyad opened the cargo door. "Out. Move it."

Faraz and the others emerged into the early morning light. They were on a dead-end street (not much wider that the SUV) that ended at the wall of a neighboring building. Iyad ushered them into a row house.

"Where are we?" Faraz asked.

"Safe house. From here, when the time comes, it will not take long to reach our destinations."

The house was abandoned. The front door opened directly into the living room, which flowed into a dining room that was separated from the kitchen and back door by a half-wall topped with a counter. On the left, a stairway led to the second floor. Some of the ceiling fixtures worked, providing an eerie low-wattage light. There were several bags of groceries and a stack of folding chairs in the dining room. In one corner, a pile of assorted luggage grew, heavy with pistols, AKs and grenades.

Faraz, Waleed and Jamal organized other early arrivals to set up the chairs and lay out the food. Ayman was not with them. He was at the rear door with a small backpack in his hand, speaking to Iyad. Faraz hung back to listen.

"You are certain?" Iyad asked.

"Yes, cousin. Finally, I am certain about something. I was with Munir when . . . when the news came. He reminded me that in jihad, we struggle to find the path Allah has chosen for us. Yesterday, I found mine. Today, I will take it."

Iyad absorbed that. "I did not expect such philosophy from you and Munir."

"Things change, sometimes in an instant."

"All right. I will make the call. This will be a great achievement. You know where to go?"

"Yes."

"Take this. It should fit you." Iyad handed Ayman a costume in a clear plastic cover. There was a mask inside—the face of a white man with blue hair. Ayman turned the package to put it into the backpack. The outfit had a shield insignia—a yellow diamond shape outlined in red, with a red "S."

Superman.

Iyad hugged his cousin and kissed him on both cheeks. "Are you sure you can do this with your injury."

Ayman touched the bandage on his head. "I must."

"*Fi amaan Allah.*" May you go with the protection of Allah.

The cousins embraced one more time, then held each other at arm's length.

Ayman looked different—somehow older. His jaw was set, he stood straight, his eyes met Iyad's. His beard looked a little fuller. He was still heavy, but no longer the doughboy Faraz met in the prison. He broke contact. "You will get word to my mother?"

"Yes, of course."

Ayman nodded at his cousin and left.

Iyad leaned out into the alley to watch him, then came back in and shut the door.

"Where did Ayman go?" Faraz asked.

"You do not need to know that. Just know that your friend, my cousin, is more courageous than we thought." Iyad walked past Faraz into the dining room. "Boys, do not eat all the food. Others are coming."

The village of Abu Qutib was a warren of narrow streets and narrower alleys, but Ayman knew it well. He had visited his grandmother here often when he was a child. He would play soccer with the local boys at the edge of the village on a pitch that was now a parking lot. They would run through the alleys playing *astagh mayat*. Hide and seek.

At the first road, Ayman stopped to check for police in both directions, then ran across to another grid of alleys. He was energized, sweating in the cool morning air. The village was quiet. The backs of the houses were all closed up. He dodged a couple of goats tied to back fences and offered morning greetings to one old woman who emerged to take out her trash.

Ayman came to the end of the village and stopped in an alley to catch his breath. The difficult part lay ahead. He would have to stay in gullies to avoid being seen, crawl in some areas, then walk up the steep road on the east side of the Old City. It would be difficult, but he would do it.

He peered out of the alley. The soccer-pitch-turned-parking-lot was to his right. The farm field between his position and the road looked clear. Ayman set out, walking along a footpath that led to a bus stop, with an Israeli checkpoint beyond.

Halfway there, he veered off to his left.

Rivka was determined that the Little Mermaid would eat some breakfast.

"I want to go now," Tali insisted, then pressed her lips together and blocked the spoonful of scrambled eggs and tomato that Rivka held out to feed her.

"Sweetheart, the parade is not until this afternoon. You must eat. Daddy will be angry if you go to Jerusalem without eating your breakfast."

Mentioning Ari made Rivka think of the night before. She shivered a little. She'd had a helluva couple of days, too. She had gone from concern that his work kept him away too much, to fear and anger when he'd been shot, to relief he was alive, and to . . . oh, what a sweet homecoming.

"Where is Daddy?" Tali asked.

Rivka came back to the present. "He left early for work. We will see him later."

The Little Mermaid leaned back in her chair and pouted.

"Now, you look like a baby. Are you a baby?"

Tali shook her head. "I am six years old. I'm not a baby."

"Then act like a big girl and eat your breakfast."

Tali glared at her mother, trapped in the logic of the argument. She picked up her spoon and fed herself a bite of the eggs.

"Good. When you finish, we will go to the school to meet up with the others and take the bus to the parade." Rivka pushed a lock of Tali's hair off her face. "You will be the best Little Mermaid in the parade. Now, eat. I will go put on my costume."

Ari gave a report on the rescue operation at General HaLevy's regular 0730 staff briefing and accepted congratulations from his colleagues.

"How is your shoulder this morning?" HaLevy asked.

"It's fine. No firing automatic weapons for a week or two, but otherwise, fine."

"And your leg?"

"I have a temporary limp. Esti tells me it's sexy."

In a chair against the wall, Sergeant Peretz shouted above the laughter. "That is a misquote."

"I believe the sergeant," HaLevy said. "Now, let's

move on to the plan for today. I will be here, monitoring everything. Colonel Ben-Yosef will be in the command trailer in Jerusalem, and hopes to get a few minutes to check in on a certain Little Mermaid."

"Right, sir," Ari said. "We have increased security for both Purim parades. The one in the Old City starts first and makes a circuit of the Jewish Quarter, ending at the central square, where there will be a festival with food and music. The later parade is in West Jerusalem, along Jaffa Street, through Zion Square to the Mahane Yehudah Market for Purim treats. The command center has been established at the staging area."

"And these increased road movements in Saudi and Jordan? Our team has confirmed some of it?"

"Yes, sir. We have increased security along the border and at the entrances to Jerusalem—well, as much as we can with large crowds expected and no reinforcements from the reserves."

"All right. Keep me posted. You also have access to the rapid reaction force if we get anything more specific on a threat."

The trip from Abu Qutib village to the Old City would normally take fifteen minutes by car. On foot, maybe an hour. The way Ayman had to go to, it might take two hours. He had no time to spare.

He tried to jump an irrigation ditch but got his feet wet in the process. He bent over so he couldn't be seen and made his way past a turn in the channel, then climbed a small rise. Ayman was past the checkpoint now. He could see the Old City walls crowning the hilltop.

He paused to admire the view, something he had never done in his years riding on that road in the backseat of his father's car. On those trips, he either had his eyes on a video game or was sleeping off the lunch his grandmother had served them.

Ayman turned left again, to avoid police monitoring traffic on the main road. He picked his way through large rocks and rough ground. Soon, he would have to walk on the road to get to the Old City's Zion Gate. It would be a long climb, but with luck he could hide himself in a tourist group heading into the Armenian Quarter for some shopping.

As the morning wore on, several more groups of five or six men each arrived at the house. There was much hollering as each team came in. The men told tall tales of their journeys and bargained over the dwindling supply of snacks. A four-a-side soccer game broke out in the living room, using a wadded-up grocery bag as a ball.

Faraz sat on the dining room floor, where he had a view of the game and both the front and back doors. He was watching for a chance to get out of there, but there were too many men around.

Iyad came into the living room. "Settle down boys, the boss is coming."

An SUV pulled up to the back door and Bashar got out of the passenger seat. He greeted Iyad and did a perfunctory check of the alley. Then he opened the vehicle's back door. Assali turned to ease himself out, coming down on his short legs and adjusting his tunic.

"Welcome, sir," Iyad said.

Assali walked past him and surveyed the living room. The men stood at attention to greet him. "Not many," he said.

"More are coming," Iyad assured him. "I have news and I must use the satellite phone."

Assali scoffed. "My headquarters?"

"Upstairs, *sayyid*."

Assali took hold of the bannister. "Bring my bag and some food."

Chapter Forty-six

Ayman struggled on the climb. He understood now more than ever why the Jews never said "go to Jerusalem," but rather "go *up* to Jerusalem." It was a physical as well as spiritual climb, especially on foot.

He had no choice but to walk on the road at this point. There was a wall of rock on one side and a sheer drop-off on the other. In the distance, he could see Abu Qutib, and to the far left, the biblical Garden of Gethsemane.

A police car approached and he turned to the wall. Was that too obvious? Would they make a U-turn and come check his ID?

Ayman stopped to calm himself. It was not yet ten a.m., but he was on the east side of the city, where there was no shelter from the sun rising in the clear blue sky. He wiped his forehead with his sleeve. The police did not come back.

He didn't want to do it, but he reached into his back-pack and took out a hooded sweatshirt. It had been part of the care package provided by the Saudis after the first camp was destroyed. The sweatshirt was great for desert nights. It was the last thing Ayman wanted to wear now.

But there would be more police cars as he got closer to the gate and lots of blue-uniformed special security forces on foot, with Uzis. He put the sweatshirt on and popped up the hood.

The rumble of an approaching tour bus forced Ayman and the few other pedestrians to press themselves to the wall. When it passed, he put his head down and forged ahead.

Ayman had worked hard to avoid such physical discomfort for most of his life. But this was the suffering he deserved for leaving his mother and sister in the care of Ra'ed. This was the struggle he must endure to find the path Allah had chosen for him—this and prison, and the air strike, and the martyrdom of his father and now his sister. They had fulfilled their destinies. With every step up the hill, he moved toward his.

At the hospital, Will had been banished to the waiting room while the medical team did Bridget's morning exam. He stopped in a men's room to wash up and had another vending machine meal—coffee and a sweet roll.

The doctor came out. "You can go back in now."

"How is she?"

"She's doing remarkably well, considering what she's been through. She should stay another twenty-four hours at least, but she put up quite an argument about that. She seems to be used to getting her way."

"Tell me about it."

"Sorry?"

"Never mind. I'll go talk to her."

But Will didn't have any more luck than the doctor.

"I need to get to the embassy," Bridget said. "No one will tell me anything without secure comms. I can't give you details, but I have to get back into the loop."

Will knew that tone. It meant he was not going to talk her out of it. "All right. I'll find the nurse and see if we can get that IV out of you. And I better call Colonel Ben-Yosef for an escort. There's a mob of reporters outside who want to meet Captain . . . Badass, is it?"

Rivka stood in the school parking lot with the other parents. Some had costumes on, others wore trendy jeans or khakis, the women adding button-down blouses and the men sporting untucked shirts opened one button too many. Rivka wore a sweater over skin-tight black yoga pants.

The lot was filling up with Toyotas and Hondas and a few Mercedes. This was an upscale Tel Aviv suburb of professionals and techies living in single-family homes with small backyards, two miles from the sea.

Nearby, Tali showed off her costume to her classmates. The Little Mermaid chased her friend Wonder Woman and posed for a picture with Queen Esther.

"It's warm for Purim, no?" Rivka said.

Her friend Batya, half a head taller with short, bleached hair, craned her neck to survey the roiling mass of children. "Yes, but it will be cooler in Jerusalem, I hope." Batya wore a shiny headband with jangly metal beads.

Rivka had cat ears on her head. She pulled her sweater over them, revealing a leopard-skin-pattern leotard with a plunging neckline.

"*Hoo-ah*." Batya shook her right hand as if she had touched something hot. "What are you? Sexy cat?"

"Wildcat, they call it. You like?"

"Ari will like."

"That's the idea."

Batya blushed. "You are too much."

"Honestly, I'm trying to get him to come home a little more often. He spends so many nights in the city, especially with what's been going on."

"As long as it's only work . . ."

"Oh, stop." Rivka slapped Batya on the shoulder, but couldn't prevent herself from blushing. Her worst fears verbalized. She deflected. "And where is Matti?"

"He is . . . well, I don't know. The Golan, I think. Reserve duty." She opened her jacket. "So, I am a gypsy girl with a peasant blouse and long skirt."

"On you, it's sexy, anyway."

They laughed. "We better get some water," Batya said. "They will keep us waiting for hours."

The women walked to a row of folding tables stacked with water bottles and snacks.

Tali ran up with Batya's daughter Sara. "Mommy, we want cookies."

"Cookies? You just had breakfast. Have some dried fruit. I'll take cookies for later."

The girls pouted but ran back to their friends.

"They are having too much fun to make a scene," Rivka said. "So, that's already a successful holiday."

In the parking lot outside the Zion Gate, Ayman caught up with the tour bus that had nearly run him over. The blue-and-white flag propped up against the windshield indicated the occupants were from Greece. He slowed his pace to allow half the passengers to disembark, then slipped into the crowd as others filled in behind him. The bus must have been chilly because several people had on jackets or sweaters, making his hoodie less conspicuous. The men even looked like Ayman, olive skin and dark hair.

They came through the outer gate to a sharp right turn inside the thick city wall, then out through a narrow passage onto a cobblestoned street. That's where the security police stood, legs apart, hands on weapons slung around their necks. Ayman turned to the tourist on his left, as if they were chatting. He pulled the hood to block his face as much as possible.

The group came to the first pottery shops, an Armenian Quarter specialty, and spread out to browse. Ayman examined a flower-pattern bowl and checked on the police. They were focused on the next crowd coming through the gate, boisterous teenagers shouting to each other in English and taking photos.

Ayman put down the bowl and walked on, leaving the Greeks behind. He turned left into an alley at the first opportunity.

Israeli press photographers scattered when the army driver laid on the horn and kept moving as the car climbed the ramp out of the parking garage. Bridget's escape from the hospital was a success, but traffic heading to the parades and other holiday events brought them to a halt.

"We'll never get to Tel Aviv at this rate," Bridget said. "Can we go to the consulate?"

"As you like," the driver said.

"Do it. Will, let me borrow your phone." Bridget called the embassy and arranged to be let into the old U.S. Consulate in Jerusalem and provided with comms. What would have been a forty-five-minute drive to Tel Aviv in clear traffic, maybe two hours in this mess, became ten minutes of lefts and rights through residential neighborhoods and briefly onto a main road to the compound gate.

The main building was a nineteenth-century villa nestled in a wooded garden near the city center. Of course, Bridget had no ID on her. And the Israeli policeman outside was not interested in her explanation.

They were rescued by a U.S. Marine who came out of the building to get them.

Inside, he buzzed them through a security door and directed them to walk through a set of metal detectors. The marine took Will's phone and pistol and let them into a waiting room. Through a large window, Bridget saw him in the bulletproof guard station comparing their faces to photos on a computer screen.

He spoke through a metal voice grate. "I've confirmed your identities. I'll unlock the far door. Someone will take you to the comms room."

Ayman got lost twice. He was used to navigating the Old City's streets and alleyways from the Muslim Quarter side. From here, everything was backward. He was sweating, rushing to make up for lost time and not daring to take off the hood. Several times, he diverted his route to avoid policemen on foot.

Finally, Ayman arrived at a familiar intersection, with trinket stands and a large coffee shop where he'd often sat with his friends and bought sweets to take home to his mother. Today, he was doing something far greater for her.

He went down the alley to the left of the shop, then two quick turns and he reached his destination—the watchmaker's shop. The metal gate was down.

Ayman moved to the other side of the two-meter-wide street and looked up toward the second-floor windows. They were closed and the shades were drawn. An air conditioner hummed in one window and dripped its condensation onto the road. The sign for NABIL SHAWKAT, WATCHMAKER was rusted. But there was a high-tech miniature security camera bolted to the wall, its red light blinking at Ayman.

"Nabil," he called out. "Nabil!"

There was no response.

Two boys on bicycles sped past him. He crossed back over the alley and knocked on the metal gate. "Nabil!" Ayman pounded harder, shaking the gate. "Nabil, open up!"

He stopped to listen. Footsteps. A muffled voice from inside. "All right. I am coming."

The lock at the bottom of the gate turned and someone lifted it. The metal rattled as the gate rolled up part of the way into its holder. Ayman saw the bottom half of a man wearing some sort of gray robe and sandals.

"Come inside," the man said.

Ayman ducked down and went through into the darkness

of the shop. The gate crashed down and the lock closed. Ayman blinked to adjust his eyes.

The watchmaker stood next to him. A full head shorter than Ayman, he was several decades older and looked it. He was thin, almost frail, and wore a knitted white skull-cap. His kaftan reached his ankles and was faded and frayed on the edges, with no pattern or embroidery. It had a V-neck with a border that looked like it had been repaired by hand.

The man put his keys into the garment's sole pocket and looked Ayman up and down with evident disapproval. "Why are you here?"

Ayman pushed the hood back, irritated at the man's lack of courtesy. "*Salaam aleikum*, honored watchmaker. How is your health?"

Nabil dismissed the inquiry with a wave of his hand. "Answer me."

"Did you not receive a call from Iyad?"

"I did. Otherwise, you would still be outside. But this is not a simple errand. You are not picking up a repaired watch or shopping for a clock. Answer the question. Why are you here?"

"I am here . . ." Ayman hesitated. Then the answer came to him. "I am here for Palestine."

CHAPTER FORTY-SEVEN

In the back of the shop, behind the counter, through a locked door, past the stairway to the watchmaker's apartment, there was a vault.

Most of the shop looked like it hadn't changed since at least the 1930s—used watches on sale for a few dollars, old clocks that ticked incessantly and chimed in disharmony on the hour and half-hour. One corner had modern digital alarm clocks and cartoon-character watches.

But here, in the back, the storage room's walk-in vault had a steel door, a combination lock, and a second keypad lock with a small red light.

Nabil opened two folded stools and put them in front of the door. Their legs formed Xs under stretched canvas seats. He squatted to sit on one and directed Ayman to sit on the other, facing him.

"My condolences and also congratulations on the martyrdom of your sister. May Allah welcome her."

"Thank you, *sayyid*."

"This is why you decided to come here?"

Ayman didn't know how to respond.

The watchmaker answered for him. "This is why you decided."

Ayman nodded. "Yes. And . . . everything."

"Motivation is good. Commitment is good. But in these things, speed is not good. It takes weeks, even months, to prepare, to be certain, to have the will to do Allah's work."

"I can do it."

"Perhaps." The old man pulled at the untrimmed strands at the bottom of his gray beard. "This is a new attitude for you, Ayman. You have come to it quickly and, in my experience, may turn away from it just as quickly."

"I will not. I believe I have been preparing for this my entire life. I understand that now. Please, *sayyid*, I have nowhere else to go. There is only one way forward for me, now."

Nabil studied Ayman's face. "I would not do this if not for your cousin's direct appeal. I was skeptical. But sometimes, Allah chooses a day for great things and a man for greatness."

"Thank you, *sayyid*."

Nabil took Ayman's hands in his. Ayman was trembling. He squeezed Nabil's hands to stop it. The watchmaker lowered his head to pray.

"*Barak Allah fikum . . .*"

May you receive the blessings of Allah.

May He forgive you from the moment your blood is shed.

May He show you your place in Paradise.

May He spare you the trial of the grave.

May He protect you on the Day of Judgment.

* * *

"That's it?" Bridget was two minutes into her call with Liz, but she was already frustrated.

She was alone in the consulate's comms room, having kicked out Will and the Israeli technician for her classified call. There were no windows and no decorations. She immediately felt claustrophobic.

"We've been focused on you, Bridge. I had one team watching for any signs of Abdallah, but there weren't any. Good news is, we've seen Saudi intel's report from the Israeli air strike. He was not identified as being among the dead."

Bridget massaged her temples. Maybe bolting from the hospital hadn't been such a good idea. "That's not much to go on."

"Sorry, it's all we have for now."

"You said there was all this traffic on sparsely traveled roads in Saudi and Jordan yesterday—possible swarming for an attack. But the Jordanians didn't intercept anyone and now all is quiet?"

"A few vehicles evaded the police. Others turned off to innocuous destinations or were found to have occupants with legitimate IDs."

"Faraz could have been in one of those vehicles."

"That's a bit of a shot in the dark."

"Not really. He's out there with these bastards somewhere. We have to find him. We have to stop them."

Liz didn't answer right away.

Bridget played her own words back in her mind. Her

tone sounded desperate, panicked. "Sorry, Liz. Rough couple of days, I guess."

"Oh, Bridget. That's got to be the understatement of the decade. Don't worry about it. We are so glad you're safe. And we are on this."

"Yeah, thanks. I know."

"If Abdallah is involved in some sort of operation, he'll make himself known when he can. Meanwhile, we switched all our resources from you to him."

"Good. Thanks. What is it for you, four a.m.?"

"Yeah, nearly."

"Okay. I know you're on top of it, but it's hard to be out of the loop. Get some rest, if you can. And make sure the team notifies me immediately of any contact."

"Sure. You got it."

Bridget ended the call, stood and put her hand on the back of the chair to steady herself. She opened the comms room door to let the technician back in. He wore jeans and an open white shirt and carried a fresh cup of coffee. "Sorry about that," Bridget said.

"No problem. I'm used to it."

"Can you possibly lend me a mobile?"

"Sure." The technician opened a locked cabinet and took a phone out of a charger. "This should work any-where in the area. The number is on the back. But you can't use it in here. I'll give it to the guard. You can get it from him when you leave."

"Thanks. Pass the number to the DIA ops center, will you?"

"Yes, ma'am."

Bridget left the comms room and found Will on a sofa in the waiting area.

"Any news?" he asked.

"If there was, I probably couldn't tell you. But no. No news."

"You don't look so good."

"Well, aren't you the charmer. But, yeah, I don't feel so good, either."

Will stood. "Hospital or hotel?"

"I think I'll lie down here, in case there are any updates."

With Nabil's blessings completed, Ayman looked the old man in the eye. For the first time since the night before, Ayman smiled.

Nabil stood and turned the dial on the combination lock. Then he entered a long code on the keypad, using his body to block Ayman's view. He turned the handle. There was a loud *clunk*. Nabil leaned back to pull the door open.

He reached inside and turned on a light. "Come." He stepped aside so Ayman could move to the back of the vault.

The space was cramped, maybe three meters by two, lined on all sides with floor-to-ceiling shelves holding an odd assortment of items—backpacks, vests, winter coats, rolls of wire, sticks of dynamite, bricks of plastic explosive and timers. Of course, timers.

Nabil directed Ayman to stand in the middle of the narrow back wall. The watchmaker looked him up and down like a tailor would, then selected a vest and held it up. "Try this."

Ayman stepped into it and pirouetted three hundred and sixty degrees.

"Good," Nabil said. "How is it?"

"Heavy, but I can handle it." Ayman's vest had four bricks of explosive lashed to the back, two more on the sides of his stomach bulge. A web of red and black wires wrapped around him and hung down in the front next to a battery pack.

Nabil gathered the wires and lashed them together with a plastic tie. "The procedure is simple to learn, but difficult to perform." He pointed to the pack's on/off switch. "This is the master power. I will connect the wires and turn it on before you leave me. After that, it is up to you."

"I will not fail."

Nabil inspected the wires one more time, then retrieved another item from a shelf—a white, palm-sized plastic handle, like the controller from one of Munir's video games. "This is the detonator. I will attach it later. You must squeeze the lever and then push the button, in that order. Otherwise, it will not function. Like this." Nabil demonstrated, then handed it over. "Do it now."

Ayman held the detonator in his right hand, away from his body. He squeezed the lever with his index finger, then pushed the button with his thumb.

"Again."

Ayman complied.

"Good. I pray that when the time comes, Allah will give you the strength to do it."

"He will, *sayyid*. He already has."

Nabil nodded, but Ayman couldn't escape the feeling that the old man was still not convinced. In the past, before yesterday, such skepticism would have upset

Ayman. He would have pouted, gotten angry, lashed out. Today, it made him more determined.

"Do not worry, *sayyid*."

"I was worried when your cousin called. I was worried when you arrived. I worry every time I hand over a device. But I see your commitment. I believe you will succeed in the most difficult task Allah puts before us in jihad. Now, where is your costume?"

Faraz was back on the floor in the dining room, picking at a bag of peanuts from the stash of snacks.

"Bashar, Khayal, upstairs." Iyad spoke from the middle of the stairway, then turned to lead them up.

They found Assali sitting on the edge of a bed sipping a glass of tea, with a map laid out next to him. The boss had taken off his *kufiyah*, exposing his bald head, with a few strands of comb-over. He was sweating even though the air conditioner in the window was on maximum. The walls were bare and half the bulbs in the ceiling fixture were out. A radio on the nightstand played Arabic music.

"Khayal, you could save me from bombs but you cannot save me from this rathole." Assali laughed, and the others did the same. But the bad joke did little to break the tension.

"We have enough men to proceed. Some were not able to cross, but our friends assure me none were arrested. Our plan is secure. The Zionists have tight security for the holiday, but we have surprise on our side.

"Iyad, Bashar, your teams will carry out phase one of the attack, in the Old City. You will enter the Muslim Quarter in small groups, as thousands of people do every day. You will gather at points I will show you on this map. You will put on your costumes and approach the Jewish Quarter. And you will strike at 12:30 exactly."

"What about me?" Faraz asked.

"Your team will be divided to replace men missing from the teams of Bashar and Iyad."

"You are with me, Disco Boy," Bashar said.

"But—"

Iyad sneered. "This is a good thing. You are not ready to lead your own team. *Sayyid* Assali has accepted my judgment on that."

Assali nodded.

"And phase two?" Faraz asked.

"Phase two is not your concern," Assali said. "But I can tell you it will be even more spectacular than planned, thanks to, well, an unexpected source. Wouldn't you agree, Iyad?"

Iyad looked troubled but said, "Yes, *sayyid.*"

"Now go," Assali said. "And Allah be with you. Send me Waleed."

Chapter Forty-eight

Bashar led prayers in the living room. When he finished, there was much hugging, handshaking and cheeks kissing, but it was low-key.

Iyad divided the men into two teams, ten for himself, Faraz, Jamal and two others for Bashar.

"We will leave at two-minute intervals," Iyad said, "and take different routes to Old City gates leading to the Muslim Quarter. From there, we go on foot. *Allah hu akbar.*"

The men responded in kind.

Bashar directed Faraz, Jamal, and another man to put the bags containing their costumes and weapons under a tarp in the bed of an old SUV parked in front of the house. They climbed into the backseat. Bashar hugged Iyad and kissed him on both cheeks. Then he got in front with the driver. "You know the route to avoid the checkpoint, yes?"

"Yes, no problem."

"Be quick. We are the first team. We must not be late." Bashar gave a half-salute to Iyad as the driver hit the gas. They sped past the entrance to an alley, dodging garbage

cans and parked bicycles before slowing to make the turn
to the village exit.

Faraz swallowed hard. There had been no opportunity
to call in. He would have to find another way to stop the
attack.

Half an hour later, Bashar paid twenty shekels to a boy
at the entrance to an open field in East Jerusalem that was
starting to fill with parked cars. He gave him an extra five
to keep their SUV near the exit and not block it in.

The men joined a stream of people heading for the
Damascus Gate. Bashar put the driver and Jamal in the
lead, with Faraz and the fifth man side by side behind,
dragging small, wheeled suitcases. Bashar was in the rear,
making sure they stayed together and on track. They all
carried backpacks or satchels.

They passed through the gate, watched but not both-
ered by Israeli police. Inside, a wide, gradual stairway
lined with produce stands and clothing shops led down
to the maze of walkways that formed the *souk*. It was
crowded with shoppers buying groceries for their Friday
mid-day feasts and taking advantage of the day off to shop
for a wide variety of goods.

Bashar forced the pace, ordering the men ahead of him
to turn left or right as they exited the market into a residential neighborhood.

As far as Faraz could tell, they were generally moving
south. He was desperate to veer off, to get to a phone. But
Bashar provided no opportunity.

The team drew a couple of looks from people they
passed, but in the Muslim Quarter, even moving fast, four

Arab men and another who looked Arab did not draw special attention. Even if someone did suspect that these guys were up to no good, Faraz wondered whether they would call the police. Could he expect help from anyone in the *souk* if he needed it? Probably not.

In an alley lined with souvenir shops, Faraz smelled lamb grilling before he saw the restaurant, positioned around a bend, just before the passage opened into a small square.

"In there," Bashar ordered. They blew past a large pile of meat spinning on a shawarma skewer and a man turning kabobs on a charcoal grill. As soon as they were inside, the cook moved two high-backed wooden chairs to block the entryway and went back to his work.

Bashar led the team past a plastic curtain into a storage room. He looked at his watch. "Here, we change."

The men pulled their costumes out of the bags—Batman, Godzilla, a skeleton, the devil, Bill Clinton for Faraz.

Bashar took five AKs from the rolling suitcases and handed them out. "Weapons check," he ordered. He reached into his backpack, took out two grenades and clipped them to his belt.

"Ready, boys?" They all nodded.

"We go left out of the restaurant into the square, then right. Stay along the wall to hide the weapons for as long as you can. In the corner, about thirty meters, there is a gate that leads into the Jewish Quarter. The festival is not far beyond. It is our job to clear the way for the others."

The driver whispered, "*Allah hu akbar.*" The men did the same.

Bashar led them in the *Shahada*, then checked his

watch again. "It is time. Be brave, my brothers. We will achieve a great victory. If Allah decrees it, we shall reap his reward. Masks on."

He left no time for doubt or indecision, no time for Faraz to do anything. Bashar opened the curtain halfway. "*Aman?*" Clear?

The cook looked right and left in the alley, then moved the chairs out of the way. "*Allah ma'ekum.*" God be with you.

Through the eyeholes of the devil mask—black and red, sneering, with curved horns above—Bashar looked toward Bill Clinton's fixed smile and shock of gray hair. "Khayal, you lead."

Faraz didn't move.

Bashar pushed him. "Go!"

Faraz thought about raising his AK and firing, but they would likely have killed him before he got them all. And Bashar said they were the first team. That meant even if he succeeded, Iyad and the others would attack, anyway. He needed to survive to call in a warning. He turned and led the team out of the restaurant, with Bashar holding his shoulder from behind.

Bashar pushed him left into the alley, then right along the wall of the square, where the Arab-owned shops were open but mostly empty. If the shopkeepers saw the weapons, they didn't say anything. Faraz heard at least one metal gate come crashing down after they passed.

Ahead, across the entrance to a passageway that led off the square, there were thick steel bars on hinges attached to the wall. They reminded Faraz of the door to his cell in the prison.

One Israeli policeman stood in front of the gate. Another

was on the far side, next to a steel guard shack with bulletproof windows and several more men inside.

"Slowly, now." Bashar ordered, grabbing Faraz's shoulder. "Be natural."

Faraz went down on one knee in front of a carpet shop.

"What's this?" Bashar asked.

"I twisted my ankle. Go ahead."

"Ach." Bashar led the odd collection of cartoon characters around Faraz. He gave the policeman a friendly wave and shouted in Hebrew, "*Shalom, chevra. Chag Sameach.*" Hello, friends. Happy Holiday.

The police officer at the Jewish Quarter checkpoint smiled, but held up a hand for the men to stop.

Bashar tossed a grenade. The team crouched down and turned to the wall.

The explosion was loud in the small square, echoing off the tan Jerusalem Stone walls.

The policeman was thrown against the gate and riddled with shrapnel. His body collapsed onto the ground. The gate swung open.

Faraz was knocked off balance onto his side.

He twisted his body in time to see Bashar fire at the second police officer. The other attackers targeted the guard shack, but their bullets bounced off.

Faraz lifted his AK and fired.

Bashar lunged forward from the close-range impact and fell on his face. Jamal turned to see where the shots came from. Faraz swept his rifle to the right and cut him down, then sprayed left to hit the other two men.

When he stopped shooting, the square was quiet. But not for long. The Israelis came out of the shelter firing.

Faraz took cover behind Bashar's body and raised his hands.

"Don't shoot! I'm American. Undercover. I stopped them."

There was an order in Hebrew and the shooting stopped. An Israeli in body armor moved toward Faraz and put one foot on his AK, the other on his neck. He reached down to pull off the mask.

"Don't move," he said in English, then issued more Hebrew orders.

"I'm an American agent. I need a phone."

The Israeli pressed harder against Faraz's neck.

"More men are coming. We have to act now. Please, let me up. Tell your men to take cover."

"You are not giving order—"

A barrage of AK fire interrupted the policeman. He took two bullets to his vest and hit the ground.

Faraz turned to see Iyad and his team coming out of another alley into the square. The policeman lying next to him got off a volley. Faraz grabbed the AK, stayed as low as he could and crawled into the shop.

He hid behind a pile of Oriental rugs, peeked over the top and fired a burst toward Iyad's men. Israeli reinforcements came through the damaged gate and formed a protective cordon around the man on the ground, blocking Faraz's view. Both sides kept up a steady barrage of gunfire.

Faraz zigzagged between stacks of carpets to the back of the shop, where he found a teenaged boy cowering under a small desk. A landline telephone sat in its cradle.

He pointed his weapon at the boy. "*Imshi.*" Get out. The boy scrambled out the back door.

Faraz picked up the phone and dialed.

Chapter Forty-nine

In the consulate's marine guard station, a red beacon like the ones on police cars came to life and started rotating. The sharp sound of a warning buzzer leaked through the bulletproof glass to the waiting room.

Will stood and moved toward the window, but the marine on duty waved him off. The young man leaned in toward a microphone on a gooseneck stand. His voice came through the consulate's public address system.

"Security lockdown. Security lockdown. Follow yellow protocols. Repeat, yellow protocols. All personnel to shelter in place. This is not a drill."

Bridget stirred from her nap.

Will shook her shoulder. "Bridget. You need to wake up."

"Hmm. What?"

"C'mon, Bridge."

The cobwebs of a deep sleep cleared. Bridget sat up fast. Too fast. She brought a hand to her forehead. "Whoa."

"Easy, now. Take it slow."

"What? What's going on?"

"That's what we need to find out."

* * *

Faraz's call was answered on the first ring. "Operator."

He didn't take the time to go through the authentication codes. He was breathing fast, speaking staccato. "Shock wave. Multipronged attack in Jerusalem. Dozens of fighters. Now in Old City. Second wave unknown." He was squatting behind the carpets, with his AK by his side under the desk.

"Received. Anything further?"

"I need egress. Carpet shop. Old City, off a square with Israeli checkpoint. Don't know the name. Gun battle in progress."

The operator said something but Faraz didn't catch it. His attention was taken by a tall man moving toward him from the shop doorway wearing a King Kong costume. Faraz dropped the handset onto the floor.

"What are you doing? Making a call?"

Faraz knew who it was before he pulled off the mask. "No, no, Iyad. I chased a Zionist."

The operator's voice came out of the phone. "Hello? Shock Wave? Anything further?"

"Traitor!" Iyad kicked the handset. "Spy!" He flipped his AK and drove the butt into Faraz's stomach. "I told Assali not to trust you."

Faraz went down but kicked Iyad's legs out from under him. He hit a pile of carpets, dropped his rifle and fell. Faraz turned his gun on Iyad and pulled the trigger. Nothing. Out of bullets? Jammed? He had no time to figure it out.

Iyad got his knees under himself and started to stand. Faraz flipped his AK and hit Iyad in the head. He went down again on top of his gun. Faraz turned and ran out the back of the shop.

He went right onto the uneven surface of the alley, running away from the square and the Jewish Quarter. He wanted to take cover in a shop but all the back doors were locked. Faraz turned a corner and came to a dead end. When he spun around, Iyad was blocking his way.

Iyad pointed his AK and shook his head. "Disco Boy. I knew it, but Assali wouldn't listen to me."

Faraz dropped his weapon. "No, Iyad. I can explain."

Iyad tossed his gun onto the ground next to Faraz's. "I will kill you with my bare hands!" He let out a crazed scream and ran at Faraz, who stepped aside and pushed him as he went by. Iyad slammed into the wall at the end of the alley.

Faraz reached for the working rifle, but Iyad got to him before he could pick it up. They each got two hands on the gun and fought for control. Iyad pushed Faraz against the wall and pressed the rifle into his throat, hissing and spitting curses. Faraz's grip weakened.

He kneed Iyad hard in the stomach. Iyad staggered back but kept hold of the rifle. Faraz punched him and he spun around.

Faraz took off running.

He came out of the alley onto a walkway lined with shops. Faraz could hear the gunfire from the square. That accounted for the fact that no one was outside. Still running, he pulled down a display stand of plastic toys as he passed to slow Iyad's pursuit. Ahead, he could see a cross street. He might find some police there, or at least use the traffic to evade Iyad.

"Traitor! Stop the traitor!" Iyad's voice came from behind, enlisting anyone within earshot in his pursuit. He raised his weapon and fired. A bullet pinged off the walls. Then Faraz heard Iyad curse.

He glanced around and saw Iyad twenty meters behind. He shook the gun and pulled the trigger again, then threw the weapon down. Before Faraz could turn his head again to face front, his feet went out from under him and he fell hard onto the flagstones.

His hands and forearms were bloodied. The right knee of Bill Clinton's suit was ripped. Faraz turned his head to see a small boy, maybe eight years old, in the doorway of a housewares shop with a broomstick in his hands.

"I got the traitor. I got the traitor." The boy sang with delight, jumping up and down. A woman came from inside the shop and pulled the boy away.

Faraz tried to stand, but Iyad's knee came down on his lower back. Iyad used both hands to take hold of Faraz's chin. He stretched his neck and spat in his face. Faraz reached back for something to grab, but Iyad stood, grabbed his hands and pulled him into the shop.

Iyad let go with one hand, grabbed a large pot from a shelf and swung it toward Faraz's head. Faraz used his free hand to deflect it, then punched Iyad in his lower abdomen. That caused Iyad's other hand to lose its grip.

Faraz jumped up, took hold of King Kong's chest and pushed him down a narrow aisle toward the shop's back door, sending pans and utensils flying, until Iyad tripped on his own feet and fell back. Faraz lunged on top of him and pummeled his face.

Iyad twisted and pushed Faraz off. He grabbed Faraz's

costume and pushed him to the floor, climbing on top and putting a knee on his chest. Iyad's hands went to Faraz's throat.

Faraz flailed his arms, punching for Iyad's face, but he couldn't reach it. Iyad's long arms were strong and he was well practiced at hand-to-hand. Faraz looked to his left and twisted his body enough to grab a metal ladle from the floor. He swung it, landing a solid blow to the side of Iyad's head. Iyad went down. Faraz scrambled out from under him and started to run to the back of the shop.

Iyad kicked and caught Faraz's right foot. Faraz stumbled but didn't go down. He righted himself and took another step toward the back door, but something heavy hit him in the back of the head. His knees went weak. Iyad caught Faraz from behind and put his left forearm across his throat.

Faraz was woozy and fought for air. His hands came up to pry Iyad's arm away, but he had no strength. He saw Iyad's right hand reach past him to grab a knife from a display. The blade flashed in front of Faraz.

Iyad pushed his forearm up under Faraz's jaw, compressing his windpipe and exposing the neck below. Faraz gasped for air and flailed his arms, desperate to find the knife. His head pounded from the blow and lack of oxygen. He felt Iyad's breath on his right ear. "Die and go to hell, infidel." Iyad brought the knife toward his throat. Faraz could fight no more. He was losing consciousness.

Something hit them hard from behind. The knife flew out of Iyad's hand and clattered onto the floor. The two of them staggered forward, but Iyad still gripped Faraz's throat.

Then, another jolt.

Iyad's head lolled onto Faraz's shoulder. His forearm fell off Faraz's throat. He slid down to the floor.

Someone caught Faraz from behind. The last words he heard before he passed out were, "I got you, little man."

PART THREE

Chapter Fifty

Bridget and Will were still under lockdown in the consulate waiting room. The marine told them there was an attack somewhere in the city and they couldn't leave. Couldn't have their cell phones, either. No amount of begging and rank pulling could change his mind or get them any more information.

Will paced the room. Bridget conserved energy, sitting on the sofa and staring down the guard when he looked her way.

His phone rang. He spoke for a moment, then knocked on the glass and leaned in toward the metal grate. "Urgent call for Ms. Davenport. Secure line in the comms room." He pointed toward the waiting room exit and the electronic lock buzzed.

Bridget took hold of Will's arm and stood. She was fully alert. The nap had worked wonders.

The technician stood outside the comms room and held the door for her. In the center of an array of computers, fax machines and telephones, a red handset lay on a table.

Bridget picked it up. "Davenport."

"Oh, thank God. It's Liz. We had a Shock Wave call. He's in Jerusalem. He asked for egress, but the call was interrupted. When the Israelis got to where he said he was, he was gone. Meanwhile, it's a real mess over there—more than a dozen bodies in the Old City, and Abdallah said there's more to come."

"Shit. All right. I'm on it." Bridget hung up and sat in the desk chair. She turned to the technician. "Get me Colonel Ben-Yosef."

The technician hit a speed dial number on the secure landline and spoke to someone in Hebrew. Then, he turned to Bridget. "It's Sergeant Peretz, Ben-Yosef's aide."

Bridget took the phone. "This is Bridget Davenport. I need the colonel now. No excuses."

"But, ma'am—"

"Now, goddamnit."

The first thing Faraz noticed was that his throat hurt. He reached for it even before opening his eyes.

When he did open them, he was immediately on alert. He planted his elbow and sat up a little, but had to lie back down when a wave of dizziness hit him.

"Easy, now."

The voice came from behind him. It was oddly familiar, but he couldn't place it. He also couldn't see who was speaking.

He was in a living room on a plush sofa, the kind with large buttons forming indentations in the fabric, the stuffing straining to get out. It was pale green with wood-topped arms. The wall behind was white, but in need of a paint job, and there was a framed Koranic quote hanging on it. To his left was a wooden coffee table with a glass top, three white doilies and a decorative ceramic bowl.

"Water?" the voice offered.

"Thanks." Faraz got himself onto an elbow and turned toward the voice.

All the blood seemed to drain from Faraz's body. His skin went cold. His head hurt. He wretched a dry heave.

The man sat down in front of Faraz on the edge of the coffee table. "That's a nice greeting."

Faraz looked away and looked back. He lunged for the ornamental bowl and vomited.

"Well, that went from bad to worse. Take it easy. Breathe."

Faraz looked up from the bowl and sat back on the couch. "What the fuck?"

"Drink some water." The man offered a plastic cup and put the bowl on a side table.

Faraz took it. His hand was shaking. He managed to get some of the water into his mouth. "Am I dead?"

"No." The man chuckled and took back the cup. "And neither am I, as it turns out." The man was thin, but filled out compared with what Faraz remembered. He looked a bit like Faraz but his skin tone was lighter. He was clean-shaven, with short black hair and, like Faraz, he had a slight hook in his nose.

Faraz reached out his hand and touched the man's face. "Johnny?"

"In the flesh."

"How is this possible?"

"You asked if you were dead. Well, you are, aren't you? Officially, I mean."

"What? Yeah, but . . . Oh, good God." Faraz put his head in his hands. "You're in the program? With the major?"

"He was a lowly captain when I met him, but yes."

Faraz looked up at Johnny, tried to see the fresh-faced eighteen-year-old he'd idolized, the cousin who let him stay up late when his parents were out, who taught him how to fix a motorcycle, who volunteered to fight for his country after 9/11 and never came home. Faraz cried at his funeral. That was more than ten years ago.

"What you did to us."

"Yeah. I think about that every day."

"We cried for weeks. It took me years to get over it."

"I am sorry about that. Really, I am. But you did get over it. And then you joined the army and said yes when the major came calling."

Faraz was silent. The lie he let the army tell his parents—that he had died in a training accident—still haunted him. They were both gone, now, barely two years later.

"We did a terrible thing, didn't we," Faraz said.

"Yeah. I won't deny it." Johnny stood and moved the bowl to a side table.

"The major convinced us it was for a greater good," Faraz said. "The major and Davenport. Or maybe you knew her as Walinsky."

"Davenport? The one who was kidnapped?"

"Yes."

"Wow. Anyway, no, I don't know her. I used up my quota of fake identities and close calls a few years ago and went inactive. That is, until I got a call that they had an agent in distress in my neighborhood."

"You didn't know it was me?"

"Not until I saw you. They gave me a rough location. I was heading toward the sound of the gunfire, looking for a carpet shop, when I came up on you and that guy fighting."

"Another second, he'd have slit my throat. You killed him?"

"Yeah, then dragged your ass through the alley. Luckily it wasn't far. You put on some weight in the last dozen years or so."

Faraz stood, unsteady. He reached for support and caught Johnny's hand. "This is so surreal."

The cousins embraced.

"When I was a kid," Faraz said, "I dreamed about a moment like this."

"I had the same dream." They hugged again. When they separated, Johnny said, "I heard about it when you . . . uh . . . died. At that time, I thought, 'maybe.' But I knew better than to ask. I wanted to call your parents, and mine, but . . . you know."

"At least, they could have told us about each other."

"No way. Nobody knows anybody. All those years in the program and you're the second guy I've met. Both were emergency protocol breaks."

Faraz tensed at a noise coming from another part of the apartment.

CHAPTER FIFTY-ONE

Bridget fidgeted on the sidewalk outside the consulate. "Where the hell is our transport?"

"It'll be here. It's only been a few minutes." Will tilted his head toward the source of the sirens that continued to wail. "They have a few other things going on."

An Israeli army jeep pulled up. Will showed his ID to the driver and they got in. "I will take you to the command post," he said.

Ayman was squeezed into Nabil's old compact hatchback—excellent for transporting watches, clocks and supplies, not so good for an overweight passenger burdened by an explosive vest. Ayman cringed at every bump in the road, fearing the bomb would go off. He coughed from the fumes that came through the floorboards every time Nabil shifted gears.

But the watchmaker knew all the back alleys of the Old City and which footpaths were wide enough for the car, avoiding the Israelis' usual patrol routes.

"Finish your food," Nabil said.

Ayman took a bite of the energy bar the old man had given him and sipped from a plastic bottle of energy drink. He hadn't eaten since the leftovers of Munir's care package that morning. And though Ayman seldom missed a meal, he wasn't hungry.

"Nerves will make you forget to eat," Nabil said. "But you must."

He drove across the Christian Quarter and exited the Old City through the New Gate—so named because it was little more than a hundred years old, in a city with a history of thousands of years. The gate opened directly into Israeli West Jerusalem, not far from the beginning of Jaffa Street.

Nabil turned right on the Street of the Paratroopers, then left at the first opportunity and found parking on a side road.

Rivka was thinking of putting her sweater back on. Jerusalem was indeed cooler than the coast, particularly in the shade of the buildings that lined the staging area. Tali and the other children were in rough formation behind a marching band. They teased and pushed each other as they waited for the parade to start.

A man's voice from behind startled her. "ID please."

Rivka turned. "Ach! Ari, you scared me."

"You didn't mind last night."

Rivka blushed. "You are impossible."

Ari smiled and shrugged. "So, no kiss, then?"

She gave him a kiss. Even with his arm in a cast and his leg bandage bulging under his trousers, Ari looked good in his uniform—the one she had ironed for him a few days earlier so he would look sharp in case the TV cameras came by.

"I like this costume," Ari said. He admired the snug bodice and cleavage.

"If you can get home before two a.m., we'll have more time than we did last night."

"Count on it."

He moved in for another kiss but she put a hand on his chest. "Please . . . the children."

"Temptress."

She touched his bad arm. "Really, Ari, how are you doing?"

"I'm fine."

Rivka studied his face. "You are usually a much better liar." She turned away and he embraced her from behind with his good arm. "Tali is over there." She pointed. "In the middle of the center row."

"I will deal with you later."

"I hope so."

Ari moved off toward the children.

Tali saw him when he was halfway there. "*Abbaaaaah!*" Daddy. All heads turned toward her shriek. She ran out of the formation and, ignoring his injury, jumped into his arms for a kiss and a neck hug. Then she wriggled away, stood back and twirled around to model her costume. "Do you like it?"

"It is beautiful. But for some reason I want to go swimming."

Tali put her hands on her hips and gave him a faux pout. "*Abba*, you are so silly."

Rivka caught up with them. "Okay, Tali. Go now. Get back in line. The parade will start soon."

"Yes," Ari said, "and I have to get back to work."

Tali blew him a kiss. "Watch me in the parade, *Abba*." And she ran back to her friends.

Ari lowered his voice. "You heard about the attack in the Old City?"

"What? No."

"We stopped them. We think it's finished now. But keep your eyes open."

"Should we leave?"

"I recommended canceling the parade, and finally your father agreed. But the government said no. Anyway, we have a big force here and the quick response team is on standby."

"It's all right," Johnny said. He put a hand on Faraz's arm and turned toward the noise in the hallway that led to the back of the apartment. He raised his voice. "You can come out. He's a friend."

A bedroom door opened and a boy of two or three ran into the living room. "*Ba!*" he shrieked. He grabbed Johnny's leg, then hid his face from the stranger.

Johnny picked the boy up. "This is Umair, my son."

Faraz looked at the boy. "This is a lot for one day."

"For one hour, even less."

There were footsteps in the hallway. A tall, thin woman in a tan sweater and long gray skirt emerged from the bedroom and took tentative steps toward them. Her hair was barely hidden under an *abaya*. Her dark eyes showed concern at first. But when she saw that all was well, she smiled, and it was as if someone had flooded the room with light.

Johnny smiled back. "This is . . ." he paused. "This is Khalil, an old friend. Khalil, meet Leila, my wife."

Leila nodded a greeting and put her right hand over her heart. "You are welcome here, Khalil. I will make tea."

Faraz made a half bow, unable to think of anything to say.

Leila picked up the boy. "Come, Umair, help *umi* in the kitchen."

Faraz watched her go, still trying to process what was happening.

"Now you know why I settled here," Johnny said.

"Yes. And you named the boy after our grandfather."

"Right." Johnny smiled. "No one knew it but me, and now you."

"And you called me 'Kahlil.' Friend. Dear friend, actually. They say Abraham was the *khalil* of Allah."

"I know. Seems right. Best to keep our secret, at least for now. Best to get that costume off, too."

Faraz looked down. He still wore the printed polyester outfit that some designer imagined would look like a president's suit. Faraz tore at the plastic fasteners and tossed the costume onto a chair.

"Might as well tell me why you're here," Johnny said.

Faraz gave him the basics.

"So, you think there's another attack coming?"

"Yeah. Unfortunately, I don't know what it is. Shit. I need to phone in."

"I tossed my cell after I got the call and I won't put Leila at risk by using hers." Johnny went to a locked cabinet against the far wall and came back with a steel box. Inside was a satellite phone and a charging cable. "Let's see if we can fire this old thing up."

* * *

Bridget and Will were delayed by the crowds streaming to the parade route and by three checkpoints. At the last one, there were four police cars parked across the road, with a portable fence in front of them hung with detour signs. They left the vehicle and a soldier led them on foot around the right edge of the roadblock to two trailers sitting in an L-shape that formed the command post. Ari was smoking outside.

"Colonel, are you all right?" Bridget asked.

"I'm fine. I wish people would stop asking me that."

"Sorry. What's happening?"

"Nothing, for now."

"Our man's report said there's a second wave."

"There was a second wave in the Old City, a second team came into the square. That seems to be it."

"You sure?"

Ari took a long drag on his cigarette, then looked at Bridget with impatience bordering on anger. "Maybe the DIA in Washington knows more than I do in Jerusalem. And I'm sure your man knows everything, except how to stop the attack, which killed four of our policemen, by the way."

"I'm sorry. That's terrible. Our man is missing, you know."

Ari exploded now. "Of course, I know! Do you think we wait for you to tell us things? We have people looking for him, but honestly, it's not our top priority. I have twenty-five thousand people at a parade."

"It's still on?"

"They won't cancel it. It's too late now, anyway. They

congratulate us for stopping the Old City attack. But they want to show that the terrorists don't create terror. Israel is unafraid. Exposed, but unafraid."

Sergeant Peretz opened the command trailer door and poked her head out. "Sir, we have a call for Ms. Davenport."

They all scrambled up the three steps into the trailer.

"It's the DIA operations center," Peretz said.

"On speaker," Bridget ordered. "This is Davenport."

"Ma'am, we have a Shock Wave call on a nonsecured line."

"Put it through."

"Ma'am, procedure dictates—"

"On my authority. Do it now."

The line beeped. "Faraz, this is Bridget Davenport. Are you okay?"

"Yes. I'm safe in the Old City. And thank God you're apparently okay, too."

"Yes."

"Has the second wave hit?"

"The Israelis think the second wave was with you in that square."

"Negative. There's another part to the attack, but I don't know what it is."

Ari took a radio off his belt and started barking orders in Hebrew.

"What's going on?" Faraz asked.

"There's a parade here in West Jerusalem. Could that be the next target?"

"Sounds right, but like I said, they didn't tell me. Also, one man is on some sort of special mission. I don't know details on that either, but I'd know him if I saw him. Actually, I heard you were held in his house."

"Al-Hamdani," Ari said.

"Yes, Ayman, the one I was put with in the prison."

Ari spewed some Arabic curses, then switched to Hebrew to issue more orders.

"How can we get you over here?" Bridget asked. "We can send transport."

There was muffled conversation on Faraz's end.

"New Gate, five minutes. I'll have one guy with me."

"Defector?"

"American. I'll explain when I see you."

"We'll send a vehicle," Ari said. He gestured at Peretz and she turned to leave.

"One more thing," Faraz said. "Al-Hamdani may be wearing a Superman costume."

Ayman sweated in the oversized jacket he'd chosen from Nabil's stash to cover the explosive bricks that bulged his costume. The front of the jacket was unzipped halfway, exposing the blue shirt and large "S" so he could blend in with the Israeli crowd. Ayman held the hard plastic mask in his right hand and played with the rubber band.

Nabil reached over from the driver's seat to make a final check of the bomb. "You saw the bus stop?"

"Yes."

"You will get on there. The bus will turn right to climb Jaffa Street. After two stops, it will be diverted for the parade. That is your opportunity."

"I understand."

Nabil picked up the detonator from the car's central console. He ran its wires through a pocket slit on the left side of Ayman's costume pants, raised the blue shirt and connected the wires to the battery pack. He flipped the main power switch to the ON position and lowered the shirt.

He gave the detonator to Ayman. "The device is armed now. Be careful. When the time comes, remember, pull the trigger and then push the button."

Ayman nodded and swallowed hard.

Nabil checked his watch, a fine one from Switzerland. "It is time." He reached into his pocket and passed Ayman a bus ticket. "Scan this when you board. Do not get into any trouble along the way."

Ayman put the ticket in his pants pocket.

"I wish I had more time with you."

"Do not worry, *sayyid*."

Nabil twisted in his seat and put his hands on Ayman's shoulders. Ayman stopped playing with the rubber band. Nabil repeated the martyr's blessings, then led Ayman in the *Shahada*.

"*La ilaha illa-lah, Mohammed rasulu-lah.*" There is no God but God. Mohammed is the messenger of God.

Nabil leaned over and kissed Ayman on both cheeks. "You must go now."

"Thank you, *sayyid*. I will not fail." Ayman opened the car door, got out and straightened his outfit. He put the detonator into his pocket, next to the bus ticket, then closed the door and looked at Nabil through the window one last time.

"*Allah ma'aak,*" the old man said. God be with you.

"*Wa ma'aak.*" And with you. Ayman put the mask on, turned toward the main road and started walking.

Chapter Fifty-two

It was a small apartment, so with Faraz in the living room and the boy, Umair, back in the bedroom, Johnny and Leila had nowhere to talk in private. They stood at the end of the hall and whispered in a mix of Arabic and English. Faraz heard most of it.

"But you said it was over," Leila said, the fear and sadness evident on her face. She leaned in toward her husband. "When you went out today, you said it was an emergency. You called it a 'one-time deal.'"

"I know but . . . I cannot explain. There's no time. I have to go with this man, make sure he is safe. Then I will come home."

Leila seemed to know she was going to lose the argument. She stared at Johnny, looked like she might cry. Then, she embraced him, squeezed him tight, and said something into his ear that Faraz couldn't hear.

Johnny kissed her, lingered for a moment, then returned to Faraz. "*Yalla.*" He led the way down two flights on a back stairway. Chained to the railing at the bottom, they found Johnny's motorcycle.

Faraz had to smile. "Of course, you have a bike."

"Damn straight."

"It's the one you always wanted, isn't it?"

"1990 Harley Fatboy. Belches smoke but moves like crazy. Only one in Jerusalem, as far as I know."

"I remember when you were fixing one of those and you taught me how to ride. We got in a lot of trouble over that. But the knowledge came in handy a couple of years ago."

"I'd like to hear that story when we have time."

"Absolutely."

Johnny unlocked the chain, slid his helmet off it and checked the fuel level. "Sorry, no helmet for you. Leila won't go near this thing."

Johnny put the chain in the cargo box. Faraz climbed onto the elevated rear seat. Johnny stepped on, kicked the starter, put the bike in gear and accelerated down the alley.

Ayman stood apart from the other people waiting for the bus. He closed his eyes, thought of Maysoon, of his mother. He thought about how proud his father would be, how impressed Iyad had been when he'd outlined his plan. Even the old watchmaker respected him now. Tonight, they would celebrate his bravery, his commitment to Allah's cause. His martyrdom.

In his fantasy, he was there, too.

For the first time, Ayman faced the fact of his own plan—that he would not be able to celebrate with them, to see his picture in the newspapers, to watch the Zionists crying on television. His death was so close and yet as unimaginable as it had ever been.

The fumes of a passing truck engulfed Ayman and he coughed into the mask. He raised the bottom to breath some fresh air. When he put it back in place and aligned the eyeholes, he saw the bus in the distance.

His hands started shaking. He put them in his pockets to steady them. He gripped the detonator, concentrated on his breathing.

Johnny locked his motorcycle to a post at the Israeli police guard shack outside the New Gate.

"What should I tell them?" Faraz asked.

"Who is Davenport, exactly?"

"She's DIA, head of the task force I'm attached to. She found me through the major."

"I guess you can tell her the truth, but no one else. The Israelis know about me at some high-up super-secret level, but we don't want to spread the word."

The Israeli army SUV sped up to them and slid to a stop. "Say the words," Sergeant Peretz said through the open window.

Faraz responded. "Shock Wave."

"All right, get in."

Faraz led Johnny into the backseat. Peretz continued north a hundred meters to make a U-turn just beyond a crowded bus stop. Faraz saw the children and adults in costume jostling for position as the bus approached. He did not see the large man near the back of the group sweating behind a Superman mask.

* * *

Ayman tensed and turned away when he saw the army vehicle make its U-turn. He thought it might be coming for him, but it passed by so fast he barely had time to move his fingers to the detonator. He moved them off as he watched the SUV speed toward the parade route.

He jerked again when the bus's brakes squeaked and hissed. It was one of the extra-long ones, articulated so it could bend in the middle. It had doors in the front, the center and near the back. They all opened. A dozen people got off through the rear door and walked past him.

Ayman's breath made the inside of the mask wet. The eyeholes restricted his vision.

"Soooperman," one teenager sang as he went by.

Ayman fell in at the back of the crowd, boarded through the rear door and held his ticket against a reader mounted on a pole.

The bus was crowded. He grabbed a handhold and turned his head so he could see forward.

A group of teenagers teased each other in loud voices—all the boys dressed as pirates, and the girl as . . . what? Bare midriff, low-cut top, short cut-offs, fingernails painted bright red. Ayman snorted. She was probably supposed to be a female pirate, but to him she looked like a prostitute. Why was this whore alive and Maysoon dead?

Ayman turned away. He needed to focus on what he had to do.

The bus lumbered through the right turn onto Jaffa Street and stopped. A family got on, parents, a grandmother and a boy wearing a skullcap with a soccer team logo. They were in old-fashioned costumes, maybe homemade. The boy, about four years old, clung to his mother's leg. He waved at Superman.

The woman turned the child away and put him behind her. She eyed Ayman, then whispered something to her husband. The man looked up, then seemed to dismiss whatever she had said. Could she suspect something? Would the bulky jacket on a warm day give him away?

Ayman could do it now. He could squeeze the lever and push the button and it would all be over. He moved his finger but hesitated. He got goosebumps. Was he really ready? Ayman felt doubt for the first time since he'd made his decision. He looked away from the family, through the bus's windshield to the large crowd ahead. He was so close to achieving so much.

He closed his eyes and recited the *Shahada* to himself. Then again. And again. Ayman allowed his head to move forward and back with each repetition. The rhythm soothed him. This was for Allah, for Palestine, for his father and Maysoon, for himself.

The bus moved off the stop and climbed Jaffa Street toward the parade staging area near Jerusalem's City Hall.

Even the parents were getting impatient now. The morning chill was gone. The sun came over the buildings and put Jaffa Street on simmer. The children's formation was in disarray, and the band's effort to keep them entertained had worn thin.

"I wish they would start already," Rivka said. She pulled her hair back off her shoulders and threaded it through an elastic band.

"Any minute now," Batya assured her. "We don't want to arrive at the market before the food is ready."

"Or start the parade before the TV networks go live." The women laughed.

"Yes," Batya said. "Today our children will be famous in a small country. Where did Ari go?"

"He is back on duty."

"At least you got to see him."

Tali's teacher came through the crowd urging the children back into formation. "The parade has started. We will be moving at any minute. Remember, stay in your lines and when I tell you, sing as loud as you can."

"It's a Purim miracle," Rivka said.

"Absolutely." Batya adjusted her headpiece. "I could not stand here one more minute."

Rivka looked back toward the command post.

"I'm glad Ari is handling security," Batya said.

"Me, too. But I wish he could walk with us."

Bridget came out of the trailer as Faraz and Johnny arrived. "I'm so glad you're all right."

"I was about to say the same thing to you."

She embraced him. It was the first time they had done that and it was awkward.

Bridget released him and he spoke in hushed tones. "Ma'am. This is my cousin Johnny. He rescued me in the Old City."

"Your cousin?" Bridget asked.

"You remember I had a cousin, don't you?"

"Killed in Afghanistan, early days, right?"

"That's what they told us." Faraz looked at her.

It took Bridget a couple of seconds. "Oh, my living God."

"So, you didn't know, either."

"No idea. But how—?"

"The major."

"Of course, the major. He would have gotten a flash message about your call."

"And happened to have a man in the neighborhood," Johnny said. "A retired man."

Bridget looked at Johnny. "The fucking major."

Johnny laughed. "It's good to be with someone who can say that."

Bridget shook his hand. "Welcome to the team."

"Let's keep it between us," Johnny said.

"Of course."

Will and Ari joined them.

"Ari, this is my agent, Lieutenant Abdallah. Faraz, this is Colonel Ben-Yosef, and I think you know Commander Will Jackson from a little dust-up in Afghanistan."

"Right," Faraz said. "In a different life."

"Good to see you, Lieutenant." They shook hands.

"And this is Faraz's . . . friend, Johnny . . . um," Bridget said.

"Just 'Johnny' is good," Faraz said.

"I would make coffee for your reunion," Ari said. "But you mentioned there could be another wave, Lieutenant."

"Yes. It could be happening any minute."

"What, exactly?"

"I was not in on that part of the operation."

"Great." Ari turned to Bridget. "As I said, he knows everything except how to stop the next attack. We will handle this on our own, as always. You three should go."

"Go? We need to fan out and help look for them," Bridget said.

"Your mission is done. You found your man. Now, go back to your hotel and let us do our job."

"My man, as you call him, is best equipped to recognize the terrorists."

"We sent al-Hamdani's photo to all our forces. This is our fight. You cannot be in the middle of it."

Will spoke up. "No time to argue. We'll get out of your way, Colonel."

He herded the others away from the command post as Ari and Sergeant Peretz went inside. Thirty meters away, the band was playing a pop tunes medley and the kids were dancing in place. Spectators were clapping in rhythm to the music. The temperature was up several degrees in the last half hour.

"May I suggest," Johnny said. "Faraz and I will go south from the roadblock, you two go west along the parade route."

"Look for young men who seem out of place in costumes," Faraz said.

Will looked around. "All the young men look out of place in the costumes."

As the bus pulled away from the second stop, Ayman held onto a seat with his right hand and slipped his left under the mask to wipe the sweat from his face. The driver accelerated up the incline toward the roadblock, where he would have to turn.

Ayman moved his head to the side so he could look past the people standing in the aisle. He saw the fence and police cars across the road and the soldiers walking back and forth with their weapons pointed at the ground. Behind them, marchers waited in formation.

The bus slowed with the traffic. A police officer in front of the roadblock directed the vehicles into a single lane to turn left. Pop music drifted into the bus.

It wouldn't be long now.

Ayman's pulse quickened. He put his hand in his pocket and caressed the detonator. There would be no more hesitation. Nothing would stop him. His destiny was right in front of him.

Faraz and Johnny went back the way they had come. They walked around the roadblock into the crowd of people on the sidewalk pushing toward the parade route. The street was packed with vehicles approaching the detour. The cousins moved as fast as they could, bucking the flow, staring down groups of young men in costumes.

Ahead of them, a bus driver laid on the horn and swerved left to accelerate past a knot of revelers who had overflowed into the road. As the bus passed, Faraz looked at the bizarre scene playing like a slide show through the long bus's windows—kings, queens, pirates, monsters.

Superman.

CHAPTER FIFTY-THREE

"Stop! Stop the bus!" Faraz's shouts were lost in the vehicle's motor noise. He ran to catch up, but he couldn't. He gestured at people farther up the street, but they ignored him.

"There's a bomb on board!"

Now, the people responded. Most started running away. Two men moved in front of the bus, waving their arms above their heads and shouting in Hebrew. The driver hit the brakes and opened all the doors. Faraz heard him say something through the vehicle's PA system. Then he bailed out through his emergency exit.

The passengers started running off the bus. Faraz would have expected some shock, even doubt, on a bus in the United States. But here, a bomb on a bus was an all too real possibility. He suspected people had been drilled on such a scenario.

Faraz fought his way against the human tide to get through the front door. Ayman stood in the back, frozen, shaking. He held a device in his left hand, with a wire that disappeared under his coat.

Their eyes met.

"No! Ayman, no!" Faraz pushed his way toward him past the last of the passengers. He ran at Ayman, forcing him to let go of the detonator and raise his hands in self-defense.

Faraz tackled him. Ayman's mask flew off and they fell hard onto the floor. Faraz could feel the explosive bricks under Ayman's coat. He groped for the detonator.

"Khayal, what are you doing?"

"Stopping you, you moron."

Ayman rolled and used his weight to push Faraz under the seats. He stood and moved toward the front of the bus, the detonator dangling by his side and bouncing off his leg.

Faraz got to his feet. Through the windows, he could see the police pushing people back from the bus while soldiers trained their weapons on it. Johnny was standing between the troops and the bus, holding up his Israeli ID and shouting something. A soldier grabbed him and pulled him out of the way.

Faraz ran forward, caught Ayman from behind and spun him around. Ayman had a wild look in his eyes, angry, determined, almost possessed. He grabbed Faraz by the neck with surprising strength and slammed his head into a pole. Faraz crumpled to the floor, dazed, next to the open center door.

Ayman reached the driver's seat, put the bus in gear and hit the gas.

With the street clear now, there was nothing to stop him. The big engine shot the empty bus forward toward the checkpoint and the parade formation behind it. The troops fired. Bus windows shattered. Ayman bent as low as he could behind the steering wheel.

Faraz got onto his knees. He saw the roadblock approaching. He saw Ayman hold up the detonator.

He heard him scream, "*Allah hu akbar*!"

Faraz dove out of the bus through the side door, landing in an awkward summersault on the pavement. He came to a stop and covered his head with his hands.

The police officer's call came through a speaker in the command center. *"P'tzah! P'tzah!"* Bomb! Bomb! On the bus below the roadblock!"

Ari hit the button on a microphone in front of him and issued a string of commands.

The explosion interrupted him, loud and sharp, with a background of ripping metal.

Then something hit the trailer so hard it nearly toppled over.

When Rivka heard the shouting from the other side of the roadblock and saw the people running, she took off toward Tali. The shooting started before she reached her. Rivka glanced back and saw the bus approaching, then the flash.

She had spent eighteen months in the army after high school, like most Israelis, so she knew what she should do. But the shock of it froze her in pace. A split-second later, Rivka was flat on her back. Her head hit the street. Her wildcat ears flew off.

* * *

The force of the blast lifted the huge bus off the ground. It flew several meters before landing hard and skidding through the roadblock as a flaming missile. Its windows blew out, sending shards of glass in all directions. Its roof opened like a sardine can and spewed seats and metal bars into the air.

The bus came to rest, crushing a burning police car against the command center trailers.

Faraz was thrown backward, rolling into the side of a car. He was stunned and his ears were ringing.

Johnny ran over to help him up and said something, but Faraz couldn't hear him. Johnny had cuts on his face and holes in his shirt.

"Are you all right?" Faraz shouted.

Johnny nodded.

Faraz looked around. Dozens of people were lying on the street, some bleeding, some apparently dead. "We were too late," he said. "Oh Allah, we were too late."

Johnny's voice came through the ringing in Faraz's ears. "You got over a hundred people off that bus. We pushed dozens more back."

"Not good enough. Not damn good enough."

When the command trailer righted itself, Ari ran out the door as fast as his bad leg would carry him. He stopped cold at the sight of the burning and mangled carcass of the bus and the police car crushed against his command center.

He couldn't see much more through the cloud of smoke and debris.

Ari nearly tripped over a soldier lying on the ground. The man was in shock, shaking. His severed arm lay next to him. Ari knelt to help him.

Farther along Jaffa Street, beyond the staging area, a second explosion sent Bridget and Will back to the ground.

Will put a hand on Bridget's back to hold her down while he raised his head to see what had happened. "Looks like something blew up alongside the command center, a vehicle gas tank, maybe."

Bridget pushed his hand off and got onto her knees. "Ben-Yosef and Peretz were over there. We need to get to them."

"No way. Look at that fire."

"We have to try." Bridget pressed against the side of a building to avoid the crush of people running toward them. As she worked her way back toward the roadblock, she could see more clearly. The command post trailers were on fire.

Rivka's chest and face were littered with fragments of glass and metal. She was bleeding and in pain. When she pushed herself up, the second explosion and a fresh hail of shrapnel forced her back to the ground.

Her yoga pants ripped and the pavement scraped her knee. Rivka raised her head a second time. Large flames shot skyward in a thick cloud of roiling black smoke at the front of the bus. It had apparently crashed through the roadblock and . . .

"Ari!" It was something between a scream and a cry.

Rivka jumped to her feet. She started to run toward the trailers, but the heat was so intense it stopped her, even though she was fifty meters away. She raised her forearm to shield her face and scanned the attack site. There was no movement. She fell to her knees.

"Riv. Help me." It was Batya, lying on the ground to her right. Her jangly headband was next to her. "I can't get up."

Rivka knelt next to her. Batya had a bruise on her forehead and blood soaking through the right side of her peasant girl blouse. "Stay where you are. Help will be here soon."

Batya pointed at Rivka's face. Rivka reached up and found a four-centimeter piece of glass sticking out of her right cheek. She removed it and winced in pain. She held her sleeve against the wound to stop the bleeding.

"The children," Batya pleaded.

Rivka looked toward the staging area. Everyone was on the ground.

Bridget and Will were making little progress against the rush of people.

"This is ridiculous," she said. "We'll never get there at this rate."

"And look at the fire. I can already feel the heat."

A black Israeli armored vehicle came from behind them, heading for the roadblock, blasting its siren and blowing its horn. Letters stenciled on its sides in Hebrew,

Arabic and English read EMERGENCY RESPONSE. The crowd parted to let it pass.

"Let's follow him," Will said.

They fought their way to the middle of the street and got into the small space behind the vehicle before the crowd closed around it.

Rivka reached the parade formation and heard the screaming.

Adults in tattered costumes called out for their children. Kings and queens and superheroes lay on the ground, some crying hysterically, others silent. The band was down, its instruments lying at odd angles along with the musicians.

She moved among the bodies, touching a head here, holding a hand there, telling the living to stay down and now sobbing for the dead.

Rivka looked around to get her bearings. The bus, police car and command post were still on fire, and the smoke cloud had doubled in size. She could smell it now. It caught in her throat and she coughed.

People around her were shouting—prayers, curses, pleas.

Then she saw Tali's class. One of the boys was up, dirt on his face, blood oozing from his nose. Rivka ran to him. She took the bandana from of his costume and held it to his nose. "Squeeze this," she said. "Sit down. Help is coming."

Rivka looked past the boy and gasped. Tali was there, lying across Batya's daughter, Sara. Rivka stepped toward them, fell to her knees and took her daughter's head in her hands.

"*Ima.*" Mommy.

Tali slurred the word, but it was the most beautiful sound Rivka had ever heard. "Praise God, you're all right."

Tali vomited and passed out. Rivka picked her up. Blood was caked in the hair on the back of the girl's head.

Rivka touched Sara's hand. "Sara, sweetie, can you hear me?"

There was no response.

Rivka put her hand on the girl's back and felt her breathing. She shook her shoulder. Sara opened her eyes. "Where is my mommy?"

"I will take you to her. Can you walk?"

"I think so."

With Tali in her arms, Rivka took Sara's hand and led her along Jaffa Street away from the carnage. Toward help, she hoped.

Tali lifted her head off Rivka's shoulder. She touched her mother's face. "*Ima*, you're bleeding."

Rivka could feel the blood trickling down her cheek but had no free hand to check how bad it was. "It's nothing, dear."

"*Ayfoh abba*?" Where's Papa?

Rivka covered the girl's eyes. "Don't look, dear. Papa will be all right. I will get us out of here."

Sara lagged behind, crying.

"Please, Sara." She pulled the girl along.

Rivka couldn't remember where she'd left Batya. City Hall was to the right, surrounded by a high fence. Ahead, the street was blocked by thousands of people running past the bodies of the dead and injured, dodging musical instruments and parade floats. Rivka pulled Sara toward the other side of the street.

She found Batya still lying in the road. If she could get up, maybe they could get the girls out of there.

Twenty meters ahead, there was an alley on the left between buildings that led to a parallel road. But its gate was closed.

As Rivka knelt down next to Batya, the gate exploded and men came out shooting.

Waleed was calm and methodical. He led his team out of the alley at a jog, then slowed to a walk and picked his targets—a cluster of people kneeling around an injured man on his right, a family running on his left, an Israeli policewoman who took a shot at him from across the street.

His vampire costume was printed with a black suit, white shirt and blue tie stained with blood. He had the mask flipped up onto the top of his head.

"*Al-yameen*," he shouted, and his men fanned out to the right, trapping people between their gunfire and the burning checkpoint. "*Allah hu akbar!*" Waleed yelled as he ran ahead, leading his team toward cover behind a newsstand.

Chapter Fifty-four

Rivka fell hard on top of Tali and pulled Sara down with her. Tali's head hit the road and she lost consciousness again. Rivka shifted her body to get the girls underneath her. She put her face to the pavement next to Batya.

The terrorists strafed the crowd, their bullets pinging off the road.

A flaming pain shot through Rivka's right leg. She cried out. There was another burst of gunfire. Batya's body convulsed and blood spattered across Rivka's face. She stifled a scream and turned Sara's head away. She was breathing hard but somehow had to play dead.

As the shooters advanced, their bullets flew over her and there was more screaming. Rivka's leg burned and she saw her blood mix with Batya's on the street. She squeezed the girls and prayed.

"There!" Bridget yelled, pointing toward the gunfire. "Let's go." She pulled Will out of the shadow of the armored vehicle.

"With what?" Will grabbed her arm. He took the pistol

out of his belt. "We have this and that's all. Those are AKs they're firing." An explosion sent them to the ground. "And grenades."

The emergency response team streamed out of the vehicle and ran past them toward the attackers.

On the other side of the burning roadblock, Faraz and Johnny were looking for a way through but were forced back by the heat.

"Listen," Faraz said.

"Gunfire."

"It's coming from the other side. We have to get over there."

"No way. Your boys did a good job of cutting the battlefield in half. And we're on the wrong half."

"Can we go around?" Faraz asked.

"It's a long way and the roads will be packed."

"Damn it."

People helping the wounded were not deterred by the shooting several blocks away. Small clusters gathered around some of the bodies. One woman's wails rose above the rest.

"Let's go down the hill," Johnny said. "It's a ways, but we can get to my bike. At least, we'll have wheels."

Faraz looked toward the burning roadblock again, but Johnny was right.

They turned around and picked their way between bodies and vehicles. There was a black strip the width of the bus where it landed and skidded into the roadblock.

Some people had not moved fast enough to get out of the way, leaving a stomach-turning debris field of body

parts and personal items. Faraz catalogued the carnage—
a man's foot in a pirate shoe, half of a knitted skullcap
with a soccer team logo, a girl's hand with bright red nail
polish. One storefront's picture window was blown in.
Faraz shuddered to think what had flown through it.

There was a crater a few meters farther back, on the
spot where Ayman had detonated his bomb. Cracked and
broken concrete slabs lay at odd angles, with fragments
of bus seats and smoldering cushions nearby.

Beyond the crater, a piece of blue fabric with bits of
yellow and red was on top of something.

Faraz stopped.

Johnny bumped into him. "What is it?"

Faraz stared. "Superman." He walked a few steps to
his right, bent down and lifted the fabric. Although he
was expecting it, Faraz recoiled.

Ayman's severed head stared up at him.

The explosion would have shattered his body, sending
his legs down into the crater, the top of his body up into
the bus ceiling, and beyond. The left side of Ayman's face
was burned and bloody. His right eye was closed, his
mouth open. His wisps of beard had been singed off.

"That's the bomber," Faraz said.

"You knew him?"

"Yeah. He was my way in. Doughboy, nerd. Put on a
front about being a fighter, but really wanted nothing
more than to sit in his room and post propaganda online.
Then they killed his sister."

"The girl in the house? I heard about that. Terrorist
family. They say she was involved in the kidnapping."

"Yeah, I guess. Hard to believe, though. I met her a

couple of weeks ago. She was in school, wanted to go to New York. I don't get it. But I guess it doesn't matter now."

"It's the life they chose."

"Maybe."

They flinched from a fresh barrage of gunfire behind them.

"We better go," Johnny said.

Faraz looked back at Ayman's head. He spat. "Asshole."

They turned and ran down the hill.

Bridget and Will took cover behind the armored vehicle with several other civilians. The Israeli force had the terrorists stuck between them and the buildings on the south side of Jaffa Street. It should have been a quick end to the battle, but an enemy who doesn't mind dying can be harder to kill. There were too many civilians around to use explosives.

The gunmen hid behind vehicles and bodies, then exposed their positions to draw fire so their comrades could respond with AK rounds and grenades. Still, it looked to Bridget like it was only a matter of time, not much time, until the Israelis finished them off.

But one of the terrorists shouted something and his men heaved several grenades. With the Israelis' taking cover, the man who gave the order led his men back toward the alley.

The terrorists disappeared past the shattered gate. An army squad moved to pursue them, but a large explosion threw the Israelis back and covered the terrorists' escape.

Smoke from the explosion blew across the road. A

commander shouted orders through a megaphone and more soldiers ran forward.

Cries and screams replaced the gunfire as the people who had pressed themselves to the ground started to move.

"There must be another way through," Bridget said. She took a step to follow the troops.

Will grabbed her arm. "The Israelis will handle it. We'll never catch up with you not at a hundred percent. And even if we did, they'd be in a firefight. We should go up the hill into the city, find our way . . . someplace. Maybe back to the consulate. This might not be over."

Bridget looked at the fire raging around the roadblock. The command trailer was all smoke and flames.

"The colonel was in there," she said.

"I know. But he's an on-the-ball guy. Maybe he got out."

"Yeah. Maybe. All right, let's go." Bridget turned and started walking out of the kill zone.

She was impressed with the level of organization already taking shape. The Israelis were using their military training to triage and provide first aid. Walking wounded sat on the curbsides. Critical cases had small teams around them. The dead were attended by family members or friends or, it seemed, strangers.

"We should help," Will said.

The shrill sound of approaching sirens reached them.

"Help is on the way," Bridget said. "We have work to do." She peered through the lingering smoke, looking for a way through the crowd.

She saw a petite woman wearing a bloodied leotard

and yoga pants struggling to stand, holding a child in her arms. "Wait. I know her."

"Me, too. It's the colonel's wife."

Faraz and Johnny finished the jog to the motorcycle, barely breaking a sweat.

"Where to?" Johnny asked. He pulled the lock-chain loose and dropped it into the cargo box.

"A phone. We need a phone."

"Roger. Hop on."

Johnny rode through the New Gate into the Old City. All the shops were closed and their security gates were down. Johnny stopped in front of a sweet shop and pounded on the metal.

"Daoud, open up," he shouted in Arabic. "Come on, my friend."

The gate rose halfway. A man bent down to speak to them. "What is it? Oh, it's you. Come in. It is not safe out there."

Johnny and Faraz ducked under the gate. "Your phone, Daoud. I need your phone."

Daoud was a small man, bald, with a moustache and wearing a baker's apron. "There is a war on and you need a phone?"

"Yes."

"All right, all right. Here." Daoud handed over his phone.

Johnny gave it to Faraz, then handed Daoud some money. "We need to take it, but we'll bring it back."

Daoud objected but Johnny shushed him and led him to the other side of the shop.

Faraz keyed the phone and moved behind a counter filled with baklava and sweet rolls.

His call was answered on the first ring.

"Operator."

Bridget started to run toward Rivka but her injuries forced her to slow down. It was true, she could never have caught up with the Israeli commandos or the terrorists.

Will jogged past her and took Tali in his arms just as Rivka staggered and fell. He laid Tali on the ground and leaned in to check her breathing.

Bridget arrived, winded, and scooped up the other girl. She knelt and checked the pulse of the woman lying next to Rivka. The woman had wounds in her back and side, and she lay in a growing pool of blood. The tips of her bleached-blonde hair were tinged with red.

Bridget shook her head. The girl screamed.

"Oh, Batya, no!" Rivka cried. Tears burst from her eyes. Then she turned and reached out to touch Tali's head.

"She's alive, but weak," Will said. "We need to get her to a hospital." He stood and waved his arms above his head to flag down an ambulance. "Hey! Over here."

The girl in Bridget's arms was sobbing.

"It's her mother," Rivka said.

Bridget held the girl tight, moved a few steps away and turned so she couldn't see. The phone Bridget had borrowed from the consulate rang. She used her free hand to take it out of her pocket. "Davenport."

"Ma'am, we have a Shock Wave call on a different unsecured line. We recommend—"

"Put it through."

"Ma'am—"

"Now!" The line beeped. "Faraz? Thank God you're alive."

"Thanks. Yeah. We got hit, but we're okay."

"There was a ground attack on this side. Any more waves coming?"

"Not that I know of. But, listen, I think I can find the house they used for staging. Any survivors will go there for egress. Assali might still be there, too."

"Oh, hell, yes, the one that got away."

"Right. But we need an assault team."

"On it. Can you meet us at the consulate?"

"I'd rather not waste the time. I have transport and it might take me awhile to figure out the location. It's somewhere east of the city. I'll call in when I find it and meet you there."

"All right. Be careful."

"Will do."

"Operator?"

"Yes, ma'am."

"End this call and get me General Hadley, priority one."

CHAPTER FIFTY-FIVE

By the time Bridget finished with Hadley, Will was helping Rivka into the ambulance. Tali and Sara were already strapped down and in the care of medics. Batya lay in the road, covered with a sheet.

Rivka looked at Bridget and mouthed the words, "Please find Ari."

Bridget nodded and the ambulance door closed.

"What was that?" Will asked.

"She wants us to find the colonel."

They looked down the street. There were only flames and smoke where the command trailer had been.

"Doesn't look good."

"No, it doesn't. And we still can't get down there. Hadley is calling General HaLevy to get a force to go with us to hit the remnants and their leader. You and I need to get to the consulate for pickup."

"It's a bit of a hike. Can you make it?"

"I'll make it."

* * *

Faraz held onto Johnny as the motorcycle took them out through the New Gate again. He reached into his pocket to be sure Daoud's phone was still there. They went right and then made the same U-turn they'd made earlier, passing the bus stop where Ayman had waited.

They passed the entrance to Jaffa Street and went left, weaving through the pedestrians still fleeing the attack. Johnny followed the road outside the Old City walls and crossed the Green Line into East Jerusalem. He accelerated past a monastery and descended into the valley below, where several Palestinian villages clustered around farm fields and edged up small hills.

They pulled into the first village, a web of residential streets around a central market square. There was no one around.

Johnny stopped the bike, and Faraz stepped off to look have a look. "Where is everyone?"

"Whenever there's a security incident, the Israelis declare a lockdown. I'm surprised we weren't stopped, but I guess the police are busy."

"This doesn't look familiar."

"It's a small village, hard to hide a large group of men here."

"Let's move on."

"Listen, Faraz. I'm not sure this is a good idea."

Faraz stood in front of the bike. "Why not?"

"Two guys who look like Arabs running around during a lockdown. And if we avoid the Israelis and find the terrorists, then what? We don't even have a handgun between us. And I'm a little out of practice fighting bad guys, frankly."

"Don't worry. It's only recon."

"Unless they see us. Then we're targets. In my time, I was as gung ho as you, probably more. But I'd like to get home tonight."

"So, you want to stay here? Or go back? Let those guys get away?"

"No. I don't want to do that, either."

"Let's continue, then. We'll find the village, hang back, call it in."

"Hang back."

"Yes."

Johnny took a moment. "All right." He cocked his head and Faraz got on. "We call it in and hang back."

"Right."

Johnny twisted the throttle and they threw up a cloud of dirt. "Hold on. The main road will certainly be blocked. We'll have to take the scenic route."

He pulled onto a gravel lane outside the village. After a hundred yards, it turned into a dirt two-track through the farm fields.

Five minutes later, they came over a rise.

"Stop." Faraz shouted over the noise of the motor-cycle.

Johnny skidded to a halt.

"That's it." Faraz pointed to the village ahead of them.

"You sure?"

"I think so. You see the fields along the highway. We came up that access road when we exited the village and turned left. If we go around, come in that way, I'll reverse the rights and lefts. Maybe I can find the house, at least the neighborhood."

* * *

As Bridget and Will approached the consulate on foot, they saw an Israeli commando unit, complete with two large armored vehicles and more than a dozen men in body armor and black uniforms.

A soldier blocked their path, his weapon at the ready. He gave them a command in Hebrew.

"We're the—" Bridget's reply was interrupted by a woman's voice from behind the soldier. He stepped aside.

"Come on through." Sergeant Peretz came into view. Her uniform was ripped and dirty. The front was stained with blood. She had a bandage on her left forearm. Her hair had fallen out of its bun and hung past her shoulders. She looked like she'd been crying.

"Sergeant, are you all right?" Will asked.

"Clearly not all right, but I'm here."

"Where's Colonel Ben-Yosef?" Bridget asked.

Peretz hung her head.

"Oh, no," Bridget said.

"Yes. He ran from the command center to tend the wounded. He was hit by the second explosion." Her voice cracked, but she continued. "I was two seconds behind, blown back into the trailer." She pointed at the blood on her shirt. "I tried to help him, but . . ."

Bridget embraced her.

Will put a hand on Peretz's shoulder. "He was a good man."

Peretz sniffed. "Yes. Some days I wanted to smack him. But for work, he was the best."

Bridget hugged her again.

"All right." Peretz broke the embrace. "There is work to do. That is what Ari would want us to focus on." She turned to an officer standing next to one of the armored vehicles. "Commander Jackson, you know Major Drucker, head of the assault team. He will take you from here. I will run comms from our field office."

"Yes, of course," Will said. "Bridget, the major led the rescue."

"Oh." Bridget shook his hand. "Thank you."

"How are you feeling?" Drucker asked.

"Not a hundred percent, but okay."

"I am glad to hear it."

"What's the plan?"

"Let me show you." Drucker led them to the back of one of the vehicles. A soldier laid out a map. "Your man said they're east of the city. Not surprising." Drucker circled a large area with his right forefinger. "Probably this valley, lots of Palestinian villages, plenty of sympathizers, no shortage of places to hide."

"So, we head over there and wait for my man to call?"

"No. We cannot go into that area unnoticed in the middle of the day with these vehicles. There will be a reaction. We could end up fighting the wrong people while the target escapes. We will go part of the way, staying in West Jerusalem so as not to raise suspicion. Then, if your man calls, we move."

"He'll call," Bridget said. "With all due respect, Major, is this the entire force?"

"Without reserves, yes. And it is a very capable force, more than enough for what we have to do."

"I guess it'll have to be." Bridget looked at Will for confirmation.

"These guys are good, Bridge, as you saw yesterday."

"Yes, of course." She turned back toward Drucker.

"Sorry. In any case, Will—Commander Jackson—and I need armor and weapons."

"You will have, but only for self-defense. You will stay back and let my men do their job."

"But—"

"No arguments. I've been through this with Commander Jackson. You are injured and cannot move fast, anyway." He turned to Will. "And, Commander, you violated our agreement twice. You will not do it again."

Will didn't answer.

"Or we can leave you both at the crossroads when we go into the valley."

Bridget turned to face Drucker. "Commander Jackson is a U.S. Navy SEAL. He has—"

Will put a hand on her shoulder. "He's right, Bridge. I wouldn't let strangers go in with my team, either. We'll be backup and watch for runners."

Bridget shot him an angry look. "Okay, okay. No time to argue. Give us the weapons. We won't get in your way."

Chapter Fifty-six

Waleed burst through the doorway of Assali's bedroom, where the volume was up on the radio, reporting the news in Arabic.

"My team hit them hard, *sayyid*. Three returned with me. The martyr Ayman al-Hamdani's bombing was spectacular."

"I know. But the Old City attack failed. They did not get past the police. Most have not returned."

Waleed's enthusiasm was not tempered. "More martyrs for the jihad. It was their destiny."

"Yes, I suppose so. In any case, we will be greeted as heroes." He didn't say the rest of what was on his mind: "and the prince will reward me, perhaps even beyond my dreams."

"Prepare the vehicles," Assali ordered. "I will leave with a team to protect me. You are the senior commander now. You will wait for the rest of the men, then follow as planned."

* * *

Downstairs, Waleed walked through the house to assess the status of the survivors. There were well over a dozen, including the six left behind to guard Assali. Some were wounded. He ordered the security team to prepare for departure in two vehicles and put others on watch at the front and rear of the house. "We will leave as soon as the rest of our brothers arrive," he told them.

Waleed went to the kitchen sink, bent down and took a long drink. He splashed water on his face, wiping off sweat and dirt from the streets. He realized he was still wearing the vampire outfit printed with dripping blood. Waleed had been too far from his targets to get any real blood on it. He unzipped the costume and left it on the floor.

He boosted himself up to sit on the kitchen counter and looked out a small window into the back alley. Waleed ran a count in his head, running through the men on Bashar and Iyad's teams. Good for them to achieve martyrdom. But some might yet return to the safe house.

Faraz and Johnny found the turnoff from the main road east of the village. The sign read ABU QUTIB.

"I'm pretty sure this is it," Faraz said.

"Can't wait to hear you tell the Ops Center you're 'pretty sure.'"

"Best I can do for now. I have to see what's inside."

"I know this village. Leila likes to go shopping here. It's a warren of streets, alleys and dead ends."

"Let's see if I can find my way through based on what I remember, just far enough to confirm this is the place."

Johnny hesitated. "All right. But no farther." He

gunned the engine and let the motorcycle coast down the embankment into a dirt parking lot.

Faraz looked around. "Far corner exit and left, then maybe ten seconds and a right on a flagstone street."

Johnny went along the row of cars, then through a narrow opening that led to a village street. After ten seconds, they came to the flagstone street.

Johnny stopped.

"What are you doing?"

"We said hang back."

"We need to be sure. We can't have them come to the wrong village while Assali gets away."

Johnny let out a long sigh. "How far?"

"A minute or so."

"All right. We leave the bike here and go on foot. When you're sure, you call it in and we wait."

"Okay."

They dismounted. Johnny set the chain and Faraz led him deeper into the village.

Bridget and Will were putting on their body armor at the staging point, a parking lot that bordered the Green Line. The Old City walls loomed above them against a perfect blue sky. To the west were the tall buildings of downtown. To the east lay the valley dotted with villages and farms that led down to the Jordan.

"You know I'm not good at waiting," Bridget said.

"I do seem to remember that."

Bridget closed the clips on her body armor and picked up the M4 Drucker had given her. She squinted down into the valley. "Damn. We can probably see where they are from here."

"Maybe. But that's good, means they're not too far away."

Faraz and Johnny were the only people out and about in the village. As they moved through the streets and alleys, Faraz kept his eyes up, searching for something he might remember from the drive out that morning—a sign, an unusual doorway. But the village was unremarkable, tan row house after tan row house, interrupted by the occasional shed or shop. With all the security doors down, nothing stood out.

Twice, they came to dead ends.

"Maybe this isn't the place," Johnny said.

"If it's not, we're screwed. Let's go back to the bike and start again."

They retraced their steps and took a different route into the village.

"This is it!" Faraz picked up the pace and went left at the next opportunity. "Yes. It's up there, I think."

"I know this street. We bought some new faucets for the apartment at a plumber's down at the corner."

They passed several shuttered stores. The last one had a rusted metal chair outside. "The owner sits there," Johnny said, "and urges people to come inside."

Just beyond was a narrow cross street. Johnny grabbed Faraz's shirt from behind and pulled him back.

"Easy, little man. If this is it, take it slow."

"Right." Faraz crouched down and peeked around the corner. Johnny stood over him and did the same. The house's front door was there, on the other side of the dead-end street, twenty meters away, blocked by a line of vehicles.

Two seconds later, they pulled back. "Confirmed," Faraz said.

"Even I could see that. Row of SUVs and pickups like that. Not likely a sewing club. Call it in."

Will and Drucker stood with Bridget when she took the call. She repeated Faraz's report. "Abu Qutib village."

"I know it," Drucker said. "Tough area, very militant."

"How far?"

"Seven, eight minutes." Drucker spoke into his radio, then turned back to Bridget and Will. "Arial recon will get there first and find the house. Let's go."

Faraz and Johnny sat on the ground in the alley to wait.

"I could go in," Faraz said. "They think I'm one of them."

"And do what?"

"Check their numbers, hit them from behind when the Israelis strike."

"Get yourself killed, too. The Israelis can handle it. We said we'd hang back. So, hang back."

They heard two vehicle engines start.

Assali came down the steps with his travel bag. The wounded sat on the living room floor. All eyes turned to the boss.

"The men are ready to take you to the crossing point," Waleed said. "*Ma salaamat.*" Go in peace.

Assali looked around the room and let loose a disapproving grunt. These men saved themselves rather than choosing the martyr's path and taking more Zionists with them. Praise Allah for the fat one, who delivered the decisive blow and secured his victory.

But Assali needed these men to cover his departure. He spoke from the bottom step. "You did well, today, my brothers. Do not stay here too long. Our martyrs are receiving their reward from Allah. You shall receive yours from me back at the camp."

"*Allah hu akbar*," came a voice from the back of the room. The others responded in ragged unison.

Assali nodded. Two men went outside to guard his departure. Assali hurried through the door to the SUVs idling on the street, with two more men behind him.

Faraz peeked around the corner to see exhaust rising and several men moving from the house to two SUVs. He pulled back into the alley.

"Shit."

"Departure time?"

"Yeah, for some, anyway. Wouldn't be surprised if Assali was getting his ass to safety, leaving the rest to fend for themselves."

The vehicle doors slammed. Johnny looked at his watch. "Still five minutes until they get here."

Faraz turned back and grabbed the shop owner's old chair.

"Hey, wait," Johnny said.

Faraz ignored him. He came back with the chair and looked around the corner again. The vehicles were approaching. Faraz stepped back and raised the chair.

"Faraz, no!"

As the lead vehicle came into view, Faraz stepped forward and smashed the chair into its windshield.

The SUV veered left and crashed into the wall. The second one plowed into it.

Faraz lunged for the passenger door of the first one and pulled it open. He had counted on them not wearing seatbelts, and he was right.

The fighter riding shotgun had flown forward into the windshield. His hands were on his face and blood dripped from his chin. The driver's head had gone into the steering wheel, and he lay slumped on top of the gearshift. The men in the backseat had flown forward into the seatbacks and now fumbled for their weapons.

Faraz pulled the passenger out of the vehicle and dragged him two steps into the alley. The man's AK fell from his lap. Faraz grabbed it, flipped it to point at the backseat, and fired on automatic.

The man on the ground grabbed Faraz's foot, but Johnny kicked him in the head and he fell back. Faraz lowered the rifle and fired a single shot into the man's chest.

All that gave the men in the second SUV time to recover from the crash. They fired their weapons, shattering the rear window of the lead vehicle. Faraz and Johnny dove to the ground and rolled farther into the side alley, coming to rest in front of the plumber's shop security gate.

"You're hit." Faraz moved to protect Johnny, who was bleeding from his left arm.

"Must have been a ricochet. Not too bad."

Assali's men continued to fire, and it sounded like they were advancing toward the alley.

"Play dead," Faraz said. He pushed Johnny flat on the ground, then shouted in Arabic, "Don't shoot. Don't shoot. It is me, Khayal." He put the AK on the ground and stood with his hands up.

The gunfire stopped. "Show yourself," came the order.

"I am coming. Don't shoot." Faraz advanced toward the street. He pointed at Johnny. "He is dead. I saw him attack our vehicles. I ran to stop him."

Faraz recognized the two fighters who confronted him, but didn't know their names. "It is me, Khayal, I know you from the camp."

One of the men grabbed Faraz, spun him around and threw him against the disabled SUV. The other man frisked him, then spun him back around. They looked down the alley at Johnny, bloodied and not moving.

"I checked him," Faraz said. "He is dead."

Faraz saw a fighter helping Assali off the floor of the backseat in the second SUV. He pushed past the two men guarding him to draw their attention away from Johnny.

"*Sayyid*, are you all right?" Faraz said. "I was coming back when I saw what was happening."

Assali got himself onto the seat. "Khayal. What are you doing out here? Who attacked us?"

"It was one man, a Zionist spy, no doubt. I killed him."

Assali grunted his approval. "Back inside, all of you."

Chapter Fifty-seven

Johnny held his breath through all of that exchange. When he heard Assali's order, he allowed himself to breathe again. He waited a few more seconds, then opened his eyes. The alley was clear. Johnny rolled over and grabbed the AK Faraz had left behind.

He crawled to the edge of the alley, put his right cheek against the ground and slid out far enough to have a look. Johnny saw three fighters with Faraz and an older man moving into the house.

Several men emerged to stand guard.

Johnny pulled back. He pressed his shirt to his wound. The bullet had only grazed him. It looked, and felt, worse than it was.

What the hell was Faraz thinking? He's in the terrorist house with the Israelis due any minute.

But there was nothing Johnny could do about that. His immediate concern was what the Israelis would do if they came upon a guy who looked Palestinian, holding an AK in an alley near the target house.

Johnny turned to the plumber's security door. He hit the lock with his rifle. It didn't budge. He hit it again. The lock held but the rusted bolt shattered. Johnny raised the door two feet and crouched down to look inside. The shop was dark. He raised the gate a little more, slipped under and pushed it down behind him.

Waleed slammed the door and pushed Faraz up against it. "What happened?"

Assali answered. "Leave him. We were attacked. Khayal arrived at exactly the right time to save us."

Waleed held Faraz in place. "How is that possible?"

"I was separated from the group. Found my own way back here."

"Nonsense." Waleed put a forearm across Faraz's throat.

"Stop!" Assali ordered. "This man has saved me more than once."

"Then who attacked us?

"One man," Faraz said. "A spy. I killed him."

"Can't be. No one would be so stupid."

"Damn the Zionists," Assali said. "They have spies everywhere."

Waleed released Faraz. "If that's true, they are coming. If we stay here, we will be trapped."

"But the damaged vehicles block the street," Faraz said. "We must prepare to defend the house."

Bridget held on as the army vehicles turned off the main road and sped along an uneven surface. From the front seat, Major Drucker issued a series of commands in

Hebrew, then turned toward the Americans sitting in the back with members of his team.

"The drone has identified the house. Lots of vehicles outside. We will go in hard. Our vehicle will be on the street in front, the other in the alley behind. You two stay back until the All Clear."

Drucker didn't wait for a response. He grabbed a hand-hold as their vehicle took a sharp right turn.

Bridget and Will braced themselves. They wore ill-fitting body armor and held borrowed Israeli M4 rifles, with the safety switches on. The vehicle accelerated for several seconds, then screeched to a halt. The rear doors opened, and the commandos poured out into a narrow street lined with doorways and shuttered windows.

They formed two lines and snaked through the small space between the vehicle and the buildings on either side. Major Drucker was in the lead.

"Come on," Bridget said. She jumped down to the street and winced in pain. She fell in behind the last Is-raeli.

"Easy, now." Will came down behind her and grabbed her arm.

Bridget pulled away. "Look. The road's blocked by a couple of SUVs. Looks like an accident."

"No," Assali said. "We cannot defend the house. We will go on foot and find other vehicles. Ten men to the back door. Slow them down. The rest to the front. We escape that way. Now."

Assali moved toward the front door. Waleed followed and barked orders for the men to cover their escape. He grabbed Faraz's shirt and pushed him toward the back, where the men stood ready to fire at any ground force that appeared. "You stay with them," he said.

Faraz threw him off. He took an AK from the floor and crouched down behind the half-wall between the dining room and the kitchen. Waleed and a phalanx of men led Assali out the front.

Gunfire came from the alley, and the men by the back door responded. Faraz turned his weapon toward them and sprayed left and right. As they fell, the Israeli commandos came into view. An explosion blew in the door. Faraz threw himself to the ground behind the half-wall, tossed the AK to the side and raised his hands in surrender.

On the front side of the house, Bridget and Will were pinned down behind the Israelis' armored vehicle. Drucker and his men were thirty meters ahead, on the other side of an alley entrance on the left, taking cover behind the damaged SUVs. They were in a gun battle with a terrorist force.

Someone shouted, "*Rimon!*" The Israelis took cover and a grenade exploded. There was more shouting in Hebrew, and the Israelis withdrew to their vehicle, two of them dragging Drucker.

They dropped him in front of Bridget and turned to defend their position.

Will knelt down. "He's alive. The armor saved him."

"I'm all right," Drucker said.

* * *

"Go now, *sayyid*." Waleed pushed Assali across the street to the back of the SUV he'd been riding in a few minutes earlier. "Move quickly with the next explosion." He tossed another grenade toward the Israeli vehicles.

With debris still flying, Waleed grabbed Assali's arm and pulled him past the vehicles and into the side alley at a run. His men followed, turning to fire their AKs to keep the Israelis pinned down.

Without the lock, the plumber's gate wouldn't stay all the way down, giving Johnny a partial view out into the alley. He was behind the shop's front counter, surrounded by an assortment of sinks, faucets and plumbing supplies.

He saw the feet go by. Then his hiding place went quiet. He eased his grip on the AK and reached into his pocket to be sure he had his Israeli-issued ID—something of a security blanket if he got arrested. Still, Johnny was reluctant to leave the safety of the shop, not knowing who he might find or whether the running battle would come back past his position.

The Israeli team in the alley streamed through the kitchen door.

Faraz raised his hands as high as he could. "I'm the American. I gave you the location. Killed those guys." He gestured toward the dead terrorists in the kitchen.

Three Israelis pointed their weapons at him. "Don't move," one of them said.

More soldiers came in through the front door, with Bridget and Will behind them.

"That's my man," Bridget said, moving to Faraz and helping him up.

The soldiers lowered their weapons.

"Are you okay?" Bridget asked.

"Yes."

"Where's Assali?"

"Went out the front just before the explosions. I thought you had him."

"Shit," Will said. "Must have gotten past us."

"Side alley," Faraz said.

Drucker spoke from the front door. "We will pursue." He issued a command and led his men back outside.

"My cousin is out there wounded. We've gotta find him." Faraz grabbed an AK from a fallen fighter and pushed past Will. "You two coming?"

Chapter Fifty-eight

Faraz led Bridget and Will past the disabled SUVs and into the alley. He saw the partly open gate and pulled it up. "Johnny?"

"Yeah, it's me."

The cousins hugged.

"This was your idea of hanging back?"

"I had to do it. How's your arm?"

"Fine. Bleeding stopped."

"Did they come by this way?" Bridget asked.

"Yeah. Then, looked like the Israelis were in pursuit."

"We should go after them," Faraz said.

Will shook his head. "We should wait here and call for reinforcements."

"Smart man," Johnny said.

Bridget stepped forward. "No. We can't let them get away after what they did."

"The Israelis will catch them," Will said.

"Not necessarily." Faraz turned to Johnny. "You know this village."

"It's a maze, as Faraz found out earlier. And there are lots of folks who will hide them and fight for them."

"What would you do if you were with them?" Bridget asked.

"I'd divide my men, force the Israelis to do the same, trap them in any one of a hundred dead ends."

"Then we really have to go, do what we can."

Johnny let out a breath and turned away.

"You don't have to," Faraz said.

"No, but she's right. I know a back way. Maybe we can get ahead of them, or at least catch up."

"Show us," Bridget said. "Please."

Assali was out of breath and sweating. Two fighters helped him keep moving through alleys and streets.

"He can run no more," one of the men said to Waleed, who was behind them with two other men, running sideways and keeping an eye out for the Zionists.

"We must . . . get out," Assali said through labored breaths, as Waleed pushed past them to scout ahead.

"Here." Waleed stopped short of the next intersection. He turned his AK and used the butt to break the doorknob of a house. He put his shoulder into the door and it gave way. Waleed led them into a darkened living room and slammed the door behind them.

Assali leaned on the back of an overstuffed sofa to catch his breath. "What is this pl—" His question was cut off when Waleed raised his left hand and pointed his AK toward the back of the house with his right.

A man appeared in a doorway. He was short and wore Western clothes and house slippers. And he had a rifle of his own. "What is this? Out of my house!"

Five rifles pointed back at him.

"Quiet," Waleed ordered.

There were footsteps and shouts in Hebrew outside. Assali crouched down behind the sofa. All the weapons except Waleed's turned toward the front door. The footsteps passed by.

Waleed waited a few seconds, then spoke to the homeowner. "We are fleeing the Zionists. We need shelter."

The man lowered his weapon. If he had any second thoughts about helping the armed men, he didn't show it. He stepped aside. "This way."

Waleed went first and pushed the man ahead of him, his finger still on the trigger.

The men followed along a short hallway and their host ushered them into a bedroom. He addressed Assali. "*Sayyid*, my family is in the room across the hall. Please, you cannot stay long."

"Yes, yes," Assali said, his breathing returning to normal. He wiped his brow with his sleeve. "We need water."

The man left. Assali turned to Waleed. "What now? We make a stand here?"

"No, *sayyid*. The Zionists will find us, use gas or drop a bomb on the house.

The man returned with bottles of water.

"We need a vehicle," Waleed said.

"I have one. It is yours for the jihad, with pleasure."

"Where?"

"It is in the lot at the edge of the village, a short walk from the back door."

"Back door," Assali said. "Perfect. Give us the keys."

* * *

Bridget was struggling to keep up with the men. Her injury and her days in captivity were affecting her more than she had expected or wanted to admit.

Will was in the lead, in SEAL mode—minus the high-tech gear.

"Where the hell are the Israelis?" Faraz asked.

"Lots of ways through the village," Johnny said. "It's good that we're covering a different route."

Will stopped and raised his left hand, then lowered it to point at a doorway. The knob was broken off. Pieces of wood and metal were on the ground.

Johnny moved forward to listen at the door.

Bridget reached for her cell phone. "We should call—"

"Shh." Will silenced her.

There was movement inside the house. Will pulled Bridget to the far side of the doorway, and put her behind him. A man said something in Arabic and another responded. The voices were muffled.

Bridget looked toward Johnny for a translation, but he pointed to his ear and shook his head.

There was more noise, people moving around maybe, but it sounded like it was farther inside the house. Will leaned forward. Somewhere in the house, a door closed.

"I think someone went out the back," Johnny whispered. "Most of these houses go through to an alley. You heard the door close."

"I need to get a message to Drucker," Bridget said.

Will nodded. "You have his number?"

"No. It'll have to go through the Ops Center and Peretz."

"That'll take forever," Faraz said.

Bridget was already dialing. "How do I tell them where we are?"

Johnny pointed to two street signs attached to the buildings at the intersection behind her. They were written in Arabic and English.

Bridget cupped her hand over her mouth and read the street names to the operator.

"We can't wait for them," Faraz said. "If Assali's men went through here, who knows where they'll end up. We could lose them."

"Could be nothing," Johnny said. "Just the family."

"Missing doorknob," Will said. "Not likely a coincidence."

"Definitely not a coincidence." Faraz kicked in the door and pulled back for cover. There was no response from inside.

Faraz raised his AK and went into the house. The owner came from the back hallway, firing. Faraz hit the floor and returned fire. The spray rattled across the kitchen cabinets and found the man in the doorway. He fell backward.

A woman screamed from a room behind. A child cried.

Faraz crossed the living room and stepped over the man. He passed the closed door to his left, the source of the noise. He checked the room to the right and found it empty, with discarded water bottles and ammunition clips on the bed.

He crossed the hall and kicked in the other bedroom door, triggering another round of wailing. Faraz pointed his weapon at the woman, who was huddled on the floor in the far corner with three young children.

"Quiet!" he ordered. He didn't bother to think of the Arabic word, but his meaning was clear.

The woman stopped screaming. The children continued to cry.

"Stay here," Faraz said. Then he moved back to the living room.

Will was standing guard. Johnny and Bridget were on their knees checking on the owner.

"They were here, but the house is clear now," Faraz said. "Woman and kids in the bedroom"

"He's dead," Bridget sat back on her heels.

Faraz turned to Johnny. "Talk to the woman before she sees this. Find out if she knows where they went."

Johnny went to the bedroom.

Bridget stood and stared at the man.

"We broke into his house," Faraz said. "I did, actually."

"He gave shelter to Assali's crew," Bridget said. "Covered their escape. You did what you had to do."

"And he did, too, I guess."

Johnny came out of the bedroom. "They went out the back with the family's car keys to the lot at the edge of the village."

"Let's go," Faraz said.

The woman came out of the bedroom and saw her husband. She screamed and fell on him, sobbing. The children came out to join her, but retreated when they saw Faraz and his AK.

The homeowner's wife launched herself at Faraz. "*Qatil!*" she screamed. Murderer. She went for his face with her fingernails.

Faraz dodged the assault, grabbed the woman's arm

and forced her back to the ground. She collapsed on top of her husband. "We gotta go," he said.

"Right." Will moved past them and opened the back door. He scanned left and right, then stepped into the alley. "Clear. Let's move."

CHAPTER FIFTY-NINE

Assali sat on the gravel of the parking lot, leaning against a van, while two men stood guard and Waleed and the others searched for the car.

The homeowner had told them it was a gray Toyota. Unfortunately, that described half the cars in the lot. To make matters worse, it was an old one. There was no remote to click, only a key. So Waleed had to go from vehicle to vehicle trying the locks.

"He has it," one of the guards said.

A car started some distance away. Assali took the guard's hand and stood. He had stopped sweating. The air was a bit cooler. The last rays of sunlight dipped behind the Old City. "*Yalla,*" he ordered.

They carved a path through the parked cars to intercept the Toyota.

As they crossed an access lane, a windshield in front of them shattered, and a gunshot echoed across the valley.

The fighter behind Assali pushed him to the ground and returned fire.

* * *

"Damn," Will said. "I missed him."

"That's Assali," Faraz said. "We'll take him. You two go after the car."

Faraz didn't wait for an answer or an argument. He grabbed Johnny's forearm and pushed him through the cars toward Assali's position.

"Cover me," Assali ordered. He pushed the fighter off him and sat up. "I will go to the car."

"*Sayyid*, you will not make it. Perhaps we should surr—"

"Never! Now, distract them." He took a handgun from the man's belt, hefted himself to his feet and ran toward Waleed and the Toyota.

The two fighters stood, taking as much cover as they could from the parked cars. They started shooting and ran the other way.

Faraz and Johnny returned fire.

"This way," Johnny said, turning a corner around a small truck to move toward the shooters.

Faraz followed. They came around the truck firing, but Assali's men caught them from an unexpected angle. Just before the bullet hit him, Faraz caught a glimpse of a bald man running.

Will reached the parking lot's main road in time to see the gray Toyota emerge from a side lane. It skidded as it made the turn and accelerated toward him. Someone stuck an AK out of the passenger's window. Will pushed Bridget out of the way and let loose a barrage from his M4.

The windshield shattered and a tire burst. The car continued toward him at high speed. He could see no one inside. Will was about to fire again when the vehicle veered left and sideswiped a row of parked cars before smashing into one of them and coming to a stop.

He moved toward it with Bridget close behind. "Stay down," he said. He pushed her to the ground behind the bumper of an old Mercedes. As Will approached the passenger side of the car, the driver's door flew open and Waleed came out, bloody and firing.

One bullet caught Will's body armor and another hit his forearm. As he fell, he pushed himself left to catch some cover from the next vehicle in the row, but his legs were exposed.

There was another volley and Will pulled the legs in, sure it was too late. But he didn't feel the burn of impact. He twisted his body to look around the car and saw Bridget advancing, in hunched-over combat position, her rifle firing on automatic.

She knelt down when she reached Will. "I think I got him."

Johnny stood over Faraz, firing at the terrorists. "How bad?"

"It's okay," Faraz said. "Just a flesh wound, left arm."

"Stay here." Johnny took off at a run and disappeared among the cars.

Bullets from Assali's men flew over Faraz and pinged off the cars. He ripped his shirtsleeve to make a bandage, then picked up his AK and moved on all fours to get a view of what was happening.

He raised himself to look over the hood of a blue Honda in time to see a fighter he recognized moving toward him. Faraz raised his rifle and cut him down.

Faraz dropped back to the ground. He heard running a few rows over. He looked around the car's bumper. A fighter was chasing Johnny. Before Faraz could stand, Johnny stopped, turned and fired at the same time the fighter did. They both went down behind the cars.

"Johnny!" Faraz moved a few steps toward him but saw something off to his right. He looked that way.

Assali.

Faraz took off after him.

Assali turned and fired his pistol from twenty meters away. The bullet went wild. He leaned against a car, breathing hard.

"Drop it," Faraz shouted, pointing his AK.

Assali fired again, then pushed himself off the car and made a hopeless attempt to evade Faraz, turning behind another row of cars.

Faraz made the same turn, now just a few car-lengths behind. "Stop, or I will shoot."

Assali ran to a car and leaned on its hood, gasping for air. He turned to look at his pursuer. "Khayal. Iyad was right about you."

"Yes, he was. Now drop your weapon."

Assali raised his head and shoulders but kept his hands on the car for support. He took a deep breath and let it out. "Did you save me at the camp to kill me here?"

Faraz didn't answer.

Assali mumbled a string of Arabic curses.

"Drop the weapon."

Assali raised it instead.

Faraz fired.

The bullet hit Assali in the side and spun him around. He dropped the gun and fell to his hands and knees, bleeding.

Faraz kicked Assali's pistol away and pointed his AK at the man's head.

"No, Khayal, please." Assali was whimpering now. "I can help you. Please."

Major Drucker and his team reached the gray Toyota and pulled two dead terrorists from the backseat. A soldier went to check on the fighter who lay on the ground on the far side of the car, while Drucker approached Bridget and Will.

One of his men shouted something in Hebrew. "They're dead," Drucker said. "Good job, Commander."

"It was a joint effort," Will said, nodding toward Bridget. She helped him stand.

"You okay?" Drucker asked.

"Just my arm and an armor bruise."

"You need to find the others," Bridget said. "Over that way." She pointed across the parking lot.

Drucker issued an order and four of his men followed. They took only a few steps before Faraz called out.

"Over here. I have Assali."

Two of Drucker's men secured Assali and tended to his wound. He was speaking to them in Arabic, already negotiating a deal.

"We have to find Johnny," Faraz said. "And at least two fighters are unaccounted for."

Drucker issued orders and his men formed into teams to start a grid search.

"Last I saw Johnny, he was this way." Faraz veered off, with Bridget and Will behind him.

He spotted the blue Honda where he'd taken cover and moved toward it. He stepped over a dead fighter and turned between two vans.

That's when he saw Johnny.

His cousin was facedown. His AK lay next to him. The ground was soaked with blood.

Faraz fell on him. "Johnny. Oh, no. No!" He turned him over.

Johnny moaned.

"Help! We need a medic over here!" Faraz sat on the ground and cradled Johnny's head and shoulders in his lap. The wound was bad, left side of his chest, just below the heart.

Faraz brushed the hair off of Johnny's face and patted his cheek. "Stay with me. You're going to be all right."

Johnny opened his eyes. "Hey, little man."

"Oh, Johnny. Hang in there. Help is on the way."

Johnny labored through two shallow breaths. "Tell Leila . . ." His eyes closed. His chin fell to his chest.

"Come on, Johnny. Don't worry. You'll tell her yourself. Please, Johnny, open your eyes."

Two Israelis arrived with a medical bag and dropped to their knees next to Johnny. Bridget knelt down and put her arm around Faraz's shoulders.

The medics moved Johnny off of Faraz. One man checked his pulse, then put his ear to Johnny's nose and mouth. The other medic cut open Johnny's shirt to expose the gaping wound. He looked at Faraz and shook his head.

"No! No! Start CPR. Get an ambulance."

"It's no use, sir," the medic said. "He is not breathing and the wound is too grave for CPR."

Faraz stared at them.

Bridget squeezed his shoulders. "I'm so sorry, Faraz."

"It can't be. He was . . . And then . . . Oh, God." Faraz leaned forward and put two fingers on Johnny's neck. He looked at the medic for some hope, but found none.

"I'm sorry, sir."

Faraz took a halting breath and let it out. He sat back on his heels. They were all silent for several seconds. Then Faraz hung his head and said the *Shahada* for his cousin.

He reached over and closed Johnny's eyes. "He got the last one, protecting me." Faraz didn't even try to stop the tears from streaming down his cheeks.

Within half an hour, dozens of Israeli military and police vehicles crowded the parking lot. Investigators collected evidence and interviewed Drucker and his team and Bridget and Will. A mortuary crew collected the bodies.

Faraz was still sitting on the ground next to Johnny.

A medic approached. "Sir, please come to the ambulance so we can treat your wound." She put a hand on Faraz's shoulder, but he brushed her off.

"I'm staying with him."

"All right, sir," she said. "I'll take care of it here." The woman put down her bag and started to work on Faraz's arm.

A member of the mortuary crew squatted next to Johnny and covered his face with a cloth. "I'm terribly sorry, sir. We'll take care of him, now."

The man and his colleague laid out a body bag, lifted Johnny into it and zipped it up.

Faraz kept staring. "Where will you take him?"

"To the Islamic Funeral Service," the soldier said. "After that, we will inform his family and they will decide."

"I am his family."

"Sir?"

"Never mind." Faraz stood and lowered his sleeve over the fresh dressing. "I'll tell them."

CHAPTER SIXTY

Forty hours later, late morning on Sunday, Bridget sat in the front seat of an Israeli military SUV. Will was in the back with a bandage on his shoulder.

Sergeant Peretz drove them north on the main highway out of Tel Aviv. The sergeant had on a dress uniform and her hair was back in the bun, but her eyes were red. Bridget doubted the woman had gotten much sleep the last two nights. She hadn't gotten much, herself.

Every few minutes, Peretz wiped a tear from her right eye. Bridget put a hand on her shoulder.

"I'm okay," Peretz said. "But I can't get that eye to stop."

"I don't think any of us is okay."

"So many dead. So many funerals already this morning." Peretz sniffed. "That's one thing we're good at. Years and decades of practice."

Peretz took an exit and turned onto a residential street blocked by parked cars.

"We can walk from here," Will said.

"All right. I will wait around the corner."

"You're not coming?" Bridget asked.

"No. I will go later with my colleagues."

Bridget leaned over and gave her a hug. Then, she and Will started the walk to the Ben-Yosef house.

The small front yard was crowded. A somber mix of soldiers and civilians stood speaking in hushed tones and sipping coffee or tea, or perhaps something stronger. A teenaged girl was walking around offering sweet rolls and cookies from a tray.

At the front door, a man in a dark suit gave them head coverings—a traditional skullcap for Will, a piece of black lace with a hair clip for Bridget.

She spotted General HaLevy on the other side of the living room with several men holding shot glasses. He was paying attention to another general, who appeared to be making a toast. Then the two generals and the others said a robust "*L'chaim*" and downed their shots.

"'*L'chaim*," Will whispered. "The colonel taught me that. He said Jews always drink 'to life.'"

"Even here."

"Especially here, I guess."

HaLevy turned and saw them. The big man's shoulders were slumped. He looked ten years older than when Bridget had first met him less than three weeks earlier. He moved toward them through the crowd and Bridget embraced him.

"I'm so sorry, sir," she said.

The general accepted her hug, then turned to Will and shook his hand.

"I admired Colonel Ben-Yosef very much," Will offered. "I wish I'd gotten to know him better."

"Yes. . ." The general seemed to want to say more but was unable.

"How are Rivka and Tali?" Bridget asked.

"Tali will recover . . . from her physical injuries, at least. She's in hospital, sedated. We will go see her again soon. Rivka is . . . well . . . how should she be? I convinced her to lie down before we return to the hospital."

"Please give her our condolences."

"I will. And thank you for helping her after the attack."

"Of course."

"You two are leaving today?"

"Yes, sir," Will said. "Within the hour."

"I wish we could have stopped it," Bridget said.

"You and your agent did a lot. Many were saved. Against this enemy, it is often not possible to save all." HaLevy gazed out the window.

Bridget took his hand and squeezed it. "Goodbye, sir."

"Goodbye. And as we say, 'Let us only meet on happy occasions.'"

"Yes, sir."

Faraz stood with Leila on the tarmac of an Israeli military airfield on the coast just north of Tel Aviv. The boy, Umair, held onto her ankle-length black *abaya*. Leila wore a widow's veil, but Faraz could see that her face was red and puffy and her eyes were still filled with tears.

She rubbed her shoulders against a chill, although the midday sun shimmered on the concrete behind them.

When the mortuary van arrived, Leila started crying again. She reached down and turned Umair's face into her skirt.

The attendants removed the metal transfer case containing Johnny's body from the back of the vehicle and carried it to a conveyor belt under the cargo door of the blue-and-white-painted U.S. military passenger plane.

There was no honor guard. Johnny had had one of those more than a decade earlier. Faraz would make sure he got another one back home, when they placed him in the grave that young Faraz had cried over that day. It already had a marker with Johnny's name on it.

The casket glided up the belt. Two crewmen removed it and carried it into the hold.

A young U.S. Army corporal came down the aircraft steps and stood at the bottom. She wore a green dress uniform. Her hands were folded. Her head was down. She was Johnny's official escort for his final trip home.

"She will take you to Johnny's parents," Faraz said.

Leila sniffed and nodded. "He told me they were dead. I always knew he had many secrets. He was . . ." She couldn't finish.

"He chose you and Umair over all of it. I dragged him back in."

Leila surprised Faraz with a half chuckle. "No one could drag Johnny into anything. Whatever you were doing, it was important to him—you were important to him. If I have any consolation, it is that he went to help you and he succeeded."

Faraz thought he might cry, now. "His parents will take care of you. They are good people and they will be very happy to meet you and Umair."

Leila nodded and raised a handkerchief under her veil to dry her tears.

Faraz squatted down to speak to the boy. "Your father

was a great man and a hero, and not only for what he did on Friday. He saved many lives. He was . . . he was like a brother to me."

Umair stepped toward him and put his little arms around Faraz's neck. Faraz picked him up, gave him a hug and kissed his cheek, then handed him to his mother.

"You will learn more about Johnny when you arrive, things even his parents did not know. Please, if you mention his old friend Khalil, tell them nothing more about me."

"You have secrets, too."

Faraz nodded.

The corporal spoke up. "Sir, ma'am, we need to go."

Faraz put his right hand on his heart and bowed his head toward Leila. "May Allah protect you."

Leila returned the gesture. "And you, Khalil." She walked past him and carried Umair onto the plane, followed by the corporal.

Faraz watched them through the windows. Leila walked toward the back of the aircraft, passing over the words painted on the side, UNITED STATES OF AMERICA.

As soon as Leila took a seat, the plane started to move. Faraz waved, but she was staring straight ahead.

The backwash from the engines hit Faraz and he turned his head to avoid it. He saw Bridget and Will alongside another American aircraft thirty yards away.

Leila's plane turned onto the runway and accelerated for takeoff. Faraz shielded his eyes and watched it go. Then he walked to Bridget and Will.

"We have the motorcycle?"

"Just loaded," Will said.

"Thanks." Faraz's voice was a hoarse whisper.

Bridget embraced him. Will patted him on the shoulder.

"The price is too high," Faraz said. "It was too high from the beginning."

"I don't pretend to know what you're going through, what you've been through," Bridget said. "But we hit them hard this time."

Faraz broke the embrace. "How many people died?"

"You stopped most of it, saved hundreds of lives. And we're already getting all kinds of intel from Assali on their operations and support system. They're crippled."

"Until next time."

Bridget started to say something, but Faraz held up a hand. "They're crippled until next time. I can tell you from the inside, they have the ideology, the motivation and the money. They won't stop."

"Maybe," Bridget said. "But neither will we."

Faraz sighed, put his foot on the first step and walked up the stairs onto the plane.

ACKNOWLEDGMENTS

The coronavirus pandemic was the "Shock Wave" that hit us all during the writing of this book. You'd think that, without children to care for, staying at home for months on end would have been a great opportunity to get unprecedented quantities of work done. That may have been true for some, but I was firmly among what I believe was the majority of writers—stuck in some sort of pandemic malaise, doing all sorts of things, and all sorts of nothing, but very little writing.

Fortunately, there's nothing like a deadline to light a fire under a former journalist.

I must thank all those who have been so supportive during this difficult year, first and foremost my wife, Audrey, on whom I inflict the first drafts of my work for her seasoned appraisal. Around the same time, the members of my critique group review selected scenes and provide invaluable input. Thank you wonderful writing partners Caryn, Kelly, Lou Ann, Marcie and Porter. Next come the beta-readers, who bring particular expertise to the table, and managed to squeeze a "read and reply" into their own pandemic schedules. My thanks to Marvin Diogenes, Mark Lavie and Marcie Tau.

With the near-final manuscript completed, an impressive array of authors stepped up to review *Shock Wave* and allowed me to attach their names to my work. Eternal gratitude to JD Allen, Brian Andrews, M.E. Browning, Marc Cameron, Avanti Centrae, Mark Lavie, Bonnar Spring, Carole Stivers, Jeffrey Wilson and Dave Zeltserman.

The team at Kensington Publishing, led by editor Michaela Hamilton, continued to provide the professional, collegial bedrock of the Task Force Epsilon operation. I am forever grateful for their hard work and support during a uniquely difficult time.

The pandemic also challenged the community of writers, which has been so welcoming to me. Deprived of our usual gatherings, the staff and leadership of writers' groups pivoted to online events, webinars and social gatherings to maintain our connections and continue our skills development. My thanks to all those who worked so hard at many organizations, especially International Thriller Writers, the Florida Writers' Association, and the Mystery Writers of America Florida Chapter.

And so, dear readers, the last and most important to thank are you. I truly appreciate your interest in the series and hope to hear from you via email or social media. Online reviews are always much appreciated. You can reach me through www.alpessin.com and find me on Twitter @apessin, on Instagram at alpessinauthor, and on Facebook at the Al Pessin Author page.

All best for a healthy 2022 and beyond.

Did you miss the first compelling thriller in the Task Force Epsilon series?
No worries!
Keep reading to enjoy the opening pages of *Sandblast*
Available from Kensington Publishing Corp.

CHAPTER ONE

When the young Arab man in a business suit got out of a black cab and breezed into the lobby bar in late afternoon, no one took any notice. This was the Marriott Grosvenor House in London, a haven for visiting delegations and business barons from around the world, in a city with a sizable Muslim population. No fewer than five of the hotel's cable channels were Arabic satellite networks.

Mahmoud ordered apple juice and took out his *Times*. If he had been arrested at that moment, and there was no reason to do so, there would have been nothing incriminating on him at all.

He perused the newspaper and sipped his juice. Mahmoud had left a message for a bellboy he'd befriended at a mosque in South London. The message said he would be in the hotel and needed a small favor. It asked the young man to please meet him near the service elevator off the lower lobby at four o'clock. He checked his watch, 3:55.

Mahmoud put a five-pound note on the bar and took the stairs down one level. The bellboy was already there.

"I was surprised to hear from you, Mahmoud," he said.

He did not appear to be concerned. The two were about the same age and had met several times. They were both five feet, seven inches tall, clean-shaven, and had olive complexions and similar builds. Men at the mosque had commented that they looked like brothers.

"My friend!" Mahmoud greeted the bellboy with a handshake and a smile. "I'm sorry to bother you, but I need your help."

"Of course. I will help you if I can."

"Thank you, thank you. But, well, this is a confidential matter." He looked around to be sure no one else was in the service hallway and then, as if he didn't know exactly where he was going, Mahmoud pretended to notice a large utility closet, its door ajar.

"In here," he said, "Just for a second."

Now the bellboy gave him a suspicious look, but it was too late. Mahmoud pushed him into the closet and closed the door.

"No, wait!" said the bellboy

"Shhh," said Mahmoud, "I have something to show you."

"No, I will not . . ." The bellboy continued to protest, but Mahmoud reached under a shelf and removed a small packet, ripped it open, and pressed a cloth to the young man's face. The bellboy passed out before he could make another sound.

Mahmoud paused. He had impressed himself; it had all gone as it did in practice. No problems. No hesitation. That gave him confidence for the work yet to be done.

Under another shelf, he found the second packet—this

one with a pair of plastic gloves and a carefully forged hotel nametag. It said "Mahmoud." Why not?

Mahmoud put on the gloves, removed the young man's uniform and put it on himself—dark blue trousers with a black stripe down the sides, a white shirt, and a pullover tunic matching the pants. It fit well, as expected. He replaced the bellboy's nametag with his, and made sure the passkey was in the pants pocket. Mahmoud took the money and two handkerchiefs out of his own trousers, now crumpled on the floor.

He opened a large plastic garbage bin and tossed in his clothes and the young man's nametag. Then he hefted the bellboy into it. The head faced Mahmoud with closed eyes, then lolled to the right.

Now, Mahmoud found the final packet under a third shelf. He took out the gun, screwed in the silencer, put it against the center of the bellboy's forehead, and fired. The young man's head jerked back and his body convulsed. Mahmoud was briefly startled. But he composed himself, put the gun and the gloves into the bin, and made sure to properly seal the lid, protecting his hands with the handkerchiefs.

Mahmoud cracked open the closet door and peeked into the hallway. Still clear. He left the closet, locked the door, and took the service elevator to the ninth floor.

Using the dead bellboy's key, he went into a small storage room filled with cleaning supplies, linens, and other housekeeping items. In the back of the room was a stack of yellow plastic buckets labeled "floor wax." He removed the upper rows until he could access the bucket at the bottom left. He opened it. It did not contain floor wax.

Seeing the black backpack in the bucket made Mahmoud pause again. Until now, he had been remarkably calm. He went through the motions of capturing and killing the bellboy as he had in dozens of practice sessions. He put the bullet into the young man's head as easily as he had fired an empty gun at the head of his trainer at the safe house, again and again. He understood now why the man had made him do it so many times. But looking at the backpack, he realized how close he was to his goal, how close he was to performing the will of Allah. He caught his breath, felt his heart race.

Mahmoud removed the backpack and put the lid back onto the bucket. He restacked the other containers on top of it and left the storage room. Carrying the backpack by its top handle, as a bellboy would, he returned to the service elevator.

On the sixth floor, he headed for Room 626. The door was open and a handwritten sign read "Delegation Baggage." No one was inside. Across the hall, several men worked behind a partly open door labeled "Control," but none of them paid any attention to Mahmoud.

Room 626 was almost empty. All the furniture, including the bed, had been removed. There were a few suitcases and other bags on the floor along the far wall, under the windows looking out on Hyde Park. The bags had delegation tags on them, each with a name, a list of destinations and room numbers, and a small American flag. The tags were tied to the luggage with white strings. Mahmoud untied a tag labeled "Mr. Goff: Brussels, Kabul, Baghdad, London" and tied it to his backpack.

He opened the top zipper. His heart pounding now, he

removed several books to reveal a metal box and reached down its side to feel for the switch. He flipped it. A red light flashed once. He put the books back in, closed the backpack, put it behind the other bags, and turned to leave. He had been in the room less than a minute.

As he left, one of the men across the hall saw him. "Hey," said the man, "Where's that other guy?"

"Went home sick," replied Mahmoud, "Can I help you, sir?"

"No, it's okay." And the man went back to his work.

Mahmoud went to the public men's room on the main floor, where he stashed the bellboy's tunic in the trash bin. He went out on the far side of the hotel, toward the park, and hailed a taxi. Within seconds he was lost in the traffic, on the first leg of a trip that would crisscross London via taxi, bus, and train before it took him back to the safe house.

Mission accomplished.

As the afternoon wore on, civilian officials, military officers, and the journalists who were traveling with them dropped their luggage in Room 626 to be sent ahead to the plane while they finished their work. Nearly everyone had an extra laptop in one of their bags. Many had other equipment—codecs, recorders, mixers, modems. By evening, when the security team came to take the bags to the plane, they were overflowing into the corridor.

Mahmoud's bag, with its metal box and tangle of wires, would have drawn attention at any normal airport security checkpoint. But it would not stand out among these bags packed with electronics that belonged to known, vetted, and trusted holders of delegation credentials.

At midnight, a police escort led the way as the delegation's motorcade rolled through a misty drizzle into Northolt Royal Air Force Base, forty-five minutes west of London. Its plane was already loaded and ready for the overnight flight to Washington. The aircraft was an impressive-looking, but aging, Boeing 747 configured for government use, white with a wide blue stripe along its fuselage, an American flag painted on its tail, and UNITED STATES OF AMERICA emblazoned on its sides.

A small, shivering team of British officials lined up on the tarmac to offer farewell handshakes and small gifts of English tea. The tired delegation members and their press corps managed weak smiles and quick thank-yous before dragging themselves up the stairs onto the plane for the last time this trip.

After takeoff, some tried to go to sleep in their seats or grabbed some floor space to lie down. Others worked on their laptops and shared the few Internet access cables. In keeping with tradition on the final leg, the boss's favorite beer was served, with pretzels.

Three hours later, when the explosion ripped the plane apart, most of the passengers were sleeping, including the secretary of defense.